IN THE PRESENCE OF WOLVES

IN THE PRESENCE OF WOLVES

THE ADVENTURES OF RANGER JACOB CLARKE

ERICK W. NASON

ARPress
ILLUMINATING IDEAS.
EMPOWERING VOICES

ARPress
45 Dan Road Suite 5
Canton MA 02021
Hotline: 1(888) 821-0229
Fax: 1(508) 545-7580

Ordering Information:
Quantity sales. Special discounts are available on quantity purchases by corporations, associations, and others. For details, contact the publisher at the address above.

Printed in the United States of America.

ISBN-13:   Softcover   979-8-89330-887-7

                  eBook   979-8-89330-888-4

Library of Congress Control Number: 2024901851

TABLE OF CONTENST

This book is dedicated to all Special Operations Forces, their lineage traced to Robert Rogers and his Rangers, to those who have served, are serving, and will serve in the future when their nation calls.

I would like to acknowledge and thank the team of Sheila Nason and Christin Perry who were able to take my story and bring it to life.

FRENCH AND INDIAN WAR

MAP OF THE SCENE OF OPERATIONS.

Map of New York

Map of Lake Champlain

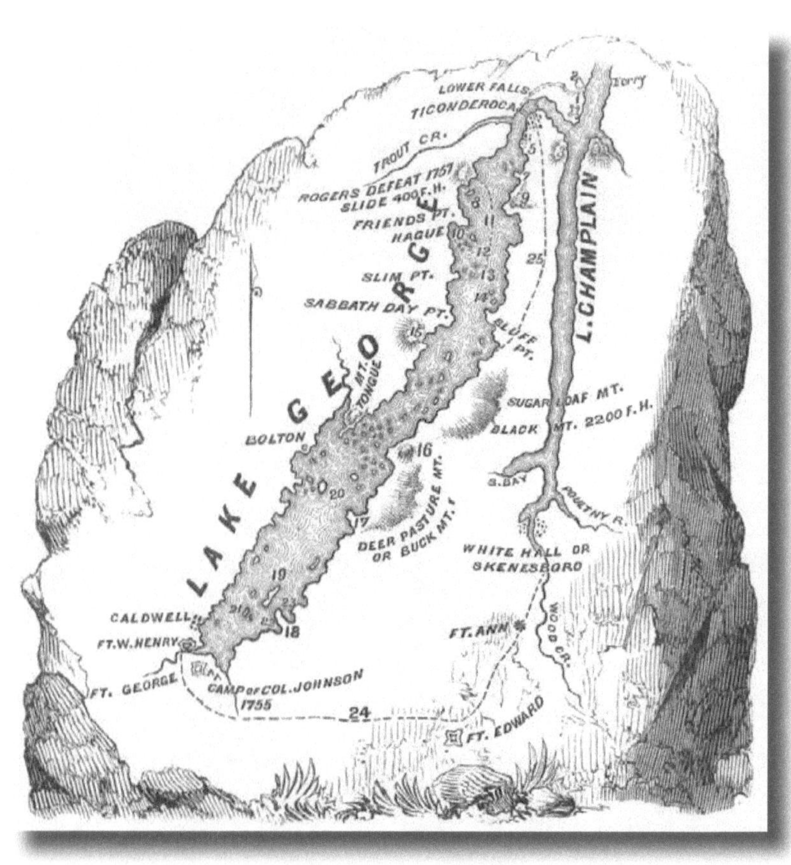

Map of Lake George

PROLOGUE

The mountains, tall and grey, are silent sentinels observing the world as events come and go. They watch over their domain bathed in the rich glow of the spring sun, covered in the white of winter, or adorned with the deep greens and the rich reds and oranges of fall as the multitude of trees that cover them take root, grow, and die with the passing seasons.

These mountains have observed much in their time, forests growing and expanding on their flanks and life coming and going in the valleys below. The blue of the lakes and rivers adds to the palette of colors provided by the trees and fields in the valleys below and between the silent peaks. These valleys pulsed with life and death as game and predators—the silent grey wolves and their prey—competed in the cycle of life, the mountains not sitting in judgment of any of their acts. It was the pattern of life.

In the measurements of man, not mountains, it was the year 1755, and a new act in the play had opened. Europeans had joined in the performance, new actors for these mountains to watch.

Conflict came with them. The great powers in Europe, mostly France and Great Britain, were once again caught in the epic tug-of-war for control not only of Europe, but of the new colonies as well. Like the great wolves, these men stalked and hunted one another in the name of their king and country, drawing in the natives to fight for their cause.

Some of the colonists had come over on behalf of their king, and others had come to escape the kings, but they all had roles in this conflict. Some had no choice, mustered into service, while others volunteered and served willingly. They had volunteered because they felt a need to do their duty, not just for their kings, but for the people they lived with. Some served for the adventure, the thrill of the hunt, and the acceptance of the ultimate challenge of facing other men in combat.

It was a small group of these volunteers that the mountains watched in silence. The men, on patrol, carefully moved among the towering pines and white birch trees, trying to make as little noise as possible. The wind blew softly through the treetops; the only sound carried along with its whisper was the cry of blue jays echoing through the forest.

Like shadows, five men moved slowly in a staggered line, about five yards between them. They moved slowly, deliberately, choosing each foot placement and keeping close to the shadows of brush and trees. They turned and scanned around them with silent eyes as they moved. They were naturals, professional hunters and trappers who had made their living from the land. They were good because they had learned to survive in this harsh country.

Now they were not hunting for game; they were training to hunt a different prey as part of a new challenge. War had returned to the valleys, forests, and lakes in the northern portion of the Colony of New York. The groups of hunters the mountains now watched were French and British soldiers, the American colonials, and their Indian allies.

These five men were dressed in different styles of hunting clothes, mostly dark green linen hunting shirts or sleeveless vests and shirts and pairs of tan breeches with knee-high leggings made of deer skin or thick woolen blue cloth to protect their legs from the ever-present thorn bushes. They all wore moccasins, darkly tanned through extensive use. Normal leather shoes would not last here.

They all carried rifled flintlock muskets. A few had the shorter versions more suitable for the thick forests, but a couple of the rifles were nearly as long as a man was tall. Their dark hunting bags and powder horns were worn close to their sides, held against their waists by belts or sashes.

Stuck in these belts and sashes were knives and tomahawks, the weapons of choice for quietly dispatching a foe or for the close-in fighting that occurred in the thickest parts of the forest. Across their shoulders were haversacks carrying their foodstuff and supplies, wooden canteens, and small blanket rolls.

Each covered his head with a different style of hat unique to the person who wore it. The man leading the patrol, his clothes more faded and worn, was Sergeant Patrick McKinney, who wore on his head a very faded green bonnet. Patrick, originally from Ireland, had traveled to the colonies to escape the harsh living conditions of the City of Cork. He stood about five foot ten, with the traditional red hair hidden under his bonnet.

Behind him, wearing a short-brimmed black leather hat, was Robert Blakefield from the Merrimack Valley in the Hampshire Grants. He was of average height and had brown hair.

The man positioned in the middle of the patrol, his darker complexion blending in with the natural shadows, wore a brown tricorn hat with most of the brim cut away. He was the Mohican named Konkapot. He was a "Stockbridge Indian," having come from the area near the Town of Stockbridge in the Massachusetts Colony. Konkapot stood a good six feet tall, and his long dark hair was properly tied up under his hat.

The fourth man in the patrol, wearing a brown jockey-style hat, was William Halley from Connecticut, also of average height. He had earned a living hunting and gathering food for his small town.

The last man, Jacob Clarke, who watched their back trail, wore a dark brown floppy hat.

All were very physically fit, faces chiseled and hardened from the difficult life of hunting and trapping across the New England frontier.

Jacob Clarke had been born in the Colony of Massachusetts, but the land his family lived on would later become known as Maine. Jacob was slightly taller than Konkapot, with light brown hair and piercing blue eyes that always seemed to have a set, determined look to them. Like his fellow hunters, his well-calloused hands and broad shoulders and chest came from the many years of hunting and trapping on the frontier. His face was weathered, lined, and tanned from living out-of-doors most of his life.

Jacob's father had brought his family over from Stratford-on-Avon, England to the new world to escape the poverty, hardships, and the constant fighting of one war after another. Wars over religion or who was the next in line to gain a throne were constantly hurling the nations of Europe at one another, and usually the common man had to pay the price, one way or another.

After traveling to the New World, Jacob's father, Richard, established a farm and trading post near the town of York, where he did well through his will to make a better life for his family. During a few years of peace, the farm prospered and trade expanded between the various Indian tribes and settlers in the area, making Richard an important townsman and member of the community. However, this peace would not last.

Once more, France and England began their political intrigue, sparring like fighters, circling and growling at one another. France was still smarting from its losses of Acadia and other possessions in the last war, known as the War of Austrian Succession or, here in the colonies, as King George's War, and the French were looking for revenge. They wanted to drive their hated adversary, Great Britain, away from their northern possessions and regain control of the northern part of the continent.

Like two large land masses grating against one another, New France and New England grinded and grated, but instead of earthquakes, wars generally broke out. Raids by French, Canadians, and Indians once more began to terrorize the New England homesteads, even though there had been no formal declaration of war between France and England. It was these raids that had eventually led Jacob to join these hardened men in this frontier area of New York.

His odyssey had begun years before. Jacob did not recall much of what had happened that fateful night; he was only eight or nine years old at the time. From what he could remember, he had just brought in a load of wood, and his mother was preparing to set the table for the evening meal when there was a knock upon the door. This was a normal occurrence for Jacob's father, Richard, because on numerous occasions a trader or farmer would arrive late at sunset to do business, and it always seemed to be around mealtime.

Richard went to the door with Jacob's younger brother, whose name was also Richard, at his side. As his father opened the door, there was a thunderous explosion and the entryway filled with smoke. Shocked by the loud explosion, Jacob looked up just in time to see his father crumple to the ground.

A large Indian in black and red war paint stepped over his body and grabbed Jacob's little brother, who was standing there in shock. Too quickly for anyone to react, the Indian pulled Jacob's brother with him over the still form of his father and disappeared into the smoke of the musket and the darkness of night.

The following morning, some of the townspeople from York arrived after hearing news of the attack. The men helped to bury Jacob's father, and their wives tried to console his mother. However, she never recovered from that night; it seemed that a part of her had died along with her husband.

When the winter came a few months later, she was overcome with sickness, and she joined his father in the ground. Once more, some of the people from York came to help bury her next to his father.

Having grown up hunting and trapping in the great forests, Jacob decided to take up the life of a long hunter, seeing no reason to stay on the farm where none of his family remained. Alone, not sure what to do, he sold the farm and trading post to one of the local merchants who had been a friend of the family.

Taking up his musket and some personal things, Jacob began working as a hunter for York, bringing in fresh meat and skins to keep the town supplied, especially in the cold winters.

He had made friends with the local Mohicans, who had come to trade at his father's place, and it was with these Indians that Jacob really learned both the craft and the art of the hunter and trapper as well as the spirituality of the land.

Living with the Mohicans, he listened to the medicine men speak of nature and the great spirits all around them, and this made some sense to Jacob. He could see and feel nature, and it brought a sense of peace which he had not felt in some time.

As Jacob grew, so did his skill as a woodsman. Only the strong and those well versed in the land survived the harsh winters in the northern woods, where there were more than bears and wolves to be concerned about. The Abenakis and other Indians friendly to the French were making their way through the woods, looking for scalps of the unwary.

Jacob traveled across New England, hunting with the Mohicans and sometimes with the Mohawks from western New York. During some of these hunts, he and his companions ran into raiding parties from the north, and quick, bloody skirmishes ensued. The rule of the northern forests was simple: learn and survive, or perish quickly in the dark woods, never to be seen again.

Jacob, having learned his lessons well, grew into a proficient hunter and trapper, known for his skills. Never settling, Jacob learned all he could from different hunters and trappers and from the Indian tribes and clans. While different in some ways, there was a commonality between the Mohicans, Mohawks, and the other tribes in the area. Jacob learned their culture, their languages, and their respect for the woods and nature.

However, deep in his heart, there was still a burning hatred for that Indian in black and red war paint who had killed his father, taken his brother, and, eventually, killed his mother. From the Mohawks, Jacob learned about one's family honor and the responsibility to avenge family members to appease and honor their spirits.

As Jacob continued to hone his skill as a hunter, rumors that war was coming to the northern woods were spreading across the land. For some, this was exciting news, especially for the young Mohawk warriors. Enthusiastic about the prospect of the warpath, they passed the news about a coming conflict between the great "fathers" of England and their enemy, the French. Down in Virginia, there had been an issue between the French and a man by the name of George Washington at a place called Fort Necessity that had sparked this next conflict.

Word from the north was that the French and Canadians were gathering their Indian allies to once more travel the warpath along the lakes and forests of the New York frontier. With war coming, there was a need for special men with Jacob's skills in hunting and tracking.

Jacob had returned to the area around Stockbridge when he first heard news of the next war. He learned that a man was recruiting in the Merrimack Valley for a special unit called Rangers. Jacob, Konkapot—with whom Jacob had been hunting for a while—and a few other hunters who knew what would be coming and wanted to stop the Indian raids gathered their belongings and traveled to Derryfield.

It was in Derryfield that Jacob met the man he had heard about, Richard Rogers, who was looking for men who could not only hunt and track, but who were seasoned in dealing with the harsh climate of the frontier forests and who knew how to fight.

Jacob felt that perhaps the time had finally arrived to avenge his family's death. He also knew what would happen if the French and their Indians began to raid once more across New England. No one would be safe.

It did not take long for Richard Rogers to convince him. Jacob signed on and was paid ten Spanish dollars for joining. This money was to be used to buy supplies, and the men who had signed up were also informed that they would receive an extra three New York shillings a day for serving. There was even a bounty for enemy scalps. Jacob had not joined for the money, but it was still a nice incentive.

Having all the gear they needed, Jacob and Konkapot, who had also signed up, purchased only some extra powder and some lead to mold into rifle balls. They planned to use much of the money to celebrate their new lives as Rangers.

That evening, a tavern called Chowning's, where Jacob and the other hunters had met with Richard Rogers and signed up to be Rangers, was now full of celebrating men sitting at well-worn tables and benches. At the end of the large common room, there was a large fireplace, with a fire crackling and snapping, its glow dancing with the light from multiple candles along the walls and on the tables. In the corner, a fiddler was playing, and the room was filled with different voices of men singing songs and shouting over one another to be heard.

It was a loud, but joyful, din, the men enjoying their mugs of local ales and brews, all trying to outboast one another about how many scalps they would take and how rich they would be at war's end.

Jacob, sitting next to Konkapot and a few other men from Derryfield, drank and toasted to the adventure to come. In the corner was Richard Rogers, sitting with a group of men, the smoke from their pipes circling about them as they discussed the coming conflict.

A young lady of fair complexion, a serving girl in the tavern, seemed to have taken an interest in Jacob, and soon was practically sitting in his lap, pouring ale and rum down his open mouth as Konkapot and the others roared with laughter deep into the night.

After a few days, the men, most of whom Jacob knew from hunting and trapping, departed Derryfield and traveled to New York to join the rest of the British and Provincial units gathering there. They spent several days on the trail before arriving at Albany, outside of what used to be Fort Orange, where they joined up with the rest of the assembling Ranger companies.

Jacob, Konkapot, and some of the other men who had traveled over to New York were assembled to meet their company commander, a Captain Robert Rogers. Captain Robert Rogers, the brother of Richard who had recruited them, carried himself like a professional, a man familiar with the forests and lakes of the frontier. Captain Rogers was also an experienced soldier, having served as a scout with Captain Ladd and also with Captain Eastman during the last war with France.

Wearing the green-colored hunting attire that Jacob would adopt, Captain Rogers addressed the men.

"You have been selected because we need you," Rogers began. "We need men who understand the hardship of traveling and the long hunt, men who have unwavering courage and fidelity."

Captain Rogers had the full attention of the group.

"I don't have to tell you what horrors will be unleashed on these people if we can't stop the French and their damnable Indian Allies," he stressed, looking each man in the eyes. "I need the best. We are heading north to assist William Johnson in building his Fort Lyman and to join the rest of the army there. Get what supplies you need, and be ready."

Rogers turned to Patrick McKinney and the other sergeants. "Train them on the march; get them so they understand the difference between hunting and ranging," Captain Rogers told them. "We won't have the luxury of time once we get to the fort."

The sergeants, all seasoned men of the frontier, nodded in agreement and went off to collect their new charges and to start shaping them into Rangers.

Now, Jacob, with Sergeant McKinney and the four other men in their section, had finished their education on the march from Albany, their classroom being the woods and valleys they had just traveled.

They already knew how to make a shelter and live off the land, to move quietly, to hunt, and to track. Patrick showed them how to apply their hunting skills to the more military-like "ranging" skills, so they could be the eyes and ears of the regular British soldiers and Provincials alike.

As the patrol moved through the trees, they caught the distinct scent of wood smoke and bacon on the wind. Patrick stopped the patrol and everyone gathered around him, taking a knee under the boughs of a large pine tree.

"Aye laddies, you can always smell their camp before you see 'em," Sergeant McKinney whispered.

Before them, they could see through the branches of the tree they were under the construction site of Fort Lyman and the gathering of the army of newly appointed General William Johnson, which stretched across a large open valley.

"Heard there is a whole bunch of Mohawks heading this way to join with us," grunted Patrick as he stood up. "Let's head over and report in."

Jacob looked across the valley, seeing the blue/gray tint of the mountains in the distance and the sun dancing off the large river called the Hudson, which ran through the valley. This place was also known as *Wahcoloosencoochaleva* in the Mohawk language, or "the Great Carrying Place" to other Indians, hunters, and trappers. Many hunters and Iroquois used the Sacandaga Trail, which led to this great bend in the river where the fort was now being built.

Fort Lyman would be a large wooden fort that would dominate the valley and control the region for his most Royal Majesty, King George

II of England. Woodsmen, protected by sections of armed men, were in the process of clearing the trees away from the fort, giving it clear lines of sight, and if need be, clear killing ground. Hundreds of men were scurrying around the work site, mostly Provincial soldiers from the different New England colonies, local militias, and civilian workers.

Standing up, Jacob once more turned to check their trail and then moved off towards Fort Edward with his section to join up with the rest of Captain Robert Rogers's Company of Rangers.

CHAPTER 1

JUNE 1755
FORT LYMAN: LEARNING THE BASICS

The fort itself was one of the largest Jacob had ever seen. Having grown up on the frontier and from living with the Indians, Jacob was more accustomed to smaller towns and villages. This site before him, the fort and all of the men moving around it, was an eye-opener, and his heart began to beat faster as the excitement of a new adventure with new sights and sounds lay before him like an open book.

Looking over to his friend Konkapot, who also had a grin on his face, Jacob nodded, ready to see this new sight, which for the time being was their new home. Jacob couldn't hide his grin as he turned around once more to check their trail as they moved down into the valley.

Jacob and the patrol were approaching the fort from the south. In the distance was the road to Albany where a column of Massachusetts Provincials, in deep blue uniforms with red facings and vests, was marching, along with several supply wagons, towards the fort.

There were long wooden walls, with logs laid horizontally, and the space between the inner and outer walls was filled with earth. The fort was relatively new; it was still being built in some places while workers were putting finishing touches on other portions.

Sentries marched along the finished ramparts and along the ditch and palisades surrounding the work site. Inside the fort, men were dragging cannons to be mounted on the completed ramparts.

Just before the Albany road crossed a creek, a wooden barricade stood guarding the approach; men from the New York Provincials were manning the picket. They wore a lighter colored green coat with blue bonnets and leggings, and they were armed with regular muskets. The Provincial men waved to them as they passed by, and the patrol followed the road up to the fort.

After they crossed the fast-moving creek, the activity around the fort became more apparent. Jacob looked around as they moved along the road towards the sprawling complex of the fort, caught up in the hustle and bustle of activities.

Men were working in a large garden that would be used to supplement the fort's rations. Most would go to the officers' tables, but the regular men would get some as well.

Jacob observed a few work details of men carrying axes, accompanied by several armed men for protection, who he assumed were heading towards the forest to cut firewood. Seeing the armed security snapped him back to reality. There was an enemy close at hand; this was not a place to let your guard down.

Along with the work details, Jacob observed both Provincials and the red-coated British regulars drilling, either in companies of around a hundred men or in smaller platoons of twenty or thirty. They went through formation changes, such as from column into lines and lines into column, and perfected their loading and firing procedures.

The sound of their officers giving commands, corrections, or instructions mixed with the noise of axes falling or chains rattling as workers attended to their tasks. The noise was deafening, but it thrilled Jacob, who became caught up in the martial spirit of the place, and he wondered if they too would have to drill like these soldiers.

As they approached the fort's tall walls, he observed several large canvas tents that had been erected where sutlers had established businesses to sell items to the soldiers working at the fort. Sutlers were always found near armies and their camps. They sold simple wares that soldiers needed such as cups and plates, as well as drinks and spirits, which was what most of the men desired.

Jacob's head was constantly swiveling, along with the other new Rangers, taking in the whole complex and the many activities. Patrick stopped them and headed off into the maze of tents, telling them to stay put. To protect the Provincial and militia camps until the fort was completed, men were building a dirt berm about a hundred yards outside the outer wall. Jacob and Konkapot stood next to Robert Blakefield, and asked about the fort and the different activities they could see.

"What are those men doing over there? They look like they're weaving baskets," Jacob asked, and Robert looked over to see what Jacob had pointed to.

"Aye, that they are," Robert responded. "They are called, ah... I believe, fascines. I am no military engineer, for sure, but I believe I heard them called that. They fill them with dirt and it makes a wall you can stand behind and not get hit."

Jacob and Konkapot nodded and watched as the men built the fascines and placed them on top of a six-foot-high berm running around the wall of the fort.

"The enemy could attack at any moment, so they have to be prepared to defend themselves if the French or their Indian friends come raiding," Robert finished.

As they stood there, Jacob continued to look around at the fort, one of the largest structures he had ever seen. The fort itself was a large, elongated square design, the western corner resting on the edge of the Hudson River. The other three corners had large bastions, and a single separate bastion called a ravelin was oriented to the north. It was detached from the fort but connected by a bridge. This was designed to add extra protection, for it was considered the most likely area the French and their allies would attack.

Jacob turned and looked at the large river just west of the fort and the island in the center of it, connected by a wooden footbridge.

Patrick returned and motioned for them to follow him as he led the patrol inside so they could visit the quartermaster to replace the supplies they had used on the march.

Inside the fort, long, two-story log buildings were being completed, which would serve as barracks, with officers and enlisted men living separately. The finished bastions were also being used for storage and, in some cases, living spaces. Only one of the barracks had a completed roof, with the other being worked on.

The inside of the fort smelled of fresh-cut logs, tar, dirt, and the sweat of many men living and working in close proximity. Jacob leaned over to Konkapot and commented on the smell and closeness of it all, and Konkapot nodded his concurrence.

The quartermaster, responsible for maintaining and accounting for the supplies used by the fort and the soldiers alike, was established inside one of the finished bastions. The cooler but darker bastion was stacked high with boxes, bundles, and barrels.

The quartermaster issued some salt pork, flour, and hard biscuits to the men, along with some powder to replenish their stock of this much-needed commodity. Jacob took his issued items and placed them inside his haversack.

After securing food and some supplies from the quartermaster, Patrick led them out of the fort, through the gate, and over the wooden foot bridge that connected the fort to a large island in the middle of the river. As they crossed the bridge and came closer to the island, Jacob could see men busy at work, but these men wore the dark green hunting clothes of the Rangers. The Rangers were living in a camp on the island, mostly in tents and lean-tos, near the log houses that were being built.

Patrick led them over to an open space. "Well lads, here's your new home," he said, pointing to the open area. "Best see to making ourselves some shelters."

Patrick dropped his equipment to go report to Captain Rogers that they had made it up from Albany. Jacob and the other men in the section began building bark lean-tos, knowing that up here in the northern forest during the spring and summer, thunderstorms appeared quickly over the mountains, and unless you liked getting wet, it was essential to have shelter.

Konkapot stayed back to keep an eye on their gear and to start their cooking fire, while Jacob and the rest crossed the bridge over to the fort's side. They headed over to where the wood detail was cutting firewood to gather limbs, pine boughs, and bark for their lean-tos.

Since they were experienced hunters and frontiersmen, they all knew what was needed, and they worked seamlessly in building their lean-tos. They began by placing sturdy limbs they had carved into poles with their knives and tomahawks; then they tied a cross beam between the posts. Next, a frame that angled from the cross pole to the ground was created. It was covered with bark sheets that they had made, and pine boughs.

They worked as a team, making small talk, mostly excited comments about the fort, since like Jacob and Konkapot, this was the other team members' first time in a major military complex.

Once the lean-tos were completed, they set up their sleeping blankets on top of a floor made of pine boughs, and hung their bags from the frame. Their rifles were always stacked nearby in case of an attack or a call to arms.

When they had finished their shelters, Patrick returned and inspected their handiwork, pointing out some areas where they could improve, but was mostly pleased with what he saw.

"All right lads, we have some free time, and from the way you were looking about, this is your first time at a fort. Go look around for a bit, then be back here before sundown," Patrick ordered.

Then he looked at each of them with a stern expression and gave one final instruction: "Stay together and don't get into trouble!"

Jacob and his fellow Rangers went over to see what was available at the sutlers' tents that they had passed. They stopped at a complex of large tents belonging to Mr. Best, a sutler who offered a wide variety of goods for sale.

In front of his tents was a wooden counter made from empty barrels and planks. Hanging from a rope suspended between two of the tents were tin cups, knives, and twists of tobacco. On wooden tables and empty crates were cones of sugar, smoked meats, and a few blankets.

The greatest interest to both Provincials and militia alike were the bottles of port and a small cask of rum that seemed to be making good business for Mr. Best. He also appeared to be making good sales of tobacco and sugar to all who were willing to pay.

While Jacob had been to different merchants as a long hunter, selling his skins and game, this was the first merchant he met that was actually in the field. All of the merchants he had dealt with before had been in towns.

Mr. Best was a good-hearted man, joking with the men as he dispensed rum into cups and sold wares to them. Jacob quickly decided he liked this man, who was open and honest with the soldiers.

From behind Jacob and the other Rangers came a loud, accented voice. Jacob turned to see who had made the demand.

"Aren't you men supposed to be working?" bellowed a finely dressed British officer, with a lieutenant and a sergeant major standing behind him. Jacob quickly sized up this officer, who had an arrogant look about him. The sergeant major had a sneer on his face, but the lieutenant who stood behind actually rolled his eyes as the captain spoke. Jacob did not like this short captain and the sneering sergeant major.

The Provincials and militiamen quickly gathered up their items, swallowed their rum, and made their way back to their camps. Wiping his hands on his apron, Mr. Best put his best face on and greeted the captain.

"Captain Reynolds, so nice to see you again. How are you this fine day?" asked Mr. Best.

Captain Archibald Reynolds of the 48th Regiment of Foot was at the fort as an observer and advisor to General Johnson. His immaculate regulation British red uniform, gold braid, and brass buttons, and a lace and silver gorget worn around his neck, stood out in sharp contrast to the shabby and dull clothing of the Provincials.

With him was Lieutenant Karl Manning, his aide, and Sergeant Major Lovewell, who carried a large halberd as a badge of his rank.

"Spare me your pleasantries, Mr. Best. How can anything be accomplished around here if these men are drunk? I should have you and your ... wares removed," scoffed Captain Reynolds.

Jacob snickered to himself and shook his head as Captain Reynolds was trying to stare down his nose at Mr. Best, except for the fact that the captain was only five feet six inches tall and Mr. Best was a good five inches taller.

Looking towards the sound of the snicker, Captain Reynolds asked, "Is there something funny, sir?" He pointed at Jacob. "Sergeant Major, see to that!"

Jacob and his fellow Rangers quickly stopped snickering and stood up from their kneeling position as the sergeant major stalked over to them.

"Who do you Provincials think you are, snickering like this? You lack the discipline to be considered good soldiers. What you need is a good taste of the cat to straighten you up. I'll have you lashed to the wheel by this evening ..."

The sergeant major seemed to focus on Jacob with his threat. Jacob calmly and coolly stared right back at him in blatant disrespect, perhaps the arrogance of youth and inexperience getting the better part of sound judgment.

"Ah ... Sergeant, these men are Rangers. Can't you see by their clothing?" Lieutenant Manning said. "These are the scouts that General Johnson uses. Let him handle it."

Staring at the defiant Jacob, the sergeant major harrumphed and backed off, but only slightly.

"Humph ... Rangers, hiding in the woods instead of facing their foe man-to-man in the open on the field of battle. We don't need them." The sergeant major walked back over to join Captain Reynolds, who was still giving Mr. Best grief about his wares and occupation. "Sorry about that," apologized Lieutenant Manning, who spoke to

Jacob and the other Rangers. "The captain and sergeant major are not used to working with Provincial soldiers."

Then he gave all of the Rangers a steady look, and said in a lowered voice, "You're new, so heed this warning. You got lucky. I've seen the sergeant major string a man up and have his back shredded by the whip for not having his stockings right. Discipline is a serious thing around here. Learn it or pay the price."

With a quick smile and a nod, the lieutenant joined the other two, who turned and departed for the fort.

As Jacob watched them go, he realized that what he had done was stupid, and it could have gotten him in a lot of trouble, not a good way to start out. Jacob looked over to Konkapot and the others, who were also breathing a sigh of relief, and muttered, "I have a feeling that those two are going to be trouble."

His fellow Rangers nodded their agreement as they started back to the island. When Jacob and the men returned to their campsite, Patrick was waiting for them with two other men, and he didn't have a pleased look on his face.

"Men, gather around," Patrick ordered.

After everyone had assembled, he let them have it. "What did I tell you before leaving here? Don't get into trouble!" Patrick roared.

Jacob and the others looked at one another abashed, but amazed at how fast news traveled.

"I heard you ran into our beloved Captain Reynolds. What were you thinking?" Patrick boomed, and as Jacob was about to open his mouth, Patrick continued on. "There is no excuse. Discipline WILL be maintained, whether it's with us or with the regulars. Do not EVER embarrass us again. Do you all understand?"

Jacob and the others sheepishly nodded their understanding, as Patrick pursed his lips.

"Even with pompous asses like Captain Reynolds," Patrick said in his regular voice. "We have to show these regulars we can be not only as good as them, but better. Believe me, Captain Rogers will handle our discipline, so don't get on his bad side.

"Do the right thing, always. Each one of you is responsible for one another. Rangers take care of Rangers, even if they are not from the same company. Don't give Captain Reynolds or his sergeant major an excuse. They would love nothing more than to have one of us whipped before the entire command."

Jacob took this lesson to heart, again chiding himself for the stupidity of staring down the sergeant major. He might have deserved it, but in the end he would win and Jacob would be bearing the punishment.

Patrick called over the two men and introduced them to the group. "This is Peter Fisch, who is joining our section," he said, indicating the man on the left. "And this is Lieutenant John Stark, who is our platoon commander."

The new man, Peter Fisch, had the look of a seasoned hunter; his clothes and equipment appeared to be well used; faded, but well maintained.

Lieutenant Stark's reputation as an experienced frontiersman was well known, Jacob having heard of him from other hunters and frontiersmen. Having been captured by the Abenaki Indians, Stark was running the gauntlet between warriors when he grabbed one of the clubs and began fighting back. This impressed the Abenaki chief, who adopted Stark into the tribe where he spent a year before returning to New Hampshire.

"Rangers, heed what your sergeant said. Take care of each other, and I don't want to hear of any more problems. Understood?" Lieutenant Stark said as he looked into all of their eyes, driving home his point by the serious look on his face. "You'll be heading out for a scout in the morning. Patrick will give you the details later."

Patrick and Lieutenant Stark walked off while Peter settled his gear, and they finished setting up their lean-tos. Jacob reflected on what had just occurred, kicking himself for being so ignorant. But he was still angry. He was proud of who he was and who he was with. How dare that regular British officer and his sneering sergeant major take that tone with them? This was their home and their fight. Who were they to tell them what to do or how to act?

Jacob could feel the anger inside him welling up, but he quickly let it go with a deep breath. Patrick was right. He could not embarrass the Rangers again, and he would remember this lesson well and try not to make the same mistake twice.

"Where you from Peter?" asked Robert Blakefield as he was helping Peter build his shelter.

While tying one of the branches as a cross bar for a lean-to, Peter replied with a heavy German accent, "Bavaria, dee southern part of a kingdom in da mountains. I was a jaeger, or as you say, a hunter."

Jacob liked this Bavarian. He carried a confidence about himself, an assurance from experience that perhaps Jacob could learn from, so he wouldn't continue to make mistakes.

Robert's eyebrows rose as he finished tying off the lashing to the crossbeam. "What are you doing here then?"

Peter looked over at him, shrugged his shoulders, and said, "I shot deer that belonged to a landlord, so I had to leave or go to jail. So I travel to England, learn to speak language, work for East India Company as a guard. Didn't like that, so I came here to become hunter again."

Peter looked up from his lashing and smiled. "And now I am here with you."

Robert thought about that for a moment, then whistled. "You go to jail if you shoot a deer?"

Peter nodded his head somberly. "Not like it is here in colonies. There, landlord owns everything: the land, the trees, the people, and the game. You taking their game is like stealing, and if you are a thief, you go to jail. I don't like jail so I come here."

After they completed the bark roofs for the lean-tos, Patrick looked their work over, nodded, and then gathered them around the cook fire.

"Captain Rogers wants us to head out towards the lake to the north of here to see if there are any French or Canadian scouts or any Indian activity in the area."

Taking a stick, Patrick drew a rough sketch of the lake and the route they would take to scout it. He drew the route from their camp generally north through the forest to the rough line Patrick drew to show the southern end of the lake. He pointed out key landmarks to help them know the route.

"Cook two days of rations, check your gear, and be ready to move out at first light."

After putting out his instructions, Patrick stayed and became involved in the small talk as they cooked their rations for the march.

He was getting to know his new men while they got to know each other.

As they sat around, Jacob thought about the scout in the morning, their first true patrol against the enemy. He was wrestling with the emotions of it: excitement of the hunt, fear of the unknown, and a deeper fear of getting killed. While he was confident in his woodman's skills, he was more afraid of making a mistake that could get Konkapot or one of the other Rangers killed than of dying himself. Shaking his head, he pushed the thoughts to the back of his mind, and focused on the present. All of the Rangers worked as a team while cooking their rations.

The salt pork was being soaked in water to remove the salt, while Robert and Peter made camp biscuits with flour, butter, and some buttermilk that Robert had been able to get from the sutler.

Once the salt was removed, Jacob and Konkapot cooked the pork on green branch spits until it was crackling and popping over the fire. The smell of cooking pork and fresh biscuits wafted around the men, giving them a sense of home and everything good in the world. The smell helped to settle Jacob's mind and the butterflies he was still feeling about the looming patrol. One thing he had learned from his years as a long hunter was how to cook.

Once all of the food and biscuits were cooked, they were distributed to everyone, and the Rangers wrapped them in cloth and packed them in their haversacks. William filled all of their canteens while everyone else was checking their rifles and sharpening their knives and tomahawks.

When William returned from the river, Patrick pulled out a ceramic jug and poured a dram of rum into the canteens to purify the water so it could be drunk. This concoction was called "grog." If they drank straight water, there was a chance they would get sick with the flux, which could kill them.

Patrick ordered them to their beds, but sleep evaded Jacob as he laid there, thoughts of the scout and ripples of fear racing around inside his mind.

"Konkapot, you awake?" Jacob whispered, and Konkapot responded he was.

"What do you think will happen in the morning?" Jacob asked, and Konkapot answered, "It's no different than when we used to go to the Mohawks in Albany and they were at war with the Hurons. Be smart, keep your eyes and ears open, and you'll do fine. Besides, I will watch your back, and I know you will watch mine."

This helped for a bit, but Jacob still wrestled with his thoughts awhile before he fell asleep.

Jacob and the others were awake and up before the sun in the morning. A cold fog hovered amongst the lean-tos and tents on the island. All of the Rangers gathered for morning formation and roll call. This was the first time Jacob and the others joined with the entire Ranger Company. There were about sixty other men, dressed mostly in the same dark green coats or hunting shirts. Jacob had adopted the Ranger-style hunting shirt and a dark green bonnet, his old floppy hat having fallen apart beyond repair.

Captain Rogers, Lieutenant Stark, and another Lieutenant, Joseph Waite, checked on the men and made sure everyone was present for duty. When the lieutenants accounted for everyone, they reported it to Rogers, who dismissed the company with instructions to the sergeants to see to their duties.

Jacob watched in fascination as the officers inspected the men and their equipment, noticing that they were very thorough. This was important, and Jacob thought about the need for good checks on the men and equipment before a scout. It made perfect sense to him.

Once the morning formation was over, Patrick led Jacob and the rest of his men from the formation area back to their camp where they put on their shooting bags, powder horns, and haversacks, and Patrick inspected them. He pointed out a spot of rust on one man's rifle or a tomahawk edge that was not sharp enough, and he made sure they all had full powder horns and shot.

"Rangers, attention to detail will save your lives. If your bags break, your knives or tomahawks are not sharp, or you don't have enough shot, you will die out here or one of your fellow Rangers will die. Learn this lesson well!"

Everyone nodded, Jacob storing this in his head as a lesson learned for later.

Once everyone was ready, Patrick led them out across the foot bridge, and they started on their first true combat patrol. Carrying their rifles easily over their shoulders, they crossed the bridge and turned northward towards the thick green forest.

Once they came around the corner of the fort and began crossing the valley towards the woods, Patrick brought his rifle to the ready. The rest of the Rangers did the same. Jacob felt exhilarated. Though the fear was still there, the excitement of the hunt suppressed it.

The sun was up and bathing the valley in its warm embrace as Captain Reynolds, who was making his rounds on the fort's rampart, observed the patrol. He shook his head and harrumphed, and the sergeant major readily agreed with his disdain.

He and the sergeant major continued on their walk around the fort, the captain making snide comments about Provincials, and the sergeant major agreeing. Lieutenant Manning watched with envy as the patrol headed out and disappeared into the woods, and then he quickly caught up with the captain and the sergeant major.

Just to the northeast of the valley, concealed on a thickly vegetated knoll, Patrick's patrol was also watched by another set of eyes with a darker intent. Laying on their bellies, concealed under the boughs of pine trees and bushes, were Tawiskara, a war leader from the Hurons, along with Wawanagit, who was a war leader of the Abenakis. Just behind them and spread out concealed in the brush were some of their warriors and one of the Canadian scouts, watching the construction of Fort Lyman and the activity in and around the place.

Tawiskara and Wawanagit spoke softly to one another in their native language. The building of this fort was a problem, as it sat in the middle of the valley they normally used when raiding the English settlements to the south. Such a large fort meant soldiers were coming into the area, and raids into English territory would be harder.

Both war chiefs watched with experienced eyes and took in the details. They observed the number of men working, how their security was placed, the number of pickets and patrols, and how well they were performing. They counted the number of cannons, at least those they could see mounted on the ramparts and those that were being moved around.

The British were coming with their Provincials and militia soldiers, and this news must be reported to their "French Fathers" to the north. This valuable information would bring them great reward, and both war chiefs relished the thought of the coming battles.

They also watched the Ranger patrol heading northward in the same direction they must travel to warn the French commander, Baron Dieskau. Switching to French, Tawiskara called the Canadian scout over and spoke of what they had seen and what must be reported. Giving one last look at the fort and the spot where the patrol had vanished into the woods, the Indians and the scout slowly backed away to start their journey back north.

Once the Ranger patrol entered the woods, the rifles which had been carried easily were now held at the ready, fingers near the triggers and thumbs close to the hammers in order to cock them quickly. They did not move with fully cocked rifles, in case of an accidental discharge that could give their position away.

On this patrol, Patrick had selected Jacob to lead, relying on his experience and sharp eyes and ears to spot the enemy early. Behind Jacob followed Konkapot and Robert, then Patrick, who pointed out the direction to take, knowing the terrain they were walking through. Behind Patrick were Peter and William, covering their trail, making sure they weren't being followed by the enemy.

The brightness of the sun quickly dimmed as the patrol entered deeper into the forest, a dark, shadowy world. The Ranger column spread out with five yards or more between them, and they were staggered left and right, each Ranger constantly scanning around for any signs of their enemy.

Jacob felt electric, his mind buzzing as he studied the ground for any tracks, listening to the sounds of birds and jays. As long as they were calling, it was considered a good sign. When the birds or animals went silent, it usually meant that someone else was in the area. He was relying on his hunting skills, but now the game was more deadly than his normal quarry. As they scanned the area, walking carefully, they looked around them and back to keep eyes on their fellow Rangers. Their moccasins treading across the soft moss and leaves made their movements nearly silent. They were taking no chances; even being this close to the fort did not mean they were safe. They knew that the enemy could also be scouting them. Patrick kept them on course, constantly watching them and making on-the-spot corrections with his hands, their classroom now more dangerous than when they had marched from Derryfield.

The patrol had moved slowly and purposely for a few hours, not seeing or hearing anything that would have alerted them to the presence of the enemy, when they came upon the ruins of old Fort Anne. More of a blockhouse with a palisade around it than a fort, it was a good place to stop. Jacob noticed the fort was in bad shape, with gaps in the palisaded wall, the wood turning green from fungus and moss.

The fort had been active during the previous conflicts, Queen Anne's War and King George's War, but the fort had been abandoned once peace returned, even if it was for only a short time. The fort now served mostly as a rendezvous location for patrols or as shelter for anyone caught outside of the fort during trouble or bad weather.

With Konkapot and Peter posted as sentries, William and Robert gathered wild raspberries from bushes that were in the process of taking over the old palisades. The raspberries were abundant and had just ripened, and their thick, thorny branches served as the only real defense in the gaps of the wall.

While Jacob and Patrick sat against one of the palisade walls and drank from their canteens, Jacob looked around at the sad and lonely place. His mind was racing once more, his active hunting confidence giving way to the uncertainty of the situation.

"Sergeant, how do you know if you're doing right?"

Patrick swallowed his grog, smiled and looked over at Jacob. "Well, lad, that comes with experience. If you're awake and above ground in the morning, then you done good."

Patrick watched Jacob nod in understanding, though he still had a puzzled look on his face.

"You're wondering what you will do if we meet the enemy?" Patrick asked and nodded his understanding after Jacob had returned an affirmative nod.

"Lad, every soldier since time immortal has thought this. Even I thought about it during the forty-five, when my clan fought the British. I was scared to death before my first fight."

Jacob looked with amazement at Patrick.

"Wait, you were afraid AND fought the British?" he asked incredulously.

Patrick laughed and nodded.

"Aye laddie, I fought the British for MY King and country. Now I fight for my new country, and no king! As for being afraid, I was more afraid of making a mistake in front of my clan, which would have been far worse than simply getting killed."

Jacob let that insight sink in, and nodded to himself, agreeing it would be far worse to make a mistake with his new family of Rangers watching than to simply get killed.

After eating some of the food they had cooked the night before and a handful of berries, Jacob and Patrick replaced Peter and Konkapot as sentries so they too could rest and get something to eat.

When they had all eaten and rested, the patrol made sure they removed any sign that they had been there before continuing northward towards the lake. The lake was known as Lac du Saint Sacrement, so named by the Jesuit priest, Father Isaac Joques, who had explored the area before being tortured and killed by a Mohawk war party. It was simply called Lake Sacrement by the English.

The lake had been used by the French explorer Samuel de Champlain, and it was a major avenue traveled by French, Canadians, and their Indian allies on their raids out of Canada into New York and the other English Colonies.

The patrol once more formed into their staggered line and continued their scout of the woods. They had not left Fort Anne for long before Jacob spotted something out of the ordinary—sets of fresh tracks. There were other men in the area wearing moccasins.

Jacob held up his hand and everyone stopped, most of the men moving up next to trees and taking a knee. Konkapot and Patrick came up to see what Jacob had found. Jacob pointed to the tracks, tracing the outline of the footprint, indicators of possible Indians or other scouts in the area.

Jacob leaned over to Patrick and asked in a whisper, "Any other Ranger patrols out here?"

Patrick thought for a few seconds and shook his head no.

"Let's see what we can find," said Patrick, pointing forward with his hand in the direction the tracks were heading.

Jacob nodded, his mind going into active hunting mode, his senses becoming more attuned to the environment, and his heart beating faster as adrenaline began to course through his veins.

Patrick cocked his hammer to full, and they all softly cocked the hammers on their rifles, checking their pans to make sure they were sufficiently primed with powder.

They moved now more slowly, more deliberately, carefully watching the woods around them. The hunt had begun. Every Ranger scanned and listened. They noticed that all they heard was the whisper of a breeze and some insects, nothing more.

As they were moving, Jacob froze in place; something just didn't feel right. It was as if several pairs of unfriendly eyes were watching them. The hairs on the back of his neck rose, and his skin was prickly.

The rest of the patrol stopped as well, quietly and slowly taking a knee behind the trunks of trees. The other Rangers were getting the same feeling, their hunting instincts kicking in. One did not last long in the wilderness without developing an almost sixth sense, more attuned than that of the average man.

It was at that moment that the trees to their front exploded in musket fire and war whoops. The Huron and Abenaki war party that had been scouting Fort Lyman had guessed right that the Rangers were using the usual route towards old Fort Anne.

Jacob's mind raced and kicked into survival mode as he instinctively dove for cover behind a large tree. Bringing his rifle up to his shoulder, he searched for the enemy opposite them in the trees, but all he saw was the grey smoke spreading from where they had fired.

As the trees splintered around them, Jacob heard the heavy impact of a ball striking someone behind him. He didn't have time to look. Automatically without thought, he was taking aim as the Indians broke from the trees and charged towards them, tomahawks and war clubs raised, their war whoops echoing off the trees.

Fear, mixed with the adrenaline rush of battle, coursed through Jacob, giving him energy and strength of purpose. His hunting instincts took charge as he slowed his breath, focusing on the lead charging warrior. Jacob sighted down his rifle, aiming at the Indian. He moved his sights slightly forward, leading his target, and squeezed the trigger. The flint sparked and the rifle recoiled, the ball hitting the warrior in the center of his chest and knocking him back. Continuing to aim along the rifle, Jacob was rewarded when he saw the Indian fall.

A variety of emotions coursed through him—excitement, rage, and wonderment, all boiling together in the moment.

Jacob had no time to reload as the enemy warriors closed on him, so his only option was to draw his tomahawk. In a split second, he was able to catch a war club being swung at him by a darkly painted Huron. Seeing the war paint brought forth a deep-rooted hatred from his past, the memory of his father's death. Enraged, Jacob spun, using his tomahawk's blade to push the warrior's club aside, and then followed through and sank his tomahawk in the Huron's head. Jacob stepped on the corpse and pulled his tomahawk free, quickly scanning the fight around him.

Breathing heavy from the fight, Jacob looked at the fallen Indian, but he wasn't the one who had taken his brother and killed his father. Disengaging, Jacob fell back. Konkapot and Patrick were also fighting hand-to-hand, each having also killed one of the attackers with rifle fire. As they were falling back, Robert picked up William, and Jacob realized that it was William whom he had heard getting hit. As they were running, there were more cracks from the Indians' muskets, the balls crashing and whistling around them through the woods.

Robert arched his back as a ball struck him from behind, knocking him and William to the ground. Jacob, horrified, turned to try and help them.

"Leave him!" yelled Patrick as he was reloading on the run. "William is dead!"

Jacob helped Robert to his feet and began pulling him along. The ball had struck him in the upper shoulder, and exited out the front of his shirt, and his blood was starting to stain his hunting shirt. Fear returned, and that helped to fuel Jacob to pull harder and stronger, making him move faster.

The Rangers ran back towards Fort Anne and took up firing positions, waiting for the pursuing Indians. They didn't need to wait long as the Indians broke from the woods, caught up in the chase and yelling their war cries.

The remaining Rangers alternated firing, with one firing as the other provided cover. Jacob was covering Patrick as he loaded. Konkapot was covering Peter, who was wrapping torn cloth around Robert's shoulder to stop the flow of blood. Once the shoulder was bandaged, Peter joined Konkapot and Jacob who were rapidly loading and firing as fast as they could.

As the fighting echoed through the woods, Tawiskara knew he needed to get the information about the English fort north to the French, and he decided to withdraw his men from the fight. He had achieved what he wanted, letting these English know they were not safe in this land. It had been achieved at a heavy price though. He would be leaving with five of his warriors dead and another four wounded.

As the firing stopped and the war whoops ended, Patrick, Jacob, and the others waited. It appeared the Indians had left them, and silence returned. The only noise at first was their heavy breathing, but soon the sounds of the birds and the forest returned.

When they felt it was safe, Peter stayed with Robert as Patrick, Jacob, and Konkapot returned to the site of the ambush. Konkapot went over to one of the dead warriors.

"Huron" was all he said before removing his knife and taking the scalp.

Patrick looked around.

"This is odd. They left their dead," he said.

Both Jacob and Konkapot nodded. Normally the Indians would have taken their dead with them.

It didn't take them long to find what was left of William. In the short amount of time since they had left the body, he had been brutally stabbed and savagely hacked apart. His heart had been torn from his chest, and he had been scalped.

Different emotions once again coursed through Jacob, sadness for the loss of a fellow Ranger and friend, anger at the enemy for killing him, and a desire to seek vengeance.

They found two more dead Indians, an Abenaki warrior and another Huron. Jacob drew his sharp fighting knife from its sheath as he stood over the dead Huron. He reached down and took the enemy dead by his hair.

Feeling no emotion, Jacob grasped the topknot of hair, surgically pulled the blade across the forehead and with a quick jerk, removed the scalp with almost a popping sound. He had learned this trick from the Mohawks in his earlier years. This small act of revenge left him with a feeling of satisfaction.

With the bloody scalp folded into his belt, Jacob helped to wrap William's remains in his hunting shirt, and then picked him up, placing William over his shoulder. Konkapot and Patrick watched the woods around them as they carried the remains back to Fort Anne. The feeling of sorrow returned, another loss from this savage war and, Jacob felt, it wouldn't be the last.

At Fort Anne, they made a travois out of branches, placed the remains on it, and began their journey back to Fort Lyman. They were cautious as they moved, making sure they would not be ambushed again.

The travois helped to carry William's body through the trees, and they all took turns pulling. Jacob pushed his sorrow to the side and resumed his hunter's habit of searching ceaselessly for an enemy hidden in the woods.

They had only traveled a short distance when they ran into a platoon of about twenty Rangers led by Lieutenant Stark.

"Heard the firing, thought you had gotten into trouble," Stark said.

Looking at the travois, he added, "I see we were right."

Patrick nodded, and they returned to Fort Lyman, with Jacob and the others in the middle and Lieutenant Stark's men making a perimeter around them.

The column of men crossed the footbridge, and one of Stark's men ran to fetch a surgeon. Patrick directed Jacob to take William over to the small cemetery on the other side of the Ranger camp. He told the others to see to their weapons and their gear, while he and the lieutenant went over to the fort to make their report.

While they were cleaning their rifles, the fort's doctor came over to work on Robert's shoulder. He had been lucky. The bullet had passed through the flesh without breaking any of his shoulder bones.

As Jacob cleaned his rifle, the emotions of the day finally burst free from the dam that had been holding them back, the weight of it all coming out. His hands shook as he wiped down his lock. He was drained and exhausted as the adrenaline left him and the reality of losing William sank in. While Jacob was no stRanger to death, no one close to him, with the exception of his father, had ever been killed in front of him.

"Well, you whelps finally saw some action, didn't you," joked a Ranger who was chuckling with a group of men who were passing by. Not knowing why, all of the emotions of the day bubbled up, and

Jacob leaped from where he was sitting and caught the Ranger in the chin with a vicious punch, knocking him to the ground. The fallen Ranger's friends jumped in and grabbed Jacob, causing Konkapot and Peter to leap up to get between them, both groups pushing and shoving.

The two groups finally separated, with Konkapot and Peter holding back Jacob, who was seething in rage. The other group, who had helped the fallen Ranger up, were also holding him back.

"Why did you do that?" demanded the Ranger, echoed by his friends.

Jacob couldn't speak, his face red and his mind blank of any thought other than a feeling of anger and loss. While holding Jacob's arm, Peter looked at the group and spat, "We lost one today, dat's vot happened!"

The group began to calm down, having learned that the remains they had seen was William. Both Jacob and the other Ranger were released. Jacob was still breathing hard, but his hostility was fading away.

"Didn't know," the Ranger commented. "Didn't mean nothing by it." He extended his hand, and Jacob took it and shook.

"Name is Francis, Francis Dawdon," the man introduced himself. "You have one hell of a punch there."

Taking a deep breath, Jacob nodded and introduced himself. "Sorry about that," he said.

Francis nodded. "Sorry for your loss, and no hard feelings?" Jacob again nodded, and the two groups returned to their duties.

Once finished with cleaning their muskets and gear, Jacob and the rest of the Rangers returned to William, carried him to an open spot in the Ranger's cemetery, and buried him. After the final shovel of dirt had been thrown onto the grave, a crude cross was placed in the ground with a small plank of wood that had William's name quickly carved on it with a knife.

Then in their own languages, Peter's Bavarian, Konkapot's Mohican, and the others' English, they said a final prayer over William's grave. Jacob was coming to terms with the loss of a fellow Ranger and friend and with his own mortality. He recognized that he was still alive and would be able to fight again.

He looked down at William's grave, and in a low voice said, "And you too will be avenged."

Shouldering the shovel, Jacob turned and returned to the camp.

CHAPTER 2

FORT LYMAN: SETTING AN AMBUSH

For the month following the ambush, Jacob and his section spent their time working on the Ranger huts that would become their barracks, conducting local patrols, and guarding work details around the construction site. More French and Indian patrols were being encountered in the area, and the entire garrison was on a heightened state of alert. Robert's wound healed, and he was able to rejoin the Rangers on their duties.

To replace William, Lieutenant Stark brought Samuel Penny and Richard Cobb to join their section. From Connecticut, Sam was both an experienced hunter and trapper like them, and he could speak French, having worked as a trader before the conflicts made trading with Canada a dangerous job. Richard was from a Ranger section in which everyone other than himself had gone home, their enlistments having expired.

"Thanks for taking me in," he said. "Was getting tired of garrison duties around the island. Need to get back out in the woods."

Captain Rogers instituted a camp routine, began instilling discipline into the ranks of the Rangers, and continued training veterans and new men alike. Because of the increased risk, he issued a standing order that all Rangers must be able to respond to the "long roll" of the drum. He explained that when the fort's duty drummer began a long roll, it was the signal for the garrison to grab their weapons and quickly assemble.

Each morning, the company formed, and Lieutenants Stark and Waite conducted roll call, accounted for their men, and inspected their platoons. Each Ranger was responsible to show up at morning formation with his rifle or musket clean and serviceable and with sixty rounds of shot and powder. Even their tomahawks were inspected to make sure they were well sharpened, had no rust, and were ready if they had to be used. Unlike the Provincials, the Rangers did not carry bayonets; their rifles were not designed to hold them. The Rangers' only close-in fighting weapons were their knives and their tomahawks.

After the inspection, the orders for the day were read, announcing who would be heading out for patrols and who would be on night watch and passing along any specific orders from General Johnson. While Jacob understood why these orders were read, it still didn't alleviate the boredom that came with the reading, which seemed to say the same thing day after day after day.

With enemy activity increasing, the Rangers had to be ready to move quickly to react to any attacks. "Turn out Rangers!" was the call to action, normally in reaction to the drummer's long roll. Jacob and his fellow Rangers always had their rifles, shooting bags, powder horns, and canteens stacked or leaning close by when they were working to be ready to respond to any calls.

Sometimes during morning inspections, Captain Reynolds, Lieutenant Manning, and the sergeant major could be seen observing from afar. Though a drill, Jacob's heart still raced when he turned out, grabbing his rifle and shooting bag.

It was during one of the morning formations that Patrick was informed that his section would be going out to set up an ambush to stop the French patrols, and if possible, to take prisoners. Once the formation was dismissed, Patrick called everyone together to give them their instructions concerning the ambush.

"We're heading back out, close to where we were ambushed, to see if we can spring a surprise on these Frenchies and their Indians," he said.

Jacob's mind began to race, hearing they were going out after the enemy who had attacked them during their last action, killing William. Doubt was starting to worm its way into his resolve. Would he come out of this fight alive? Would he make a mistake? Jacob shook his head, pushed the thoughts to the back of his mind and focused on what Patrick was telling them.

As before, Patrick knelt down and, using a stick, drew a rough sketch of their route in the dirt.

"Time to make these bastards pay for killing William," he began. "We're going out to set up an ambush to stop these bloody bastards' freedom of movement and see if we can take a prisoner to get information about the enemy."

Patrick looked at each of the men to make sure they understood their mission. The stern expressions he got back from them showed they understood. Jacob felt good inside, though he had to admit it was strange that he would feel good about going out to kill other men. But in his mind, it was justified because of what they had done to William.

Patrick continued, "We're going to be heading out for a couple days, so we're going to draw provisions from the quartermaster, cook it up, and get our kits together before starting out first thing in the morning."

As the section broke up to go get their haversacks, Patrick pulled Jacob off to the side.

"You seem to know what you're doing, and I could use a hand in leading these men," Patrick said. "I've already spoken to the lieutenant and the captain, and they both agree, you're to be my new corporal."

Jacob shrugged his shoulders and nodded his head. Inside his mind though, thoughts tumbled about as doubt raised its ugly head. Corporal? Could he really do it? Could these men place their lives in his hands? Would he be able to lead under fire and not make mistakes that could get them killed? Instead of worrying about himself, now he would have to worry more about them.

Patrick could see by Jacob's expression that he was wrestling with the notion.

"I'm not sure I'll make a good corporal. I can still keep fighting, right? Don't have to wear anything fancy like an epaulette on my frock?" Jacob asked as he pulled out the right sleeve of his frock.

Patrick just snorted and shook his head. "No, laddie, I need you doing what you do best: shoot straight and true, find them before they find us, and help me lead these men. I may need you from time to time to help train and lead."

Patrick looked seriously at Jacob and placed a hand on his shoulder. "Lad, I know this is a lot to ask. I felt the same way when I was promoted, especially to this here sergeant job. Some have to learn to be a leader, others have the gift of being a natural leader."

Patrick looked Jacob in the eyes. "You, laddie, are a natural leader. The men already follow you even if you don't know it. Trust your instincts and your gut, no different than what has kept you alive up to this point."

Jacob nodded that he understood and could see Patrick's point. He had been a leader even if he hadn't realized it.

Patrick could see the idea had sunk in, and he nodded.

"As a corporal, if you want some extra stuff, maybe the quartermaster can give you an extra ration of fatback or something."

Patrick squeezed Jacob's shoulder, Jacob nodded, and the two Rangers shared a good laugh as the anxiety drained from Jacob.

"C'mon corporal." Patrick pointed with his head. "The men have to get their rations of this fine food so we can cook it up right and head out."

Patrick and Jacob caught up with the rest of the men and headed over to the fort to be issued their provisions. As before, the quartermaster gave them their staple of rations composed of flour, salt, some beans, some salt pork and beef, and a pint of beer.

Once they had received the rations and placed them in their haversacks, they returned to their island and to their newly constructed field kitchen. The field kitchen was a circular ditch about three feet deep and three feet wide. On the inside wall, holes were dug into the side where the fires were built, and above them a chimney was dug down to the fire. Firewood was stacked off to the side, and one of the additional responsibilities of the night watch was to keep the fires burning.

Some of the men went over to their lean-tos to grab cooking pans, while the rest of the Rangers occupied a couple of the fire holes and started cooking their beef and pork. They were sharing the field kitchen with other Rangers from the company who were also cooking rations to head out.

Patrick had divided the labor up amongst the men. Peter and Robert made biscuits while Samuel and Konkapot focused on cooking the meat, and Richard boiled the beans. Everyone congratulated Jacob on his new promotion and gave him a hard time about it.

Once all of the rations were cooked, the men went back to their lean-tos to finish preparing their gear. After making sure their gear was serviceable, they returned and sat in a circle around their squad fire.

Samuel pulled out a small metal pot and after placing it on the fire, dropped in some small lead ingots. The Rangers were issued the lead in ingot bars, and had to melt them down to be poured into the molds. Allowing the fire to heat the pot and melt the lead, they all sat back, leaning on their arms or against logs while Peter told them stories of the fine established houses of "ill-repute" in Munich and how they compared to the colonial ladies he had met in Boston.

As they waited for the lead to melt, Jacob watched his fellow Rangers banter back and forth in good humor, mostly excited about going out on a patrol instead of being stuck with local garrison duties.

Jacob still was trying to deal with the reality of being a corporal, wondering if he was ready. As he listened to his friends, and they truly were friends as well as comrades-in-arms, Jacob was feeling a comfort, a brotherhood he hadn't felt in a long time, a sense of belonging. He felt safe with them, and in that security, he was growing confident about his abilities.

As Jacob watched his comrades, he also mused on his feelings about killing the enemy. He had killed before, more game than men, but he had killed a few men before he joined the Rangers. These had been Hurons who were trying to kill him, and he had defended himself.

Deep in his heart though was the specter of the painted warrior who had killed his father and taken his brother, and his thirst for revenge was there. Jacob wondered if he could control that rage before it consumed him.

Now he was fighting in this war, and the enemy would try to kill him, his comrades, and his friends. So he would kill them. While he did not take pleasure in it, fighting was his job now, like hunting had been before. It was a matter of survival, so killing his enemy would help him live through this, and if he could, help some of his friends as well.

Jacob was concerned about what would happen if he began to like killing too much. Fighting was brutal, and he had to become savage and brutal to survive. As long as that beast did not take over his soul, he would win.

Jacob recalled back when he had lived in a Mohawk village for a short time during his long hunter days. A Shaman for the village had explained the balance of life as the Mohawks viewed it. With the Mohicans and Mohawks, he had experienced their connection to nature and their religious beliefs, understanding although not really accepting anything other than what he saw before him. Jacob understood the difference between good and evil, and he hoped that what he did, while brutal and savage, was for the greater good.

Jacob returned to the present as his comrades were laughing with Peter as he told his outrageous stories. He was part of this close-knit family of Rangers, and if being savage would keep them, as well as himself, alive, then that's what he would do.

Looking over, Jacob observed that the lead had melted. Now it was a bubbling silvery-grey liquid, and they pulled bullet molds from their shooting bags. Konkapot also pulled out a ladle, and Jacob used a thick branch to pull the pot from the fire and set it near them. Each man had a wooden bowl next to him.

Scooping out some of the liquid lead with the ladle, Jacob poured it into the bullet mold, and then passed the ladle around to the other Rangers, who took their turns pouring the lead into molds. After waiting long enough for the mold to cool, Jacob tapped it a few times and then opened it, dropping the new ball into the wooden bowl.

The Provincials carried muskets that were normally the same caliber, either .69 or .75, and they could be issued manufactured balls. But every rifle needed a specific mold for its bullets, which made it difficult for the quartermaster to supply balls to the riflemen. Balls for the guns the riflemen carried had to be well formed in molds that matched their rifles. It was the responsibility of the rifle's owner to make a sufficient number of balls before heading out.

Once the ball cooled enough to be handled, they snipped the residue of lead, which had been created by the spout of the mold. Using a file, they then smoothed the balls. Jacob inspected each one to make sure there were no deformities; any found bad were thrown back into the pot and re-melted.

The following morning dawned grey and windy, with a wetness on the wind that spoke of impending rain. Jacob knew the weather was going to be a benefit as well as a challenge.

The Rangers got their gear ready, making sure they brought some extra waterproofing to protect their rifles' firing mechanisms as well as themselves from the looming rain. Jacob scanned the sky and shrugged; while he might not like getting wet, there was little he could do about it, and so he didn't dwell on it.

Patrick and Jacob checked everyone before they departed the island. Jacob checked to see if the canteens were full and everyone had their shot and powder, while Patrick observed Jacob and made sure that all was in order and ready to go. Once Jacob nodded that everything had been checked, Patrick led them out. They cradled their rifles and marched off, with Lieutenant Stark wishing them good hunting.

As they crossed over the bridge, there was a good breeze whipping up some white caps on the river. They headed once more northward into the thick forest that was even darker today than normal.

Before reaching the wood line, the patrol spread itself out, Jacob and Konkapot in the front, followed by Robert, then Patrick and Samuel, and finally Richard and Peter. Rifles were all carried at the ready, but hammers were still only half-cocked. As soon as they entered the forest, they quickly began their habitual scanning of the area for signs of any tracks or sounds of other people.

After a few minutes in the woods, Patrick stopped the patrol and had them all take a knee, facing outward and listening, blending in with the brush. Since they had been ambushed on their last patrol by an enemy scouting force, Patrick wanted to make sure there was no one near them as they entered the woods. In silence, the Rangers scanned and listened to the world around them. Jacob's anxiety slipped away, replaced by the focus he always had while hunting.

After a few minutes, the bird calls and other normal sounds of the forest returned, which meant there was no one nearby. After this listening halt, Patrick signaled for Jacob to begin moving. He had told Jacob the route, which followed a northwest-running trail towards a large creek, halfway between the fort and the large lake to the north. It would be at that creek that the ambush would be placed.

As the patrol moved deeper into the woods, the clouds became darker and thicker, and the wind started to pick up slightly. Jacob could sense there was a storm coming. He welcomed it because he knew it would help hide their movements as they set up their ambush, though they would get wet in the process.

He was worried they would find no enemy. Who in their right mind, he wondered, would be out in one of these northern summer storms? Then he snickered to himself, well ... we are out in it, so are we of right mind?

They followed the trail, but from a distance in the woods, to see if any enemy patrols had set up ambushes of their own. After an uneventful march, they arrived near the creek, halting on some high ground and taking up positions behind trees while Patrick and Jacob went forward to look at their prospective ambush site. They stopped down slope at the tree line to look at a small open field with a stream about five to six feet across meandering through the center. Numerous game and other trails seemed to crisscross this field.

Patrick nodded and whispered to Jacob, "Well this is it. Where should we put the men? Where do you think the enemy will come from?" Jacob looked around and spotted a small rise off to their left that appeared to have a good view of the field and provide concealment and cover for their patrol. It was defendable as an elevated position if the enemy was larger than they expected. Jacob pointed and whispered, "Over there."

Patrick nodded in agreement. "We're of the same mind; I was looking at that spot meself."

They went back to where they had left the men and moved the patrol over behind the rise that they had selected, approaching it from behind. They took up two-man positions that Patrick pointed out. One covered while the other slowly moved debris and branches to allow them to hide without disturbing the front, which could warn the enemy of their presence.

In the distance, a peal of thunder echoed off the mountains. It was going to be a wet night.

After the three positions were ready, the men rotated between watching the field and eating their cooked but cold rations. Jacob and Konkapot were together with Richard and Peter in the middle and Robert and Samuel on the other end. Patrick was in the middle so he could give directions.

As the sun set, the rain began to fall softly. All of the Rangers took sections of leather and tied them around their firing mechanisms to keep them as dry as possible. As the night progressed, the men pulled out painted cloth that was water resistant to help them stay mostly dry so they could try to catch a little sleep. While on patrols or in ambush sites, they didn't really sleep, but rather snoozed. A man who slept deeply on patrols was a dead man.

The men quietly rotated between watching and sleeping. The rain began to fall harder, the wind picked up, and lightning and thunder crashed around them. The thick boughs of the trees and their painted blankets kept them dry for the most part, but not entirely.

Jacob was watching the field, the rain splattering against his hat, and sure enough, a cold trickle of rain found its way down the back of his neck and between his shoulder blades. He gave an involuntary shiver as the cold hit him, hoping this rain would be to their advantage if the enemy was close by.

Jacob had nothing but time on his hands as he watched and waited for the enemy to arrive, if they arrived. This was a large forest with many trails, though this was well known as an area the enemy used.

With all of this time, Jacob's mind began to mull over his different feelings and thoughts about being a Ranger. The excitement of the fight, the adrenalin rush from the action, and living life on the edge were all feelings Jacob now associated with being a Ranger. Also there was the thought of death; his own or his friends. He still wondered if he would do the right thing and not make mistakes.

As he watched and listened to the constant low pitter-patter of dripping rain on the leaves and limbs, Jacob accepted that he couldn't control death. If it was his time, there was nothing he could do about it. But if he could do anything to prevent himself or his friends from dying, he would. He would learn and adapt, taking in everything he could from Patrick and the other experienced men so he too would become proficient, and, with this, smart enough not to make mistakes. He would focus on the now, and this satisfied him. With a nod, he accepted it, and then he heard the sound of Konkapot coming up. His time to sleep had arrived. When Konkapot softly shook Jacob awake for another turn at watching the field, the rain had stopped. There was still a good breeze blowing, with the trees creaking and their rain-soaked branches dripping on them as they lay in their ambush position. The clouds were moving away, and the flicker of lightning was now far off in the distance.

The moon and stars were coming out, and the men could hear night insects, which included the hum of the ever-present mosquitoes and black flies searching for the Rangers. Soon an owl hooted, and even the distant sound of thunder faded away into the night, replaced by nothing more than the sound of the wind in the trees.

The rest of the night passed uneventfully for the patrol, and soon Jacob was finding it hard to stay awake. While he was watching the field, he would catch himself nodding off or his eyes would slowly begin to close. Jacob shook himself and, in a way, hoped the enemy would show up or dawn would arrive to break the boredom of the wait. As the grey of pre-dawn approached, Patrick made sure everyone in the ambush was awake.

They all took turns dumping their pans and using cloths to dry them. They then loaded new and drier priming powder for their rifles. As one cleaned, the other watched the woods in case the enemy arrived. No sooner had they finished checking their rifles than Jacob noticed several deer running across the field, breaking out of the woods opposite them, quickly crossing the clearing, and going past them into the woods. Jacob alerted Patrick, pointing his fingers at his eyes and then pointing to where the deer had just come from. Patrick nodded and soon they all settled deeper into the ground, wiggling on their stomachs, their rifles aiming at the far side of the field and resting on logs to steady their aim. Dawn was slowly approaching, and the field was becoming a little brighter, when Konkapot spotted the first Indian warrior moving along the far tree line. He slowly kicked Jacob, who looked to where Konkapot was pointing and soon spied more of the approaching Indians.

Soon, all of the Rangers were tracking the Indians, who were now coming out of the woods and stopping at the stream. Silently and slowly, seven rifles followed the approaching Indians, each pointing at a different warrior. Even though the Indians were only fifty yards away, they didn't spot the Rangers because the Rangers' dark green clothing, which had become even darker in the rain, blended perfectly with the trees and shrubs they were hiding in. The rifle barrels slowly continued to follow the Indians as they moved towards the stream in the middle of the opening.

The only sound was the echo of a woodpecker tapping on a tree in the distance and some birds chirping. Stopping in the middle of the field were ten darkly painted Indian warriors, two Canadian scouts in regular huntsmen's clothes, and three men in white coats and blue breeches, with black tricorn hats. These finely dressed men were Lieutenant Louis de Coulon, Ensign Pierre Joseph, and Sergeant Paul Marin of the Troupe de la Marines, who had accompanied the Canadian scouts and Huron warriors.

They had been sent here by their commander, the Baron Dieskau, who was planning an attack against Fort Lyman to prevent its completion. The report provided earlier by the war chiefs Tawiskara and Wawanagit concerning the progress on the fort and the number of Provincial soldiers gathering there had alarmed the Baron. He wanted these men to identify any weaknesses in the defenses and to plan a route for the army to take to get to the fort.

Jacob concentrated on slowing his breath, carefully aiming to make sure his first shot was true. Remembering their objective was to take at least one person alive as a prisoner, Jacob was aiming to hit what he suspected was a French officer in the shoulder; he thought that a shoulder wound would be enough to take him prisoner without killing him. He guessed he was an officer by the silver gorget he wore around his neck and the silver trim along the edge of his black tricorn hat.

The air was almost buzzing with tension as the Rangers waited until Patrick gave a simple command of "now!" All seven rifles barked nearly as one, and seven enemies spun and flopped to the ground in twisting motions. Jacob could see that the officer he had aimed at was still moving, so at least he was still alive while the other six were lying still. The Rangers burst from their concealment, drawing their tomahawks. Konkapot, Samuel, and Peter were quickly loading their rifles on the run as Patrick, Robert, and Richard moved quickly across the field.

They wanted to capitalize on the shock of the ambush to get into a good position before the enemy rallied.

Jacob moved fast to take the officer prisoner. As he broke cover, he pulled his tomahawk and sprinted through the tall wet grass towards where the officer was lying.

The shock of the ambush was wearing off, and the surviving Hurons and Canadians were beginning to fight back. Wanting to make sure his quarry wasn't pulled off by the Hurons, Jacob rushed out and stood over the wounded Frenchman, who he noticed had curled up into a fetal position, his eyes squeezed tightly shut. He was silently moving his lips, perhaps in prayer.

Jacob saw where his ball had passed cleanly through the shoulder, making a neat but bloody hole on the man's uniform. As Jacob looked down at his fallen quarry, a Huron warrior was closing in on him. Jacob had failed to notice the warrior because he was focusing on his prisoner and not the fight around him.

Konkapot had just finished loading his rifle when the Hurons and Canadians counter-attacked, and he spotted the charging Huron heading towards Jacob. Konkapot quickly brought his rifle up to his shoulder and fired, his ball passing close to Jacob's right shoulder to catch the charging Huron in the chest.

Konkapot's shot brought Jacob to full attention, and he looked up in time to meet a second Huron by quickly lowering his shoulder and twisting under the Huron as he swung his tomahawk downward, flipping him over his shoulder.

In a fluid motion, Jacob followed through by sinking his tomahawk in the chest of the warrior. A third Huron was hit from Peter's rifle, and one of the surviving Canadians was hit by Patrick's thrown tomahawk, which was followed up by Patrick burying his knife into the Canadian's chest. Patrick stood up, pulling his tomahawk and knife out, wiping the blood from both on the dead Canadian's shirt.

It was enough for the rest of the Indians, who decided to make a break for it and run back into the woods, leaving their dead and wounded to the Rangers. Wiping his tomahawk on the dead Huron, Jacob returned it to his belt in the small of his back. Then he drew his knife to remove the scalp of the dead Huron for the bounty it would bring him. As it popped off, Jacob looked over and saw the Frenchman had rolled over and was staring at him, his eyes wide in horror.

Putting his bloody trophy in his belt, Jacob approached the wounded Frenchman, who was trying to wiggle and crab away from him in the tall grass. Jacob knelt down, pinning the man in place with his knee, returning his knife into its sheath. He turned the Frenchman over and looked at the shoulder wound as the Frenchman stared up at him in shock.

Jacob yelled for him to stop fidgeting, and it seemed the Frenchman understood, though his eyes stared at Jacob and the bloody scalp in fear. Keeping his rifle close at hand, Jacob pulled some cloth bandages from his haversack and began binding the Frenchman's wound.

"You understand any English?" Jacob asked, but the Frenchman only cocked his head, and then shook it no. "Of course not," Jacob muttered.

With a heavy sigh, Jacob looked for Samuel, who was talking to the wounded French sergeant. Patrick was with him. Samuel indicated that the sergeant wouldn't last long.

Patrick looked over to Jacob, and sent Samuel over with a nod of his head while he finished off the sergeant quickly with his knife.

Though brutal, it was better than leaving him to the wolves. They had to move fast, and he wouldn't have made it back to the fort anyway.

"He doesn't speak any English, Samuel. Let him know he is safe as long as he follows our instructions," Jacob said.

Samuel explained to the prisoner that he was safe. The French officer seemed to respond with a sigh of relief. He nodded and accepted that he was their prisoner.

"Finish up here, and get ready to move," Patrick commanded. Konkapot and Peter went back to their ambush position, gathering up their blankets and other items, while Patrick and the others searched the bodies for anything that would be of use to them. Jacob reloaded his rifle.

Patrick looked at Samuel.

"Samuel you take care of him as we move, since you can speak to him, and we can't."

Samuel nodded. Once everyone was gathered in a tight circle, Patrick waved to move out, and the Rangers rose up and began their quick journey back to the fort.

Because of the Frenchman's wounded shoulder, they didn't bind his hands, but they placed a noose around his neck, which Samuel controlled. Jacob and Konkapot led, with Patrick, then the prisoner and Samuel, followed by Peter, Richard, and Robert.

The Rangers moved as quickly as they could as a bright sun finally broke through the morning clouds. The enemy dead were left where they fell, minus their scalps and equipment, which Patrick and Robert had bundled up to carry back to the fort to see if there was anything with information value.

The fort was alerted that they were coming in with a prisoner by the pickets, who had sent a runner ahead. When Patrick and the patrol reached the sally port to the fort, General Johnson himself was waiting with some members of his staff, including Captain Robert Rogers.

The fort's surgeon took charge of the wounded prisoner as Patrick reported the results of their ambush, and then followed General

Johnson and Captain Rogers into the fort, yelling to Jacob to take the men back to camp to clean their gear.

Jacob hefted his rifle and led the rest of the Rangers back to the island. Robert stayed behind to drop off the captured equipment at the fort, but he quickly caught up with them at the camp. They were greeted with warm hellos and welcomes from the other Rangers who had seen them enter the camp, and they waved back in response.

The first thing they did after dropping off the gear was to make hot water to clean their rifles. They placed their tin cups with water in them next to the fire. Dipping rags in the warm water, they cleaned the powder residue from the firing mechanisms. Then they used whittled sticks in the touchholes, poured the hot water down the barrels, and swished it around before pouring out the foul-smelling black water. They repeated this until the water came out clear. Then using their ramrods and cloth patches, they dried out their barrels.

As they cleaned and wiped down their gear, they talked with other Rangers who had stopped by to learn about the ambush and the fight. Jacob felt he had done well, though he did blame himself for not paying attention and almost getting his head split open if it hadn't been for Konkapot. He had to work on paying better attention.

With that as the only exception, Jacob realized fear and doubt no longer clouded his mind, that he was becoming more accustomed to the action, and that he was trusting and relying on his comrades' and his own skills. Perhaps he was starting to get the hang of this Rangering.

Word had spread quickly through the camp on the success of their ambush, and more fellow Rangers, including Francis Dawdon, stopped by to congratulate them and to hear about the ambush.

Once their weapons and gear were cleaned, they had stripped out of their wet clothes and hung them out on the lean-tos or lines strung between them to dry in the sun. They sat naked on their ground cloths, drying their wrinkly skin in the sun while sharpening their tomahawks or knives.

It was at this time that Captain Reynolds and his men arrived to make a snap inspection of the Ranger camp. As luck would have it, they came upon Jacob and his fellow Rangers drying off.

"What on earth are you naked men doing? This is a disgrace," stammered Captain Reynolds as he spotted the hanging clothes and naked Rangers lounging around their camp.

Jacob and Konkapot looked up and couldn't believe what they were hearing.

"You heard the captain you bloody rabble," hollered the sergeant major. "Stand up when an officer is addressing you!"

Jacob and the rest of them looked at one another, shrugged, and stood into a squad formation, naked as the day they were born, while the captain continued his diatribe.

"Undisciplined, unprofessional soldiers," he said. "How can these men stop the French if they have no discipline, just sitting here relaxing in the sun?"

While Jacob stood as rigidly at attention as he could, he couldn't believe what Captain Reynolds was spouting about. He tried to determine what he had done to draw this man's ire on himself and his comrades.

Jacob lost some of his discipline when Captain Reynolds talked about their relaxing in the sun. He stepped out of the line, went over to their gear, and returned with a bundle which he threw on the ground at the captain's feet. All of the scalps they had just taken fell out as the bundle opened.

"We had a busy morning, sir; these Hurons and their friends won't be bothering anyone ever again. We stopped them from getting to you and the fort."

The captain was at a loss for words, and the sergeant major looked aghast at the scalps lying on the ground. Jacob could see over the captain's shoulder to where Lieutenant Manning was standing, and he noticed that he was silently laughing to himself at the expense of the captain and the sergeant major. He was the only one who seemed "normal" among these three professional British soldiers. Jacob also saw the approach of another officer, this one in a blue coat.

"Perhaps, Captain, you should see to your duties and advise the commander on how to defeat his enemies rather than pester these

Rangers," a voice said from behind the captain. "These men did a great service for our commander today and deserve better of you."

Captain Reynolds turned to see a tall man in the deep blue, redfaced uniform of the Massachusetts Regiment. Colonel Ephraim Williams, who along with Captain Rogers and Sergeant McKinney, had approached unnoticed by the captain and his sergeant major. The Rangers had spotted them, and they stood even more rigidly at attention, though still with slight grins on their faces.

Captain Reynolds turned and saw that it was Colonel Williams. He said, "Well, that may be, but under what authority do you give orders to an officer of one of his Majesty's regiments?"

Colonel Williams looked down at Captain Reynolds, cocked an eyebrow, and said, "If you have questions concerning my authority, take it up with General Johnson, who was appointed to his position by his most Royal Majesty. I have the same authority that he does as granted by his Majesty, Captain."

Closing his mouth, Captain Reynolds harrumphed and started back towards the fort with the sergeant major right behind him. Lieutenant Manning walked up, looked at the scalps, reached out and shook Jacob's hand, winked, and quickly marched off to catch up with the captain.

"I think that one will be all right in time," Jacob commented, "if we could ever get him away from the captain."

"That man has a lot to learn, or he won't survive out here," said Captain Rogers about Captain Reynolds. "Either from the French or from us."

Colonel Williams agreed, and turned to the assembled Rangers. "You did fine work today. Keep it up, and we'll have these bastards on the run soon enough!"

Colonel Williams returned to the fort as Rogers addressed Jacob and the men.

"Good job this morning. Not only did it send a message to the French and their allies that they can't move freely about, but we're learning a great deal from that lieutenant you captured about the

Baron and his plans. Seems we're going to have some hot business soon enough."

Captain Rogers turned to face Patrick. "Get them ready and cleaned up. We're going to start training the company in the morning." Then Rogers looked at the men. "And perhaps get them dressed like proper Rangers."

Smiling, Captain Rogers again congratulated the men on their ambush and returned to the fort. Patrick turned to Jacob.

"What did you ever do to that captain to earn his special attention?" he asked.

Jacob shrugged his shoulders. "Just lucky I guess. Wrong place at the wrong time. Never met him before other than here. Guess we'll never be friends."

Patrick let out a good laugh, and slapped Jacob on the shoulder.

"I bet you lose sleep knowing you and he won't be best of friends, eh?"

They all finished cleaning their gear and dressed in spare cloths while their other clothes dried.

Back inside Fort Lyman in the one finished barracks, General William Johnson, appointed Indian Superintendent in New York and General in command of the operation, was reviewing the information they had gathered from the prisoner, who was being led away to the fort's hospital tent.

General Johnson had a map stretched out on a table, candles holding the corners down. In the room with him was Colonel Nathan Whiting of the Connecticut Regiment, soon joined by Colonel Williams, Captain Rogers, and Captain Reynolds.

"Gentlemen, it seems we may have to move our timetable up and go after the French sooner than we had thought. From what I learned from our guest, provided to us by Captain Rogers's men, it seems that the Baron Dieskau will move south to the top of Lake Sacrement and will establish a base there."

William Johnson pointed out this position on his map, a spit of land between Lakes Champlain and Sacrement, a placed called Ticonderoga, and then traced his fingers down to their position.

"My plan, once the Mohawks arrive in the next couple of days, is to march north and put a stop to this Frenchman's plans. I will strike first and strike fast. You have these days to get your men ready, gentlemen. I intend to take the entire army north, keeping only the New York Provincials here to protect the work parties and garrison the fort."

General Johnson looked over at Captain Rogers.

"Captain, I will need the use of your Rangers along with the Mohawks to scout ahead of this army as we march, screening our advance and protecting our flanks. See to your men. Get with the quartermaster to ensure all have rations, powder, and shot for the expedition. Dismissed, gentlemen."

Captain Reynolds was eerily silent throughout the entire discussion, observing from the corner of the room as the details of the plan were discussed.

Far to the north, deep in French-controlled territory on a small finger of land that pointed into Lac Champlain, was Fort Saint-Frederic. Its construction had been started in 1734 by Gaspard-Joseph Chaussegros de Léry, and it now served as the French main base of operations against the English and their colonies to the south.

This was the line between New France and New England, and it was here that the French and Canadians, along with their Indian allies, were encamped and preparing for the next stage of their campaign to wrest control of these colonies from the British.

Within his large room in the fort, Jean Erdman, Baron Dieskau, who commanded the combined force of regular French regiments, Canadians, Hurons, and Canadian Mohawks and Abenaki Indians, was studying his map, his hand stroking his chin in thought.

Standing around the map were the commanders from the regular Régiment de la Reine and the Régiment de Languedoc, as well as the Canadian Militia commanders and Indian war chiefs, including Tawiskara, Wawanagit, and Tehwehron of the Caughnawaga Mohawks.

"From what our stalwart allies brought us," Dieskau gestured to Tawiskara and Wawanagit, who nodded in return to the compliment, "the English have a sizable force south of us that we need to eliminate in order for us to march on Albany and remove this English boil from our borders. From what our scouts have described, their defenses are not yet complete and the garrison is mostly Provincials and militia, with a small detachment of British regulars."

Using a dagger, Dieskau pointed to their position at the top of Lac du St. Sacrement.

"We'll march south to Ticonderoga and establish a base of operations there that will support our thrust against Fort Lyman here," he said as he stabbed the map with the dagger, leaving it embedded.

"We will crush the English in one violent stroke and clear our path to Albany. The army will march in three days. Ensure all men are provisioned and ready to march."

The officers, having observed what Dieskau had pointed out on the map, saluted and returned to their regiments, while the Indian war chiefs thought of the glory and spoils that soon would be theirs.

CHAPTER 3

FORT LYMAN: THE CAMPAIGN

Fort Lyman became a hive of activity as Provincials began more intensive training and drilling, gathering of supplies, and getting their equipment ready to prepare for the upcoming campaign. The field kitchens were constantly being used as groups of men cooked their rations, and the quartermaster was busy issuing supplies. Work also intensified on finishing the fort and getting the numerous cannons mounted on the ramparts.

It was no different for the Rangers, with Captain Rogers leading his company through a rigorous training program based on his experiences in the last war. This was the first time that the company as a whole was operating as a unit. The Rangers for the most part had been operating in small, independent sections.

Jacob's mind was like a sponge, taking in all he could as he learned from the expert himself. He found that many of the skills Rogers showed them were no different from those he had learned as a long hunter, but they had been adapted to military use.

Captain Rogers led the men out into the forest to work on movement techniques, which were necessary to survive against a hostile force that was also familiar with woodcraft. Rogers stressed the importance of traveling in single file as small units and keeping the spacing between Rangers to prevent one ball from hitting two men. Rogers stressed how important it was for everyone to make sure they were paying attention to their surroundings to spot the enemy before he spotted them. Jacob recalled that hard lesson from the time they were ambushed, an event that was now seared into his memory.

The company practiced moving through marshes, which they might find along their campaign north. Here Rogers showed them how to move in line abreast when crossing soft ground, returning to the file once again on hard ground. Rogers stressed that they should constantly be looking for the enemy, who could ambush them in tough spots like swamps.

One of the main missions for the Rangers was scouting and screening, and they would be expected to scout enemy positions and forts for the general. Rogers had them practice near one of the outer blockhouses how to scout for a good position, before occupying it to conduct the reconnaissance. They practiced moving techniques, approaching their target in a straight line instead of moving parallel, which would make it easier for the enemy to spot them.

With their recent success in ambushing and taking a prisoner, Rogers instructed them on how prisoners were to be treated. They were to be kept separate from fellow prisoners, and those Rangers escorting prisoners were to take a different route back, to prevent the enemy from following with superior numbers to attack and rescue their comrades.

Because the Rangers would be moving with the large Provincial force with General Johnson, they practiced how to support the march. The Rangers would separate into columns that marched on the flanks or fronts of the Provincials to provide early warning if there was an enemy force in the area waiting to ambush the columns.

In the open field near the fort, they practiced marksmanship, including how to work as a pair with one firing and the other covering so there would always be one loaded rifle in case the enemy decided to charge. Rifles took longer to load than the regular smoothbore muskets of the Provincials and regulars.

Captain Rogers had them practice covering one another by actually firing. Not only did he want them to do it correctly, he checked the targets to make sure their shots had been accurate.

While the Provincials practiced maneuvering their columns into line and firing as a massed formation, the Rangers practiced firing from a knee or even prone so the enemy bullets would fly over them. Rogers continued to preach the importance of teamwork.

With such a crafty adversary, Rogers instructed his Rangers to be cautious of anything that looked too good to be true, such as pursuing a retreating enemy. He recounted numerous times in which the retreating enemy was a ruse, used to lure the pursuers into an ambush.

Because their enemy was also well versed in tactics, Rogers had his Rangers work on escaping in case they were overwhelmed by superior numbers. He had the men break away to retreat to a better position at which they could rally and defend themselves.

He showed them how to form either a square or a circle, using high ground or thick terrain to assist in their defense. With the enemy skilled in ambushes, Rogers had his Rangers practice reacting to enemy fire, either breaking away or trying to flank the enemy and take them under fire.

Rogers took the platoons out at night to practice night movement and taught them how to establish a camp during a patrol. Most of the regular European armies and the Provincials did not operate at night. Rogers intended to make the night and the darkness their own.

He made sure they knew how to set sentries and rotate duties between sleeping, eating, and standing guard, and then told them to make sure everyone was awake and packed and listening for enemies before the dawn, a practice known as stand-to. They had already seen that the French, the Canadians, and their Indian allies liked to attack at dawn, hoping to catch their enemies while sleepy and easy to overwhelm.

Rogers also had them practice clearing any sign showing that they had stopped for the night. Prior to departing, they were to send out scouts to see if there had been any enemy movement near their encampments. During their practice patrols, Rogers instilled in them the routine of placing sentries when they stopped to drink or gather water from streams. Their safety depended on the sentries' constant vigilance. As the Rangers practiced their scouting techniques, they also were sweeping to the north of Fort Lyman. As they were moving through the valley, they found a landmark which was easily identifiable, a lone mountain in the valley. "Does it have a name?" asked Samuel as they took a rest break, looking at the lonely mountain. "Not sure," replied Patrick. "but the French probably own it, seeing we're between territory."

Samuel nodded, looking at the mountain, as well as Jacob and some of the others. There was a bald rock face on the western side of the mountain that Jacob filed away in his memory, to use as a navigation aid here in the forest. Rogers motioned for the break to be over and to form up, "We'll see you later, French Mountain," groaned Samuel as he got to his feet and readied to move on.

As the Rangers returned to the fort, Rogers instructed the men not to use the regular roads and trails in case the enemy was waiting for them in ambushes. If ambushed near the fort, the Rangers were to pursue, but by different paths, not using the one the enemy had made their ambush on in case they had laid another ambush along the trail to surprise any force reacting to the attack.

Jacob and his fellow Rangers returned to their island to clean their equipment and rifles after these practice patrols. The fort was nearly complete due to the herculean efforts of the workers, the walls solid and mounting around thirty-five cannons pointing out of the ramparts. Most of the barracks were finished, and the large Union Jack flag of Great Britain was flying in the breeze from a center flag pole.

Most of the log huts on the island were nearly complete, while Jacob and his section continued to sleep under their lean-tos. They would probably move into the huts when winter came and the snow began to fall.

Another garden was started on the southern end of the island, and a blockhouse was being constructed in the center of the island as part of the fort's growing defenses.

During a break from training, Jacob, Konkapot, and the other Rangers were sitting on logs near their lean-tos, sewing up holes in their clothes and patching their gear. As they were talking about the training they had received, there arose a commotion from the southern side of the fort and island.

Jacob and the other Rangers rose up to see what was happening, and they spotted a large body of Indians approaching the fort from the south on the Albany Road. The Mohawks had arrived, and leading them was their War Chief, Hendrick Theyanoguin, wearing a British officer's red coat.

Jacob had met Chief Hendrick in his younger days during his time with the Mohawks. He knew that Chief Hendrick was a strong supporter of the English, having been one of the four "Indian Kings" who had gone to visit England.

General Johnson came out of the fort and met Chief Hendrick, grasping forearms and welcoming him to the fort. Chief Hendrick had brought with him about two hundred warriors, who broke off to set up camp near the fort's southern-facing wall.

That evening, Jacob, Konkapot, and some of the other Rangers went over to visit the Mohawks in their camp. In the center of the camp, a large fire had been built, and suspended over it were two butchered cows, a gift from General Johnson to the Mohawks.

Sitting on blankets, Jacob and Konkapot, with the other Rangers sitting around them, visited with several of the Mohawks they knew while a few curious Mohawks stood or sat behind them. Jacob spoke Mohawk, and translated for the Rangers, especially Peter. The conversation ranged from hunting, to their military actions so far, to the upcoming campaign. When the conversation centered on combat and warfare, Jacob and Konkapot showed the scalps they had taken in their fights. Jacob thought that one of these days he should turn them in for the bounty money, but they had been so busy training, and the quartermasters had been too busy to accept them anyway.

The Mohawks and the Rangers showed each other their knives, tomahawks, and rifles. Jacob had brought some of the items they had taken from the dead Hurons and Frenchman, and he gave them as gifts to the Mohawks, who in turn presented gifts of beads and wampum to the Rangers. Seeing the Mohawks, Jacob felt like he had returned home to close friends he had not seen for a while, and in a sense, he had.

Like artisans talking about their craft, the Indians and the Rangers boasted, telling of great and impossible deeds to the enjoyment of their fellow Rangers and the warriors who sat and smoked their pipes, smiling and laughing.

As the sun set, the fire grew higher, the beef was distributed, and another gift from General Johnson, a cask of rum, was opened and distributed. The Mohawks and the Rangers were bonding as warriors and professionals do. After a late night of drinking, singing war chants, and watching war dances, the Rangers stumbled back across the bridge to their lean-tos and quickly dropped off to sleep.

With no specific duties the next day, Jacob and the other Rangers returned to the Mohawk camp. In the open field where they trained, the Rangers and Mohawks had shooting contests for accuracy and range as well as tomahawk throwing contests. The Rangers did impressively well in the rifle marksmanship, both in long range and in accuracy, but the Mohawks owned the tomahawk throwing competitions, with the Rangers making good attempts but not doing as well.

Then the Rangers joined the Mohawks for a game of lacrosse, which was a learning experience for some of the Rangers who had never played, but it was a good bonding moment between comrades.

Standing on the fort's ramparts, Captain Reynolds shook his head and scoffed at the activity.

"Do they really think to defeat the French with these savages and Provincials? Is this what we have fallen to?" lamented Captain Reynolds. "Sir, this is their way. It may be difficult for us to understand, but at least they are on our side," said Lieutenant Manning.

"Lieutenant, if I want your views on these savages, I will ask for it, which I do not."

Captain Reynolds turned to face Lieutenant Manning.

"Once General Shirley's expedition against the French at Fort Niagara is complete, he will surely come here and put this upstart General Johnson in his place, and with the regular regiments he will bring here, he'll show this rabble how true, disciplined soldiers perform."

Lieutenant Manning shook his head in wonder. How could this man be so stubborn and short-sighted, failing to see the reality of the military situation?

For one thing, he did not appreciate the fact that being assigned as advisors to General Johnson had actually saved their lives. Because of this assignment, they had not been with their regiment when it took part in the failed expedition under General Braddock against the French Fort Duquesne in the Ohio Valley.

Their "disciplined and professional" regiment had been torn to pieces by the French and Indians in a well-established ambush, against a commander who only knew the tactics of fighting on the open European battlefields, using linear tactics instead of adapting to a new breed of combat.

The remnants of the 44th and 48th were being rebuilt, but with raw recruits. General Shirley, who had assumed command of the Royal forces in the colonies with Braddock's death, had requested additional regiments to be sent to the colonies, but none had yet arrived. Captain Reynolds was going to have to get used to the Provincials and militia units for a while longer until the British regiments arrived.

Lieutenant Manning also recalled from the reports how a Provincial dofficer, a Colonel George Washington from the Virginia Blues serving as an advisor, had helped to rally the broken British forces to save the day. This was the way these colonials fought, and if they wanted to survive and win, the Rangers needed to learn their style of fighting.

As the British and Provincials trained and prepared for their campaign to the north at a place that the Indians called Ticonderoga, located between Lake Sacrement to the south and the longer lake which the French called Champlain to the north, Baron Dieskau had encamped his army of French, Canadians, and Indians and was in the process of building a fort, which he named Carillon.

It was fitting that the new fort was on this very spot where the French explorer Samuel de Champlain, accompanying an Indian war party, had encountered an Iroquois war party. Supporting their new Indian allies, Champlain and two of his men, armed with muskets, turned the tide against the Iroquois, who were normally the superior fighting force.

This encounter in a way sowed the seeds for the current conflict: a power and arms race for the new world. Fort Carillon would serve as Champlain's base of operation, from which he could use the lake to transport his men and supplies southward instead of hacking through the thick wilderness.

Dieskau planned to accomplish the same victory that Champlain had earned there at Ticonderoga, except Dieskau's victory would be against the entire English forces, and he would drive them all away.

Tawiskara and Wawanagit entered Dieskau's command marquee with news.

"The English appear to be making ready to move. Our scouts saw many Mohawks arriving to join the English," said Tawiskara.

Tawiskara and Wawanagit's ability to speak decent French was also a product of the Champlain expedition. Because of their desire to procure muskets for their tribes, the Indians had learned to speak French to enable trade between the two nations.

"Were any of your warriors spotted?" asked Dieskau.

Tawiskara shook his head no. "No one was detected, and as you instructed, we took no scalps to let them know we were there. This is making my warriors angry; they have come to fight, not watch."

Dieskau raised his hands in acceptance and reassured both war chiefs that the time for battle was soon approaching.

"I plan to march quickly southward and get between the English and their fort, which I will destroy by moving behind them," explained Dieskau, using his dagger to trace the route from Ticonderoga to Fort Lyman.

"Then when the English turn to try to save their fort, we'll destroy them as well. This is a great opportunity for our victory. I couldn't have planned it any better myself. Tonight, have your war dance, have your warriors ready their tomahawks and knives, for soon they will have their scalps and their victory."

As Dieskau and his staff planned for the march, the Hurons, Abenakis, and Canadian Mohawks held their war council. A great fire was built, and all were addressed by their war chiefs, Tawiskara, Wawanagit, and Tehwehron. Promises of scalps, plunder, and the deaths of their English foes, and predictions of a great victory were repeated through the night, punctuated by the loud war cries of the assembled.

With drums beating and the fire crackling high in the center, the three tribes of warriors mingled and danced their war dances to appease their gods and spirits, asking to be granted victory and honor in the coming battle.

In the morning, Dieskau gave the order for half of the force, consisting of some two hundred French regular grenadiers from the Régiment de la Reine and the Régiment de Languedoc, six hundred Canadian militia members, and over seven hundred Indian allies, to travel south on the lake, and then follow Wood Creek to the east to get around the English.

The rest of the army would work on Fort Carillon and be ready to march south to support Dieskau's push to Albany once he had destroyed the enemy and their fort.

As Dieskau was preparing to move his expedition south, General Johnson was forming his expedition to march north. Assembled outside of the fort, the army was drawn up for his inspection: the Massachusetts Provincial Regiment under Colonel Williams, the Connecticut Provincial Regiment, and Captain Robert Rogers' Company of Rangers, and the Mohawks under Chief Hendrick. The Provincial force numbered around two thousand men, with the New Hampshire and New York Provincials staying behind to garrison the fort and finish construction.

General Johnson inspected the gathered army with Captain Reynolds muttering under his breath that "vagabonds and rabble in uniforms do not make an army."

Pleased with what he saw, Johnson ordered the Rangers forward to scout and send flankers to protect the columns of soldiers and supply wagons. Following close behind the Rangers, who moved off into different positions to cover the advance, were the Mohawks. Then the columns of Provincials turned and began their march north towards the lake. The campaign was now under way.

Patrick, Jacob, and their group of Rangers were part of the right flank screeners, accompanied by about twenty Mohawk warriors, who moved like shadows through the trees. The army would march along the old road towards the lake, but the Rangers and the Mohawks would make sure that no French or Indians ambushed them while they were using such an obvious route.

Captain Rogers and a small detachment of his Rangers under Lieutenant Stark accompanied General Johnson's command in the column, which included Captain Reynolds, Lieutenant Manning, and the sergeant major. Rogers found it interesting that both Captain Reynolds and the sergeant major had apprehensive looks on their faces. Chuckling, Rogers focused on the march. The column stopped at old Fort Anne, the Rangers providing an outer security ring with the Mohawks while the rest of the army rested and allowed time for the supporting wagons to catch up.

Once rested, the army was ordered to resume the march, with the Rangers and Mohawks spreading out to the front and flanks. They passed by French Mountain once again, now becoming a familiar landmark as they moved toward the lake. As the sun was beginning to set, the column arrived in an open, marshy area at the southern end of Lake Sacrement.

The Rangers scouted around the area and found no recent sign of French or Indian activity, though Jacob spotted some cranes and loons taking flight from the water. The French column was making its way southward along the eastern shore, but it could not be seen from the southern end of the lake.

Rogers pointed out to General Johnson that near the center of the marsh was some high ground that would make a good and defendable camp position. Johnson agreed, and the army occupied the high ground and settled in for the night. The Rangers and Mohawks camped around the Provincial soldiers who were in the center with the supply wagons and command staff.

In the morning, General Johnson began establishing his base of operation for the coming campaign. He started by sending out work details to cut down trees to fortify the high ground they occupied. Once finished, he could use the fortified area as a supply point to support the next phase of northward movement towards the French Fort Saint-Frederic.

Patrick, Jacob, and the other Rangers were sent out on patrols to scout the area around the new encampment, accompanied by some

Mohawk warriors, to make sure the enemy was not watching them. They were progressing eastward in a wide sweeping circle away from the camp when they detected movement. The Rangers and the Mohawks dropped to the ground and crawled forward through thick brush up a small rise. From the top of the rise, they saw below them the long columns of Dieskau's expedition. They had landed their boats in a bay away from Johnson's camp and were marching overland towards Fort Lyman. The Rangers observed the moving column, composed of uniformed French regulars in their white coats and black military cocked or tricorn hats,

Canadians in their typical civilian/hunting clothes, and a large number of Indians.

The Mohawks who were with the patrol pointed out the three different tribes, the Hurons and the Abenakis, and then their hearts sank as they noticed their northern cousins, the Caughnawaga Mohawks.

This was no scouting expedition; this was a major movement by the enemy.

Patrick whispered in Jacob's ear, "We need to get out of here and report back to the general. He will want to know this."

As they slowly crawled backwards, they spotted the approaching Huron flankers. Patrick turned to the patrol and placed his finger to his lips, then slowly pulled his knife and drew it across his throat. Jacob and the others nodded their understanding; this would be a silent kill. He pulled his knife and passed the silent command back to the rest of the patrol, who readied their knives and tomahawks.

When the flankers reached their position, the Rangers sprang from their hiding places, making quick work of the Hurons. Jacob caught his target from behind, covered his enemy's mouth as he sank his knife into his kidneys, and held him tight until the warrior stopped moving, then slowly lowered the body to the ground.

Jacob didn't dwell on the fact that he had just killed another man. It was becoming so automatic that he didn't have to think about the action required. After hiding the bodies in the brush, the Rangers and the Mohawks returned quickly back to their camp at the lake.

While Johnson was working on his new encampment, the French expedition under Dieskau had landed at an area known as South Bay. Moving away from the bay with the Canadians and Indians leading the column, Dieskau and the French regulars began their march towards Fort Lyman. The French had left a small force at the bay to protect their boats in case they were detected.

They were using an unfamiliar route, having been ambushed on numerous occasions by these English "Rangers" along trails they had used before. But Dieskau did not know that he had been spotted by the Rangers and the element of surprise had been lost.

As they were moving towards Fort Lyman, the Canadians and some of the Indians, including Tawiskara, were concerned that they didn't see any signs of the Rangers or any other Provincial activity in the area.

The French still moved quietly and cautiously towards their objective, not wanting to warn their prey. They moved so slowly that it took two days to travel approximately fourteen miles from the bay to the fort's location. Concealing the army, Dieskau sent Tawiskara and some of his warriors and French engineers to observe the fort.

What they found shocked them. The engineers, using telescopes, observed that the fort walls were complete, as were the outer works of ditches and palisades. They could also see the numerous mouths of cannons pointing out of the ramparts along the fort's wall and bastions. Numerous smoke columns rose above the walls, and a large Union Jack was flying from the flag pole.

Tawiskara looked at the fort, recalling how it had looked during his last visit, and he knew they were too late. It would not be good for his warriors to attack the fort now with the cannons on the completed and sturdy walls; many of his warriors would die.

The French engineers also concluded that it would be difficult to take the fort. They had not brought any artillery to batter down the walls or conduct a proper siege. They shook their heads in disappointment.

They reported to Baron Dieskau that it would not make military sense to attack the fort without artillery. Somehow his English adversaries had outpaced his plans, finishing their fort ahead of schedule. Now with a completed fort, it would be foolish to attempt an attack with the forces he had, especially without artillery.

During the discussion, Wawanagit and Tehwehron arrived with their warriors and brought with them a Provincial deserter they had captured along the way. From this deserter, Dieskau learned that Johnson had in fact arrived at the lake and was in the process of erecting entrenchments and building a base of operations to attack northward against the French fort. They also found out that their little secret was no longer a secret, because a Ranger and Mohawk patrol had spotted their column and had warned Johnson.

Dieskau shook his head. "No matter. I had intended to destroy this English force and will do so, just not here. We'll set an ambush for them, and when they march this way, we will destroy them, and then return with cannons later to destroy this fort."

Dieskau knew that General Johnson's new position at the base of the lake was not yet finished and it would be easier to assault than the fort. Dieskau instructed the Indians and the Canadians to make haste towards the lake and to find a suitable place from which to ambush the English.

Tehwehron wanted to destroy the hated English, but he did not feel comfortable when he learned the Mohawks were with the English. To Tawiskara, it did not matter; a dead enemy is a dead enemy, and if their cousins had chosen the wrong side, then they were enemies.

CHAPTER 4

THE BLOODY MORNING SCOUT

Following the report provided by Patrick about the French movement, General Johnson assembled the army within its new encampment. Johnson centered himself and began speaking to the assembled men. Jacob prepared himself for the long, boring lecture to come and resigned himself to his fate.

"First of all, I hereby name this body of water Lake George on behalf of his most Royal Sovereign, King George II of England."

Most of the assembled men gave three rousing cheers of "huzzah!" as Jacob and Patrick looked around and coughed. They noticed they were not alone as other Rangers and Provincials did the same. The Mohawks just cheered to cheer, not really understanding what was being said.

"The French are here. We have them caught between us and the fort. I have denied them their lake, naming it for the King. Now, I intend to deny them this land by destroying their force.

"Colonel Williams, you will lead your regiment with Colonel Whiting's regiment in support. You will head back towards the fort and when you find the enemy, drive these invaders from our land. Crush them between your men and the fort!"

After his speech, Chief Hendrick approached Johnson and said he would accompany the men with some of his warriors. He had learned that their northern Mohawk cousins were with the French; maybe he could convince them to switch sides or at least not to fight.

Johnson agreed and wished Chief Hendrick the best of luck, and then returned his focus to making their encampment more secure.

Having not been assigned to the column, Rogers asked for volunteers to go with the Provincials to help out while he stayed with the rest of the Rangers to protect the encampment.

Patrick had volunteered them and, with Jacob, returned to get the rest ready to move. Knowing they would be moving fast, Patrick, Jacob, and the other Rangers stripped down to the bare essentials for fighting. They would go with the column as it set off to meet the French.

With Colonel Williams on horseback and Chief Hendrick alongside, the column marched out of the encampment and headed south. The date was September 8, 1755.

Patrick, Jacob, and the other Rangers were leaning on their rifles, watching the column pass by. It felt strange that they were now marching south to face the French instead of the more typical northward movement. Once the column began to snake down the road that they had created by marching to the lake, Patrick waved them forward and the Rangers took up a position at the rear of the column.

What bothered Patrick was that he did not see any scouts going before the column or any flankers being pushed out.

Colonel Williams was an experienced fighter, having tangled with the French and Indians before. Perhaps he was waiting until they were deeper into the woods before sending scouts out, or maybe he felt confident that the French would not surprise them, or that their greater number would make a difference. It didn't matter to Patrick; the colonel was in charge, and Patrick was only responsible for his own men.

As the Provincials entered the woods south of the lake, another force was deploying to meet them halfway between the lake and Fort Lyman. Dieskau, with Tawiskara and Wawanagit, spotted a ravine with the trail the English had made passing through its middle. The ravine was in sight of a lonely mountain. Dieskau silently wondered if it had a name before dismissing the thought and returned to the preparation for the ambush.

Dieskau had brought a combined force of French regular grenadiers from his two regular regiments. He deployed them to be the blocking force in the ravine.

He placed the Canadians and the Indians on the high ground on both sides of the ravine. They would serve to protect his force from any enemy flankers or scouts, and then they would shoot down upon the enemy in a crossfire that should decimate the Provincial soldiers. Then his elite grenadiers would charge and finish the job.

This was perfect, the right kind of position from which to ambush the foe and secure his victory. The grenadiers deployed in line, deep in the ravine, two ranks deep and shoulder-to-shoulder, just around a bend on the trail so they were hidden from the approaching English. This should surely shock these Provincials and halt them long enough for them to be caught in the crossfire from above, Dieskau thought.

The Canadians and Indians took up their positions along the rise. All they had to do now was to wait for the English to walk into their trap. Tawiskara was painted in dark red and black war paint across his chest and face; his Huron warriors were also painted for battle. Wawanagit and his Abenakis were wearing their dark war paint, looking forward to the coming battle and thinking of the scalps and plunder promised to them by the French.

The only reluctant warriors were Tehwehron and his Mohawks, having learned that their southern cousins were marching with the English. They all felt the same; they had no problems with waging war and killing the English, but they did not want to kill their brothers.

Tehwehron was not sure what would happen, but he knew they would be the first to spot the approaching English column. The Canadians took cover behind the rocks and trees where they had a good aim at the trail that the English would soon be traveling.

The entire ambush party began the wait, keeping still so as not to alert the approaching prey before they greeted them with fire and steel.

Dieskau would wait for the right moment to spring the trap.

As the column wound its way through the woods, Patrick, Jacob, and the Rangers moved along the rear and flanks of the column, listening to the shuffling gait of the Provincials as they marched, the clank of tin cups and canteens keeping time with their steps. They were still surprised not to see any scouts leading the column or on the flanks to protect the column.

As Jacob scanned the woods around them, he wondered what Colonel Williams was thinking. He began to get mad at the stupidity of this march. Why were they being placed at risk by not doing something as simple as placing out flankers and scouts?

The colonel knew there were French, Canadians, and Indians out there. Why was he not taking any precautions? Shaking his head, Jacob continued watching the woods for any sign of the enemy, but the anger remained. He might be new to this whole military thing, but even he knew it was bad business not to have scouts out. Captain Roberts had drummed that into their heads.

Yet, Colonel Williams did not understand these same rules that the Rangers followed. Jacob mistakenly thought these precautions were a common practice. Because all of the Rangers used scouts, he thought the other Provincials did the same.

The trail they were following began to wind down into a small ravine and the ground began to rise on either side of the column. The trail wound through the trees and followed the natural drift line of the rolling terrain. They spotted their newly found landmark of French Mountain (as they had begun calling it), to their front.

Jacob scanned the area, only noticing deer in the distance bolt away and the sound of the breeze in the trees, their limbs creaking. No sign of any French, Canadians, or Indians, but from the rear of the column it would be hard to spot anything that hadn't already engaged the column. Jacob was getting an uneasy feeling, and when he looked at his fellow Rangers, they too seemed to be edgy. Something didn't feel right. The column continued to march along the trail, entering the opening of a ravine. This didn't make sense to Jacob, but he thought Colonel Williams must know what he was doing.

Jacob could see they were moving into a natural choke point. He shook his head and kept scanning the surrounding area, now starting to fill with boulders of differing sizes scattered among the trees. Jacob couldn't shake the uneasiness he was feeling. He didn't like marching into this ravine.

To the front and unseen by the Provincials, Tehwehron watched the approaching column, the head of the column actually entering the ravine with no scouts out in front. From his concealed position, Tehwehron could not see any flankers either, but he did see the Mohawks moving with the English, and he made a quick decision.

He whispered to his warriors to fire their first volley into the air as a warning, which should be enough of an alert for honor's sake before engaging the English with his fellow Mohawks. He felt it would be bad luck to fire on their brother Mohawks without warning them first.

His warriors gravely nodded, and they began to raise their muskets high, aiming to shoot over the Mohawks in the column, most aiming at the English instead. Across the ravine, Tawiskara and Wawanagit pointed to the column, and their warriors, along with the Canadians, started to aim and follow the advancing English and their Indian allies with their guns. They had no problem with aiming at the Mohawks. More scalps and booty for them!

Dieskau heard the rhythmic pattern of the approaching column's footsteps, and the clanking of their gear echoing through the trees and boulders. A smile slowly rose on his face in anticipation of the victory to come.

Quietly, he ordered his grenadiers to shoulder their muskets, already tipped with their fixed bayonets. Drawing his sword, he gave the command to make ready and present, the muskets leveling straight down the ravine at the approaching Provincial column. Soon the column would turn the bend, and he would begin the slaughter.

Colonel Williams felt confident in his regiment and the men under his command. They would make quick work of these French, Canadians, and Indians as they had done in the past. He was watching the head of his column begin to turn a bend when he spotted what he thought were white uniforms in the distance. He couldn't see exactly who they were from his position in the column because there were trees in the way. He rose up in his saddle to get a better view.

Then high and to his right, Colonel Williams heard a loud whoop of several voices yelling in the Indian language and a volley of musket fire that only struck a few of his men. It was enough though and the column froze, either because of what they saw or what they had just heard. The Mohawks were all looking up at the edge of the ravine.

At the rear of the column, Jacob stopped and looked to Konkapot. "Did you hear that? It sounded like, 'Be warned brothers.'"

Konkapot nodded just as they heard a volley of musketry in the distance. Patrick yelled, "trouble," and the Rangers picked up their pace and started to head towards the sound of firing.

Baron Dieskau was just as surprised when he heard the Indians shout and fire the volley. The damn Indians had fired too soon. And yet, just as quick as it happened, there before them coming around the corner was the head of the column, the soldiers looking up and to the side of the ravine instead of to their front. Perfect.

They had stopped and presented an excellent target. Not to look a gift horse in the mouth, Dieskau gave the order to fire and the grenadiers unleashed their massed volley of over two hundred muskets. The bullets slammed into the head of the column, just as the rest of the ambush party began firing downward into the compact column. The timing was nearly perfect as the Provincials were hit from three sides.

It was a deafening roar as hundreds upon hundreds of musket and rifle balls impacted on the stopped column. Along with striking the bodies of their targets, the bullets also tore into trees and rocks, sending splinters in all directions along with ricocheting balls. In addition to the roar of the volley, all of the Indians raised their war cries, adding to the noise and confusion of the attack.

To Colonel Williams, it seemed the whole world had just opened on top of him, and before he could realize what was going on, he was toppling over as his horse was shot from beneath him.

As the horse screamed and fell to the ground, Colonel Williams saw the men of his regiment falling around him, almost in slow motion. The ground rushed up as his horse finished falling to the ground.

Panic began to spread through the entire column. The Mohawks, who had heard the warning, had dove to what cover they could find as the bullets shredded the trees and the leaves about them, but soon some of the balls began falling about them, killing and wounding the Mohawks.

Raising their muskets to their shoulders, they began to return fire at the enemies who were firing down upon them. Some of the Provincials, who had not immediately been hit, were also seeking cover and bringing their muskets to their shoulders in this chaotic fight.

Some of the platoon commanders were issuing orders to make ready as more men began to fall where they stood. Panic was starting to set in, and some of the least experienced men broke and began running into or around the men behind them in the column, causing even more confusion.

The ravine was filling with the choking grey smoke of hundreds of muskets and rifles firing at each other, blinding the combatants.

Above, Tawiskara, his warriors, and the Canadians were firing as fast as they could reload, picking their targets carefully. Tawiskara observed the man in the dark blue uniform on horseback tumble as his horse was hit several times and dropped screaming to the ravine floor. He saw the officer recover from the dead horse and begin making his way forward in the column, drawing his sword and issuing orders, appearing to attempt to rally his panicking men.

Then he spotted a Mohawk chief wearing a red coat come up next to the officer. Tawiskara spoke to the warriors close to him, telling them to shoot the officer. He would take care of the Indian traitor who had sided with the English, even wearing their clothes.

The officer could be seen pointing his sword and yelling at his men, climbing a large boulder to direct the defense. Raising his rifle, Tawiskara took careful aim at the chest of this red-coated chief as his men did likewise with the Provincial officer in blue. Slowly he let out his breath and squeezed the trigger.

The sound was intense, the ravine amplifying the noise of battle. Colonel Williams had pulled himself free from under his dead horse, drawn his sword, and begun giving orders.

"Take up firing positions, fire by platoons!" he yelled as he pointed his sword in the direction he wanted them to shoot. He pushed men who were wandering around in the direction they needed to go.

He was having difficulty communicating with his commanders. The smoke was making it hard for his men to see him and for him to spot his officers. The leaves were falling like snow as the bullets flew through the air, some making pinging sounds as they ricocheted off the rocks and trees, causing both wood and rock splinters to spray the men, injuring them as well as the rifle and musket balls.

Colonel Williams was trying to rally his men. He had seen the early signs that panic had begun to set in. He was trying to make his presence known in the noise and confusion of the battle, attempting to stop the rush of the terrified Provincials towards the rear.

He spotted a large boulder. Atop it, he would be able to see what was going on, and his men could see him. As he began climbing the boulder, Chief Hendrick approached, trying to help stem the panic and provide guidance to his warriors.

Colonel Williams just had enough time to turn and see Chief Hendrick arrive when the first bullet hit him in the chest. That bullet was quickly followed by two more as he twisted from the impact and fell onto the boulder, dead before his body finished its fall, looking up into the sky.

Chief Hendrick saw Colonel Williams get hit. As he approached the fallen colonel, Tawiskara's first bullet struck him, followed quickly by two more. The old warrior's life ended as his blood was absorbed into his red coat. He fell alongside Colonel Williams, their blood mingling.

Tawiskara lowered his rifle and gave a victory shout which was quickly picked up by his warriors, who had seen the officer and the chief fall from their well-aimed bullets. He began loading his rifle for the next target, feeling this was going to be a great day for the Hurons. With the fall of their leaders, the English began to break and run from the fight. All too easy.

From his position, Tehwehron saw Chief Hendrick fall, knowing this warrior by his red coat and by his reputation. He believed he had met the requirements of honor by giving a warning shout and a volley in the air for his brothers, but now seeing his fellow Mohawks fall increased his concern that this day would bring bad luck to them all. Fellow Mohawks should not be fighting one another. He was superstitious that their spirits would hunt them and bring them down for being involved in their deaths.

With the loss of Colonel Williams and Chief Hendrick, the front of the column began to break apart and run to the rear, leaving many from their ranks dead or wounded on the trail.

As the front of the column began running by with no leadership, the other companies thought a retreat had been ordered, and they began to fall back as well. In the rear of the column, where the Connecticut Regiment was located, Colonel Whiting began organizing a defense by placing one company on one side of the ravine, and another just to the rear with another on the opposite side of the ravine. This allowed the men running to pass through without disrupting their firing lines, and he began to provide covering fire for the fleeing men.

One of the Massachusetts Regiment's captains found Colonel Whiting and told him that both Colonel Williams and Chief Hendrick had been killed and that he was now in command. Nodding, Colonel Whiting thought to himself, in command of what? A disintegrating column still caught in an ambush?

Colonel Whiting acknowledged the news and instructed the captain to form a firing line down the trail, but it seemed the captain was thinking more about running than fighting. Shaking his head, Colonel Whiting returned to commanding his troops as the column disintegrated in front of them.

As the column began to fall apart, Baron Dieskau gave the order for one more volley and then a charge with bayonets. He was tasting victory. His foe was falling before him and beginning to run away. It wouldn't take much more than a charge to break them and rout the enemy, he thought. Victory was close at hand. All he had to do was reach out and take it! As soon as the muskets fired, Dieskau raised his sword and yelled, "Charge!"

The French grenadiers, having fired their volley, stepped off with their bayonets lowered and began to advance down the trail, shouting their war cries. Tawiskara and Wawanagit, seeing the French begin their charge, pulled out their war clubs and tomahawks, and letting loose their own blood-curdling war whoops, charged down the ravine to begin the slaughter of the English and gather their well-earned booty and trophies. The Canadians too pulled out their knives and tomahawks and raced alongside the charging Indians, closing in on the retreating English. They caught them quickly, tomahawks and war clubs impacting with the backs and heads of the running Englishmen. Stopping only to take scalps, and sometimes to load their muskets, the combined French force was exploiting its advantage and destroying its adversary.

As he led his grenadiers forward, his sword pointing the way, Dieskau thought to himself that it was all coming together just has he had planned and that a great victory would be his.

Patrick and the Rangers could hear the crash of the musketry as the battle began in front of them. They were breathing heavily, the adrenaline beginning to kick in with battle close at hand. Angling away from the ravine, the Rangers took up a position behind some rocks. They could see one or two Provincial soldiers run by, and then the trickle turned into a torrent as the numbers began to grow. Jacob shook his head; this was not a good sign.

Then like a flood, it seemed the whole column had turned around and begun to run from the ravine, scattering in all directions, with the exception of a few companies and platoons that were leap-frogging back in good order and firing at the advancing enemy.

Next they saw, coming from around the bend in the ravine and running after the Provincials, the Canadians and Indians closing in with tomahawks and war clubs, sometimes firing their muskets at close range into the backs of the retreating soldiers.

"Pick your targets, lads. Make them count!" Patrick yelled as he squeezed the trigger on his rifle and began to reload. "We're going to have a lot of company soon. Be ready to fall back."

The Rangers followed their training, one man firing while the other covered. Jacob moved and reacted automatically, though he felt a growing anger as he watched the Provincials break and run instead of fighting.

As the flood became a tide of running Provincial soldiers, Patrick gave the order to break away. One Ranger would run back while his partner fired, then he would turn and cover his partner. Their accurate fire was effective, but it was not enough to turn the tide.

The battle, which was quickly turning into a rout, saw all the combatants intertwined in the dance of death as fighting became up close and personal. There was little to no cohesion in the Provincial ranks.

Only a few elements of the Connecticut Regiment were still holding their ground, but they too were quickly becoming surrounded and had to break away before becoming completely encircled.

The Rangers kept up a steady pace of firing and falling back, weaving from tree to tree to protect themselves from the flying bullets. Jacob was taking aim at an approaching Canadian when he felt like he had just been punched in the face with a blow that spun him into the ground. Shaking his head to clear his watery eyes from the impact, Jacob sat up on his elbows and gingerly felt his right check. A spent bullet had hit him under his eye and had gouged a chunk of flesh from his right cheek.

Konkapot ran up. "You alive?"

Jacob held his hand up and nodded. He got to his feet and kept moving. This battle was getting hotter than what they had wanted or expected, with no quarter asked or given. Jacob was controlling his growing fear and channeling it to fuel his survival instincts as the fight grew more intense around him.

As Jacob and Konkapot supported and covered one another, the Indians were moving through the fallen soldiers. Tawiskara and Wawanagit with their warriors entered the ravine and went over to the prone bodies of Colonel Williams and Chief Hendrick. Wawanagit and his warriors stripped Colonel Williams of his sword, gorget, personal items, and hair while Tawiskara took Chief Hendrick's bloody red coat.

"This is the price for siding with the enemy," he said, as his men also stripped the old chief of his personal items and his hair.

Raising the bloody coat over his head, Tawiskara gave a loud victory whoop, joined by his warriors. They were followed by Wawanagit and his warriors, holding over their heads their plunder and prizes. This was what they had been waiting for, to see their enemies destroyed.

Baron Dieskau was caught up in the moment, the rush and thrill of battle and victory, urging his grenadiers and men forward. He would push these Englishmen all the way back to their encampment and finish them off there.

He could even force the fort to surrender without artillery, if he could finish off the force here at the lake. Once his victory was complete, he would gather his men from Ticonderoga, and they would march unopposed to Albany. He could taste the ultimate victory to come.

Once both the Provincials and the French had emerged from the ravine, the fighting broke apart into smaller, more personal actions as the Provincials ran in different directions, hotly pursued by the Canadians and the Indians. The Rangers were moving away from the fight, and they found a place to hold up and catch their breath for the moment. Patrick looked at Jacob's face. The gouge the bullet had left was the length and thickness of a finger and it ran along Jacob's cheek back to his right ear.

"You'll live. You just won't be as pretty as me anymore," Patrick said as he swabbed the dry blood away from the wound.

Jacob chuckled and thanked Patrick. A quick check showed everyone else was uninjured, though breathing hard. They checked their powder and shot, which they distributed across the section before heading back out towards the lake and the encampment.

The woods had quieted some, with only sporadic firing and war whoops in the distance, but as they moved forward, the sound of a new battle could be heard ahead. Patrick pointed in that direction.

"Let's go see if we can help them out."

The Rangers came upon the scene of the new fight, members of a lone platoon from the Connecticut Regiment, based on their uniforms, who were trying to hold their ground. They had taken some cover behind fallen trees and boulders. However, they were being encircled by the more numerous Canadians and Hurons, who were beginning to pick them off one by one.

Patrick brought his Rangers together.

"We'll line up and fire, moving forward by teams and see if we can give these fellas some help. Shoot fast. Shoot true."

Everyone nodded, and the first three, Richard, Jacob, and Peter, took aim at the Canadians who were in front of them. They all fired at once, and three Canadians fell, the sound of the Rangers' rifles masked by all of the firing that was occurring and the fact that the Canadians were not expecting to be attacked from the rear.

The first three began reloading, as Robert, Samuel, and Konkapot advanced forward, picked their targets, and fired. Patrick added his rifle when a target appeared. This continued until the Rangers actually cleared a path and rushed down to the beleaguered Provincials.

Lieutenant Israel Putnam was having an extremely bad day. His company commander had been hit when the regiment fell apart, and his last instruction was to give the column supporting fire to cover their retreat.

Now they seemed to have attracted the attention of what felt like the entire French Army. They had been able to extricate themselves from the ravine and take up a defendable position, but there were just too many enemy fighters, and his men were getting low on ammunition.

Then through the smoke and haze they saw several men running towards them, but they were wearing green.

"Hold your fire! Rangers are coming in!" yelled Putnam.

Patrick and his Rangers skidded to a halt as they ran into the center of the Provincials and dropped to the ground.

"Where could you use some help, lieutenant?" asked Patrick, who was breathing heavy.

"Here is good as any," answered Putnam, who returned to directing the fire of his platoon.

The Rangers spread out, seeking cover and taking up good firing positions. This time, they all fired when they had a target, and they were beginning to take a heavy toll on the enemy. The Provincials fired in volleys while the Rangers picked their targets—one shot, and one kill.

As the Rangers and the Provincials fought for their survival, Tehwehron was leading his warriors forward, looking for a way to vent his anger and frustration at having to fight brother Mohawks. In the distance, he heard what sounded like an organized fight, and he headed in that direction. Perhaps there he could find satisfaction fighting with a suitable enemy, not his brother Mohawks.

The Indians came upon what appeared to be a group of Provincials, some wearing dark green and others in blue, defending themselves. He hurled his warriors forward at these hated foes, placing the blame on them for his having to fight his fellow Mohawks and the bad luck it would cause.

His warriors began to pour fire into the group, and he observed some of the Provincials fall, but he also saw some of his warriors fall from the more accurate shooting of these men dressed in green. Rangers, they were called. Raising his tomahawk, Tehwehron ordered his warriors forward to close with and hack these beasts to death. He gave a war whoop and pressed forward.

As they charged forward, Tehwehron's blood began to boil. Here was a chance to avenge his Mohawk brothers and Chief Hendrick, who had been killed because of these Englishmen. He placed the blame for their deaths squarely on the English. Perhaps their blood would wash the shame and potential bad luck away, appeasing the spirits of the Mohawks who had been killed.

As the fighting swirled around them, Jacob spotted the charging Indians and shouted a warning. Both Provincials and Rangers turned and fired as one at the charging Indians. It wasn't enough. Even though a good number of the Indians fell, the volley didn't stop the attack, and some were closing in with their tomahawks and war clubs raised.

After he fired his rifle, Jacob quickly slung it over his shoulder, pulled his knife and tomahawk from behind his back, and met the charging Indians. As he swung his tomahawk, it was met by his attacker's own tomahawk with a loud "clank," but Jacob used the momentum to spin and catch the Indian across the throat with his knife, a splash of warm blood hitting him the face.

Jacob didn't stop. He knew he had to keep fighting and moving to survive, his instincts taking over as he fought without thinking.

The battle for survival was brutal and savage. Men were locked in close combat, using everything they had at their disposal—tomahawks, knives, clubs, muskets, and even their bare hands or rocks picked up from the ravine floor.

Lieutenant Putnam thrust his sword into an attacking warrior, and brought his own tomahawk up in time to block a war club from another warrior. Jacob saw this and threw his tomahawk, striking the warrior in the center of his back.

As Jacob moved to pull his tomahawk free, he felt a heavy blow against his back, which threw him down, knocking the wind out of him and causing sparkles to dance before his eyes. Shaking his head to clear it, Jacob saw the Lieutenant standing over him, pulling his sword out of the stomach of the warrior who must have attacked him. Then he felt something heavy slide off his shoulder. He reached up, pulled his rifle down and saw that it had been broken by the tomahawk, which had struck its center, saving his life but bending the rifle into a useless mess.

Shrugging off the destroyed rifle, he looked up to see Patrick wrestling with a warrior, and yelling, "Get them out of here!"

Jacob grabbed the Lieutenant and yelled, "Fall back, fall back to the camp!"

Rangers and Provincials alike began to break away. As Jacob turned to run, he came face-to-face with Tehwehron, the warrior's eyes raging with burning intent through his dark war paint, which was smeared by powder and sweat.

Jacob reacted automatically and with quick reflexes. Catching Tehwehron's tomahawk on its downward arch and using the momentum, he pivoted and went down on his knee, throwing Tehwehron over his shoulder. Following through, Jacob's tomahawk impacted into Tehwehron's chest. The warrior, with a slight shudder, gave out his last breath and died with a strange, almost satisfied look on his face.

Jacob had no time to reflect. Pulling out his tomahawk and grabbing the lieutenant, he took off running through a gap that opened into the woods with some of the Provincials following.

"Keep going," yelled Patrick, but then there was a wet thwack as a bullet hit someone. Jacob looked over his shoulder, and saw that Patrick was falling face down with his arms at his side. There was no time to check. The Canadians and Indians were pouring over their old position, closing on them, and they had no choice but to run.

With no time to think or react, Jacob was sprinting and weaving through the trees. The Rangers assembled on the run, followed by some of the Connecticut Provincials, including Lieutenant Putnam.

When the sound of fighting became distant, they stopped running to catch their breath. Jacob took stock of who had made it and of their situation. Konkapot was unhurt, but Peter had a severe gash over his left eye which was bleeding heavily. They were the only Rangers left.

"Did anyone see Richard?" panted Jacob.

Konkapot nodded his head and said, "Saw him take a bullet between the eyes, killed him quickly. What about Patrick?"

Jacob shook his head. "Saw him get hit, not sure if he survived; they were swarming the area." Then Jacob asked, "What about Samuel?"

Konkapot and Peter both shook their heads; no one had seen him in the confusion. Jacob counted eleven Connecticut Provincials, who were looking to him for instructions.

"Let's make our way back to the lake and the camp," Jacob said, motioning them to follow him.

The fight was not over yet. There was more work to be done.

Jacob felt a heaviness on his heart, believing Patrick was dead, having seen him fall, and not knowing where the others were. No time to despair—he had to get these men back and regroup; he'd have time to mourn once it was over.

The Provincials eagerly followed the Rangers, confident that even with only a few green-clad men, their chances of survival were much better than on their own. At the trot, the survivors made their way to the fortified camp and the rest of the army.

CHAPTER 5

BATTLE AT THE LAKE AND BLOODY POND

General Johnson knew something bad had just happened because the sound of firing was close enough to be heard from the encampment. Fearing the worst, he began organizing the defenses to prepare for whatever came out of the woods. The men who had stayed behind began overturning the supply wagons and adding them to spots in the barricade not yet finished. Men who were not working on the barricade were checking their muskets, readying them for the coming fight.

General Johnson then decided to play the ace up his sleeve, ordering his artillery out from behind the barricade and into position to cover the field. They had brought three pieces of artillery with them, and he had the gunners train them on the trail coming out of the woods. If the enemy was closing on them, they would surely come from there.

Some of the militia and Provincial soldiers who had stayed with the wagons began piling wood, barrels, and boxes into improvised firing positions as others helped drag the cannons from the center of the camp to the opening where they could face down the road.

The guns, light three-pounders, were pulled into position on an open, flat piece of ground. After the men had dragged them into place, they detached the ropes they had used to pull them and laid them off to the side.

They then ran back to help the other gunners bring the ammunition boxes forward, as well as the equipment necessary to load and fire the guns. The artillerymen, helped by the militia and Provincials, placed the ammunition boxes to the rear of the guns, each holding about twenty prepared rounds. Some of the rounds were solid shot, and others were grapeshot—cloth bags filled with musket balls wrapped around wooden sabots.

The crewmen took up their positions and their tools. The gun commander gave the command of "load" in which the crewmen went about the business of loading their guns with their deadly shot. Once the guns were loaded, the commander made one final look over the barrels to make sure they would cause maximum damage, then turned and looked towards the general in anticipation, waiting for his order to fire.

The guns were loaded and ready; now they just had to wait for the enemy. The rest of the camp was manning the barricades and wagons, cocking their muskets with numerous clicks up and down the line. In the center, General Johnson waited for the enemy to appear.

Johnson didn't have to wait long as the French, Canadians, and their Indian allies were in hot pursuit of the running Provincials. Baron Dieskau was pressing his men forward, wanting to secure this complete victory. The Canadians and Indians were charging before his column of grenadiers, but they stopped at the edge of the forest.

Baron Dieskau moved forward to see why they were stopping with victory so close at hand. At the forest's edge, he could see the open field and marsh, and in the distance on the rise was the hasty barricade and what appeared to be overturned wagons, as well as the remnants of the Provincial forces running across the field to the safety of the barricade.

"Why are you stopping?" Dieskau addressed the Indians and Canadians. "The victory is at hand. All you have to do is reach out and take it!" The Canadians and Indians began to gather around the Baron.

The Caughnawaga Mohawks said that their war chief, Tehwehron, was dead, and they would not lose any more warriors. Wawanagit said that if the Mohawks would not advance, neither would they. Too many of their warriors were dead, and they did not want to attack a prepared position.

Dieskau turned to the Canadians, who also refused to go. Disgusted, Dieskau turned to his grenadiers and gave the order to form close column and prepare to charge. He turned to the Canadians and Indians and said, "If you will not take this victory, then I will take it all for myself."

Tawiskara looked at the Abenakis and Caughnawagas and couldn't believe what he had heard. They did not want to continue the fight against their hated foes. Looking with disdain at his allies, Tawiskara began to move his Huron warriors forward alongside the French grenadiers. All the glory would now belong to him and his warriors alone. Baron Dieskau himself led from the front with his sword drawn.

Tawiskara called to his men, saying all of the scalps and plunder was theirs alone, and they responded with a resounding war whoop and began to jog forward. The grenadiers were six men abreast, marching in lock step.

Baron Dieskau had thought this martial display would be enough to humble or embarrass the rest of the Indians and the Canadians so they would join in, but it seemed only the Hurons wanted to share in this victory. No matter, more glory for him and the allies who marched with him, he thought. The column broke from the forest and marched into the open, Dieskau leading the way as they topped a small rise.

As they got closer to the Provincial barricade, he noticed three cannons pointing right at him. He realized this might not be as simple as he had thought.

General Johnson's belief that the enemy was upon them was confirmed as the survivors from the ambush began to trickle from the forest. The trickle soon turned into a torrent of running men, some alone and some in the remnants of units.

Shouting that the enemy was right behind them, the survivors entered through the barricade's opening or just simply climbed over the top to get inside. The defenders were manning their improvised wall and barricade, muskets at the ready, though they were becoming increasingly concerned looking at the shape of the survivors, who were taking positions along the barricade.

Jacob and his survivors broke out of the forest a little further down to the west of the trail and moved quickly to the barricade. As they approached, he could see the gunners getting ready so he led his men behind the cannons.

The Rangers, with Lieutenant Putnam and his Provincials, followed Jacob and manned an opening in the barricade, readying their muskets and rifles. All of the men were breathing heavy from the run and from the fight, and now they were trying to catch their breath before they were attacked again.

Jacob found a musket and extra shot and powder to replace his destroyed rifle. He loaded and joined his men on the wall. There was an eerie silence as the number of survivors entering the enclosure got smaller and smaller, then stopped entirely.

Jacob's mind raced as he waited for the enemy to appear. He was still caught up in the emotions of the fight, and the loss of Patrick and his other friends was there, but he didn't dwell on it. Jacob would have to mourn them later if he survived this next fight. He let the loss fuel his anger, and he would take it out on the approaching enemy.

A few minutes later, a yell of "Here they come!" was passed from down the line, and everyone looked down their barrels, taking aim. Hundreds of hammers were pulled back.

In the distance, Jacob saw that a column of white-uniformed French regulars was advancing down the trail led by an officer in the front.

Jacob also spotted some Hurons on the flanks, but this was a surprisingly smaller force than the one they had just been fighting. Many Canadians and Indians appeared to be missing or were holding back. Jacob thought maybe they had all shot better than he had thought, making more enemy casualties than he had estimated.

They all held their fire until the French and Hurons got closer, determined to make every shot count.

Jacob began settling his breath, slowly breathing in and out, calming himself as he looked down the barrel of his musket. He could almost hear the tension as a buzz and feel the energy building as the French came closer, their footsteps stomping in unison as they marched down the road in their tight column.

The air was electric as everyone waited in anticipation for the enemy to close and the command to fire to be given. When the French and their Indians were less than one hundred yards away, General Johnson gave the order to make ready. The riflemen and musket men all aimed at the advancing Frenchmen, and the gunners on the cannons started to blow constantly on their slow matches to keep them glowing.

Johnson simply looked over to the battery commander who was watching him and nodded his head. The commander raised his sword and gave the command to make ready. The gunners with their slow matches raised them up, signaling they were ready to fire.

With a final "Give... fire!" all three cannons roared, the sound echoing off the trees. The grapeshot flew from them, decimating the front of the French column and some of the advancing Hurons, some balls impacting flesh and others stirring up the dirt in front of the attackers as they struck and bounced up from the ground.

Jacob and his men were surprised to see that the officer leading the French was still standing as his men behind him fell like rag dolls. "Lucky devil," Jacob commented.

General Johnson gave the command to open fire, and the Rangers and Provincials pulled their triggers. The barricade roared with a sheet of flame reaching out towards the enemy.

This time Dieskau was not so lucky, balls striking him in the abdomen and legs, and he fell, along with more of his men. As he went down, the French grenadiers stopped to return fire at the barricade and at the artillery men, who were going through the procedure of loading another round.

A third volley from the barricade punctuated by the cannons was all it took for the grenadiers to break and turn, withdrawing from the fight. As Jacob was reloading his musket, he caught a motion out of the corner of his eye. General Johnson had just been hit by a lucky shot and was being supported by an aide.

Provincials, militiamen, and the Mohawks were all jumping over the barricade to chase after the French and Indians. The Mohawks seemed to have focused their interest on the fallen French commander and were in the process of trying to take his hair when General Johnson, supported by an aide, stopped them from killing and scalping Dieskau.

Jacob observed this, and wondered if the situation were reversed, would the French commander have spared one of them.

Looking over at Konkapot and Peter, Jacob nodded his head towards the field, and they jumped over the barricade and began heading to where Patrick and Robert had fallen. They knew they couldn't leave their fallen comrades and had to go back out and find them, hopefully preventing them from being brutalized or desecrated.

"The Provincials can chase after the French," Jacob instructed. "We're going to go and take care of our own."

Lieutenant Putnam and some of his men were behind them, feeling they were now part of Jacob's men and following his lead. The more the better, Jacob thought, because as they ran into the woods, he didn't know whom they would run into.

The sound of firing in the distance told him the Provincials had become the hunters instead of the hunted, and the table had now been turned against the French. There didn't seem to be as much activity on the side of the forest from which they had come, however, and it was not difficult to find their way back to where they had made their stand. All they had to do was follow the trail of dead Canadians, Indians, and Provincials.

The forest became silent as they came to the rocks and trees where they had made their fight. The three Rangers quickly spread out, with Lieutenant Putnam and his men mirroring their actions. They entered the site where they had made their fight, carefully watching and listening for any sight or sound of the enemy.

Jacob found Patrick lying face down in the dirt, his arms out and a bloody spot in his back where the bullet had hit him. He still had his rifle, his equipment, and his hair. Apparently the Indians had had no time to loot the body and take his scalp, moving fast to try to catch Jacob and his surviving men.

Throwing his procured musket to the side, Jacob took Patrick's rifle and collected his gear and his bonnet. Jacob felt a stab in his heart, seeing his friend and mentor now dead. Anger started to well up inside him, and he wanted to go find the enemy and make them pay for what they had done to Patrick.

As if his thoughts had been answered, Jacob picked up the sound of approaching men and signaled to everyone to find cover in the jumbled trees and brush.

Taking cover behind some trees and rocks, Jacob reprimed Patrick's rifle, hoping it was still loaded. Calmness settled over him as he anticipated dealing destruction on those who had killed his comrades and friends. Looking over, he could see similar fierce looks on Konkapot and Peter, who were determined to finish the enemy. He looked over his shoulder to Lieutenant Putnam who nodded back, and then Jacob waited for the voices to appear.

Entering the clearing were five Indians and about ten Canadians who seemed to be avoiding the fight. They were looting the dead instead, taking gear from both the Provincials and from their own dead.

Controlling his anger, Jacob aimed at one of the Canadians who was laughing and joking with the others as he took items from a dead Provincial. While it was bad enough what they did to one another in battle, seeing their dead being desecrated seemed worse and made Jacob angrier. Taking a deep breath and slowly letting it out, Jacob aimed and pulled the trigger and the rifle fired, the bullet hitting the Canadian in the head. The rest of the Rangers and Provincials opened fire, which dropped several more Canadians and Indians, forcing the rest to flee.

Anger boiling over, Jacob let out a blood curdling war cry and then screamed, "For Patrick!" which was echoed by Konkapot, Peter, and the Provincials. Rising up, Jacob led the pursuit of their quarry, loading on the run. He was followed by the others. Jacob's heart was racing as he sought vengeance.

Gritting his teeth, he led the pursuit of the running Canadians and Indians, determined not to let any of them live to see tomorrow. Legs churning, brush whipping past him, Jacob focused on the running quarry, closing the distance.

Jacob and his men continued to chase the Canadians and the Indians through the woods, firing when they could and loading on the run. A few Indians and Canadians were hit, and they fell, dropping the loot they had taken.

The rest were running so fast and were so fearful of the Rangers and Provincials that when they broke into an open area with a pond in the middle of it, they didn't see the other Provincial soldiers who were already there.

Though surprised when the Canadians and Indians burst into the opening, the Provincials all turned and fired. Caught between Jacob and his men and the Provincials, none of the Canadians or Indians survived the crossfire.

Jacob yelled that Rangers were coming in, wanting to make sure they were not accidently shot by the surprised Provincials. He entered the clearing with his rifle held over his head. Spotting their signature green uniforms, the Provincials waved them in.

Jacob and Lieutenant Putnam went up to the group of Provincials.

Jacob could see by their uniforms that these men were from the New York Provincials.

"Thought you boys were back at the fort?" Jacob asked, and a sergeant of the group nodded.

"We were, but we decided to come out and give you all a hand."

The New Yorkers explained that they had heard the firing from the fort and their commander, Captain McGinnis, had ordered them to come out and try to give aid to General Johnson if they could.

"We were moving along the military road when we found the French baggage train and captured it. Then we heard the Canadians returning through the woods, and we decided to give them a surprise of their own. Once that business was done, we began clearing the woods, securing any French and Canadian survivors as prisoners."

Jacob nodded and asked if they had found any prisoners. The New Yorker answered with a sly grin, "Very few."

Jacob nodded and saw that the New Yorkers were dragging the dead Canadians and Indians over to the pond and throwing them in.

There must have been numerous bodies already in the pond because the water was beginning to turn a brownish, bloody red.

Jacob took a deep breath and suddenly felt tired, all of his anger seeping out of him, exhaustion taking over, along with remorse. A feeling of satisfaction washed over the other emotions though, as he watched the New Yorkers drag the dead enemy into the bloody pond. Maybe it was enough payback for the loss of his friends. Only time would tell.

Jacob and Lieutenant Putnam returned to Konkapot, Peter, and the Provincials, who had begun to collect their dead. Jacob knew it was the right thing to do; Captain Rogers had pounded into them the need to take care of one another.

Building a travois out of branches, Jacob prepared Patrick's body to be moved as Konkapot and Peter searched for the rest of their friends.

After a short search, they found Robert's body with a large, bloody hole in his forehead where the ball had exited. Like Patrick, he still had his hair and gear, the enemy moving too fast to scalp and strip him. They brought him over to join Patrick's body on the travois that Jacob had finished.

"Any sign of the others?" Jacob asked, and the two shook their heads no.

Jacob gave a heavy sigh, hoping they had made it.

Lieutenant Putnam came over to Jacob as he was finishing securing Patrick's body on the travois.

"Good idea, this," Putnam commented. "You best head back. We're going to be here for a bit collecting up our dead. Thanks for saving us. I won't forget it."

He reached out and shook Jacob's hand. Nodding, Jacob wished them well and with Konkapot and Peter helping, pulled the travois back to the encampment.

When they left the woods and entered into the open field, they could see that the rest of the Provincials and militiamen had been busy as well, collecting the remains of at least twenty dead French grenadiers, who had been torn to pieces by the grapeshot.

They also spotted Dieskau, leaning against the barricade. He had been shot through the bladder and couldn't move very well.

When Jacob saw their surgeons working on the wounded French commander as their own wounded were being carried past, his thoughts turned dark. Why should that man live while his friends and comrades were dead?

After entering the barricade, they took their dead and placed them with the others, long rows of Provincials, militiamen, and some of their green-uniformed Rangers. Jacob looked over the rows of the dead, but didn't spot any of his missing friends.

Jacob and Peter joined the other injured at the field hospital and waited their turn to be seen, as Konkapot went off to find the rest of the company. The two found some boxes to sit against and rested, observing the chaos of the hospital.

Jacob watched in fascination as the surgeons worked on the wounded, including General Johnson. The general seemed to be doing okay. He was giving instructions to General Lyman on what to do next.

Leaning over to Peter, Jacob asked how he had been wounded. Peter shrugged his shoulders and said he had turned and apparently had run into a Canadian's tomahawk. Luckily he was so close, he received only a glancing blow off his face and cheek, saving his eye from harm.

Jacob chuckled and said, "perhaps we should call you 'Hawked-eye,'" because of the injury. Peter looked at Jacob and just shook his head no. Then Jacob asked if sparks flew when it hit, and the two chuckled. Jacob fingered his own close call, probing the bloody gouge under his eye and cheek.

While waiting for a surgeon, Jacob spotted Captain Reynolds who, even after all of the action and fighting they had just gone through, was somehow still clean. It appeared that the captain was scolding Lieutenant Manning, whose clothes were covered in dirt, mud, and blood. It appeared from a distance that the captain was criticizing the condition of the lieutenant's uniform, waving his hands and pointing at the new stains.

The sergeant major, who was standing off to the side, also looked no worse for the wear. It appeared the lieutenant had gotten involved in the fight and was now taking grief for it.

Jacob was physically and mentally exhausted, both from the hard fighting and the loss of his friends, which was now starting to sink in. He reflected on the stupidity of it all, the senseless loss from poor leadership. He thought that if the column had been properly deployed with scouts and flankers, they perhaps would have avoided walking into the trap.

While this was enough to get Jacob riled, seeing Captain Reynolds, who Jacob knew had been nowhere near the fighting, giving Lieutenant Manning so much grief for doing his job caused his anger to boil over once more.

Jacob wanted to do something to the captain, but he reined in his desire to kill the man. He spotted a pile of bloody rags left by the surgeon. Without thinking, he took a wadded bloody ball of the rags and threw it at Captain Reynolds with all of his might. Fate must have smiled on him, because the ball of rags arced perfectly through the air and struck the captain with a bloody plop.

Captain Reynolds's face became bright red as he began to spin around sputtering and yelling, demanding to know who had thrown the rags. Luckily for Jacob, he was masked by the working surgeons, and the captain did not see him. Jacob leaned back against the barricade with a satisfied look on his face. Peter looked over at him, winked, and then closed his eyes to rest.

It was later in the day when Peter nudged Jacob as Samuel was being helped into the surgeon's area by two Provincials. Jacob and Peter stood up and went over to see him, and Samuel's face lit up, happy to see them still alive. Helping Samuel walk, Jacob and Peter led him over to their spot against the boxes.

"How did you get hurt?" Jacob asked, and Samuel looked away disgusted.

With a deep sigh, he explained that as he was turning to run back, he stepped into a hole and twisted his ankle. Loosing balance, he fell and rolled down a small hill, hitting his head on a rock and knocking himself out.

Jacob looked at Samuel's head and under his hat was a bloody cloth. Then with a heavy sigh and a shrug, Samuel said, "That's not all." He pulled his hat and the bloody bandage off, showing a large bald spot on top of his head.

"Lucky for me, the poor bastard who tried to scalp me wasn't very good or this would be a lot worse."

Both Jacob and Peter tried hard not to laugh, but after all they had been through that day, they couldn't help themselves. They both began to giggle, which quickly grew into a fit of laughter.

Samuel looked angry, stammering, "Damn it. It's not funny, and it hurts like hell."

This only added fuel to the fire, and the two were laughing so hard, they had tears in their eyes.

Caught up in a way to vent the emotions of the day, Samuel also began to laugh long and hard along with his friends, the tension of the day rolling out of them as they laughed until tears were streaming down their dirty cheeks.

As the surgeons worked, they couldn't help but look over at three crazy Rangers, who were laughing and rolling on the ground. The surgeons shook their heads, thinking war does strange things to men's minds. After a while the laughter stopped, and the mood changed. The three talked quietly about losing Patrick and Robert, supporting each other in their grief.

CHAPTER 6

FORT EDWARD: AFTER THE BATTLE

The three wounded Rangers continued to wait their turn for the surgeons to look at their injuries. Waiting didn't bother them; there were others who needed the surgeons' attention more than three simple Rangers who seemed to have had a bad case of the giggles.

Jacob and Peter sat back, leaning against the side of an overturned wagon, watching the carnage around them, with Samuel adjusting his hat to hide most of his bandage.

The Provincials in their red or blue uniforms mixed with the French and their white uniforms, some Rangers in green, and other militiamen in their regular clothes. All of these conflicting shades had one color in common, blood red.

The surgeon's mates, with help from both Provincials and militiamen, were carrying the wounded to the surgeons, who had stretched boards across boxes and barrels and were up to their elbows treating injuries. The blood was pouring off these tables like rain water, the screams and moans echoing off the barricade. Jacob decided it was a horrible sound and promised himself that he would avoid getting seriously injured again.

He just stared, seeing but not seeing at the same time, looking off into the distance. The exhaustion after the fight, the loss of Patrick and Robert, even the pain of his own injury left him numb to what was happening all around him. General Johnson had been carried off to more "comfortable" quarters, as was the French commander Baron

Dieskau, who was moved inside a tent. Jacob's heavy eyelids closed, and he quickly fell asleep, exhaustion taking over even in the din and chaos of the field hospital.

The butcher's bill for their victory had been heavy. The surgeons' white and brown aprons were heavily smeared with blood, and they were busy sawing off limbs they could not save, the bones shattered by shot and shell. The piles of arms and legs started to stack like firewood off to the side of the tables and were a gruesome sight to behold. The surgeons' mates, who were running back and forth bringing instruments and carrying off the baskets of severed limbs or bloody bandages, were in constant motion.

Peter shook Jacob awake. He looked around and spotted Konkapot and Lieutenant Putman walking up, Konkapot carrying some food and tin cups. He knelt down and handed Jacob, Samuel, and Peter some dried meat, biscuits, and in the tin cups, a strong grog of mixed rum and water "Told the captain you were over here, and I see you found Samuel, so that's all of us," said Konkapot, who looked inquisitively at Samuel's bandages.

Samuel retold his story about being semi-scalped, and Konkapot snorted and was soon laughing. Samuel simply shrugged. He was getting used to it now.

Lieutenant Putnam looked down at Jacob.

"Just wanted to thank you for saving my hair and skin back there," Putnam said as he held out his hand to each of them. "I won't forget it. You boys need anything, look me up."

Jacob, Samuel, Peter, and Konkapot all shook the lieutenant's hand and wished him the best of luck. Smiling and waving, Lieutenant Putnam turned and returned to his men.

After Lieutenant Putnam left, they started to eat the food they had been brought and slurp down their grog. After finishing their food and grog, the three just sat there, Konkapot staying to keep Jacob company. "Did you ever think we would be caught up in things like this?" Jacob asked Konkapot.

Konkapot leaned his head back as he thought about the question. They had come a long way together. The two had been inseparable since shortly after Jacob left his home.

He had met Konkapot when he was younger, and the young Indian stopped at his family's trading post on hunts with the Stockbridge. To Jacob, they were as much family as any aunt or uncle would have been. It had seemed natural to Jacob to join with the Stockbridge Indians when his family was no more, and they became his surrogate family.

It that sense, Konkapot became his brother, filling the void of his lost brother, who had been taken during that fateful night.

"No, not really," Konkapot replied, answering Jacob's question. "But if I recall, don't you always get us into some sort of trouble?"

Jacob looked over and asked, "Trouble? No more than you did."

Shaking his head, Konkapot replied, "Wasn't it you and the niece of the sachem at Fort Hunter that almost had the both of us running the gauntlet? Then there was the daughter of that war chief at Canajoharie, and then there was …"

Jacob didn't let him finish. "Yes, yes, I admit I sometimes don't think straight," Jacob said, holding his hands up in surrender.

"Sounds like you were thinking, but not with your head," commented Peter, and all three started laughing again.

The three comrades continued to watch the activity in the field hospital as the shadows grew long with the setting sun. Helpers came out with lanterns to try and give the surgeons some light.

Jacob dozed off and was asleep when a surgeon's mate arrived to look at his wound. He snapped awake, grasping the mate's hand while drawing his fighting knife without thinking, instincts taking over again.

"Easy, easy now, just want to look at the gouge in your face," the surgeon's mate quickly stammered, staring at the sharp blade hovering just in front of him.

Jacob looked around quickly, realized where he was, looked sheepish, and apologized. Peter was being looked at by another surgeon's mate, with a militiaman helper holding a lantern, while it looked like Samuel had a new bandage around his head.

Jacob hadn't realized the sun had set and night had arrived. He released the mate's wrist, who shook his hand to get the feeling back into it before looking at and probing the wound on Jacob's right cheek. The mate was very careful how he treated Jacob's wound, fearfully staring at the location of the knife on Jacob's belt.

"Well, not much I can do," the surgeon's mate said as he pulled a wet rag from a bucket, squeezed the water mixed with blood out of it, and started to clean the wound. Jacob looked down in the bucket, but was glad he could not see how much of the content was water and how much was blood.

The mate instructed Jacob to try to keep it clean, and moved on without even bandaging it. Jacob looked over to Peter, who was also finished. Jacob nodded, stood up, and grabbed his gear. Peter and Konkapot also stood, grabbed their own gear, and followed him away from the carnage.

Samuel had to stay behind. His leg injury was making it hard for him to move quickly, and the surgeon was going to look at it again after he had rested for bit. They wished him luck, said they would look for him back at the fort, and then disappeared into the night.

After finding a more suitable place to sleep, away from the sight and smell of the surgery, they dropped to the ground and decided to camp right there. They were so exhausted, they fell asleep where they fell, still wearing their gear, cradling their rifles close to them.

It was a dreamless night, and Jacob woke just as the sun was beginning to rise. He kicked Peter and Konkapot awake, and then they went looking for the rest of the Rangers. They found Captain Rogers and Lieutenants Stark and Waite with most of the company on the other side of the encampment.

Jacob reported in and informed both Rogers and Stark that Samuel was still in the hospital with a leg injury, unable to move. Konkapot had already reported their losses of Patrick and Robert while Jacob was in the field hospital. Rogers looked Jacob over and nodded his head.

"Heavy losses yesterday. Are you fit?" Rogers asked, as he pointed to Jacob's wound.

Jacob nodded that he was.

"Good to hear. Rejoin the company then," Rogers ordered, and they turned and joined the rest of the company.

Jacob could see that their numbers were fewer, and like himself, the Rangers were dirty and they all showed signs of the recent vicious fight. They nodded to acknowledgements from their fellow Rangers, who welcomed them back and said it was good to see them alive. They also asked questions about Samuel and offered condolences on the loss of Patrick and Robert.

Although he was still emotionally tired from the fight and the deaths of Patrick and Robert, Jacob felt good as his comrades welcomed him back. It felt like being part of a large family.

Rogers addressed the assembled men:

"Rangers, you have won a great victory over the French, and I am proud of how you all fought. We lost some good Rangers, but we must not let this dampen our resolve. We will not allow our honored dead to have fallen in vain.

"We are going to keep bringing the fight to the French and their allies until this fight is won. We will also continue this tradition of not leaving our fallen comrades behind. We will always bring them home if we can."

With that, Rogers formed the company into a column of twos.

Leading them from the front, Rogers started them on the journey back to Fort Lyman.

Along the way through the woods, they ran into some of the New York and Connecticut Provincials, who were still gathering up weapons and equipment from the fallen as well as the baggage and equipment taken from the French when they had counter-attacked from the fort.

As the Rangers passed by, they saw Lieutenant Putman, who was watching them with an almost envious look in his eyes. Jacob, Peter, and Konkapot tipped their hats to him as they walked past, and Putnam responded with a salute of his own.

By midday, the Rangers arrived at the fort, and they returned to their island. Rogers gave orders to clean and fix their gear.

By late afternoon, the bodies of Patrick and Robert had arrived along with the rest of the dead. Jacob, Peter, and Konkapot were part of a burial detail that added Patrick's and Robert's remains to the other fallen Rangers in their growing cemetery.

After pounding in wooden crosses with Patrick's and Robert's names carved on them, Jacob pulled Patrick's bonnet out and draped it over his cross. There were a lot more crosses and fresh graves in their cemetery on the island, Rangers and Provincials alike.

After everyone left, Jacob sat on a stump, looking at the growing cemetery that was filling with some of his friends. Jacob thought about his life and his mortality. He wondered if he would join his friends and comrades under the earth here on the island.

Doubt was starting to wriggle its way back into his mind, and Jacob quickly squashed it. No, he wasn't done yet. He made a promise to himself to survive, to keep fighting, and to stop this enemy from winning and taking over their land. He would honor his friends by stopping the enemies that had put them there in the ground.

As Jacob reflected on his present situation, he observed Samuel arriving with the rest of the wounded. He hobbled over to the island, assisted by some of his fellow Rangers.

After a few days to rest and recuperate, Captain Rogers ordered Jacob and a few other Rangers to head to Saratoga as an armed escort for Mr. Best. What Rogers was really doing was giving them some time to get away from where they had suffered their losses and to let off steam. Jacob, with Peter, Samuel, and Konkapot, along with a few others from the company, walked to Saratoga with Mr. Best and some of his workers who were driving the wagons and carts. Mr. Best was picking up supplies not only for his store, but also on behalf of the fort. With the recent attacks, it was considered prudent to send an armed escort for the supplies.

It had been awhile since Jacob and the other Rangers had gone south. Most of their time had been around the fort or northward. It was a pleasant break, with new sights and sounds to take their minds off their losses. But the Rangers still remained vigilant on the march, escorting the creaking wagons and carts. As they walked alongside the carts, Jacob got to know Mr. Best.

"You can call me Frederick, son. Don't have to be so formal out here," Mr. Best said.

He was originally from Lancaster in Pennsylvania and had always been a tradesman.

"When everything was pointing towards this war, I decided to follow the army and set up shop near them. Soldiers need wares, and having been a militiaman myself, I know how messed up the quartermasters can be."

Jacob looked at Frederick in surprise, and he could read Jacob's thoughts.

"I know I don't look it, but I fought during this here, what they call King George's War. Served with the Provincials after Saratoga was attacked and burned by the Indians, and I was at the taking of Louisburg. I remember how bad the food was, and little to no rum. The officers were always well fed, but not us foot soldiers. So I decided to go into the trading business, and whenever I can help the common soldier, I do."

Jacob nodded. He had a better appreciation of Frederick Best and of all he tried to do for the men. Many a good time had been had at his sutler tents around a cask of ale or rum, as they all tried to escape from the reality of war, even for a short time.

Jacob looked up at Frederick. "Well Mr.—I mean Frederick, we do appreciate what you do for us, especially us Rangers."

Frederick nodded his head and looked evenly at Jacob.

"I like you, son. You remind me of myself when I was younger," he said, and then looking down at his slight paunch, "and a bit thinner."

The trip south to Saratoga was uneventful. Jacob smiled and looked over to Konkapot who was smiling too. They had been to this region before, which was a hunting area for the Mohawks, and they had visited the town to trade, but that had been some time ago.

It took a few days to gather and load the supplies for Frederick's wagons and carts. So for two nights, the Rangers occupied a corner of Shields Tavern, where they held an impromptu wake for their departed friends and comrades.

The Rangers included Mr. Best and his men in the celebrations, since they also felt a close attachment to these wild Rangers. It felt good to celebrate the lives of their comrades and escape the war for a few moments.

The rum and ale flowed, the men toasted to the memory of their fallen friends, and then toasted to their victory over their enemies. There was, unfortunately, a lot of toasting for the large number of friends lost, and soon all of the Rangers were drunk, but for the most part they were happily drunk.

Jacob was sandwiched between Konkapot on one side and Samuel on the other. They sang drinking songs horribly off-key, swaying back and forth. Peter joined in, though he sang German drinking songs in German. The Rangers didn't notice and sang along with him, even if they didn't know the words.

There were only a few scuffles with some locals who tried to interfere with the Rangers' wake, becoming upset with the loud noises and bad singing. In time, the locals learned to leave the Rangers alone as they drank and sang, and gave toasts on behalf of their honored dead.

Those who tried to interfere were met with vicious-looking knives and tomahawks, even if they were not held very steadily. Finally, the locals gave over the corner of the tavern to the Rangers after one of them had foolishly grabbed a Ranger, who quickly knocked him out with a single blow. The locals, who now knew better, dragged their unconscious friend away from the wild pack of fighters.

However, some of the locals joined in, buying drinks for the victorious fighters and sharing their songs. In return, the Rangers bought them drinks. After a short while, Rangers, farmers, and local tradesmen were singing songs together and having a good time of it.

Near the end of the second night, a shaky Jacob stood and, in a loud, if slurred, voice, honored their old "Mic" Patrick, and their friend Robert.

"Here's to ya, lads. May you drink in heaven or wherever you are dry!" Jacob toasted, and the other Rangers cheered and joined in. Jacob drank deep and then fell backwards into the Rangers who caught him, slowing his drop to the floor.

In the morning, Jacob and his Rangers felt somewhat better despite their hangovers when they escorted the now loaded carts back to the fort without incident. It was something they all had needed, to celebrate and let loose, helping them deal with their losses while away from the sights and sounds of the battlefields.

The Rangers all walked with a bounce in their steps, even when they entered the valley and saw the fort in the distance. Jacob nodded when he saw the fort.

"Time to get back to work," he said, and Konkapot and Samuel agreed.

For the next couple of days, the Rangers fixed or replaced weapons, allowed wounds to heal, and got ready for their next patrol.

Jacob took Patrick's rifle, which had replaced his destroyed one, out to the practice field to set the sights. After nailing a wooden target to a tree about a hundred yards away, Jacob set the rifle's stock against his foot and while holding the barrel against his side, poured some gunpowder out of his horn into a smaller horn tip, which was used to measure the amount. Jacob had scratched lines inside of the measure for different amounts of powder, depending on the range.

After filling the horn tip to the level for a hundred yards, he poured the gunpowder into the barrel and tapped the butt against the ground. He then placed a small piece of cloth as a patch and pressed a bullet into the patch. Luckily, Patrick had had some bullets left, and the bullet mold for his gun had still been in his bag, which Jacob had also grabbed. Using a smaller patch knife, Jacob trimmed the patch so it only surrounded the ball, and then he pushed it into the barrel.

It was a good, tight fit. Jacob drew the ramrod and rammed the ball home. Patrick had also scratched lines on the end of his ramrod, which showed when the ball was seated correctly. It was essential for the riflemen to know when the ball was set all the way to the bottom of the barrel. If not set properly, the ball might not come out or perhaps it might even cause the rifle to explode.

Once the rammer was returned into the slot under the barrel, Jacob brought the rifle up and held it at chest level, opening the frizzen, the flat metal piece in front of the lock that covered the pan, which held the priming powder next to the touch hole in the barrel. The lock, which held the flint after it was cocked and the trigger pulled, struck forward, the flint rubbing against the hardened steel of the frizzen to make the spark which fired the rifle.

He poured some more powder into a small pan and then closed the frizzen over the pan. He brought the rifle up and sighted at the target. The rifle felt well balanced. Letting out his breath slowly, he pulled the trigger, and the rifle barked and bucked against his shoulder. After several shots, Konkapot joined him at the wooden target, observing the nice grouping of holes. Too bad they were all three inches to the right of center.

"Well, you can always aim a bit to the other side, and you should hit your target in the middle," commented Konkapot.

Jacob snorted and walked back to the firing line. He pulled out a small hammer and began tapping the rear site to move it. Soon, Jacob was tearing up the center of the target. Lieutenant Stark walked up.

"That's Patrick's old rifle. I heard it could shoot the eyes off a gnat."

Jacob nodded that it was.

"Good. The captain wants to see you," Lieutenant Stark said.

Jacob grabbed his gear, and Konkapot followed along as he walked over to a hut that Captain Rogers used as his headquarters. Leaning his rifle and his bags against the wall, Jacob entered the hut with Lieutenant Stark while Konkapot sat outdoors in the shade next to Jacob's gear.

Rogers was busy writing a message. After finishing and folding it, he passed it to a messenger, who quickly left to deliver it.

"General Johnson wants to know what the French are doing, and he ordered patrols to scout out the French near the top of the lake."

Rogers stood up and looked Jacob in the eyes

"I want you to take out a patrol and scout the western side of the lake and see what they are up to, sergeant."

Jacob looked up, unsure of what he had just been called, and he saw that both Stark and Rogers were smiling.

"I need a new sergeant to replace Patrick, and you were his corporal. I know you can handle not only yourself, but your men. The lieutenant recommended you as his new sergeant. Do you accept?"

Jacob nodded to accept the promotion.

"When are we to leave?" he asked Captain Rogers.

"In four days. We have to reorganize the company and get you two more men."

He nodded, and Captain Rogers shook his hand, followed by Lieutenant Stark. Then he went outside of the hut, and noticed that Konkapot had taken his gear, hopefully back to their camp.

When Jacob arrived at the camp, Konkapot, Samuel, and Peter congratulated him on his new promotion as did some of the other Rangers who arrived. Jacob looked over at Konkapot, who tried to put on an innocent face, but he couldn't hold it and broke out laughing, slapping Jacob on the shoulder.

Jacob told them they were heading out on a scout in four days and that Captain Rogers was getting them some replacements.

"Vat do we do until then?" Peter asked.

Jacob just shrugged his shoulders and answered, "Get ready."

"Den we must celebrate!" Peter yelled as he pulled out some tin cups and a ceramic jug of rum.

The celebration continued later that evening when more of the Rangers who were done for the day and some of the Mohawks stopped by their fire, bringing rum and joining in. As the sun went down, more Rangers and Mohawks arrived and the party grew, with the festivities continuing into the late hours. Songs were sung, rum flowed freely, and sparks from the fire mingled with the stars in the heavens above.

Jacob still was in shock about the promotion, but it felt right, like it was supposed to be this way.

The following day, the Rangers joined the rest of the Provincials in a large formation in front of the fort. General Johnson addressed the assembled men, declaring that the fort would now be named Fort Edward and that a fort to be named William Henry would be constructed at the site of their victory over the French at the southern end of the lake.

The assembled men gave three loud "Huzzahs!" before they were dismissed to continue their duties for the day.

Once the formation was over and Jacob was back on the island, Lieutenant Stark arrived with the two new men. James Cooke and Charles Matthews were both seasoned scouts from New York, having trapped and hunted in the very region in which the Rangers were fighting.

Jacob, Peter, and Konkapot welcomed the new men to their section. Jacob went over his plan for the scouts, and then they began gathering supplies and getting ready. As they had done in the past, they drew their rations and then cooked them in the field kitchen. They checked their gear and ensured they had enough shot and powder.

Both James and Charles knew the area and the trails that ran along the lake, and they began to describe what type of terrain they would encounter. Jacob listened intently, asking for the best routes to avoid the enemy, and both James and Charles described the area in detail.

Jacob nodded to himself. These two were going to work out fine.

The Rangers packed their cooked rations, extra clothes, and powder into knapsacks made from deerskin with the hair left on to make them more water resistant. Wool blankets were rolled up, tied off, and slung along with their haversacks, shooting bags, powder horns, and canteens. Extra powder horns were carried, as were their trusty tomahawks and fighting knives, cleaned and razor sharp.

Lieutenant Stark met with Jacob and his Rangers before they departed, telling them that their scout was important because General Johnson needed the numbers and activities of the French. He needed to know what they were doing at the northern end of the lake, because he still wanted to attack and drive the French further north after their victory at the southern end.

Stark pulled Jacob off to the side.

"This is your first scout as sergeant. Are you ready?" Stark asked.

Jacob nodded.

"I can't stress how important this is to the general. Good luck out there."

Jacob returned to the waiting Rangers

"Did the lieutenant kiss you on the cheek goodbye?" Samuel asked.

Samuel was the section's joker, and his nonsense sometimes helped to lessen the stress and get the Rangers through a difficult moment.

"No, but he told me to take extra special care of you, Samuel."

Everyone chuckled, even Samuel, as Jacob led the patrol across the bridge and once more into the forest to make their way north. Konkapot was first, followed by James and Charles, then Jacob and Samuel, and finally Peter. Jacob was keeping an eye on the new men, and he told them to watch the others and learn as they marched. It was going to have to be a crash course on Ranger training until they got back to the island.

It was now getting close to the end of September. The pine trees were still a deep earthy green, but the oak and birch trees were turning shades of yellows, oranges, and reds. A crisper, cooler breeze was blowing through the valley, a precursor of the winter to come. "West Mountains", the name the Rangers gave to the range of mountains to the west of the valley, shimmered in the reds and oranges of the turning leaves.

As they traveled along the trail to the southern end of the lake, they kept a good spacing, every Ranger scanning to his front and sides with his rifle at the ready. This might be their territory, but they had learned that the French or their allies could appear anywhere and attack. It was a reassuring sight when they spotted French Mountain, and even Samuel whispered, "Hello, old friend" as they passed by.

It was an eerie feeling as they moved through the ravine where the ambush and battle had occurred, almost expecting the ghosts of Patrick and Robert to be waiting for them. Jacob, Konkapot, Peter, and Samuel stared hard as they went through the ravine and wooded area and then as they passed "Bloody Pond." It looked normal now, dark waters sitting placidly over the unknown remains of their enemy, concealing them from passers-by.

They finally arrived at the southern end of the lake, which was a hive of high-energy activity. The men who had built Fort Edward were beginning on the new fort, which would be named Fort William Henry. They spent the night near the old encampment, which was being used as a base of operations. They passed the evening getting to know Charles and James, and telling them about the fight that had taken place right there where they were resting.

Jacob had the men rotate guard duty through the night to stay in practice and to be ready just in case the enemy was out there. He got them up in the cold predawn and then started off before the sun had risen, entering into a new part of the forest that Jacob had never been. He placed Charles and James up front to lead, since they had more experience in this new area than he did.

They moved silently in single file, spread out and staggered. The new men had learned quickly. They had to adapt their hunting skills to these Rangering skills if they wanted to survive. They fell into a rhythm as they moved. They searched and their rifles followed their eyes, knowing they were no longer in friendly territory. They scanned an area until they saw the eyes of the Ranger behind them, and then they reversed the scan. Their mission was to scout and report, avoiding a fight if possible.

When they got ready to stop for the night, Jacob always looked for a thicket or defendable position that would conceal them. He and one other Ranger scouted out the site and the area around it before moving the men inside.

The Rangers made slow but steady progress and after a week on the move without being detected, James said they had arrived in the area north of the lake. James and Charles led them up a small mountain, and from the top they could see the shimmering reflection of sunlight off the waters of Lake Sacrement, or Lake George as the English now called it. They carefully traveled around near the summit, following game trails and ensuring they did not expose themselves. They followed the mountain around to the east, then north. Charles led them to an area where there was an opening in the trees, but there were still enough shrubs and bushes to conceal them.

Below them were the French and what appeared to be construction of a large fort and military camp. It was time to scout and get General Johnson the information he wanted. It was time for the Rangers to go to work.

CHAPTER 7

FORT CARILLON: THE FRENCH BASTION

Michel Chartier de Lotbinier, the engineer tasked to build a fort on this finger pointing into and between the lakes, felt the bugs would certainly be the death of him. Hopefully, with the weather becoming cooler, these bugs will go away, he thought. He also thought it was rather strange that he was actually hoping for cold, even though here in the northern wilderness, cold winters could be brutal.

Lotbinier glanced up from his plans and looked at the activity as work crews moved around the perimeter. It was a good position, surrounded by the lakes on three sides, which would force their enemy to attack from only one direction. They had hacked down all of the trees where the fort was to stand and had used the logs to begin the first wall. Even though the site was surrounded on three sides by water— Lake Sacrement, Lake Champlain, and the La Chute River—a work detail was beginning to construct a moat on the landward side of the point. Other work details were building the first of the batteries, which he hoped would be done in time for the cannons. They should be on the way and would be arriving soon on barges sent south from Montreal.

However, Lotbinier was concerned, having not heard from Baron Dieskau's expedition to the south. He was also worried that the supplies that had been brought with him at the beginning of the campaign were starting to run low. Even if the Canadian hunters and the Indians were to supplement their rations with game and fish taken from the lakes, there were other necessary supplies that had to come from Montreal and Quebec.

This actually concerned him more than the lack of news from the Dieskau expedition, because he understood the current politics of the French Government in the Canadian provinces. His cousin was the Marquis de Vaudreuil, the Governor General of Canada. His cousin had personally recommended him for this assignment, which would "be great for his career and prestige." Prestige, he snorted, as he slapped another black fly biting his shoulder.

Lotbinier knew about the corruption that was embedded within the entire government of Canada. The success and survival of these men depended on these petty officials putting their own self-interests aside and supporting this operation. He shook his head, knowing those fine gentlemen would never do that.

As for news from the expedition, the Baron could be marching triumphantly into Albany, and he would be the last to know with these damnable thick forests making communication difficult.

Suddenly, there were excited voices coming from the shore. Lotbinier looked over in time to see several canoes pulling up with a mix of French uniformed men, Canadians, and Indians, who were being met at the shoreline by their comrades. Perhaps some news from the triumphant Dieskau had finally arrived. Maybe Dieskau would ask for his engineer to come to Albany, and he could leave this miserable place to another engineer.

After a few minutes, he was approached by one of the returning French soldiers. Lotbinier looked up and was shocked by what he saw; the normally crisp white uniform was smeared and stained with mud, powder, and blood. Coming to a semblance of attention, the soldier saluted. "Ensign Joseph de Villiers cares to report that the expedition is no more."

Lotbinier stood and returned the salute and then asked the ensign to stand easy and tell him what had happened. A camp stool and a stiff drink of rum were brought for the ensign and after he sat, he began his tale of the disaster at the southern end of the lake.

He recounted how they had found Fort Lyman completed and heavily defended, and the Baron had decided to ambush the English in the ravine. He described how the ambush had appeared to be successful, with many of the Provincials falling or running. He ended with the description of the slaughter of their men before the barricade, the Baron either dead or captured.

Across the LaChute River in a thicket, Jacob, James, and Samuel, with Peter watching to their rear, were in an observation position that gave them a clear view of the activity across the river but was far enough away to give them security. Still, Jacob had posted Peter to keep a watch for any French or Indian patrols while they observed the French. Jacob could see all of the activity, having witnessed the canoes and what appeared to be survivors from the fight at the barricade. They had taken a long time to return to their position here.

Carefully opening a small telescope and then wrapping a cloth around it to prevent any of the brass from shining, Jacob observed the activity in the French camp. He spotted the meeting between a French soldier, who he assumed was a survivor from the fight, and the men in the camp. One of the men began giving instructions to messengers, who scattered around the camp. This soon produced extra guards who marched off to patrol and protect the work parties on the landward side of the point.

"I guess news of our little welcome to the French down at the other shore has just reached these folks," Jacob commented softly.

He also spotted the Indian survivors heatedly speaking with their comrades and making large gestures that pointed to the French. Jacob focused in with his telescope and could see the Indians did not look pleased.

"Maybe a little love lost between the French and their friends."

Satisfied with what they had observed, Jacob decided to return back to their concealed camp. With such a large area to scout, Jacob had decided to split his force with Konkapot, who led Charles and James. They would switch off, with Jacob leading a scout one day and then Konkapot the next. They would scout an area, and then move to a new one on the following day until they had scouted the entire point.

At night, they compared their notes, and Jacob consolidated their information and continued to work on a sketch of the French positions. They estimated the number of French soldiers and identified the various units by observing the different colors of the facings and cuffs of their white coats, as well as the different regimental flags displayed. It was hard to get an accurate count of Indians, who seemed to be coming and going, but mostly going.

"Guess they didn't like what happened at the southern end of the lake," Jacob speculated.

After spending about a week scouting the area, Jacob decided it was time to return to Fort Edward with their information. Besides, they were running low on food, and the chances of their being detected were increasing as more patrols were observed around the work site.

Jacob led the patrol out of the base camp, once more concealing any sign of their presence. They wrapped skins over their firelocks to protect their rifles from the light drizzle, just in case they did make contact with an enemy patrol.

The rain didn't last. The sun came back out just after midday, and the Rangers slowly began to dry out as they moved. After traveling a day and believing they were far enough away from the French, Jacob decided it was time to replenish their food supplies.

Everyone agreed, since they had already eaten the last of the dried or cooked meat and biscuits. Konkapot spotted a large deer and quickly fired, bringing it down. While Konkapot cleaned the deer with James's assistance, Jacob and the rest of the patrol provided security in case someone unfriendly had heard the shot.

As Jacob was scanning the woods, he heard low whimpers nearby and taking Samuel with him, scouted out the sounds. They came across the carcass of a dead grey wolf, which appeared to have somehow slipped and gotten its head caught in a tree stump that had snapped its neck.

The whimpering was coming from three pups nearby, who went silent when Jacob approached. The pups were more curious then scared, their eyes watching the men approach. From what Jacob could guess, they were only about six or seven weeks old, and they would have no chance of survival out here. Looking over at Samuel who was smiling and nodding his head enthusiastically, Jacob returned the nod.

Jacob and Samuel picked up the pups and brought them over to the rest of the patrol.

"Look what we found," announced Jacob as he handed one of the pups to Konkapot and kept one for himself, while Samuel was scratching behind the ears of the third, which he had carried.

Cutting some meat from the freshly cleaned deer, they fed the pups, who wolfed down the meat. Samuel looked up at Peter, Charles, and James to see if they were interested, but they shook their heads no which made Samuel's face light up.

It was common practice for Rangers to have dogs, and sometimes wolves, as pets. There were a few running around their island back at Fort Edward. As he sat leaned up against a log, Jacob looked into the eyes of the pup he had chosen, a grey-colored pup that looked back with its golden eyes.

"Well little guy, seems we're kindred spirits here," Jacob said to the wolf, who cocked his head at Jacob. "You lost your mother too, and need a family," Jacob said, and the wolf barked. "Well you're now part of our family, just like me. We'll take care of you."

Jacob scratched the pup behind his ears, and it was enough for the wolf pup, who seemed to accept him and his new fate.

Once they were ready to move, Jacob placed the pup in his haversack so that its head could stick out but it would still be secure. The pup didn't seem to mind and fell asleep, content with a full belly of fresh deer meat and the swaying of the haversack. Konkapot and Samuel did the same with their pups, who also fell asleep, having been fed fresh deer meat. They too seemed to have accepted their new fate with these Rangers.

Jacob led his men away from where they had killed the deer in case there were unfriendly ears in the area. They moved southward for a bit until they found a rock overhang where they could make camp and build a small fire to cook their fresh meat. Jacob posted a guard, and they began to skewer the deer meat on green branches they had stripped with their knives. They hung the branches over the fire.

Soon the sound of the crackling fire was joined by the snapping and popping of cooking meat, the smell the sweetest they had experienced in a while. The only smell they had noticed lately had been their unwashed bodies in close confinement.

Using some cord, the Rangers made leashes for their wolf pups so they would not go far. The pups stayed close, happy with the fresh meat that was being given to them and the warmth from the fire. They frolicked and played with each other and with the Rangers, who were relaxing. Having not spoken louder than whispers for some time, they were now able to talk, even if in low voices.

"What do you think of that French position?" Samuel asked Jacob. "Think we will have to take it?"

As Jacob scratched the ears of his dozing pup, he nodded slowly. "Yes, in time we'll have to try and take it, hopefully before it gets any stronger. That's a good position they have picked. Will make it a tough fight."

Then the conversation switched to Samuel and his new hair style. James and Charles, being new to the section, had heard mentions but didn't really know the story. Taking his hat off, Samuel showed them that the small circle where the scalp had been taken from him was healing, but no hair was growing. Still, it spoke highly of Samuel; not very many men could get scalped and live to tell about it.

After he placed his hat back on his head, Samuel said, "This is why you two," pointing at Charles and James, "watch what we do and learn from your sergeant there, or you could end up worse off than this."

The compliment surprised Jacob, but he took it in stride. What Samuel said was true, and he would make sure these two learned to survive.

After all of the meat was cooked, they allowed the fire to die down and the patrol settled into sleep, still taking turns keeping watch. During Jacob's turn, he sat watching the woods around him while scratching behind the ears of the pup he had taken for himself.

Looking at the deep grey and white fur of his wolf, Jacob said, "Your name will be Smoke."

The pup just cocked his head to look at Jacob, not understanding. "Does that work for you, Smoke?" Jacob asked the pup who simply barked, but seemed more interested in whether he was going to get any more of the cooked deer meat.

The night was quiet, but a breeze whistled through the leaves, which were beginning to flutter down to the forest floor. The stars twinkled through the crisp, clear air, but the moon was off to the side where Jacob couldn't see it through the trees. Flights of geese were passing over, their light honking softly drifting on the night air.

Konkapot was feeding some meat to his wolf that he named Raven, for the dark almost black color of her fur, and Samuel was playing with his rambunctious pup whom he had named Otto. Smoke cocked his head at Jacob, waiting for his meat for the morning, which Jacob fed him, nearly having his fingertips bitten by his sharp teeth.

The breeze was a chilly one. Winter's fingertips were starting to stretch out into the valleys, to take the grip that would soon cover the mountains and forests with ice and snow.

In the morning, they cleared away any sign that they had been there, scattering the ash around the rocks and burying their fire pit. Once all was secured, the section resumed its travel back down the lake.

The trek took another couple of days of slow but cautious movement, but they arrived at Fort William Henry's construction site without any contact with the enemy. Their mission had been successful, and Jacob gave a sigh of relief. His first time being in charge of a scout was nearly over.

Fort William Henry was starting to take shape. The inner parts of the walls were complete, and the outer portions were being built up as men shoveled dirt from the surrounding moat into the space between the outer and inner walls.

They were still using their hasty barricade fortification left from the battle as their camp site while men worked on the fort. The Rangers waved at some of the Provincials, who recognized them as they continued down the trail. It now seemed to be more of a road than a trail as a result of all the wagon and foot traffic to and from Fort Edward.

Jacob had decided to use the road for speed, which would be their security as well, to get the information that the general wanted to Captain Rogers. After they made their way over to the island, Jacob placed his gear in his lean-to, passed Smoke to Konkapot to watch, and reported to Captain Rogers.

Immediately after Jacob reported in, Lieutenant Stark and Captain Rogers walked with him over to the fort to meet with General Johnson. "The general will want to hear it from you," Rogers told Jacob. "He may ask you specific questions about the position."

The fort was completed now. All of the buildings and barracks had roofs, and there was smoke rising from the many chimneys.

They were shown into General Johnson's office, and after the other colonels arrived, the meeting began. Johnson was sitting in a large chair, his leg still wrapped in a bandage and propped up on a smaller stool with a pillow on it.

Gathered in the room were General Lyman, Colonel Blanchard, the fort's commander, Colonel Whiting, and of course, skulking in the background was Captain Archibald Reynolds, with Lieutenant Manning and the sergeant major.

Jacob presented what they had observed from their scout of the French construction of their fort. He showed his sketch of the works and recounted how many French units he had observed and also what was being built around the site.

"Gentlemen," Johnson began, speaking around his pipe stem. "I believe it would make more sense to wait to take the fight to the French. We're not ready. We do not have enough men to defend Fort Edward, work on Fort William Henry, and begin a campaign against the French to the north."

Tapping his pipe against his shoe heel, he added, "And it's starting to get cold. Winter is coming soon, and we're definitely not ready to wage a winter campaign. I am concerned that if we were to launch an attack now, we could get caught in a snowstorm or our supplies would not be able to make it to us through the weather. I propose we wait until spring to increase our numbers, finish Fort William Henry and have it serve as a secure supply base, and then launch a spring campaign against the French. "Sergeant Clarke, thank you for your information. We do not require you to stay for the rest of the meeting."

Jacob saluted General Johnson, nodded to Captain Rogers, and took his leave of the assembled commanders. He hadn't stepped very far from the office when he heard, "Ah, Sergeant Clarke, may we have a word."

He turned and saw he was being approached by Captain Reynolds, with the sergeant major and Lieutenant Manning behind him.

"How can I be of service to his most Loyal and Royal servant to the King?" Jacob asked. Captain Reynolds looked taken aback by Jacob's civil inquiry.

"Well, yes. I am not sure of what you Provincials do," began Captain Reynolds as he approached. "But to arrive looking and …" Reynolds pulled a handkerchief from his wrist and held it to his nose, "… smelling like you do. In the British Army, I would have you flogged."

Jacob shook his head. He had tried to be civil to this man, and it didn't matter. He moved a little closer to Captain Reynolds, who wrinkled his nose and held his perfumed handkerchief closer to his nose as a shield.

Jacob simply said, "Guess I am lucky that I am not in your British Army."

The sergeant major broke in. "You Provincials will be, soon enough. You'll be put under our control, and soon you will taste British discipline and wear proper uniforms. Regular British officers will be in command, with no more of these Provincial play-acting officers. They'll be lucky if they hold a captaincy. Provincial generals and colonels, bah," scoffed the sergeant major.

"If I may sir, Sergeant Clarke was probably asked to give the commanders the scouting information as soon as he arrived, and he didn't have time to change clothes or clean up," said Lieutenant Manning.

Captain Reynolds and the sergeant major both turned slowly towards the lieutenant. "Being around these Provincials will be the end of you, lieutenant. As I have stated before, when I want your opinion, I will ask for it, and I am not asking for it."

"You're always welcome to come with us sir, and see how it's done," Jacob said.

With a look of horror in his eyes, Captain Reynolds shook his head no.

"That is not a proper way for a regular officer and gentleman to conduct himself against the enemy; he must apply the gentlemanly principals of war and meet on the field on equal terms. How dare you practice such an ungentlemanly way of waging war, sir?" huffed Captain Reynolds, who turned and stalked off with his trusty sergeant major trailing him.

"Besides, I have a duty to try and advise these officers of rabble on how to conduct a proper military campaign," the captain added as he walked away.

As Lieutenant Manning was turning to go, Jacob touched his arm and said, "You seem more intelligent than our beloved captain and sergeant major here. Why don't you come with us and learn about ranging and scouting?"

Manning smiled and nodded his head.

"Who knows? Maybe I will once I can separate myself from Captain Reynolds. Have a good evening, Sergeant."

Leaving the fort and crossing over to the island, Jacob could see the bonfire that had been started, and he was soon welcomed by Rangers, Mohawks, and some of the Provincials who had gathered around to pass the rum and to hear the story of their scout.

The Rangers were celebrating Jacob's surviving his first scout as a sergeant. They sat on stumps and logs, told what they had seen of the French fort being worked on and what had appeared to be the news of their victory arriving to the French at the lake. Samuel brought Smoke over, who jumped around and nipped at Jacob's fingers.

The other Rangers described their scouts around the area and told what had happened at the fort while they were away.

"We put into that there Ticonderoga place a few years back," commented one of the Rangers. "Thought it would make a good place for a camp. Guess them Frenchies thought so too."

Jacob nodded, then asked the assembled group what they all thought about Captain Reynolds, which evoked a lot of hacking and spitting on the ground. Everyone was of the opinion that he was not worth the uniform he had purchased and that he was steadily becoming a royal pain in their asses, Rangers and Provincials alike.

Soon the stories got bolder and more flamboyant as the rum flowed and the night wore on. Each Ranger, Provincial, or Mohawk tried to outboast the others on their many exploits in which they had single-handedly saved the day in one place or another. The Rangers, Provincials, and Mohawks laughed and joked, returning to their normal ways after the harsh recent fight against the French at the lake.

Peter was busy explaining about a Bavarian custom of hunting "Wolpertingers," a strange breed of rabbit with wings, fangs, and duck's feet. He told them how the hunter must lure this elusive animal into a trap, using a candle only when the moon is right.

As Jacob and Konkapot translated this odd tale to their Mohawk brothers, they all shrugged and mentioned wood spirits. Jacob believed spirits were involved in Peter's story, either beer or this thing called "schnapps" that Peter also spoke of. As tall as his tales appeared to be, they made Peter more a true Ranger and a stronger part of their section with every telling.

Sitting back against a log, with Smoke sitting in his lap, Jacob sniffed his clothes. Perhaps Captain Reynolds was right. He did need to change his clothes. He smelled like he had been on a long scout, or crawled through a slop pit, or probably a little of both.

CHAPTER 8

FORT EDWARD: THE COMING WINTER

The seasons slowly but steadily marched on, the air becoming cooler and crisper, the trees changing into their multi-hued glory, and the leaves beginning to fall. The mornings arrived frosty, and the sentries' breaths formed a light mist as they walked and watched the woods around them. The cooler wind gently blew through the forests and valleys, the leaves dancing as they fluttered down to cover the ground in a golden-red carpet. It was becoming cool enough at night that Jacob and his Rangers decided to move from their lean-tos into one of the completed log houses. Jacob and his men took their turns working on the other log houses in preparation for the coming winter, and they helped complete the blockhouse in the center of the island. When they were not building, they patrolled or provided security for the workers who were constantly restocking the firewood for the fort and its garrison.

Captain Rogers himself went out on patrols. General Johnson wanted to be kept informed of everything the French were up to as he and the other officers planned their spring offensive. Rogers and a few Rangers traveled by canoe to the north end of the lake and then traveled northward past the construction at Ticonderoga to observe the French at Fort Saint-Frederic, located on a spit of land known as Crown Point.

After being out for ten days, Rogers returned, called all of the Ranger officers and sergeants together, and told them what he had seen. "The French are staying very active, working on improving their position at Fort Saint-Frederic. I saw they were adding another battery of cannons and reinforcing their barricades. Perhaps they know we're planning to come after them up north."

The other Rangers, smoking their pipes, nodded their heads in agreement.

"I also saw a large number of Indians encamped there, shooting at marks. From the regimental flags and different uniforms, I estimate there are about five hundred French regulars camped there with the Indians."

Rogers continued, "On the way back south, I stopped to pay a visit to our old friends at Ticonderoga. I saw a lot of smoke from cooking and warming fires. It also sounded like the French were drilling and practicing their musketry.

"From these two camps, either they are really concerned we're coming north…" Rogers paused to look at his gathered men "…or they are getting ready to come south. In either case, expect to be taking more patrols out to keep the French under observation so there are no surprises. I am heading back up to Ticonderoga. Lieutenant Stark, you will be in command while I am out on this scout."

Lieutenant Stark nodded, and the meeting broke up. Stark then leaned over to Jacob and informed him that his task for the day was to report to the quartermaster and then go hunting. Jacob headed back over to where Konkapot and the men were finishing shingling one of the log houses.

He told his men to grab their shooting bags and rifles; they were heading out to help restock the fort's supply of meat. Freed from the routine duty of building huts and going hunting instead, all of their faces lit up and they gave a slight victory "whoop" as they grabbed their rifles and shooting bags.

Once everyone had his rifle and was ready, Jacob led the Rangers over the bridge and reported to the quartermaster. Jacob's men joined a gathering of other Rangers and even some Provincials. Most were tasked to go hunting, but some carried poles for fishing. Jacob nodded to the other men as the quartermaster instructed that they would need a couple of deer and ducks or geese from each of the groups.

"Fellas, I think we're in for a cold winter this year. We're going to need to smoke a lot of meat and fish to weather through it," he explained. "Good luck out there."

The groups of hunters gathered quickly, dividing up the valley so they were not running into each other while hunting. A good-sized group with cane poles and lines headed towards the river to fish, with some carrying their muskets for security just in case.

Jacob pulled the other Rangers together and in a low voice, said, "Keep your eyes open out there. See if we have had any visitors in the area."

The other Rangers nodded their understanding, shouldered their rifles, and headed out. The Provincials for the most part headed north along the river, because their smoothbore muskets would serve better at shooting ducks and geese, while the Rangers and their rifles would go after the deer. Jacob led his men south to try their luck in that direction. As they followed the wall of the fort southward, they passed by Frederick Best, who was in the process of building a permanent log house from which he would operate his shop. The foundation and base were being built by a few workmen. Frederick, who was watching the construction, spotted Jacob and waved him over.

"You boys heading out on a hunt, perhaps?" Mr. Best inquired, seeing they were not heading northward while carrying their rifles. "If you happen to find an extra deer, I would be willing to give a trade for it. Interested?"

Jacob placed the stock of his rifle on the ground and leaned on it.

"What are you willing to trade for a poor deer that happened to lose its way from the fort to say, you?"

With sparkling eyes and a smile, Frederick answered, "Oh, I bet I could find something to trade with ya for a poor, lost deer."

With a wink and a snort, Jacob nodded and led his Rangers into the woods to see if they could find a lost deer along with others for the fort.

Even though they were hunting, they treated it like they were on a patrol. They spread out in their staggered line, taking up their fields of observation. Konkapot was leading, followed by Peter, then Jacob, with

Charles, James, and Samuel watching their trail. With the increased French activity, it was always better to treat any outing like a scout, and it was also good to keep their skills honed.

The day was clear, if not crisp, leaves fluttering and falling around them. Jacob noticed that their green attire was not blending in as well with the forest; many of the trees whose leaves normally concealed them now offered only barren branches. There was no sound in the woods except for the breeze whispering and the blue jays and other birds. They heard the knocking of a woodpecker in the distance.

After traveling southeast for a bit, they broke out of the forest into a small clearing where a lonely cabin sat. The clearing stood behind large clumps of yellowish grass and remnants of corn stalks, standing brown and silent.

Jacob spread the men out in a line and carefully approached the cabin. The field they were crossing was once gardens, but they had not been attended to in a long time. The Rangers were on their guard, scanning their surroundings, noticing no sound or smoke coming from the cabin or its chimney.

They came upon a small pen near the cabin, which may have been used to hold animals, but there was no sign of whatever had been kept there.

The Rangers spread out around the cabin while Jacob and Samuel approached the door. They stood to either side of the door, and Jacob reached down and grasped the handle and slowly opened it. As the door opened inward, Jacob and Samuel entered a very empty and dusty room.

"Doesn't look like anyone is home," commented Samuel. Jacob nodded his head in agreement.

"Can't blame them. With all of the raiding going on, it wasn't safe for these people out here."

Jacob looked down into the dust and dirt and saw that the door had been opened before. There were other tracks in the dirt and dust, animal and some human footprints.

"Sam, it looks like someone else was here."

Sam looked down and also observed several sets of footprints moving around the house like they were looking for something. Scattered on the floor was a pewter plate and some wooden spoons, but little else.

Jacob and Samuel went outside and conferred with Konkapot and the others, who also said they had found footprints around the cabin, but it had been some time since these visitors had been here. As Charles and James watched the field around them, Jacob, Peter, Samuel, and Konkapot shared their thoughts.

"The footprints are moccasins, not shoes or bare feet," Jacob said as he traced one of the footprints with his toe. "Could be one of our patrols, or could be our friends from the north."

Everyone nodded.

"Psst!" caused everyone to take a knee and face out. Jacob looked over to Charles who had made the sound and was pointing off into the field. Jacob moved in a crouch over to Charles to see what had alerted him. Charles, with a grin, pointed across the field, "Some deer just entered the field, and it's our lucky day!" Charles whispered.

Relaxing slightly, Jacob snorted and looked to where Charles was pointing. Sure enough, six deer, two large bucks and four does, had entered the field and were grazing on the tall grass.

Jacob waved everyone over and pointed out the deer. They picked their targets, and then slowly and carefully spread out into a line. Then, as one, they slowly stalked forward towards the grazing deer. They were downwind from their targets as they advanced until they were about fifty yards away.

While covering their locks, they slowly cocked their rifles. With a quick nod, Jacob rose followed by his Rangers, and they all fired as one. The deer lifted their heads as the Rangers rose, and then all six balls struck true, the deer falling not far from where they were grazing. The Rangers reloaded and waited to see if their shots had attracted anyone's attention.

As Jacob observed the woods around them, he thought, how are we going to drag six deer back to the fort?

As if reading his mind, Peter winked and said he would be right back. He headed over to a shed near the cabin, and in a few minutes, he returned with an old, squeaky pushcart that wobbled a little, but looked solid.

With a shake of his head, Jacob waved his men over to the deer as Peter pushed the protesting cart over. As Peter and James watched the woods, Jacob and the other Rangers quickly cleaned the deer with their sharp knives, and then loaded them into the cart, hoping it didn't collapse. Peter and Charles pulled the cart, Konkapot and Samuel led, and Jacob and James followed behind.

They found an old wagon trail from the cabin that wound its way through the woods and came out on the Albany road. With wheels screeching, they turned the cart towards Fort Edward. At least they didn't have to be worried about being quiet, considering how loud the pushcart was.

It was after midday when Jacob and his Rangers broke out into the valley and saw Fort Edward in the distance. They pushed the cart up to where Frederick had his tents and the beginnings of his log hut. The sutler was with a couple of Provincials when he saw Jacob stop and with a large smile, he walked over to the Rangers.

As Charles and James lifted one of the large bucks from the cart, Jacob, with a look of pure innocence stated, "I believe this deer lost his way, and we brought him back to you."

With a hearty laugh, Frederick shook Jacob's hand and whispered in his ear, "You boys come back later, and we'll settle up. I am a man of my word."

With a wink, Frederick called for some of the workers to come over and help the lost deer find its way behind his large tents.

With a smile and a nod, Jacob led his Rangers into the fort where they dropped off their five deer. They also left the push cart with the quartermaster, who would put it to good use.

"Good job lads. Head over to the cask and draw you each a cup of rum for a job well done." The quartermaster said.

After thanking the Rangers, the quartermaster, with his men, pushed the old cart over to where other game was being prepared, either smoked or salted, and then put into barrels for storage. The men, after drawing a cup of rum, moved off to the side and enjoyed their reward from the quartermaster.

"Ah, I see you Rangers are hard at work as ever," came the sarcastic voice from behind them.

Jacob turned to see Captain Reynolds and his ever-faithful sergeant major, but the lieutenant was absent. Jacob had to admit, the fact that the captain could continually show up unobserved at the most inopportune times was uncanny. He would be a good Ranger with those skills, Jacob thought, then quickly erased that idea from his mind. The captain would never be a good Ranger.

"So good to see you this fine day Captain Reynolds, Sergeant major. Anything these poor Provincials can do for you?" Jacob commented, giving a mock bow to the captain.

The captain approached Jacob, looking up into his face.

"The day I need the use of you 'Rangers,' will be the day I eat my hat," he sneered.

Jacob looked down at the captain. "I'm looking forward to watching you eat your hat, sir."

With a harrumph, the captain turned and walked away, followed by the glowering sergeant major. Shaking his head while the other Rangers snickered, Jacob finished his rum. He placed his cup in his haversack and led his men out of the fort and then over to Frederick's shop.

Sitting behind the large tents, Frederick shared some of his rum with the men as they discussed the trade for the "lost deer," which was in the process of being cut up and dried. Supervising the work was Frederick's wife Martha, and a woman with reddish-blonde hair that Jacob had never seen before.

"Who is that?" asked Jacob, pointing to the young women.

"Ah, that is Maggie, an indentured girl who is working here with her sister, Audrey," explained Frederick as another girl, slightly older and with red hair, came out from one of the tents to help with the deer.

"With business doing so well, I thought I would get some extra help that's softer on the eyes, if you know what I mean."

Jacob nodded as Frederick winked and went back to bartering with the other Rangers on what they wanted in trade for the deer. Jacob watched Maggie for a bit as she worked on the deer. She looked up, saw Jacob was watching her, smiled, and carried a platter of meat over to a drying rack set up near a fire.

The other Rangers settled with Frederick, securing some new knives, and best of all, woolen mittens and hats, all in trade for the deer. These would be helpful when the weather got colder. Jacob on the other hand, watched Maggie as she moved back and forth, working on the deer meat. He was fascinated with her. Something about her tugged at his heart and soul, and Jacob wasn't sure what to do about it.

Granted, Jacob had been with women before, which previously had gotten him in trouble with some of the Mohawk elders. Konkapot had rescued him from that unpleasantness.

But this was the first time he had seen a colonial woman who almost made his heart skip a beat. There was something about Maggie that stirred something inside him that he hadn't felt before. Since he had left home, he had never had a true relationship with any girl, so he was navigating through unknown territory.

Seeing that Jacob was intently watching Maggie, both Konkapot and Samuel walked up behind him and looked over his shoulder to see what had caught his attention. Samuel began grinning as Konkapot blew into Jacob's ear, causing him to jump.

"What you looking at Jacob?" Konkapot asked innocently, already knowing the answer.

"Well, ah," Jacob stammered, which made both Samuel and Konkapot smile even more. In response, Jacob closed his mouth tightly and turned red.

Konkapot laughed and slapped Jacob on his back, enjoying the uneasiness Jacob was feeling.

"Seems you have a new campaign," Samuel suggested. As Jacob glared back at him, Samuel winked.

"It is definitely worth campaigning for."

With a deep sigh, Jacob smiled and nodded.

"We're here to help if you need us," Konkapot offered.

Jacob snorted and nodded towards the island. "Let's get back to it," he said.

As they were gathering up their things, Jacob turned to look at Maggie one more time and was surprised to see that she had been watching him. She quickly returned to her work, causing Jacob to smile.

The Rangers continued to hunt for the fort for the next couple of days until Captain Rogers returned from his scout and called all of the officers and sergeants to a meeting.

"Men, I just returned from my scout up at the northern end of the lake, visiting our friends at Ticonderoga. They have also been very busy, still working on their fort. I observed a lot of cut timbers in the area, and about a thousand men or more."

Rogers let that sink in before continuing, "We also followed a canoe with Indians and Frenchmen heading south from Ticonderoga. They landed on an island in the middle of the lake. We caught them as they headed north, reducing their numbers by half before they got away.

The Rangers hooted and huzzahed with that news. Rogers nodded and raised his hand to quiet them down so he could continue.

"They appeared to be scouting the islands on the lake. I'm not sure why, so I will be leading a platoon in boats from Fort William Henry, and we'll head north to try and take some prisoners to see what they're doing. Lieutenant Stark, I will be taking your platoon. Have your men ready to depart in two days and have them prepare about a week's worth of rations."

Lieutenant Stark acknowledged the instructions and called for Jacob and the other sergeants to follow him outside where he would give them their orders.

"You heard the captain. Have your men pack a week's worth of rations, shot, and powder. Make sure they carry knapsacks or packs that keep the water off. We're heading out on the lake," Stark said.

"It also would be useful to identify anyone with experience handling whaleboats."

Jacob and the other sergeants nodded their heads in understanding and left to gather their men and ready their gear. Jacob and his Rangers drew rations of salt beef and pork, powder, lead for making balls, biscuits, potatoes, and onions, which they packed away after wrapping them in skins to keep them dry. They gathered around the fire to make enough rifle balls to total at least sixty rounds each. Some carried a little more, and extra powder horns were also packed away.

The following morning after formation, Captain Rogers and Lieutenant Stark led the platoon in two columns from the fort, and they traveled along the now-improved military road to the construction site of Fort William Henry. From Frederick's store, Maggie watched the Rangers march off towards the north, fascinated by the Ranger who had stopped by and whom she had caught watching her.

Smoke, the other wolf puppies, and some other Rangers' dogs followed alongside and scampered about as they marched with the Rangers. The dogs and the wolves stopped at the beginning of the forest and watched the men leave.

As the Rangers disappeared into the forest, the dogs and puppies scampered back to the camp, playing and chasing one another while awaiting their masters' return. They would be watched by some of the Rangers who were staying behind.

When the Rangers arrived at Lake George, they noticed much work had been done. The walls were almost complete and the frames of the long barracks were being worked on. Perhaps knowing that winter was coming soon had motivated the workers to complete the barracks quickly. As they passed through the woods and the former battlefield, Jacob couldn't help but think of Patrick and the others lost here.

The Rangers marched past the work site and continued on to the shore. Passing between the barricaded camp and the fort, Rogers led the platoon down to where several long bateaux boats were waiting. The long rowboats used to transport goods on the local rivers and lakes would now be used to transport Rogers and his Rangers.

After setting up a quick camp near the shore, the Rangers gathered to learn how to use these large boats from experienced men from the area. These men were professional sailors who had come up from Albany and New York and who gave the Rangers a quick course in seamanship.

Jacob and his Rangers along with another section manned one of the boats as the entire platoon divided up and took boats out to practice rowing and maneuvering them on the lake. Some of the boats handled well, while others were circling one way or the other as the Rangers learned to row as a team and to steer the crafts with a tiller.

Each boat had an experienced sailor giving instructions on how to row as a unit and how to use the oars to turn and stop the boat if need be. The sailors also helped show them how to use the tiller in steering the boats.

As Jacob worked on using the oars and learning how to steer with the tiller, he thought that it made sense to learn how to use these boats. Lake George was one of the better ways to get up north quickly without trudging through the mountains and thick forests. Through trial and error, the Rangers finally became proficient in rowing and maneuvering the boats. They beached their craft, built cooking fires, and settled for the night, talking about their mission and undertaking any final preparations for their departure in the morning.

"Jacob, think they will give us naval pay along with our Ranger pay?" Samuel asked, which caused the other Rangers to laugh.

CHAPTER 9

LAKE GEORGE AND TICONDEROGA: MARITIME SCOUT

The morning dawned grey and cold as the Rangers rolled out of their blankets. All of the Rangers were moaning and groaning from sore muscles caused by the new experience of rowing.

Jacob took out his flint and steel, and using some charred cloth, caught a spark and placed the glowing ember into a small ball of tinder and pine. Blowing gently, he got the ember to glow and then the tinder to smoke until it caught fire. He placed it in the fire pit and began arranging the smaller limbs and tinder until a fire was growing steadily.

The Rangers warmed themselves around the fire, hands holding cups of tea. Even Jacob was shrugging to get the kinks out of his shoulders, and he wondered how they would feel later. With the expedition heading out at dusk, the Rangers spent the time checking their gear, resting, and have a warm dinner. Once the whole platoon was up and fed, the Rangers packed their gear and loaded their boats. A light, cold drizzle began to fall as the men pushed the boats into the lake and took up their oars for the journey north, Jacob wondering why it always chose to rain when they began a journey northward.

Jacob and the Rangers made their way northward, hugging the coastline as they watched for any signs of the enemy. Similar to what they do during their patrols in the forests, the Rangers pulled into shore, concealed their boats and watched for any signs of the enemy, before traveling again at night.

While a good learning experience for the scouts to come, the Rangers saw no sign of the enemy and Rogers grudging accepted they were not about, and decided to return to Fort William Henry. The tired, sore and blistered Rangers were happy to see the southern shore and Fort William Henry, columns of smoke reaching into cool fall sky.

Rogers gathered the men together after they had secured the boats and their gear, and praised them for enduring the mission as true professionals and Rangers. He was also proud that with the boats, his men had demonstrated another capability the Rangers could use to scout and raid their French foes to the north.

"Lieutenant Stark, you will remain here with the platoon, provide security, and scout around the fort while I go report to General Johnson."

Stark acknowledged his instructions.

"Have one section ready to go north. I plan to return to Ticonderoga once I am finished reporting to the general," Rogers said.

Lieutenant Stark nodded and turned to Jacob.

"Find a place in the camp, but don't get too comfortable. You'll be going with Captain Rogers on his next scout."

Jacob nodded and led his Rangers into the old encampment where they found a place to build some lean-tos. Much had changed since they had last been there. All signs of the battle had been removed by the constant construction. With the fort nearly complete, Jacob mused, much had changed since the fight there and in the nearby woods.

They had not been there for more than a day or so when Captain Rogers returned from reporting to General Johnson at Fort Edward. Rogers had not returned alone. A familiar face was with him, at least familiar to Jacob and his Rangers. Newly promoted Captain Putnam, whom they had rescued not far from this very spot, was being introduced to Lieutenant Stark. Stark waved Jacob over, and along with his men, he walked over to the officers.

"I believe you men know each other?" asked Captain Rogers.

"Yes sir, we have passed one another previously," replied Jacob as he and his men took turns shaking Putnam's hand.

Rogers explained that Putnam had just volunteered to join the Rangers to learn their skills so he could create a similar Ranger company for Connecticut. Stark was going to show him what it took to be a Ranger officer while Jacob and his men went north with Captain Rogers. Putnam wished them luck and then walked off with Stark to be introduced to the rest of the platoon.

Rogers, cradling a musket called a fusil in his arms, asked Jacob if they were ready. Nodding that they were, he and his men headed down to the lakeshore and loaded their gear into canoes.

"Thank God it's not those damn whaleboats," remarked Charles as they loaded their gear into the canoes. Canoes were much easier to handle than the large whaleboats, and were not so tiring. His comment was quickly followed up by an "Amen" from James, and Jacob had to nod in agreement, although his shoulder and back were no longer sore, and the blisters on his hands from rowing were starting to heal.

They placed their gear in the middle of their canoes, and James and Konkapot took one, Charles and Peter the second, and Jacob, Samuel, and Captain Rogers the third. Before they climbed into the canoes, Rogers gathered them together to give them their instructions.

"After talking with General Johnson," began Rogers, "he wants more information concerning the French, so much so that he has instructed us to take a prisoner as well as gather information. We are heading up past Ticonderoga to observe the French near their Fort Saint-Frederic at Crown Point."

Rogers used his ramrod to draw a sketch on the shore, mapping out their route.

"Everything clear?" Rogers asked.

The Rangers nodded and manned their canoes. Taking up their paddles and keeping their rifles close at hand, they began their journey northward, following the western shore of the lake.

Jacob noticed that the mountains were all covered in different hues of reds and oranges as fall took a firm grip across the land. This meant Old Man Winter would be closing on them soon.

The Rangers paddled north, again not seeing any signs of the French, the Canadians, or their Indian allies. Near the lake's midpoint, they put into shore, concealed their canoes, and camped for the night.

The next day dawned cold but clear, and the Rangers put their canoes into the water and continued their journey northward. Just before the lake narrowed and joined with Lake Champlain, the Rangers put to shore, dragged their canoes up into the forest, and concealed them.

Leaving James and Charles to watch the canoes, Rogers led the rest of the patrol westward. They skirted around the French position at Ticonderoga while they made their way north towards Fort Saint-Frederic.

The Rangers arrived at an area that was a little more than halfway to the fort just as the sun was sinking to the west. Rogers led the way through the growing darkness. They were able to travel easily as the moon shone brightly in the cold, clear night. Like silent, ghostly shadows, the Rangers moved stealthily through the night until they found a suitable thicket in which to camp.

The next day, the Rangers continued towards their objective and finally arrived just outside of the French fort. Rogers led the men into a thicket of willows, which they would use as their observation base camp. The Rangers were about a thousand yards from Fort Saint-Frederic, which was an imposing site. The fort's walls were made of stone, and the main tower in the northeast corner near Lake Champlain was almost four stories tall, mounted with cannons at each level. Jacob appraised the fort and assessed it would be a tough position to take.

This was the line between the two opposing nations, the furthest south the French were established until they finished their fort at Ticonderoga. Hundreds of French regulars in their white uniforms marched around, with additional hundreds of Canadians and Indians coming and going around the fort. Jacob was amazed they were able to get as close as they had with all of the activity.

As the Rangers settled into their concealed position, they observed the activity in and around the fort until the sun set, and a cold darkness settled over them. Each Ranger carefully pulled on his warm long coat, hat and gloves, and began taking turns pulling watch and sleeping as best they could. Rogers took his turn along with the others. The only sounds were the night birds and a few insects as the fort's fires and lanterns sparkled in the distance.

The night retreated from the rising sun, and the Rangers shivered in their concealed observation point as the fort started to wake up.

Inside a warm room in the fort was Major Joseph-Antoine le Fèbvre, commanding the regular battalion of the French Franches de la Marine, as well as the entire force of Canadians and Indians gathered at the stronghold of Fort Saint-Frederic. The major was busy studying a map of Lac du St. Sacrement showing the new British positions of Fort Edward and Fort William Henry.

If their scouts were correct, it seemed the English had been busy. What he wasn't sure of was whether the English were building defenses against the campaign planned by the French for early spring, or whether they were themselves getting ready to launch a campaign against the French. In either case, as commander of the front line of the French Empire here in the colonies, he had better ensure the men and the fort were ready.

"Captain de Brisay!" commanded Major Fèbvre, and the captain entered the room quickly from the adjoining office.

"Sound the long roll. I want to see how fast they can assemble. Time them, Captain. We must be ready. The English may already be around us."

Looking at the map one last time, Major Fèbvre thought that if he were in the same position, he would be out scouting his enemy's camps. As the sun rose and the fort's activities became easier to observe, Rogers was not satisfied with what they could see. He crawled over and whispered to Jacob that he was moving forward for a better look and Jacob was to cover him.

Nodding his head in understanding, Jacob asked if he wanted one of them to come with him, and Rogers shook his head no. As Rogers started to crawl forward, the rest of the Rangers took up firing positions, just in case. Konkapot had crawled up next to Jacob.

"Crazy bastard," whispered Jacob, and Konkapot nodded his head in agreement. "Keep an eye out for Frenchies in case they spot our brave leader."

Then Jacob whispered to the rest of the Rangers in the thicket. "The captain has gone forward to look around, so keep your eyes peeled. Samuel, watch our rear in case we have to make a quick exit."

The other Rangers nodded and intensified their scanning of the area to protect Captain Rogers. Jacob watched as Rogers, grasping branches in his hands, began crawling forward, holding the branches in front of him as camouflage, attempting to conceal his movements.

Once again, Jacob shook his head and muttered, "Crazy bastard." When the sun rose above the mountains and bathed the valley in sunlight, Rogers had positioned himself behind a large log ahead of them.

Suddenly, large numbers of French came pouring out of the fort and assembling into their companies to the sound of the long roll. Rogers had no choice but to stay put, because he would surely be spotted now if he tried to crawl back to them. The Rangers were seriously concerned.

"How in the hell did they not spot him or us?" whispered Jacob as all of the Rangers took up their rifles and sighted over their barrels, expecting to get attacked at any moment.

Jacob and his Rangers watched their areas, surprised that no one attacked. Konkapot whispered over to Jacob, "Perhaps it was a drill like we do," and Jacob nodded. It made sense, but still they remained on heightened alert. The sun was about halfway to midday when sure enough, Jacob spotted a lone French soldier walking around, and he was heading towards Rogers.

"Ah damn," Jacob whispered. "Wouldn't you know it, we have a morning walker and guess where he's heading?"

Konkapot whispered back "Us?" to which Jacob responded, "No, the captain."

Peter looked over to see where Jacob was aiming and following his line of sight, spotted the white-uniformed soldier slowly walking with not a care in the world, not suspecting that a rifle barrel was slowly following him from the thicket.

Jacob took up a good sight along his rifle at the approaching Frenchman. Then in a flash, Rogers broke from his concealment and confronted the soldier. They could not hear clearly what Rogers was saying, but the Frenchman didn't seem to be following his instructions. Perhaps Rogers was taking him prisoner.

While Rogers was bold, the Frenchman had a clear advantage with the looming fort behind him filled with soldiers and Indians. Jacob and the others had been as shocked as the Frenchman when Rogers broke from cover, contrary to how he had trained them.

Jacob continued to mutter under his breath, "Damn crazy bastard."

The Rangers watched to see what would happen next, not wanting to give their position away. Just as quickly, the Frenchman pulled a knife and attempted to slash Rogers, who blocked it with his musket and then placed the barrel against the Frenchman's chest.

Swiping the musket away, the Frenchman took another stab at Rogers. Having no choice, Rogers pulled the trigger and ended the brave Frenchman's life. That definitely got the garrison's attention as Rogers sprinted back towards the Rangers.

"Here we go, get ready!" Jacob commanded.

In the distance, Jacob could hear the long roll continuing, calling the French soldiers back to arms. Luckily, the Frenchmen were in the middle of eating and having just finished a drill, were wondering if the roll was for real or another drill.

That hesitation was all Rogers needed as he quickly turned and ran back towards their thicket. Rogers, legs and arms pumping, closed the distance, and as he passed, Jacob and the others picked up and ran after him.

They ran for a bit until they found an elevated position where they could gather their breath and wait for the pursuit. Turning around toward where the French should be coming at them, the Rangers took up firing positions, crouching behind logs.

They didn't have to wait long; several Indians and Canadians were running towards them. As one, the Rangers all fired and dropped seven of their pursuers. This shocked them enough that Rogers and the rest of the Rangers were able to take off running again while their pursuers sought cover.

The Rangers loaded on the run. French and Indians were firing at them, but their balls were not falling anywhere near the Rangers, instead whistling harmlessly by.

After running for an hour or so, the Rangers took up a concealed position on a small rise covered with thick pine trees. They stayed still, even after a few groups of Canadians and Indians ran by, unaware of the Rangers hidden in the pines. Rogers had Jacob and his men rest for a bit, and they waited for darkness to fall so they could begin their movement back to their canoes.

By morning, they arrived at the location where they had left the rest of the Rangers and the canoes. Using bird calls, Jacob signaled Charles, who replied with a different bird call, indicating it was safe to approach. Quickly uncovering their canoes, they loaded and started paddling south back towards their camp. Rogers had them travel only at night and make camp as the sun was rising.

They rested in their concealed position, recounting for James and Charles their scout of Fort Saint-Frederic. They continued on the next evening and arrived safely back at the southern shore of Lake George. After pulling their canoes ashore, Rogers complimented Jacob and his men on their performance. They hadn't brought a prisoner back, but Rogers blamed himself for that.

Captain Rogers departed, and Jacob and his men joined Stark and Putnam in the encampment and told them about their scout of the French.

"He did what?" asked Putnam as Jacob retold how Rogers had crawled forward, using the branches in his hands for concealment. Even Putnam shook his head and commented, "Crazy bastard," and Jacob replied that he had said the same thing.

The Rangers remained at Fort William Henry as October turned into November, and the season became colder and more blustery. Like Fort Edward, Fort William Henry was an irregular, square-shaped fort, with bastions in the four corners and log walls about thirty feet thick. Inside were four two-story log barracks, and a dry moat surrounded the fort on three sides, with a drawbridge to enter the one set of doors in the wall. The walls facing the lake had a sharp drop-off to the shore and did not require a moat. Cannons were mounted on the bastions and along the wall.

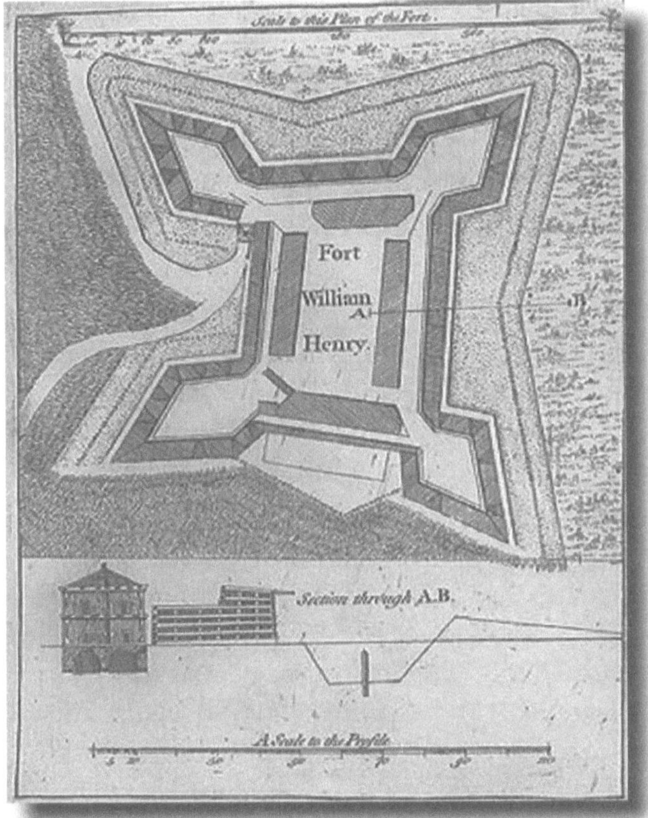

The Rangers rotated between the camp on the island and the old encampment at the lake, while the Provincials and British regulars moved into the barracks. It was a trying time for the Rangers. The number of scouts performed around the fort and up north was wearing them down, and they also suffered from the increasing cold.

Tempers flared, and from time to time, there were heated arguments that sometimes came to blows, Rangers brawls that often spilled into the camp's streets. Captain Rogers put a stop to each incident as quickly as he could, usually roaring at the top of his lungs for the men to stop fighting amongst themselves. "Save it for the enemy up there!"

Rogers growled at his offending men, pointing to the north. "We Rangers take care of one another; we do not fight one another."

Then to drive his point home, he asked, "Do you want them," pointing towards the fort and meaning the Provincials or British regulars, "to discipline you? How many of you could last under their lash?"

Unfortunately a few Rangers didn't get the message, and a couple had to face Rogers' discipline. Eventually, two of the Rangers were kicked out of the company for not behaving themselves.

While Jacob and his Rangers were tense from time to time, either Peter or Samuel would do or say something that would help drain the tension away.

As their time at Fort William Henry continued, friction was building between the Rangers and some of the Provincials and British regulars. This came to a head for Jacob and his Rangers one day when they were assigned to protect a wood detail of New York Provincials.

Jacob and Konkapot, having gone to the encampment to get food for their men, were entering the glade where the wood detail was working when they came across a group of ten New Yorkers confronting some of Jacob's men. He could see the New Yorkers were challenging Peter and Samuel as Charles and James stood behind them. Jacob could also see a fairly large New Yorker doing all of the talking and poking Peter in the chest.

As Jacob and Konkapot approached, he could hear the big ring leader's snide comment, "We're just as good as you fancy pants Rangers are. We don't need you," and he poked Peter in the chest again. Jacob could see that Peter and the other Rangers were getting mad, but holding back.

"What's the meaning of this?" Jacob yelled, getting everyone's attention as he walked up to the group.

Knowing where the trouble lay, Jacob walked right up and faced the ring leader as he turned to see who had yelled. Peter and the others had relieved looks on their faces when Jacob arrived.

"Who's asking?" was the smart comeback from the ring leader.

Jacob, who was about the same size as the New Yorker, stared coldly into the man's eyes.

"That's who's asking, Sergeant," Jacob returned, not taking his eyes off of the New Yorker.

The man turned to his compatriots and snorted, "Sergeant, ha!

Guess they put stripes on pigs too!"

He turned back to face Jacob and glared, "There is no rank out here, fancy pants."

The tension that Jacob had been dealing with began to bubble up and mix with his growing anger at this offensive New Yorker. Not backing down, Jacob glowered back at him.

"I'd watch that mouth of yours," Jacob warned in a low voice, "before you get into something you don't want."

"Your mother didn't seem to mind my mouth when I bedded her at the brothel the other night," the New Yorker sneered back.

He never saw it coming as Jacob's fists caught him in the stomach and face. Jacob hit him three times before he fell back. Jacob followed him to the ground and continued to pummel him.

It was enough to snap the tension, and the other Rangers fell on other New Yorkers who had been part of the confrontation and began to strike them hard and fast. All of the tension that had been building in the Rangers poured out as they vented it on the hapless New Yorkers. It was a quick and vicious fight, and the Rangers stopped when they could see the New Yorkers had learned their lesson, the hard way.

Pulling the battered ring leader's now swollen and bloodied face up, Jacob leaned over and simply said, "I warned you," before letting the ring leader's head fall back onto the ground, where he lie, moaning. The New Yorkers who had not been involved in the fight and had come up to watch raised their hands to show they didn't want any trouble, and they began to drag their semi-conscious mates away from the Rangers.

Jacob looked up to see their relief arriving.

"Perfect timing," he said as he gathered his Rangers and headed back to the encampment. Jacob had to admit, all of the tension was gone, and he felt better.

"What do you think the captain is going to say when he hears about this?" Konkapot asked as they made their way along the trail.

Jacob nodded his head and wondered how much trouble he had just gotten himself and his men into.

"Didn't the captain warn us to not fight one another?" Samuel asked.

Peter responded, "Ya, dat vat the captain said, nothing about dem," pointing over his shoulder back towards the New Yorkers.

What they had said was true, in a fashion, Jacob thought. The captain had only warned them not to fight one another.

"Besides, didn't the captain say we had to take care of one another?" Samuel continued, supported by a chorus of "yes" from the other Rangers.

"Hopefully the captain sees it that way, but does anyone want to take bets?" Jacob responded, and no one took him up on his offer.

Still, it did seem the fight was the pressure valve they had needed to let out the growing tension, and the section actually walked with a bounce in their steps as they recalled the fight. While it was one technique for relieving stress, Jacob hoped it wouldn't have to come down to finding a fight every time they were stressed, though he didn't cancel the idea entirely from his mind.

It wasn't long afterwards that the news of their little skirmish must have reached the fort, and Jacob was summoned to see Captain Rogers. "Good luck," Konkapot, Peter, and Samuel all said as Jacob made his way over to Captain Rogers.

Reporting to Rogers, who was sitting on a crate as he was going over some messages, Jacob waited for the captain to explode on him for their fight with the New Yorkers.

Not looking up from his papers, Rogers asked, "Heard there was some sort of disagreement between you and your men and some soldiers from New York?"

Jacob simply replied, "Yes, sir."

Rogers continued to read his papers with an "hm...hmm."

There was an awkward silence as Jacob waited for the captain to tear into him, the anticipation making it difficult for Jacob to maintain his composure, wondering what punishment Rogers would deal out to him.

Rogers finally put the message down and looked at Jacob directly.

"Any of your men hurt?" Jacob shook his head no.

"Sergeant Clarke, you are aware of my policy about fighting, correct?"

Jacob nodded his head yes.

"You and your Rangers messed them New Yorkers up a good deal," said Rogers as he stood from his crate.

Jacob braced for the coming sentencing, as all sorts of visions raced through his mind about what could happen to him. Would Rogers actually have him flogged, or even worse, would he be thrown out of the Rangers for fighting?

Pursing his lips, Rogers stared directly at Jacob, and asked, "What do you have to say for yourself?"

Jacob resolved himself to face whatever punishment came from Rogers, and replied plainly, "Sir, they were instigating a fight with my men, and they outnumbered us two to one. We showed as much restraint as we could, but we couldn't help ourselves. We took care of one another, and that's all."

Rogers nodded his head as Jacob explained.

"That's how I see it as well," returned Rogers, "and I am glad you showed restraint and didn't kill any of them. That would have looked bad for us."

Jacob was shocked at how Rogers was handling the incident.

"I spoke with their commander who said they were troublemakers, and actually thanked us for setting his men straight."

Jacob looked relieved.

"Still," Rogers continued, "we must maintain discipline, or we will turn into an unruly mob."

Jacob stiffened, again waiting for Rogers to set his punishment. "For violating my directive against fighting, Sergeant Clarke, you and your men are docked two days' pay. Any questions?" Jacob quickly nodded and replied with a "no sir." Rogers accepted it and dismissed Jacob.

As he turned to leave, Rogers said, "Sergeant Clarke," and Jacob turned back to face Rogers.

"Good job."

He winked, sat back down on the crate, and picked up another message. Saluting, Jacob turned and walking away, returned back to his waiting men.

"Well, he still has his back so he wasn't flogged," said Samuel.

Jacob shook his head and told them what Rogers had said. As a group, they were all relieved, and they went back to talking about their fight, joined by some of the other Rangers who had heard of their skirmish with the New Yorkers.

Jacob and his men didn't have to wait long before Captain Rogers called the platoon together. The Rangers, standing in a half-circle, listened as Rogers gave his instructions for their next mission.

"General Johnson still wants more information about the French; he is concerned about their large numbers north of here. In the morning, we're heading back up north along the lake in the bateaux. We will scout out how many French are at Ticonderoga, and we will determine whether they are a defensive garrison or if they are preparing for a campaign south."

The Rangers returned to their lean-tos, inspected their gear to make sure it was all serviceable and waterproof, and cooked their rations. Once everything was in order and they had gathered their gear, Jacob led his Rangers to the shore. As they were walking, Captain Putnam caught up and joined Jacob and his men.

"Mind if I tag along with you?" Putnam asked, and Jacob nodded and welcomed the captain to the section.

The bateaux were similar to the whaleboats they had used before, but they were even bigger, and some of the men could be heard griping about even sorer backs and shoulders. The other difference between the bateaux and the whaleboats was that two of the bateaux had small swivel cannons mounted on their bows. Samuel looked over at Jacob and smiled. "Now that could make a difference," Samuel said, pointing at the guns.

Jacob looked over to where Samuel was pointing. "Then Samuel, you'll be our gunner" he replied.

Like a kid at Christmas, Samuel clapped and rubbed his hands together and moved forward to check on the gun. Smaller than a regular cannon, it fired two-pound balls, which Samuel found in a small box, along with the powder bags and tools to load and fire the gun.

It didn't take long for the Rangers to put into the lake and start their journey north. They were now experienced mariners. It still took two days to carefully make the journey to the northern end of the lake, with Rogers having them travel at night. It was just before sunrise when they landed their boats on the enemy shoreline.

Rogers called Putnam over, and after a quick discussion, Putnam returned to Jacob.

"You boys interested in doing some scouting?"

Jacob nodded and received the instructions that Rogers had given.

Putnam with three Rangers was to scout out the French advance camp on Ticonderoga. Jacob selected Peter and Konkapot to accompany Captain Putnam and himself, while the rest of the Rangers helped to conceal the boats.

Taking only what they needed, Jacob and the small scouting expedition took off towards where the French were building their fort.

Jacob was impressed with how Putnam carried himself. He must have had some experience at this, plus learning quickly whatever Lieutenant Stark had passed on to him. They moved quickly and carefully through the woods, keeping a good spacing between them but still covering one another.

Just before midday, they came upon the French encampment, just south of where the French were building their fort. White tents were in evenly spaced but rigid rows, with command marquees and larger tents on one side. What the Rangers noticed was that there were no entrenchments, barricades, or walls around the camp. It was entirely open, except for a few guards pacing around the perimeter.

They made a quick count of the number of tents, and estimated there were about two hundred or so French regulars encamped there. While this might seem a great opportunity for a raid, the small platoon of Rangers was still greatly outnumbered. Satisfied with what they had observed, Putnam and Jacob led the Rangers back to the shore and reported their findings to Rogers.

Captain Rogers agreed that this would be a great opportunity, but he was also concerned about being outnumbered. He sent one boat back with instructions to press all the way to Fort William Henry and bring back reinforcements. The Rangers stayed in concealed positions around the shore, waiting for the reinforcements to arrive before engaging the French.

However, after waiting a full day, luckily not being detected by a French patrol that had passed by, Captain Rogers made the decision that it would be safer to withdraw instead of waiting there. The chance of being detected, especially with such a large French force nearby, was growing the longer they stayed.

In frustration, Rogers ordered the men to get the boats back into the water and load. Carefully withdrawing from the shore, the Rangers started back towards the southern end of the lake. They didn't get very far, however, before they ran into the boat Rogers had sent, leading several other boats with Provincial troops that Johnson had sent as reinforcements. Turning the expedition around, Rogers returned to the shore and quickly sent two more scouts back to make sure the sentries had not been alerted to their presence as he organized the attack.

Unfortunately, Rogers' luck had run out. In the distance, the sound of musket fire could be heard.

"To arms!" ordered Rogers as the Rangers quickly fanned out and the Provincials formed into their two-rank lines.

Soon the Rangers who had been sent forward as early warning began to fire, as the two scouts came running into the camp. The men breathlessly explained they had run into a large column of French, Canadians, and Indians, when another shout alerted the Rangers that two large canoes were coming around the bend of the lake.

The French were pursuing with both infantry and men in canoes, trying to catch the Rangers between them. Jacob, whose boat was still in the water looked up to see the approaching canoes, each large enough to hold about thirty men.

"Sam, now's your chance, get your cannon ready!" Jacob yelled as he brought his rifle up to aim at the approaching canoes.

Rogers instructed Putman to hold the shore while he dealt with the canoes. The Provincials began volley firing, their officers yelling out the commands, and the Rangers began selecting their targets and shooting. Rogers jumped into one of the boats and waved at Jacob to follow him. Lowering their rifles, Jacob and the other Rangers began pulling on the oars to get the boat out into the lake, as Samuel finished loading his swivel gun. The boat that Rogers had jumped into was the other one armed with a swivel gun.

As Samuel blew on his slow match to get it glowing, Konkapot and the others took aim with their rifles, and Jacob steered the boat so the bow pointed towards the approaching canoes, the other Rangers pulling with all of their might on the oars.

The Canadians and Indians in the canoes, yelling their blood curdling war whoops, began shooting, the balls splashing around Jacob and Rogers' boats. The noise of firing from the shore intensified as Putnam poured musketry into the advancing French. The smoke from the battle began to drift from the woods onto the lake.

Jacob waited until the canoes closed to within a hundred yards before giving Samuel the command to fire. With a large smile on his face, Samuel fired the cannon with a thunderous roar. The shot was well aimed, and the two-pound ball punched through the canoe in the front and near the water line, as the Rangers fired their rifles, sending a few Canadians and one Indian falling into the lake. From the right, Rogers' swivel cannon roared, firing grapeshot, which shredded the other canoe and caused more Canadian causalities.

The damage was enough that both canoes began to quickly sink, with the Canadians and Indians splashing into the water and making for shore. Jacob turned the nose of his boat to face the shore; he had spotted the white uniforms of Frenchmen heading towards their positions, attempting to flank the Provincials and Rangers.

He yelled to Samuel, "Fire on the flankers!" pointing to the French. Samuel nodded happily, reloaded, and began shooting the swivel gun at the flanks of the French as they moved through the trees. There was something odd about seeing Samuel with a big grin on his face as he loaded the swivel gun, spun it around, and aimed along the barrel at the French with James and Charles helping.

Soon the gun was barking in a sustained rate of fire at the French, with Samuel, James, and Charles giving their own whoops and yells. The flanking attack was faltering, with the French shocked to be hit by cannon fire from their flanks.

Rogers' boat came alongside, and he added his swivel gun to the barrage and ensuing carnage. The small cannons, along with Putnam's handling of the Rangers and Provincials on the shore, forced the French to withdraw. Both Rogers and Jacob's boats covered the force as they reloaded their boats and pushed off for the return trip to the southern end. Rogers looked over at Jacob.

"Well, maybe it wasn't how we planned it, but I think we hit them hard enough to let them know it's not that safe for them here!"

Jacob nodded his agreement as he continued to watch for either more canoes or more Indians.

Once the force was on the water, they headed back to Fort William Henry. As the boats cut through the water, the sergeants checked their men and reported to Captain Rogers that all men were present, with no injuries except for some cuts and scrapes.

Trying to maintain noise discipline was given up as the Provincials excitedly talked of the fight. For many of them, this had been their first taste of combat, and the excitement of surviving made them gush.

Jacob at the tiller observed that the Rangers were more reserved, having been in action many times, but he recalled their first action and how the excitement of it had gripped them. The Rangers did talk amongst themselves and joke, but not to the same degree as the Provincials.

The trip south was uneventful. They continued through the night without making camp and arrived at the fort in the morning. After speaking to the men, praising them for their performance in action, Captain Rogers headed back to Fort Edward to report to General Johnson.

The Rangers returned to the encampment and began cleaning and drying their gear. Captain Putman stopped by, and Jacob and the Rangers congratulated him on his command of the action.

"I think I am going to like this job leading Rangers," said Putnam.

"You all like to fight, and you fight well."

He nodded to them before continuing his rounds around the encampment.

Once their gear was clean and fires had been built large enough to dry their clothes, which were hanging from lines and lean-tos, the Rangers sat and relaxed as best they could, swapping stories of their exploits in the last battle. With the French appearing to be building up their forces, there would be little time to rest before they headed out for their next scout.

Jacob was knocked over as Smoke charged into him next to the fire, and they started wrestling around, just as Konkapot and Samuel were knocked around by their happy wolves. They had been brought from the island by some of the Rangers who were joining the band at the fort. After playing with their pets and feeding them some meat strips, they all settled down for the night. Jacob laid back against a log, scratching a contented Smoke behind his ears, as they tried to outbrag Samuel, who insisted he had done more damage with his swivel gun than the entire force did with their muskets.

CHAPTER 10

FORT EDWARD: WINTER SCOUTS

Jacob and his men had only been at the encampment for one night when Captain Rogers arrived from Fort Edward and asked for him by name.

"You must have made an impression on him," said Lieutenant Stark, "or he likes how you pulled his bacon out of the fire."

Jacob raised his eyebrows in agreement and left to meet with Captain Rogers. Rogers explained that General Johnson was still concerned about the French presence, especially after their engagement a few days before, and he wanted another scout of the French positions at Ticonderoga.

"Sergeant Clarke, you will take your Rangers and put in at a different spot than our last action. You will scout the enemy, determine their numbers, and attempt to identify how many different units are present and the condition of their works before returning and reporting back to me here. Any questions?"

Jacob shook his head no. This would be a normal scout of the enemy, if there were such a thing as "normal."

After receiving the last of his instructions, Jacob returned to Konkapot and the others and explained what they were going to do. They began to get their gear ready. They only had to restock some dry rations, because they still had enough shot and powder to support the mission.

Smoke, along with the other wolves and dogs, watched the Rangers head down to the water, and then returned to the lean-to and curled up next to the embers of the fire. Jacob and the Rangers joined Rogers, who was waiting to see them off at the shoreline and then loaded the canoes for the journey back to Ticonderoga.

"You think we could borrow some of those large canoes we saw the other day?" asked Samuel. "Now those would make these excursions easier, using just one canoe instead of a couple."

Jacob thought about it and made a mental note to see if they could find one of the large French canoes and liberate it for themselves.

They pushed off, traveling all day and into the night to arrive at a different landing spot farther up the lake from where they had landed before their brief battle with the French and Canadians. The air was definitely colder now, and the mountains had turned into grey sentinels, their colorful leaves gone. It wouldn't be long before snow fell.

After hiding their canoes and leaving Peter and Konkapot to guard them, Jacob and the others skirted along the shoreline, keeping to the brush as they moved to a suitable observation position. They were all on extra guard, having just engaged the enemy not far from where they stood.

Soon, they found a great site for observing activity around the French position without drawing notice of their presence. The French had definitely been busy. The Rangers observed three new completed barracks buildings inside of the now-completed walls of the fort. Additionally, they spotted four new storehouses. Satisfied they had met their mission objective, Jacob led the Rangers back to the fort.

After spending the entire day on the lake, happily without any contact with the French, the Rangers pulled their canoes up onto the shore and returned to the encampment while Captain Rogers went once again to Fort Edward. Jacob did feel bad that they had not found one of those large canoes; perhaps they could acquire one on the next trip up north. The morning after their return, the platoon was called into formation, where several wagons with the quartermaster from Fort Edward had pulled into the encampment. The men were issued thick green blanket coats, snowshoes, wool hats, and thick gloves. Even though Jacob and his men still had their hats and gloves from their trade with Frederick, it was always good to have spares, especially if they were given for free.

It was clear the coats couldn't have come at a better time as the month of November marched on. The weather had become much colder during the day and downright frigid at night.

In addition, they received some of their pay from the paymaster, and the Rangers signed their names in the orderly book for receiving their clothing and pay. As all good soldiers do, once released from the formation, the Rangers headed over to the line of sutlers' tents to spend their newly acquired coins.

As they browsed the tents, Jacob thought about Maggie back at Fort Edward and wondered how she was doing, or even if she was still there.

"Looking for something these sutlers don't have?" Samuel asked.

Jacob looked over at him and glared, then nodded and laughed along with Samuel, who slapped him on the shoulder.

For the next couple of days, Jacob and his men went out on hunting expeditions, which also served as scouting expeditions to look for any signs that the French or the Indians were in the area. They brought their wolves with them, who were big enough now and who would sometimes point out deer before the Rangers could spot them. On a few of the hunts, Captain Putnam accompanied them, still learning his craft as a Ranger officer.

Jacob and his Rangers also tried their hands at fishing. Jacob still posted sentries even though they were only a few hundred yards from the fort while they tried to catch fish along the lakeshore.

Konkapot and Peter seemed to be the best fishermen of the group, competing with one another to see who could catch the most fish, or the largest, or the most colorful. The boasts went back and forth as each held up his catch, the other Rangers voicing their assessment of whose fish was the best.

Other groups, both Rangers and Provincials, joined them to try to catch more fish for smoking and salting before the winter set in and the lake froze over. Jacob could read the mountains and the icy chill in the air, and they told him it wouldn't be long before the lake would ice over. Large smoking racks were built near the shore, and the quartermasters had the barrels and salt out, packing the fish.

Soon a messenger arrived from Fort Edward, and the garrison, including the Rangers, was assembled on the fort's parade ground to hear the message.

"From his Excellency, General Johnson, commanding," read the messenger. "I hereby release all of the New England Militia to return to their homes, but to remain ready if called out to meet a French incursion. The general thanks you all for your service."

There was a loud huzzah from the militiamen, but dour looks from the Provincials and regulars who envied the militiamen and did not look forward to spending the winter at the lake.

The following day, the columns of New England Militia, men from New York, Massachusetts, and New Hampshire, shouldered their muskets and bags and began their journey home. The Provincials wished them all well on their journeys, even though there were looks of envy and even some looks of hostility towards the departing men.

The rest of the garrison, about six hundred men, began what was known as "going into winter quarters."

Lieutenant Stark and Captain Putnam moved the Rangers into the fort, occupying one of the barracks buildings that had been vacated by the departed militia. Jacob had to grudgingly accept that these barracks were actually nicer than he had thought and would be warmer than wintering under a lean-to. The barracks room was large enough for the entire platoon, with wooden bunk beds and with large stone fireplaces at each end of the room.

Jacob and his men stowed their gear, and then went down to the parade ground to gather firewood to get the large fireplaces restarted. In their haste to pack and leave, the militiamen had let the fires go out and hadn't restocked the firewood.

Samuel and Peter went to the fort's quartermaster to get fresh candles to replace the short, stubby ones left in the room. Jacob, Charles, and James brought fresh straw for their beds, replacing the old smelly straw that had been left by the militiamen. They rolled out their ground cloths and then they rolled out their blankets.

Jacob thought their new quarters would keep them safe from the cold wind, but it remained to be seen how stuffy and, eventually, smelly the barracks room would become once all of the men had settled in. Smoke didn't seem to mind the new quarters, and he curled up under Jacob's bunk.

The following day, the Rangers were pleasantly surprised when Frederick, with Audrey, Maggie, and a few hired workmen, rolled up in some large wagons and carts and set up shop just outside of the fort. Word was quickly passed, and the men who were not on work detail or guard duty made their way over to Frederick's wagons to see what wares he had brought.

Jacob and his Rangers were coming in from a morning wood cutting protection duty when they spied the wagons, recognized Frederick's voice, and made their way over. It looked like Frederick was having a good morning, wheeling and dealing with several of the men as both Audrey and Maggie were fetching items and making sales on their own.

Jacob, along with his Rangers, walked towards the wagons, Smoke and the other wolves coming along to see what was going on. The men were paying Frederick with shillings or trading skins and other items. Frederick was bartering with the best of them as each man was trying to get his attention.

Watching from a distance, Jacob was looking to spot Maggie as Charles, James, and Peter went over to browse the goods Frederick had bought. Konkapot and Samuel remained behind with Jacob.

The two knew why Jacob had paused, and they knew who he was looking for, and they decided to stay put and wait to see what would happen. With mischievous grins on their faces, they watched Jacob literally raise up on his toes to try to see over the heads of the men crowded around the wagon.

All three spotted Maggie at the same time. She was busy pouring some ale into the tin cups the men from the fort were holding out.

Both Konkapot and Samuel looked at Jacob who was just standing there.

Konkapot punched Jacob in the shoulder, which made him jump and stopped him from gazing at Maggie.

"Well?" Konkapot said, and Jacob testily replied, "Well what?"

Samuel jumped in. "Aren't you going over to say hello to the fair lady?"

Looking at his two friends with a frown, Jacob replied, "I will when I'm ready."

The two looked at one another, reveling in Jacob's uneasiness, and Konkapot pushed him forward.

"Don't tell me our brave fighter here is afraid of that woman," Konkapot said. "You didn't seem so afraid of the Mohawk sachem's niece."

Taking a deep breath and turning away from his laughing friends, Jacob set his jaw and walked forward to join the line of men looking at Frederick's wares and getting ale from Maggie.

Having recognized Charles and James, Frederick raised his hand and waved at Jacob. "Ho, Jacob, good to see ya in one piece still lad!"

That helped to ease Jacob's tension, and he waved back. "Good to see your business is doing well," Jacob shouted over the din of the competing men as they haggled with Frederick's helpers.

Frederick, along with Konkapot and Samuel, smiled as Jacob made his way over towards Maggie. As she was pouring another ale, Maggie saw Jacob, and recognized him as the one she had seen watching her while sitting and talking with Mr. Best back at Fort Edward.

She remembered him: such a serious and intent look on his face, with striking blue eyes, and that scar on his cheek. He might not have been the most pleasant one to look at, but there was something about this Ranger. Maggie had secretly hoped to run into him here at the lake.

She smiled at Jacob and was shocked to see this brave Ranger blush and look away.

"Maggie, why don't you take a break?" Frederick said from behind her.

Taking two mugs of ale from Frederick, she boldly walked up and handed one to Jacob, who had a shocked look on his face when she handed him the mug, but he quickly recovered.

Jacob led Maggie over to a log and sat down, and Maggie joined him on the log. Smoke padded along and sat down, almost as interested as Konkapot and Samuel, who were watching from a distance.

Taking a sip of his ale and wiping his mouth with his sleeve, Jacob held his hand out and introduced himself to Maggie, who shook his hand. Jacob marveled at how soft her hand felt. Then Maggie, after taking a drink of her ale, let out a deep burp, which was enough to break the tension.

"So, what's your story Jacob? How did you end up here on the frontier fighting these savages?" Maggie asked.

Jacob recounted his life up to that point—the death of his family, living with the Stockbridge Mohicans, and joining the Rangers. Maggie listened intently to Jacob as he recounted his life— she was fascinated by this Ranger who seemed a little afraid of her, but yet who would go bravely into harm's way to fight the enemy.

After finishing his story, Jacob asked how Maggie and her sister had ended up there with Frederick on the frontier. With a deep sigh, Maggie explained that they were indentured servants, who now worked for Frederick.

"Well, Audrey and me had traveled with our parents to Boston, but they were indentured to pay for their passage from England. My family had worked in Boston for about two years, when both of our parents caught smallpox and died."

Maggie paused and took a long sip of her ale before continuing, Jacob waiting intently.

"The family we had been working for took mercy on us I guess," Maggie continued, "and sold our contract to Mr. Best, who was looking to expand his business in upper New York. So we came with Mr. Best and three wagons of wares from Boston to Albany, and then up to Fort Edward."

Jacob took a drink from his mug, looking at Maggie with understanding.

"Must be tough," he commented, understanding what it was like to have family die off and to be left on your own.

Maggie laughed and scratched her nose. "Oh, it's not a bad life, except for being out here on the frontier surrounded by Indians, bears, and wolves."

Maggie looked down at Smoke's golden eyes, which were watching her, and she bent down to look closely at Smoke. "Present company accepted, of course," she added.

Jacob was amazed when Smoke looked up and licked her nose in response, sitting back down on his haunches, tongue lolling out the side of his jaws.

Giggling, Maggie wiped her nose then looked at Jacob. "I should get back to work. I don't want to keep Mr. Best waiting."

Maggie stood and Jacob followed. She reached out, and Jacob shook her hand.

"It was nice to meet you Jacob. Perhaps we could speak again later?"

Jacob nodded and said only, "I would like that."

Smiling, Maggie took the mug from Jacob's hand and returned to the wagon. Jacob watched her go, then turned and couldn't hide the smile on his face until he saw that Samuel and Konkapot had stayed and watched his conversation with Maggie. Jacob quickly shifted his smile to a frown and glared as he approached his grinning friends.

"That must have been nice," Samuel remarked as Jacob stomped by, but then broke back into another smile.

Looking at his two friends, he answered, "It was nice."

Both patted him on the shoulder as they made their way into the fort. Maggie, as she poured ale again, watched Jacob and his friends enter the fort and smiled to herself.

November changed to December. The wind blew cold and harsh from the north, stripping what few leaves were left from the trees. Only the enduring pines were still green. While the valley remained cold, the only snow was on the tops of the mountains, where some white wisps could be seen.

When the Rangers went out on their scouts or hunts, they were now wearing the thick green blanket coats, or capotes, and fur caps. They all started to make "snow moccasins" of thick deer or cow hide, lined with wool and waterproofed. Their summer moccasins would not keep the wet and cold from their feet.

Jacob, Konkapot, and Samuel were sitting around the fireplace in the barracks as they sewed their boots together. Jacob had a feeling they would need them soon. From their years of long hunting, they knew the importance of keeping their feet warm and dry in the winter. They knew many a man who had not taken precautions and whose feet had turned black and a few who had died from the infection that had set in from their frozen feet.

Smoke and the other wolves were chewing on the scrap skin from the snow moccasins.

Jacob and the others, who had all spent many days hunting and trapping, held a deep respect for the winter and the icy snow it brought. If you didn't respect it, it would kill you quietly and quickly, leaving your frozen corpse to be consumed by animals in the spring when it thawed out.

When they were not out scouting, hunting, or guarding work details, Jacob was over visiting Frederick in the hopes of getting some time with Maggie. Frederick had become a father figure in a way to both Jacob and Maggie, and Jacob wanted to do the right thing, not act in the rash way he had shown in relationships with women before. There was something about Maggie that told him he had to be different, not just a rough and ready Ranger, but more.

Luckily for Jacob, Frederick liked him and took a fatherly approach to watching over Maggie and her sister, Audrey. There had been a few occurrences in which Frederick had straightened out some of the Provincials and some of the British regulars, as well, who had not been respectful to the girls. Frederick always had a stout cudgel close at hand when the rum and ale began to flow freely and some of the men lost their sense of propriety.

When time permitted, Jacob and Maggie walked around the fort or the encampment area.

"So, you were here when the big battle took place, with General Johnson?" Maggie asked during one of their walks. She could see there was a hurt deep in Jacob's eyes when she asked, but he told her the story of the fight.

"Over there was where the encampment was," Jacob pointed to the small hilltop. "This was nothing but open fields and marshes; that hill was the only real defendable location. Even though we spotted the French on a scout," Jacob continued, spinning and pointing to the east, waving his hands to show it was a good distance away, "the general did nothing until we learned the French were between us and Fort Edward."

"He did nothing?" she asked, and Jacob nodded.

"He ordered the Provincials out as he strengthened the hasty defenses here."

"What did you do in the fight?" Maggie asked, and Jacob pursed his lips, trying to find the words to explain the fight without bravado or going into the gory details.

"We went with the Provincials, on our own accord. We weren't asked for. We stayed in the rear until we entered the ravine and all hell broke loose upon us."

Jacob pointed to the southwest in the direction of the ravine where the fight had occurred.

"You mean that ravine we passed through to get here was where the fight happened?" Maggie asked, and Jacob nodded somberly.

"Brutal fight there, and we were fighting for our lives, all the way back here," Jacob again turned and pointed to the encampment, "until the French pursued us and we stopped them right here where we're standing."

Maggie could see Jacob's thoughts go back to that moment.

"Did you lose some friends in the fight?" she cautiously asked.

Jacob nodded. "Sergeant Patrick McKinney and Robert Blakefield were lost during that fight, good men."

Seeing the loss in Jacob's eyes, Maggie reached out and hugged him, which surprised him, but he hugged her back.

"Well, you and your friends made it, revel in that," Maggie said, after she let him go. "You're alive, and I am sure you have learned from it, or else you wouldn't be standing here with me, telling me about it."

Jacob nodded and admitted Maggie was right. He needed to focus on the now. He could honor the memory of his friends, but he should not dwell on their loss.

Jacob was again surprised when he felt Maggie take his hand, and the two walked back to Frederick's wagons hand-in-hand.

It was mid-December when Jacob and Konkapot were called to the room that Captain Putnam and Lieutenant Stark used as an office. When they entered, Captain Rogers was there speaking to the two officers.

"Ah, our two volunteers," said Lieutenant Stark, who almost fell over laughing at the shocked looks on both Jacob's and Konkapot's faces. They had just realized they had walked into an ambush.

Stark raised his hands in defense as Rogers spoke up.

"I asked for you two by name. I am heading up to Ticonderoga," explained Rogers, "and from what I heard throughout the company, you two are experts at pulling my bacon out of the fire."

Both Jacob and Konkapot coughed and looked slightly sheepish as they stared at Captain Rogers.

"I haven't had very good luck in getting information about the French. You two have kept both my luck and me alive, so will you come?"

Jacob looked at Konkapot, who nodded. He turned to Rogers and also nodded. What else were they to do? Say no?

"Fine, fine. Here is the plan."

Rogers pointed out their route up the lake.

"This will be a small scout of the enemy's position at Ticonderoga. The general wants to know what kind of winter quarters the enemy are in and how many men are there. We need to determine if they have sent most of their army home like we have, or if they are maintaining strength at their encampment. Any questions?"

Jacob looked at the map and the route they were taking, and wondered how deep the snow was up where they were going. Snow could be an asset, or a hindrance. It all depended on the situation.

Jacob looked at Konkapot who shook his head no, and so Jacob responded with, "No questions."

After receiving additional instructions, Jacob and Konkapot returned to the barracks to pack and ready their gear.

The following morning they met with Captain Rogers at the lakeside near a canoe. The lake was a smoky steel grey, cold but not yet frozen. After they had loaded their gear, Rogers sat in the front to paddle, Konkapot in the middle with the gear, and Jacob in the rear with another paddle. They pushed into the cold, grey lake and started their journey northward.

There was no sound on the lake with the exception of their paddles biting into water as it flowed around the canoe. Jacob knew they had to be careful; if they made one false move and spilled into the lake, it meant a cold death for them all.

The sky was dark grey with heavy clouds that Jacob knew were snow clouds. They had not traveled far when they noticed a fire built on an island along their path. They floated by, trying to figure who would be on the island, most likely French or Canadians. Indians wouldn't make a fire to announce their position, and no civilians were this far north of the fort.

Still, they didn't want to alert anyone to what they were doing. Rogers reached for his bag and pulled a couple of fishing lines and handed them out to Jacob and Konkapot. They floated for a bit, fishing, to keep anyone who might be watching them from guessing who they truly were.

They floated by on the currents until they were away and could paddle over to the other side of the lake and take a different route to Ticonderoga. After a full night on the lake, Rogers pointed towards shore and they landed in a small cove, pulling the canoe in.

Jacob and Konkapot carried the canoe into the woods. Knowing they couldn't leave a guard, they covered the canoe in limbs and then used pine boughs to wipe away their tracks as Rogers watched the woods for the enemy.

The three took off from the shore and headed towards a small mountain, the same one Jacob and Konkapot had used before as a landmark. Rogers led them around the mountain so they could approach the fort from the north to get a different view. They had to stop a few times to avoid Canadian and French patrols that were passing by.

When they found a good observation position around dusk, they decided to rest for the night and scout the French in the morning. They pulled themselves deep into a thicket of brambles and saplings. After making a small hole in the vegetation, they wrapped themselves in their blankets and went to sleep, taking the risk of not posting a watch and hoping luck would look over them.

The morning broke cold and misty, with a light drizzle falling on the Rangers as they packed their gear and started for the fort. Crawling forward, cradling their long rifles and trying to keep them dry, they moved to an observation position.

Below them, the French were hard at work on the fort. They had been busy since the last time the Rangers had been there, only a few months before. The fort now had cannons mounted on three of the bastions—four pieces of cannon mounted on the southeast bastion, two on the northwest towards the woods, and two on the third. The fourth bastion, near the river, was too small to hold guns.

There were many cooking and warming fires around the fort and amongst the long straight lines of soldiers' tents. They also observed that the French and Canadians were building log huts. They estimated there had to be around five hundred soldiers at the fort and camp.

While this was the best information they had obtained in a while, Rogers was not satisfied. He nodded his head back towards the rear, and they crawled away from their observation position.

"We need to get accurate information for the general," whispered Rogers. "We need to grab a prisoner."

Jacob looked at Konkapot who shrugged, then back to Rogers and nodded he understood while thinking, "Here we go again."

Rogers led them over to a new spot and set up a small ambush position along a trail to see if they could capture someone. They lay concealed in thick brush along the trail, but no one approached for a while.

Then, the drizzle changed to snow, which began falling softly but became harder over time, the flakes growing in size. Even though they were laying there in capotes, the cold found its way into their skin, and they shivered, their bodies unable to move to warm themselves. They pulled branches over their heads to help mask their wispy breaths.

Eventually, there were sounds of movement, and the Rangers readied themselves, but a platoon of French regulars marched by. Jacob held his breath, hoping Rogers wasn't crazy enough to ambush this much larger force and breathed out when he let them pass. After a little while longer, about twelve Canadians marched by with two dead deer they were carrying to the camp. Still outnumbered, Rogers let this group march past as well.

As the snow continued and the sun dropped, Rogers whispered, "This isn't a good spot, we need to get closer."

He led them, crawling closer to the fort. Rogers was hoping that he would be lucky again and get one soldier walking alone like at Fort Saint-Frederic. They slowly crawled forward and got closer to the fort, watching another trail. Jacob hoped their luck held and they didn't come upon a large force as they crawled forward. Of course, who in their right mind would be out in a cold snowstorm?

They still lay concealed, but snow was starting to layer on their backs and shoulders, which helped in their camouflage. It also made it colder for the three Rangers, who tried everything they could to not shiver violently or make any noises.

The cold was starting to set into their bones. His bones aching, Jacob was becoming concerned that parts were starting to lose feeling. Rogers finally had to accept that they were not going to get lucky and grab a prisoner.

The Rangers could smell roast meat and bacon on the breeze from the fort and the camps, and their stomachs growled. They hoped no one had heard them. Accepting defeat, Rogers motioned for them to crawl back.

Slowly backing away from their concealed positions, the Rangers moved away from the fort. The sound of singing could be heard from both the fort and the camps on the cold night breeze. Jacob was amazed and amused at the same time, perhaps befuddled by the cold.

The Rangers took a different route away from the fort, heading northwest and then to the south towards their hidden canoe. The snow was coming down very hard, making it difficult to move. The found an abandoned shack, and after making sure no one was in it, the Rangers moved inside. Konkapot used branches to obscure their footprints, but the snow was falling hard enough that footprints were soon covered anyway.

They still did not light a fire, but they changed their shirts. Jacob and Konkapot also changed their hats and gloves for dry ones, thankful they had brought the issued hats and gloves along with their personal ones. At least the shack kept the snow and wind off them. They slowly massaged their numb feet and toes, warming them gently and bringing them back to life.

They rolled up in their blankets and ate cold rations before falling asleep, once again letting luck pull watch for the night. With the snow falling hard, they hoped the French would not expect that anyone would be out scouting them. Besides, the French were singing. Perhaps they were having a party and were too busy to look for a few spying Rangers. They tried to catch what sleep they could, the cold making it difficult with their bodies shivering to stay warm. Jacob, who had awakened to relieve himself, sat there for a while and listened to the wind whistle through the loose logs and boards of the shack.

The storm had passed, and the sun was starting to rise when Rogers woke them and decided it was time to leave. They opened the door, pushing it out through the newly fallen snow, and stepped into a crisp morning, the sun reflecting off the blanket of snow that covered everything. The air tasted cold but fresh as the Rangers departed and continued on their journey to their concealed canoe.

The snow was not deep enough to make it difficult to move forward, but they were concerned that their tracks would attract someone. With the exception of a hawk circling lazily off in the distance, there was no sign of life. The snow shimmered like a thousand diamonds in the morning light and crunched under their feet as the Rangers slowly made their way across it.

Travel was becoming difficult, because their bodies were exhausted by the cold and by their having to trudge through the snow. They saw the shore in the distance, heard no sound of pursuit, and were thinking that luck had finally smiled on them once more when two deer came out of the tree line just in front of them.

It was Rogers who said, "Why not?" and brought his rifle up.

Jacob also brought his rifle up, and they both fired, dropping the two deer. They quickly dressed the deer as Konkapot worked at uncovering their canoe, which by now was under a thick layer of snow, and got it into the water. They put their gear and the deer meat into the canoe and quickly pushed out into the lake in case someone had heard the shots.

They paddled down the lake until they thought they were a safe distance from the French. Spotting a small island with trees, they pulled in to cook some of the deer. Konkapot built a small fire, using the tree limbs over them to break up the smoke, as Rogers and Jacob skewered some of the deer meat and started cooking it.

The wonderful smell that came from the venison, accompanied by the snapping and crackling noise of the meat cooking, made their stomachs growl in anticipation of a warm meal. Jacob felt like his stomach was trying to chew its way through him to get to the roasting meat.

Not waiting for the meat to completely cool, they pulled it off and began eating what they considered one of the best meals they had had in a while. Perhaps it was due to their being cold, exhausted, and hungry, but they enjoyed every bite.

As soon as they were done, they extinguished the fire and scattered the ashes before climbing back into their canoe. The rest of their journey was uneventful and soon in the distance, they observed the long columns of smoke rising from Fort William Henry, which was also covered in snow.

After they landed their canoe on the shore, Rogers pulled his gloves off and shook Jacob's and Konkapot's hands, thanking them for a good mission.

"Perhaps one of these days we'll get lucky enough to take a prisoner so we can get more accurate information," Rogers said. Jacob nodded, but thought, "If we keep going out with you we'll end up chasing somebody."

Jacob and Konkapot grabbed their gear as men came down to get the deer from the canoe, having observed the scouts' arrival from the walls. They walked up from the shore, crossed the drawbridge across the moat, and entered the fort.

There was much activity there. Cook fires were burning, and some of the wives of the fort's garrison were putting up pine boughs around the barracks. Jacob and Konkapot looked at each other, puzzled, and climbed the steps to their barracks. Inside, James and Charles were playing checkers while the others were sewing clothes and snow moccasins.

"Well, look who finally made it back from their expedition," announced Peter, who walked over to the fire and from a small cauldron, ladled out a steaming liquid into two cups, which James brought over to Jacob and Konkapot.

With a big grin, Peter hoisted his own cup and said, "A good Weihnachten my friends!" Confused, Jacob looked over to Samuel, who looked up and said, "Merry Christmas, lads."

The Rangers had no duties or responsibilities the next day, December 25th, but the Ranger officers and sergeants were called down into Putnam's office. Captain Rogers was there with a note in his hand.

"Men, General Johnson has retired to Albany for the winter. He instructed me that the commissioners would be forming a new regiment of Provincials to garrison the fort here and at Fort Edward for the winter. The regiment will be commanded by a colonel from Boston, a lieutenant colonel from Connecticut, and a major from New

York. Rogers looked around the room to blank stares; the men were more concerned about what would happen to them.

"General Johnson also felt that it would be wise to leave a company of Rangers under my command to continue our excursions towards the enemy's forts during the winter. Looks like we're still in business lads. Pass the word to the men to enjoy themselves. We're going to be busy soon enough."

Captain Rogers and Lieutenant Stark left for Fort Edward, leaving Captain Putnam in command. Putnam walked around and shook each of the sergeants' and remaining officers' hands, wishing everyone a Merry Christmas and told them to see to their men.

With the downtime, Jacob repaired his gear and made sure everyone's equipment was repaired and ready to go. It might be winter quarters, but they could be called upon at any moment to scout.

They also knew that the coming spring meant a return to the fighting, as both sides would strive to meet their military objectives. Jacob knew they would be right in the middle of this renewed fighting. He was trying to figure out how he could head back to Fort Edward so he could call upon Maggie, who had returned with Frederick back to his log home/shop for the winter.

CHAPTER 11

1756
FORT WILLIAM HENRY: FINDING THE LOST

It was bitterly cold. Old Man Winter took the northern frontier in his iron fist, and snow and ice began to envelope the valleys. Lake George froze over thick enough that men could walk out onto the ice. The sky was a crisp blue, with white clouds streaking the cold skies and the sun sparkling on the snow and ice covering the fort and the ground around it. The sentries at the fort were walking their posts along the walls and bastions, feet crunching on the packed snow, bodies wrapped in thick capotes and fur hats. The walls and bastions had become so covered in ice that a few of the men had slipped and injured themselves. Smoke columns from all of the fort's chimneys rose into the clear blue sky.

Jacob was sitting next to the fireplace in the platoon's barracks on a homemade stool, the fire snapping as he sewed up a tear in one of his shirts. Smoke was curled up in a corner, golden eyes watching from behind his tail, which covered his nose.

All of the Rangers were repairing clothing or fixing equipment. The other wolves and the Rangers' dogs were snoozing in front of the fire or at their masters' feet.

"You think Captain Rogers is crazy enough to take us up north now to scout the French?" Samuel asked from between his teeth as he bit down to cut the thread he had been using to sew up a pair of his breeches.

Jacob put his sewing down and thought about it.

"Yes, he's crazy enough, and the French wouldn't think anyone would head up there in this cold."

Peter scoffed from his side of the room. "Cold, you think dis is cold?

I would think men like you would be used to cold vinters here."

Samuel looked over at Peter, who was smiling around his pipe stem, head wreathed in smoke.

"Well, yes," said Samuel, who looked over at Jacob, who was nodding his head. He had been through some severe winters here in the North. "I've seen some good winters in Boston and the like, but not like this, deep in the woods," Samuel said.

Peter nodded. "You will, trust me, you will."

Smoke observed the conversation from his corner. What did winter matter to a wolf? He had been fed, and he was in a warm room out of the weather. To a wolf, this was the good life.

Samuel nodded and returned to his sewing.

There was shouting from the fort's parade ground, quickly followed by a Ranger running into the room, yelling, "Turn out, Rangers!" as he sped through the barracks room and out the other door.

The wolves looked up as Jacob and the others dropped what they were doing.

"Perhaps the French are as crazy as us," shouted Samuel, as he ran to get his gear.

They grabbed their green capotes and pulled them on, throwing their shooting bags, powder horns, haversacks, and canteens over their shoulders. They grabbed their rifles and ran down into the parade ground with the wolves running alongside.

The platoon formed quickly. Captain Putnam, who was standing with a Provincial officer, addressed the assembled Rangers.

"Men, we have a problem. Several men from the New York Provincials may be missing between here and Fort Edward. We don't know if they are lost, or if the French or Indians got them. We're going to spread out and look for these men, or any signs of them."

Putnam called Jacob and the other sergeants up to the front of the formation to divide up the search area. Once they received their instructions, the sergeants returned to their men.

"We're heading towards Fort Edward," Jacob told his men as he used his ramrod to sketch a map in the snow.

He drew two squares representing the forts, a line for the military road, and a circle. "Here is us, here's the road, and here is Fort Edward," he said, "And here is Bloody Pond." He pointed to the circle near the road, "and of course, French Mountain is here."

"We're going to move along the western side of the road and head over to Bloody Pond, move towards the mountain then head west and move along the river to Fort Edward. Sergeant Carpenter and his men will be to the eastern side of the road and will follow alongside us towards Edward. We're not sure how far they may have wandered, and we can also see if there are any signs of Indians over there. Everyone still have two days' rations packed and canteens full?"

Everyone nodded, indicating they were ready. Jacob led the men to where their snowshoes were stacked, and they headed out of the fort into the snow. The other Rangers were spreading out in different directions as the New York Provincial officer and Captain Putnam watched them go.

Smoke and the other two wolves raced out in front of the Rangers, churning up the powdery snow before them. Jacob hoped they could help; perhaps their keen sense of smell, sight, and sound could help locate the lost soldiers before Old Man Winter claimed them.

The snow wasn't deep until the Rangers started to enter the woods. While one Ranger watched the woods, another pulled on his snowshoes, then covered his partner as his partner put on his snowshoes. This might be a search and rescue, but they still were not taking any chances in case there were enemies in the woods watching them.

Konkapot and Peter led the way, followed by Jacob and Samuel, then Charles and James. They were bundled up in their thick coats, fur hats, and gloves, but the Rangers made sure their ears were clear to hear, and their eyes searched for any signs or tracks in the snow.

The Rangers now were able to stay on top of the snow with their snowshoes. As they moved deeper into the woods, there was no sound except for their snowshoes crunching on the snow and the wind blowing through the trees. Now and then, snow fell from the branches. The wolves moved around, sniffing the air and the ground, but not detecting anything.

They traveled past the clump of fallen trees where they had met and fought together with then-Lieutenant Putnam. Snow now covered most of the old trees, turning them into white mounds. They still used this spot, along with Bloody Pond and French Mountain, as landmarks. The snow made the area look serene and harmless, covering any signs from the bloody engagement. Jacob paused to remember Patrick before moving on with the scout. The Rangers always seemed to pause quickly at this location to remember the fallen.

They saw only a few game tracks, but no footprints as they moved through the woods and came out by the now-frozen Bloody Pond. They could barely recognize it as a pond, except that no vegetation marked the snow over the frozen water.

They stopped to take a break, chew on some biscuits, and drink from their canteens, always keeping a watch around them for signs of the soldiers or of their enemies. Off to their east was the white and grey face of French Mountain watching over them, like a tired old man.

As they chewed and watched the woods, Samuel said, "You'd think these fellas from New York would know better than to head out here."

Everyone nodded in agreement.

"Maybe they were townsmen and not used to wilderness winters," said Charles, and again all of the Rangers nodded.

Jacob hoped they would find them safe and sound, but as they moved deeper into the woods and time passed, he knew their chances were getting smaller. Once everyone had finished eating and resting, Jacob motioned the Rangers on, with the wolves again leading the way.

They crunched through the snowy woods, but still the Rangers did not see or hear anything that could help locate the lost soldiers. The wind creaking in the trees was the only sound heard.

Their progress was slow, even with snowshoes. They continued generally westward until they could see the Hudson River, its rocks covered in a frozen blue and white mantle. The sun was beginning to sink behind the mountains, and the Rangers stopped for the night.

As the sun dropped, so did the temperature and Jacob decided to have a fire built. It would help them stay warm, but it would also serve as a beacon if the lost men were out there. He set a watch though, in case the fire served as a beacon for any unfriendlies.

After an uneventful but frigid night, Jacob decided to parallel the river, staying in the woods and moving towards Fort Edward. The sun, at its peak height and with no clouds to block its beams, was creating a blinding glare off the snow and ice along the river. Even the wolves were staying to the shade of the trees, avoiding the glare.

After an hour or so of moving along the woods, Konkapot stopped the scout, and Jacob moved forward to see what he had found. Konkapot and the wolves, whose ears were perked up, were staring at what looked like two figures, huddled together and stumbling through the snow.

Jacob had Konkapot move forward, and the rest of the Rangers moved into a line and approached the figures cautiously. The wolves fanned out but stayed near Jacob and the others.

The men did not appear to be armed, but they were stumbling and tripping as they walked, holding on to one another. As Jacob and the others approached, they could see they were wearing Provincial uniforms, and Jacob breathed a sigh of relief. These stumbling figures were the lost soldiers.

"Who's there? Are you a friend?" yelled one of the men, who was looking all around, as if he couldn't see.

"We're Rangers from the fort. Are you well?" Jacob replied. The man who had spoken smiled.

"Oh, thank the heavens! We found someone, John."

John moaned and looked around blindly for their rescuers.

Jacob moved closer and saw that the men were suffering from snow blindness and from the cold. The areas around their eyes were sunburned, and they were squinting or moving with their eyes closed.

Jacob and Samuel provided security as the other Rangers each took one of the soldiers by the arm and led them back into the woods. Jacob could see that some of their fingers were already turning black from the frost, as well as the tips of their ears and noses.

He led them to a spot where the snow was thin, sat the two Provincials on a log, and began to try to ease their suffering. The Rangers shared their rations and canteens with the rescued soldiers, who wolfed them down quickly.

"We were traveling from Fort Edward to Fort William Henry when a snowstorm just snuck up on us. We somehow got off the road and ended up going into the woods, and then it got dark. The snow began falling even harder, so we huddled together under some trees. Davie and Robert left to go and try to find help, but we didn't see them again."

The spokesman for the group, Daniel Kipp from Albany, continued to talk about what had happened to them.

"When the morning came, we kept walking and couldn't find the trail with the snow covering everything. We saw the river, so we headed towards it, knowing it ran by the fort. We followed it for a few hours, and the snow became very bright, and soon, we couldn't see anything but a bright white."

Jacob and his Rangers knew that one of the challenges of hunting and trapping in the winter was understanding snow blindness, in which the sun reflecting off the snow burns the eyes and temporarily blinds.

Daniel continued, describing how they had kept wandering, falling, and staying wet, shivering so hard he thought his bones would break.

The Rangers had built a fire to dry the rescued soldiers, and they covered their burned eyes with cloth.

"James, Charles, keep an eye on things here," instructed Jacob.

"The rest of you come with me to find the other two. Smoke, let's go!"

Ears perked, Smoke led them through the snow in a bound, already beginning to hunt for the lost men.

The two Rangers nodded as Jacob led the other four with Smoke, Konkapot's Raven, and Samuel's Otto ranging out in front on a search moving eastward into the woods. They were able to reacquire the tracks that Daniel and the others had made. Smoke detected the trail before Jacob saw it.

They followed the three wolves along the wandering tracks in the woods, and then the wolves stopped at a lump of snow with some uniform green showing through. Samuel moved up and brushed the snow away to uncover one of the lost soldiers, who appeared to have curled up under a tree and fallen asleep, freezing to death. It was what Jacob had feared; Old Man Winter had claimed this man for his own.

"We need to bring him back to the fort," Jacob said, and they went to work to free the body from the snow and ice.

They made a travois to drag the body as they continued looking for the other soldier. They hadn't gone far when the wolves found him tangled up in some tree trunks. It looked like he had stumbled and struck his head against a trunk, and had either broken his neck or had knocked himself out and frozen to death.

In either case, he too had been claimed by Old Man Winter. Jacob and Peter loaded this body onto the travois with the other one while Konkapot and Samuel went back to get the rest of the Rangers and the rescued Provincials.

Once everyone had arrived, the whole group continued to push on to Fort Edward since it was closer than going back to Fort William Henry. James and Charles helped the blind soldiers, and Peter and Samuel pulled the travois with the bodies of the two dead soldiers. It was close to sundown when the party finally arrived at Fort Edward.

Soldiers from the fort ran out to help Jacob lead these rescued soldiers back. After passing them to the surgeon, with Daniel thanking them over and over for their salvation, the Rangers went out to the island and entered their hut.

It had been a while since they had been there, having spent more time at Fort William Henry than at Fort Edward this winter. A layer of dust covered everything.

Charles crouched by their little fireplace, his flint and steel clicking, which soon led to the glow of a fire. They hung their snowshoes outside of the cabin and brought their gear inside. Jacob had just sat down on a stool and was starting to relax with his eyes closed, when a Ranger stuck his head inside.

"Captain Rogers wants to see you, Sergeant Clarke." Jacob opened an eye, sighed, and nodded.

"Boy, news travels fast around here," he groaned as he got to his feet. The three wolves stared at him, but remained curled up near the fire. The exception was Smoke, who wagged his tail for a few seconds before covering his nose with it and going back to sleep.

"Give our best to the captain," said Samuel, whose eyes were closed as he leaned back on his bunk.

"I'm sure he will feel all warm and fuzzy knowing you care, Samuel," Jacob said as he departed and headed over to Rogers' hut. On the way, Jacob waved and greeted the other Rangers he passed, who welcomed him back and asked how things were up at the lake.

"Cold," he answered truthfully, and the Rangers laughed and waved.

The platoon streets, which ran between the cabins, were well packed with mud and snow, the glow of candles and the light of fireplaces spilling from the doors and showing the way. Cooking and warming fires were dotted along the other sides of the cabins, and sounds of fiddles and men's voices laughing, singing, or talking came from all around the camp.

Ducking his head into Captain Rogers' cabin, Jacob kicked the mud and snow off his snow moccasins before entering.

"You wanted to see me, Captain?" he asked as he removed his hat. Captain Rogers looked up from his map.

"I heard you found the lost Provincials. If I was a betting man, I would have bet that it would be you to find them. You have good luck, and I want to use your luck again."

Jacob nodded. "Where and when are we going?" Rogers smiled.

"We'll head back to Fort William Henry in the morning, grab some of the platoon, and head back up to the French forts, and, by God, I will have my prisoner this time!"

It was as Samuel had predicted. He was crazy enough to try again to take a prisoner in this weather. Typically crazy.

Jacob returned to the cabin, and told the men not to get too comfortable because they were heading back to the lake with Captain Rogers in the morning.

"Where and when are we going?" Samuel yawned, and Charles and James repeated the question.

"How'd you guess, Samuel?" Jacob was pleased when Samuel sat up, awake now.

"We're heading back up to our favorite place, and the captain intends to get his prisoner this time."

Charles and James groaned from their bunks, and Samuel shook his head.

"Maybe I shouldn't have said anything," Samuel said with a sigh.

"Fate was listening this time."

Peter smiled from around his pipe. "Another adventure, here we go!"

They made sure the fire was going and there was an ample supply of dry wood in the cabin, before they rolled up in their blankets and went to sleep. They knew they had better get rest, because they wouldn't get much once they started north, especially in the cold.

When one of them got up to relieve himself at night, he would throw some wood on the fire to keep it going. As dawn approached, Jacob grabbed a small bucket, went outside and filled it with snow, and placed it next to the fire to melt the snow so they would have hot water in the morning.

It was a good night's sleep, the search having exhausted them, and when the morning cannon fired, the Rangers rose and put on their now-dry gear while drinking some hot tea. After packing their gear, they turned out and headed over to the command hut.

Jacob wondered when he would be back to their cabin. As they walked across the camp, he looked over to the sutlers' area where Maggie was, and he sent a thought, hoping she was well.

They met Captain Rogers at his cabin. He had Sergeant Anderson's section of Rangers with him, who he said would be traveling with them to the lake. Jacob and his men shook hands and stood leaning on their rifles, talking in low voices with the other Rangers as they waited for Captain Rogers to lead them out.

Rogers led the two columns of Rangers across the footbridge and then took the military road back to Fort William Henry. They made better time walking on the road, but they still kept their watch on the wood line alongside the road.

The wolves moved along the wood line, darting to and fro, sniffing and following tracks. Perhaps in time Smoke and the other wolves would help detect enemies who might be hiding in ambush. Jacob placed that thought in his mind to try out on one of their upcoming scouts.

They had an uneventful march and broke out of the woods to see the fingers of smoke from the fort rising up into the air, beckoning to them in the breeze.

Rogers led them into the fort, and Jacob sent his Rangers to their barracks room while he reported to Captain Putnam about finding the lost soldiers. Putnam thanked him, told Jacob he would inform the New York captain, and then turned to speak with Captain Rogers when he entered the office.

They would not be called on for a couple of days, which allowed Jacob and the others to continue going out on hunting expeditions to keep the quartermaster stocked with food.

Smoke, Konkapot's wolf, named Raven because she was now blacker than grey, and Samuel's Otto were growing bigger and stronger. The Rangers took their wolves with them as they hunted. They moved silently through the snow and woods, their instincts taking over and helping them to find game.

When they were back in the fort, just like the human Rangers, the wolves became playful and wanted to wrestle or at least to stay near Jacob and the others as if they were members of the Rangers' pack.

It was mid-January when Jacob was called down to a meeting with Captain Rogers, who said it was time for them to head north to scout the French positions and, if they could finally get lucky, take a prisoner. They would use the lake, but not in the normal sense. It was frozen, so they were going to use skates.

Jacob and his Rangers, along with two other Ranger sections, joined Captain Rogers at the lakeshore with their skates. Most of the Rangers who had experience as winter trappers and hunters had used ice skates before. Some Rangers had not, so just as they had had to learn how to use the bateaux boats, they now put on their skates and tried to learn how to use them on the frozen lake.

The Rangers experienced in skating watched their comrades fall several times on the ice and roared with laughter, but after some time, the new skaters seemed to get the hang of it.

Some of the British regulars came down to see the skating, and Jacob noticed Lieutenant Manning was watching and nodded to him. He wasn't surprised that Captain Reynolds and his sergeant major were not there.

When Rogers was satisfied, the Rangers put on their gear and their skates and started up the lake. Before leaving, the Rangers tied scarves around their heads with small slits for their eyes to help fight the glare from the ice and prevent snow blindness.

They skated in two long columns, keeping a good spacing between them. They used the same tactics they would have used in the woods, except there was more distance between men.

One of the inexperienced skaters fell, and there was a sickening snapping sound as he hit the ice. It looked like he had broken his arm when he had tried to stop his fall.

Rogers checked on him and saw that he could not continue with the scout. He ordered him back to the fort to see the surgeon.

Two other Rangers got him off the ice and helped him back to the fort on land. Rogers watched them go, knowing he had just lost three valuable Rangers. He waved the others forward to continue on the scout.

The Rangers traveled about a third of the way up the lake before they made camp. They moved deep into the woods and set up a camp, rotating between guard shifts, eating cold rations, and wrapping up in their blankets. Summer or winter, the Rangers applied their tried and true tactics while on their scouts.

Jacob took his turn on watch during the cold and cloudy night, hoping it wouldn't snow on them until they got off the lake. Some of the Rangers were snoring lightly, used to the cold conditions, while others shivered as they readjusted their blankets to try to keep their heat in and the cold out. Just before dawn, Rogers made sure everyone was awake for stand-to.

After packing their gear, they all faced out and watched the woods as the grey of the early morning turned to gold, and the sun rose over the trees and mountains. Positive there were no French, Canadians, or Indians in the area, the Rangers returned to the lake after concealing the signs of their camp and continued on the next leg of their journey.

They cautiously moved up the lake, keeping constant watch on both the lake and the woods on either shore. So far their luck had held, and there had been no signs of any enemy, just the occasional flock of birds over the lake. The Rangers knew the enemy used the lake as they did, as a frozen highway to move men, so they remained wary.

The ice on the lake was very thick. There was no sound of cracking or creaking as they moved along it. This relieved Jacob, who didn't like the thought of falling through the ice into the deep, dark, cold water.

"What a horrible way to go," he mumbled to himself while looking down at the black ice.

They made camp just before the lake narrowed. The steep cliffs on either side of the narrows would have made camping harder.

With no sign of the enemy, the Rangers endured another cold night keeping watch and catching some sleep. The next morning, they followed the same stand-to pattern of packing and listening for the enemy before doing anything else. Rogers then led them back out on the ice, and they skated to the spot where Lake George connected to Lake Champlain.

Resting at the frozen waterfall, with only a slight trickle of water running through the different shades of frozen blue hanging ice, they ate some more cold biscuits and dried meat and washed it down with water from their canteens, which had been refilled from the trickle of water.

Securing their skates in their packs, the Rangers put on their snowshoes and followed Rogers as he led them towards the French position. They moved around to the west away from Fort Carillon and found a nice thick area of brush and trees in which to set up a base for the night, as the sun wasn't staying up very long during these winter months.

Making sure they removed any signs of their tracks, they moved deep into the brush and once again took turns watching the woods, eating, and sleeping.

When it was Jacob's turn to stand watch, now and then his mind wandered, and he thought about Maggie back at Fort Edward. This was a new experience for Jacob. Previously on scouts, Jacob kept his thoughts on just being a Ranger, going after the enemy, and surviving. Thinking of Maggie, who had captured his heart, was a new feeling that Jacob was getting used to, and he found he liked it.

A cold wind blew over Jacob and the resting Rangers, weaving its way through the tall trees and along the mountains, sinking down into the valley and along the frozen lake.

The blowing wind caused loose snow to shimmer and dance along the walls of Fort Saint-Frederic, and a bundled sentry, who shivered from the cold embrace, growled "Zut!" through his scarf in a burst of steamy breath.

Inside the command barracks, Major Joseph-Antoine le Fèbvre, who was an early riser, listened to the cold wind dance around the roof of his office. The major was normally up before his staff and most of his soldiers. Stoking up the fire in the fireplace, Major Fèbvre dressed warmly. The stone construction of Fort Saint-Frederic protected its inhabitants from enemy fire, but it was ghastly cold in the winter.

He stepped into his office and once again stared at the map, hoping it would tell him something new about the enemy. Major Fèbvre took a seat in his chair and picked up several reports about his troops' disposition and the English disposition at the southern end of the lake.

The door opened, and his aide brought in a platter of warm bread and eggs and a large tankard of steaming tea. The major motioned for the platter to be set at a corner of the table as he continued to read the reports and then look at the map again.

The winter would pass, and then they would try again to remove the English from the lake and from the area to the south, finally taking Albany as their own.

Major Fèbvre sat back with satisfaction, his stomach grumbled from the smell of the bread and eggs, and he realized he was indeed hungry. Taking a savage bite, he chewed and smiled as he thought of leading his troops through the streets of Albany, a hero of France.

Now that has a nice ring to it, he thought as he sipped his warm tea.

Cutting through the frigid air and chasing the cold wind were the first golden rays of the sun as it crept over the lip of the mountains. As it climbed, the sun's glow bathed the frozen valley, lake, and forest, and what little life that was there stirred and greeted the dawn.

The Rangers continued with their practice of standing-to before sunrise. It was even more important to be ready to fight if they were attacked at dawn now that they were deep in French territory. There was no sound, just the wind through the trees, and it was still dark. The sun hadn't reached them yet in their sheltered area of trees and brush.

Rogers, believing they were safe, led the patrol out of their base and, after concealing all signs of their presence, moved towards the fort until they came upon a well-used trail. Doing a quick check and determining they were on a good piece of ground, he placed his Rangers in an ambush and waited to see if he would finally get lucky.

Konkapot who was next to Jacob on the line, whispered, "Think we'll get lucky today?"

Jacob shrugged as he continued to scan the area for a target.

Konkapot whispered again, "Think we'll rotate back to Edward soon?"

Jacob thought about it before slowly nodding. "It's about our time to rotate I think," was his whispered reply.

"You going to see Maggie when we get back?"

Jacob turned quickly to look at his smirking friend, then looked around to make sure he hadn't caught Rogers' attention. Turning back to Konkapot who was still grinning, he hissed, "What are you, my mother?"

Konkapot simply raised an eyebrow. "Why, yes. It seems someone needs to look out for you, and I have been doing it for a bit."

"So?" Jacob hissed in return as he turned back to watch for the enemy, but Konkapot continued in a whisper. "You, my friend, need a good girl, and Maggie seems good for you, better than the sachem's niece." Jacob snorted, holding back a laugh at the memory of the Mohawk sachem's niece and all the trouble he had gotten into because of her.

Looking around to make sure no one had heard his snort, Jacob looked back at his friend and broke into a smile.

"Yes, you're right, as always," Jacob said, and Konkapot winked and returned to watching for the enemy.

"Of course, I'm right," Konkapot whispered back. "I know what's best."

Trying to get back to the business of the scout, Jacob couldn't help but think of Maggie, and he knew he would see her again once they got back to Fort Edward.

Rogers and his Rangers did not have to wait very long, for just as the sun was climbing over the woods and mountains, they heard the sound of approaching men. The sun was behind the Rangers and shone brightly in the eyes of the approaching men, simply perfect.

There were two sleds being pulled by six men, who were walking as if they had not a care in the world. They definitely did not know there were any Rangers about. In fact, only one carried a musket; the other muskets appeared to be in the sleds.

As the men and sleds came even with them, Rogers and his Rangers burst out from the snow and quickly surrounded the men. Caught completely by surprise, the two Frenchmen and four Canadians didn't have time to yell as these shapes appeared out of the woods, shadowed by the rising sun, and leveled their rifles at them.

Rogers quickly bound the men and looked inside the sleds, which contained fresh beef.

After binding the captives, the Rangers took turns pulling the sleds with the fresh meat, beginning their journey back to Fort William Henry. Because the prisoners could not skate, the Rangers traveled overland next to the shore and took three days to return to the southern end of the lake.

Rogers was extremely pleased. They had finally captured prisoners that could be questioned to gather information about the French intentions, and there was no one in pursuit. They had pulled it off, and as a bonus they had secured two sleds of fresh meat, which would deny the enemy and restock their own supplies.

It was to jubilant cheers that the Rangers entered Fort William Henry a few days later with their prisoners and their prize. That evening, the quartermaster and his cooks prepared some of the captured beef, and the men of the fort enjoyed the extra ration of fresh, unsalted beef with their evening meal.

As they savored their meal, with sounds of fiddles playing in the background, Jacob and his Rangers were approached by Captain Rogers, who shook their hands and thanked them for a job well done before moving on to the other Rangers. They shrugged, appreciating the recognition, and went back to their beef and drink.

The next morning, Captain Putnam met with Jacob and the Rangers in the barracks and told them to pack their gear, for they were returning to Fort Edward. Captain Rogers wanted to make sure all the platoons rotated through Fort William Henry and spent a month doing scouts while the other Rangers supported operations at Fort

Edward. Jacob had thought their time for rotation was close, and he had been correct.

Jacob and his Rangers packed up their gear and formed up with the rest of the platoon, which would march with Captain Rogers back to Fort Edward. There was a Lieutenant McCurdy now in charge of the platoon, as Captain Rogers had sent Lieutenant Stark off to recruit more men.

The platoon shouldered their rifles and, with the wolves running alongside, they began their march back to Fort Edward. Once on the road, the rifles came off the shoulders and went into the ready position as the Rangers resumed watching the tree lines.

They were walking along when Smoke suddenly stopped, his ears perked up, and a low growl escaped from his throat. The other two wolves and a few of the dogs all picked up on what Smoke had sensed and charged into the woods, barking. Jacob looked at Konkapot, and then they, with the rest of the section, took off behind the wolves and dogs.

Running through the woods, they could hear the dogs barking, and soon there was a deep growl as a wolf sounded like it was biting something or someone. The Rangers came upon a man dressed in a white capote on the ground with Smoke biting down and shaking his arm. The other wolves had another man, also wearing a white capote, pinned against a tree, and a third man was raising his musket to fire.

Both Jacob and Konkapot fired at the same time, dropping the third man, who flew back from the impact of the rifle balls that had struck him in the chest at close range.

Samuel and Peter ran up to the man the wolves and dogs had cornered, and he quickly threw up his arms in surrender. James and Charles aimed their rifles at the man on the ground as Jacob called Smoke to him. Smoke had a bloody but satisfied wolfish grin as he trotted over.

"J'abandonne…J'abandonne!" yelled the one man who was standing as the man on the ground clutched his mangled arm to his chest.

"What is he saying, Samuel?"

"He wants to give up," Samuel said, and then spoke to the man in French.

"They're Canadians. They want to surrender, and they want us to stop the wolves from attacking them anymore."

They searched the dead Canadian, took his gear, and left him in the woods, except for his hair. The remaining two were added to the other prisoners, and the entire column resumed marching to Fort Edward.

Captain Rogers walked over to Jacob.

"See, I told you that you bring me good luck. Two more prisoners. Perhaps having these wolves and dogs around can help us bag some more." Jacob nodded and scratched Smoke's head. The wolf was walking with a bounce as if he was strutting. Perhaps he had earned the right to strut.

The platoon approached Fort Edward, with Rogers and a section taking the prisoners into the fort while Jacob and the rest of the platoon returned to their cabins on the island. It didn't take long for Jacob and his Rangers to get resettled in their cabin, having come from there quite recently. Soon the fire was crackling as James and Peter brought in an armload of firewood to add to their stack.

The Rangers stowed their equipment, hung their ice skates and snowshoes, and went in search of new straw for their beds. Unable to find any, they went out and gathered pine boughs to make their beds.

The following morning, after formation and straightening up their cabin and platoon street, Jacob, Konkapot, Peter, and Samuel went over to call on Frederick to see how his shop had turned out. Of course, Jacob had another reason, and it seemed Konkapot had told the rest of the group, who were smirking and smiling at Jacob as they approached Frederick's shop.

After crossing the bridge over the Hudson River, which was still flowing but with chunks of ice visibly floating by, they made their way around the trail which followed the fort's wall and came out at Frederick's sturdy log cabin.

As they approached, Frederick himself came out and greeted them. "Heard you and your men would be heading this way."

"Looks like you're doing well, Frederick," commented Jacob, who shook his hand. "What's over there under the snow?"

Looking over, Frederick smiled and said, "Growth my boy. That is the foundation for my real house and shop; this is just temporary and will serve as my warehouse."

Samuel whistled. "Your cabin is bigger than three of ours!"

"Aye, that may be true, but I have better stuff in mine than there is in yours," Frederick replied with a wink.

Maggie came out as Samuel and Peter followed Frederick into his shop to see his wares. Konkapot only delayed a second to smile as Jacob observed Maggie before entering the shop. Jacob's face was a little red, and Konkapot wasn't sure if he was blushing or if he was red from the cold.

Konkapot was happy to see his friend finally showing an interest in a woman. He was concerned that Jacob had been consumed with his quest for vengeance for his family, which seemed to have burned out all of his softer side. Now, he was being caught up in this conflict with the French, which was fueling his desire for revenge.

Konkapot believed that it was unhealthy for a man to focus so intently on vengeance that he did not find companionship with women. Now with Maggie in the picture, Konkapot might not have to do anything more and could allow nature to take its course.

She was better than the sachem's niece, not so vain. And she was strong-willed, someone who could match Jacob's iron will. Maggie was also better looking than the sachem's niece, Konkapot thought.

Squaring his shoulders, Jacob went over to Maggie to say hello. Smoke, who had accompanied them, made his own greeting by licking her hand and rubbing his head against her skirt for a pat. Maggie was nearly knocked off her feet as Smoke rubbed up against her legs.

"I see you're back from up at the lake," Maggie said with a giggle as she rubbed Smoke.

Blushing slightly, Jacob nodded his head. "Well, I didn't want you to get lonely all by yourself here."

Maggie smiled and looked at Jacob, who was still blushing, but only slightly.

"Well, Smoke wanted to say hello. He missed you," he said. Looking at Jacob, Maggie replied, "Oh, he did, did he?"

Then she knelt down and hugged Smoke, who rubbed his head against her, and promptly licked her face.

"Well, I missed him," Maggie said. She then looked at Jacob, and added, "too."

Smoke didn't seemed to mind what was going on. He was getting his head and ears scratched, and that was fine with him. Maggie stood up and Smoke ran off to join the other wolves since Martha was feeding them some scraps of deer meat.

Maggie moved up close to Jacob.

"How bad did poor Smoke miss me up there at the lake?" she asked.

Jacob stuttered a few words, "Well, um, er, he seemed to think of you a lot when, ah, we were up there at William Henry and out on scouts."

Maggie placed her hands on her hips and looked at Jacob. "Oh, did Smoke tell you this himself, or can you read his thoughts? I heard you Rangers can do magical things."

Jacob didn't hesitate or stutter, but replied, "No, he made it clear to me, ah us, that he couldn't stop thinking of you, every day."

Maggie smiled and moved even closer and whispered in Jacob's ear. "Well, let him know I thought of him every day too."

Then she kissed Jacob on the cheek before stepping back.

"Have to get back to work," she said. "But it's nice to see you." Then she winked and added, "and Smoke."

Konkapot watched Jacob from the door and smiled. Then in the distance, he saw three red-coated individuals on horses leave the fort and head along the trail to the road. Konkapot whistled and nodded his head towards the outside to Peter and Samuel, who stopped talking with Frederick and followed Konkapot out the door.

Jacob, who had been busy talking to the smiling Maggie, did not notice the approaching men until Smoke began a low growl in his throat. Jacob turned to see Captain Reynolds, Sergeant Major Lovewell, and Lieutenant Manning ride up.

As usual, Captain Reynolds made a beeline for Jacob, followed eagerly by the sergeant major and reluctantly by Lieutenant Manning, who hung back a bit.

They rode with their gear and bags tied behind them on their horses as if they were departing for good. Konkapot thought that would be a good thing.

"Best do something about that beast, Ranger. It simply confounds me how dogs are allowed in the camps of these Provincials. As usual, you men are here, shirking duties and responsibilities," sneered Captain Reynolds.

Smoke continued to growl at the captain, who seemed to pull back on the reins of his horse, backing it up. Konkapot, Samuel, and Peter all came out and stood behind Jacob.

"At least Smoke here has captured a prisoner. I haven't seen you capture anyone or do anything helpful in this fight yet," Jacob said while staring coldly at Captain Reynolds.

Konkapot looked over Jacob's shoulder and saw that the sergeant major was staring at Maggie with a hungry look. This could be a problem, he thought, and he realized it could be dangerous for Jacob.

"Why…you…disrespectful Provincials, I'll have your hide!" choked

Captain Reynolds, whose face was turning several shades of red.

The sergeant major was so busy staring lustfully at Maggie that he didn't hear his captain's protests. Once more to the rescue, Lieutenant Manning spoke up.

"Sir, if we are to arrive at Albany in good time, we should be on our way."

With a harrumph, Captain Reynolds turned his horse and started down the Albany road, followed by the sergeant major.

Walking up to Lieutenant Manning, Jacob said, "Watch yourself around him. You seem to be a good man, and we hate to see good men go to waste or be killed because of the incompetence of others."

Jacob stared at Captain Reynold's back, and the lieutenant understood what he meant.

Manning nodded his head and reached out to shake Jacob's hand. "We have orders to report to Albany. It seems we may be assigned to a new regiment that is being organized." Jacob took his hand. "You can always volunteer to join us."

Manning nodded. "We'll see. Good luck."

He spurred his horse to catch up with the other two.

"That man is a ganz arschloch," commented Peter. Jacob nodded, not understanding what it literally meant, but figuring it couldn't be good. As they were heading back to the island, Konkapot spoke to Jacob, warning him about the sergeant major and the way he had looked at Maggie. Jacob's eyes became cold and focused, almost deadly, as he stared in the direction the three had ridden.

"Don't worry. We'll help you by keeping an eye on the sergeant major if he does in fact return here," said Peter.

Jacob nodded and looked down to see Smoke looking up at him, like he too agreed that he'd help watch Maggie.

It's nice having friends like this watching out for one another in the field, and here in the camp, Jacob thought. Rangers need to stick together and face all challenges, no matter what they are.

He let his anger subside concerning the captain and his ever-faithful sergeant major, and took his ribbing from his friends concerning Maggie. They too rejoiced in his budding relationship with her, but they did it in the Ranger fashion of giving him a hard time.

CHAPTER 12

FORT EDWARD: NORTHERN SCOUTS

Jacob and his fellow Rangers spent most of the winter at their camp next to Fort Edward, while Captain Rogers continued to scout the French positions around Fort Saint-Frederic and the now-named Fort Carillon, a name they had learned from the prisoners taken at Ticonderoga.

The Rangers and the Provincial soldiers settled into their winter encampment with the Rangers going out to hunt for food and to conduct local patrols. They developed a routine of work details, guard details, hunting details, and some time for themselves.

The hunts were more and more urgent, as supplies from Albany were becoming scarce. Wagons and sleds from Albany that would normally have carried supplies to the forts were having difficulty crossing the Hudson.

Worse yet, the supplies were being used as political pawns by the different colonial governments as they schemed and maneuvered against one another. Jacob observed that these politicians were well fed and warm in their grand homes in Albany and Boston while the soldiers defending them were quartered in their huts or cramped barracks, living off what they could hunt.

The quartermasters at both Forts William Henry and Edward had begun rationing supplies, and the Rangers were forced to spend most of their time hunting rather than scouting.

It wore on the men, and from time to time, tempers flared. While

Jacob and his Rangers might have had some friction, they didn't come to blows, whereas some of the sections had men who ended up fighting and wrestling one another in the muddy streets between the huts.

Captain Rogers put a quick end to these fights. However, there still remained tension, and there were more shouting matches and arguments between the Rangers and the British Regulars.

Rogers still enforced their discipline, and a few Rangers spent time in their guard house on the island. Unfortunately, he could not save a couple men from facing the lash from the British for failing to follow orders or for gross insubordination. Like the regulars, the Rangers stood in formation while the lashes were administered to the guilty men.

Rogers continued to stress that they must take care of their own, and he tried to protect the Rangers whenever possible by not allowing the regulars to punish them.

A break in the winter routine came when Captain Putnam told a few sections, including Jacob and his men, that they were needed for an expedition being launched by Captain Rogers, a return to Fort Saint-Frederic.

"Thank God," said Samuel as he packed his gear. "I never thought I would actually look forward to heading back up north to break up this dull routine."

Jacob nodded, but the expedition would take him away from Maggie. This time back at Fort Edward had allowed more time with her, and he was more confident now, and to be honest, more relaxed. He no longer stuttered or blushed when he saw her.

He had strong feelings for her, and he believed she had feelings for him as well. This must be true, he thought, judging by the way both Konkapot and Frederick smiled at him every time he went over to visit Maggie.

After packing their gear, including their snowshoes and ice skates, and ensuring that they had warm clothes and several days of cooked food, the Rangers shouldered their packs and started off for Fort William Henry. As they crossed the bridge from the island, Jacob was pleasantly surprised when Maggie met them, bundled up in a deep green cloak. Konkapot and the other Rangers in the section watched as Jacob went over and spoke with her.

"How long are you going to be gone?" she asked, and Jacob shook his head.

"Don't know, but I will be back when I can." Maggie nodded and looked intently into his eyes. "You stay safe out there, you hear me?"

He took her hand and squeezed it tight. "Smoke and the others will watch over me."

Maggie pursed her lips. "They better!" she growled, then quickly kissed Jacob on his lips.

Konkapot and the others had raised eyebrows and slight smirks on their faces, but they all replied, "Yes, ma'am!"

"Sergeant Clarke, can we leave now?" called Captain Rogers, who too was smiling at Jacob's expense, and both Jacob and Maggie blushed. Jacob quickly kissed Maggie back on her lips before rejoining the column. Konkapot and the others hooted when Jacob rejoined the ranks, but their smiles quickly faded as Jacob scowled at them. Then he too smiled, and they all laughed as they started out on the military road.

Jacob waved his men forward, and they joined the end of the column of Rangers. Maggie waited until the Rangers had faded into the distance, their green clothes blending into the forest, and then she turned and went back to work.

By midday, Jacob's section had joined with their fellow Rangers at Fort William Henry. Captain Rogers and the other Rangers had returned to the original walled encampment and made it their own.

Living conditions inside the fort were worsening as the crowding caused sickness to spread quickly among the Provincial soldiers. Rogers and the Rangers had decided it was healthier to stay out in the old encampment in lean-tos and log huts where at least there was space between the structures for fresh air.

Jacob and the other sergeants from Fort Edward reported to Rogers while their men made temporary lean-tos for the evening and started their cooking/warming fires. Rogers briefed them that Colonel Glasier, the newly appointed acting commander at the fort, had instructed them to conduct another scout of Forts Carillon and Saint-Frederic.

"Rangers," Rogers began, and using an old ramrod as a pointer, he drew a rough sketch of their route on the ground.

"We'll head along the eastern shore, staying to the woods. I have received reports that the lake is thawing, and I don't want to lose any Rangers through the ice. We'll make our way north, then cut across at the falls near Bald Mountain, and pass between Carillon and Saint-Frederic. We'll scout and collect information to assess the enemy's strength and to determine their intentions. We will also attempt to take a prisoner or two. Any questions?"

The assembled sergeants looked around at each other and shook their heads in unison. Rogers nodded in acceptance.

"See to your men. Dismissed."

As Jacob returned to the lean-tos, he was greeted by Konkapot next to their fire holding up a tin cup of steaming liquid for him. The others were already sipping theirs. Sniffing first, Jacob took a sip of warm, spiced wine.

"Where did you get this?" Jacob asked.

Konkapot simply shrugged his shoulders, and replied, "Scouting." As they sipped their warm wine and went over their gear, Jacob informed them they were returning once again to the north to scout out positions, and, if their commander had anything to say about it, they would take at least a prisoner or two.

Samuel just shook his head and muttered, "Crazy bastard," under his breath. Once everything was ready, Jacob settled in with the others.

After making sure his bedroll was set up, Jacob returned to the crackling fire that was throwing great shadows against the wooden palisade and the lean-tos as the sun quickly sank behind the mountains.

Wrapped in their blanket coats and wool caps, the men sat on logs around their fire and ate their rations as men from other Ranger sections joined them.

"Hey, Jacob," commented Michael Murray, a Ranger from a different platoon. "Heard you got yourself a good deal at Mr. Best's shop."

It seemed that the story of Maggie and Jacob had even made it up to Fort William Henry. Nodding his head, Jacob said, "Aye. She's much better to look at than your tired old face, and she smells ten times better!"

Michael raised an arm and sniffed and nodded his head, which got the rest of the Rangers laughing. A bottle of rum came out and toasts to Jacob, Maggie, and Michael's worn and tired face were given as the bottle was passed around.

By morning, the Rangers were all business as they prepared to march out. Captain Rogers had collected about fifty-six men for their scout. "Are we scouting?" asked Peter. "Or going out looking for a fight?"

Looking at all of the assembled Rangers, Jacob had to agree. They definitely had enough men to do a thorough scout, but it was also enough to get them into or out of trouble.

Captain Rogers ordered them forward, and the Ranger column snaked out around the lake and followed the eastern shore. The snow was not as thick as it had been. Temperatures were warming up as winter began its transition to spring.

The Rangers were staggered and spread out in a column, their eyes scanning the trees for any sign of the French. While not as thick, the snow still crunched under their winter moccasins, and their breath drifted as grey wisps around them until the sun was high enough to warm the air.

Rogers led the Rangers towards the hills and small mountains that were west of Fort Carillon, and as their luck would have it, it began to snow lightly. Rogers moved the patrol into a thick depression and sent out several smaller scouts to determine how far the fort's construction had progressed.

The French and their allies had been busy, steadily improving the fort. Captain Rogers determined that Fort Carillon was now so strong that if Johnson wanted to make a spring push against Fort Saint-Frederic, he would have to reduce or capture Fort Carillon first.

Carillon now had two strong outer works made from oak instead of the pine that had been used to build Fort William Henry. That would make a siege tough, even with artillery. New construction included enough stone barracks to house three to four hundred men.

The fort was not impregnable though; the walls were fairly short and they appeared to be thin, even though mounted with heavy artillery. Some of the walls were made of stone, while at least one was observed to be still made of wood. Due to the rocky terrain, the fort was not completely surrounded by a ditch or moat.

They noted that the fort was still garrisoned by French regulars, Canadian Militia, and some Indians. Captain Rogers collected all of the information that the different scouts brought in and consolidated it for his notes.

Satisfied, Rogers continued the patrol northward towards Fort Saint-Frederic. They waited to move until the sun was just about to rise. Captain Rogers led them to a steep mountain overlooking Saint-Frederic, and the Rangers slowly climbed to the top where they were able to get a clearer view of the French positions and the work they were doing on their fortifications.

Rogers called up a few Rangers who had skills at sketching to make a diagram and map of the French positions.

They had been lucky so far, having had no contact with any French patrols. Again satisfied with what they had gathered, Rogers led them down the mountain to a small village he had observed from the mountain top. He spread the Rangers out into a large semi-circle ambush near the village and waited to see if they could catch anyone.

Jacob and his men had hunkered down in some trees and brush near a road that led into the village. It was a well-situated village, with cows out in snowy pastures digging for grass and smoke rising from farmhouse chimneys.

After a time, a Frenchman was observed leaving the village and walking down the road towards the fort, which was only a half-mile away. The man passed by one of the other Ranger sections, and the men jumped out and captured him. Jacob and his men continued to cover and scan the area for more Frenchmen or Canadians who might come from the village.

In the distance, the firing of two muskets echoed through the trees. After a few minutes of silence, a cry of "Rangers, to me!" was heard, and the Rangers rallied to Captain Rogers.

One of the sections had spotted two more men, but when the Rangers jumped out to capture them, the men had turned and run towards the fort. The Rangers had tried to shoot them, but they had missed.

"We don't have much time," said Rogers. "Half of you will set an ambush here for the French who will soon be joining us; I want the rest of you to set fire to the village and deny the French any supplies that are stored there."

The Rangers turned and went to work immediately.

Jacob's section was one of those selected to destroy supplies. As some sections moved towards the village and others set up firing positions, Jacob and his men shot the cattle in the fields.

Jacob thought this was a waste, but he knew they couldn't capture and herd the cattle away before the French arrived. Meanwhile, new columns of smoke began to rise from the village buildings.

At least the Rangers were pulling the people out of the village before setting fires to their homes and barns. Having just shot and killed a cow, Jacob thought this was a strange way to wage war. Then again, the French, or more precisely their Indian allies, would have done the same, the exception being that they wouldn't have warned the people first. It still didn't sit right with him, but he continued shooting the cattle.

From the far side of the village, the sound of rifle and musket fire began to thunder as the French turned out in reaction to the warning brought by the two men who had escaped capture. Jacob had his men take up position near a barn that had not yet caught fire, and they took aim towards the sound of battle.

Ranger sections were beginning to fall back, leap-frogging with one section covering and firing while the other bounded back to a supporting position. Jacob held his position as a section of Rangers ran by. He nodded and yelled that they'd take over, urging the men to get out of there. As the last section ran by, they were pursued by both white-uniformed French regulars and white-capote-wearing Canadians.

"By pairs, pick your targets and fall back!" ordered Jacob as he brought his rifle up and aimed at an advancing Frenchman.

The sun was reflecting off a gorget around the officer's neck, and Jacob aimed at that. Letting his breath out, he squeezed the trigger and the rifle cracked. As he turned, he saw the French officer fall. Two other rifles fired, and Peter and Charles fell in right behind him.

They ran down a smoke-filled road. The fires were beginning to pick up in the houses and barns. Loading on the run, Jacob, Peter, and Charles turned and rested their rifles on a fence.

"Go!" Jacob yelled.

Konkapot, James, and Samuel fired their rifles, turned and began to load and run by. The smoke from the fires was masking them from the French as balls whistled by and splattered against some of the walls of the barns and houses. The smoke was also making it hard the Rangers to see their targets.

"Not liking this. Can't see!" yelled Samuel as he ran by. "Hell of a way to fight a war!"

Jacob had to agree. The white uniforms were blending in with the smoke and making it hard to see them. But if they waited for them to get closer, it might be too late.

"Let's go. Everyone out of here!" yelled Jacob.

He led the rest of the section as they charged down the snow-covered road away from the French. They were starting to breathe hard as they ran along the road, which was now turning into mud from the heat. The Rangers themselves were starting to get hot, with all of this activity while wearing their thick blanket coats. Huffing and puffing, Jacob and his Rangers ran through the smoke and out the other side of the village. They joined up with the rest of the Rangers, who were taking up new firing positions.

As Jacob and his men ran, balls whizzed and buzzed by, and something tugged on Jacob's coat, but he didn't stop running. As they passed the line of Rangers, "Fire!" was heard, and a roaring volley drowned out any sound.

Jacob and his men turned panting to see a bunch of dead French and Canadians the volley had just dropped not too far from there. The rest of the French and Canadians were running back towards the village. Cradling their rifles but bent over with their hands on their knees, Jacob and his men were catching their breath when Rogers jogged by with his original prisoner and a new one in tow.

Shrugging, Jacob and the others joined the column and jogged with them, and the Rangers withdrew as the village and barns burned heavily behind them, the smoke blocking out the sun and casting a dark shadow across the clearing.

The Rangers traveled back to Fort William Henry without further incident, except for Konkapot pointing out the hole a French musket ball had made through Jacob's blanket coat.

"Glad to see your luck is still holding, my friend," he said. "Besides, I don't want Maggie mad at me."

Once they were finished at Fort William Henry, Jacob and his Rangers returned to Fort Edward, where they resumed their winter duties of patrolling and hunting. With the exception of a few more scouting missions conducted by Rogers and other Rangers, there were no other actions against the French, the Canadians, or their Indian allies.

Winter was loosening its grip on the valley and the mountains. The snow and ice melted, and soon the temperatures rose and the vegetation began to return. Spring was a time for change and a time for planning the next moves against the French.

Jacob contented himself with visiting Maggie when he was not working on the new Ranger barracks on the island or going out on patrols. A spark had started between them that was slowly growing into a tiny flame, but many changes were coming that could affect them. Plans were being made that would send the two great nations' armies once again to hunt one another in the green forests of the North.

Spring bloomed and blossomed, and June arrived warm and clear in New York. The Rangers were spending most of their time, when not out on scouts, working on their island. The company streets that ran between the huts were a thick, gooey mud that the Rangers tried to harden with straw. Many Rangers fell in the mud, to the merriment of their comrades, as they tried to dry up the roads.

The island was cleared, and new latrines were dug as garbage and broken items were thrown into the old latrines and buried. Provincials and some of the Rangers cleared the gardens next to the fort and on the island and began planting for the coming year. Buildings and huts were repaired, and Rangers accompanied work details as protection against any enemy scouts.

Far away from Forts William Henry and Edward, other changes were occurring. William Shirley, former Commander in Chief of British Forces in America and Royal Governor of Massachusetts, had lost favor with the crown and was removed from office.

In Albany, a meeting was being conducted in a large room in the home of a wealthy merchant, which was now being used by the British as their headquarters. Here, they were planning their next move against the French and their allies in the north.

In the center of the room, on the once polished wooden floor that now was scuffed by the officers' many booted feet, was a large table covered with maps and letters from various commands.

Standing around the table were regular British officers in their fine, well-tailored scarlet uniforms with gold braids and buttons. Joining the British officers were Provincial officers from New England in their deep blueand red-faced uniforms, and New Yorkers in their green uniforms. Sitting in tall chairs around the edge of the room were men in the normal, but still well tailored, clothing of government officials and some militia officers.

The men were in heated discussions, with the British officers reading dispatches and speaking to one another, while Provincial officers were deep in their own arguments. The loudest of the groups were the politicians, representatives of the newly appointed Royal Governor of Massachusetts, Thomas Pownall, and another group representing Sir Charles Hardy, the Royal Governor of New York.

Smaller groups of politicians were moving freely between the larger groups, including men who were representatives of Thomas Fitch, Royal Governor of Connecticut, and Benning Wentworth, Royal Governor of New Hampshire.

While the noise rose and fell in a cascade of different voices, the topics were the same: What were they going to do about the French? There were concerns that the enlistment times of both the Provincial troops and the militia would expire soon. There were other reports concerning the lack of supplies coming from the colonies to support the military operations at Forts William Henry and Edward, and there were numerous reports from British observers and others about the alleged lack of discipline and order at Fort William Henry.

The room suddenly became silent, and the British officers all rose and stood at attention as the new arrivals entered, one officer passing his cloak and gold-trimmed bicorn hat to a waiting aide.

Major General James Abercrombie, second-in-command of the Royal forces in America, and Lieutenant General Daniel Webb had recently arrived in New York. They had traveled to the colonies with General Campbell, who was assuming command of the Royal forces in America from Governor Shirley.

Both officers walked into the room, and Webb pulled from a pouch a stack of dispatches, which he handed to General Abercrombie. The other officers, Provincials, and politicians gathered in a semi-circle around the map. Abercrombie took stock of the assembled men, noticing the divides between the regular British officers, the Provincial officers, and the politicians.

"Gentlemen," began Abercrombie, "I bring instructions from Lord Loudoun."

He opened the first dispatch, which was the official notification from the King concerning the appointment of Major General John Campbell, 4th Earl of Loudoun, to the posts of Governor General of Virginia and Commander in Chief of all forces, British and Provincial, in the American colonies.

After passing that document to a waiting aide, he read the next dispatch.

"By the authority of King George of England, I hereby relieve General William Johnson from command of forces in New York and appoint General John Winslow of Massachusetts to assume the role of Commander of Provincial forces serving in New York."

This announcement appeared to sit very well with the delegation from Massachusetts, who seemed not to like General Johnson. However, their cheerful exclamations were soon silenced as General Abercrombie read the next document.

"On behalf of a grateful King, William Johnson is appointed as Superintendent of Indian Affairs for our northern colonies, awarded 5,000 pounds, and will receive a Baronet from our hands at his earliest convenience."

The glee of the Massachusetts politicians had quickly turned to dismay. While they had achieved their goal of getting a Massachusetts officer to replace him, William Johnson's new authority allowed him to speak directly to the British Parliament concerning Indian affairs in New England, and he would no longer be answerable to the colonial governments. "With that out of the way," remarked General Abercrombie, "let's get down to business as to why we're actually here."

The British and Provincial officers moved closer to the table and map. While some of the politicians closed in, the rest went off into corners to continue their debates and maneuver to get their respective colony an edge in one deal or another.

"General Webb, could you please tell us what Shirley's plan was for the spring offensive?" General Abercrombie asked as he oriented himself to the map and specific locations of key areas, mostly in New York.

After sorting through some of the documents, Webb began reading: "The army is to contend itself by conducting a maneuver up the Chaudière River towards Quebec City, demonstrating as a threat in order to draw French and allied forces away from the main efforts. These efforts are the capture or reduction of Fort Duquesne, the destruction of the French and their allies near Lake Ontario, and the taking or reduction of the French position at Fort Saint-Frederic. This operation will require a combined strength of Royal and Provincial forces to number ten thousand."

General Webb stopped reading and pulled a second document out of the stack and continued:

"Royal regiments will be increased from two to five to support these operations in the northern colonies, to be dispatched from Great Britain with recruitment to be conducted within the American colonies."

With a deep sigh, General Abercrombie stood up and stated, "Right… I don't think we'll follow that plan."

Pausing as he picked up a stick to use as a pointer, Abercrombie began. "I believe the key to victory is taking the French positions here."

He pointed with his stick to Fort Carillon and Fort Saint-Frederic. "But if the scouting reports are accurate, we will need to take Carillon first before Saint-Frederic. We will begin moving forces and supplies north while we reinforce our positions along the west near the great lakes and the Oswego frontier."

Abercrombie tossed his stick onto the map and picked up one of the reports from Fort William Henry.

"Then there is this issue about the Provincials, the militia, and the lack of discipline and order."

Abercrombie looked up and asked who had brought these reports, and Major Eyre, the engineer responsible for the construction of Fort William Henry, stepped forward.

"Sir, I brought some of those reports. Most were from a Captain Reynolds, 48th Regiment of Foot, who was an observer at both Forts Edward and William Henry."

Abercrombie nodded and picked up a letter and read aloud, "Fort William Henry is nastier that anything I could conceive, a great waste of provisions, the men having whatever they please, and no great command kept up."

Major Eyre nodded and looked at General Abercrombie.

With a shrug, Abercrombie instructed, "Major, by my authority, I promote you to acting commander of Fort William Henry until I can find a colonel to command it. Additionally, I will send two companies from the 44th Regiment of Foot with you to reinforce the garrison. I want this problem fixed, Major. See to it!"

Major Eyre saluted and moved off to the side to an aide who was sitting at a table and drawing up the proper papers and orders. "Ah…sir," began a politician from Massachusetts. "We already have a commander at Fort William Henry, a Massachusetts colonel."

General Abercrombie turned to face the politician, who went silent and stepped back at the stare he received.

"Yes, that. I will also remedy that."

Abercrombie asked General Webb for the Royal Order, and Webb pulled it from the pouch.

"By order of King George, all Provincial officers, including generals and colonels, are to revert to the rank of senior captain when serving with Royal forces, submitting to the direction and command of regular British officers and commanders."

There was a short moment of stunned silence, before both the politicians and the Provincials began voicing their outrage. Demands were voiced about procedures, with the politicians arguing that Provincial commanders led their respective colonial Provincials and militias, whose time was about to expire anyway, on behalf of their colonial governments.

General Abercrombie looked around the room and found General Winslow.

"Would your men serve faithfully under the command of a British officer?"

General Winslow thought for a moment before shaking his head no. "No matter, from this time forth, Provincial and militia units serving the crown are now subject to the same regulations as the regular British Army. This should stiffen discipline and restore order," said Abercrombie as he returned to his map to study his next move.

Back up in the frontier and at Fort Edward, there was also a changing of rank and position. Captain Rogers had received instructions that he was now a Captain of an Independent Company of Rangers, a decision made by Governor Shirley just before he had been replaced. This placed

Rogers and his Rangers in a unique position. While still a captain, he now technically outranked any Provincial officer.

The order also moved his Rangers from just Provincials to "His Majesty's Independent Company of Rangers." This meant his Rangers were neither Provincials nor regulars. They could operate "free of the line," but were still subject to regular British rules and regulations.

This now allowed Rogers to operate more freely, and to accept his assignments and execute them in the manner he saw fit without having to deal with the politics and bureaucracy of the Provincial governors. He sat the order down and smiled to himself. This was all part of his plan to eventually gain a regular commission in the English Army.

With his new independent company, Rogers called for Lieutenant Stark and his brother Richard.

Along with his new orders, Rogers had also received instructions from the New Hampshire Governor. Rogers, with Lieutenant Stark, was to take half of the men and travel to one of the furthest frontier towns in New Hampshire, simply known as Fort Number Four, in the Connecticut Valley. The governor was concerned that with all of the activity in New York, the French and their Indians would try to come through New Hampshire.

While they were there, Stark was instructed to recruit more men, if possible. Rogers made it very clear that these new recruits were to be especially selected for their survival and hunting skills. No amateurs were to be recruited. He needed good quality men. Let the Provincials and the regulars worry about numbers.

Richard Stark would take charge of the Rangers at Fort William Henry, and he was to keep up scouting patrols of the enemy. Lieutenant Waite would remain at Fort Edward.

CHAPTER 13

QUEBEC AND ALBANY: PLANNING THE NEXT MOVES

The wind snapped and whistled through the ropes and canvas sails on the French frigate, which was making its way down the broad river towards the imposing cliffs in the distance, topped by the city of Quebec. Standing on the foredeck, the sailors busily working around him, Major General Louis-Joseph, Marquis de Montcalm-Gozon de Saint-Veran, stared at the city, which was becoming clearer as the ship sailed closer to the cliffs on which it stood.

Gripping one of the stays, he turned to look at his companions, Brigadier le Chevalier de Levis and Colonel le Chevalier de Bourlamaque, and smiled while pointing towards Quebec.

"There, gentlemen," he instructed. "That is where our destinies lie, and soon we'll be bathed in glory!"

Both officers smiled and concurred enthusiastically; the great adventure was about to begin. France was concerned about the lack of progress in the colonies against the English. King Louis XV of France wanted this stalemate over and the English driven out of the northern colonies.

The King also had made it clear that Marquis de Vaudreuil, the Governor General of New France, was in command. Montcalm would do his duty as any good soldier would, while this colonial-born Vaudreuil remained in charge.

If he could win enough victories, or even drive the English away and take Albany, perhaps there would be a new Governor General,

Montcalm thought. "Governor General Montcalm of New France"—it did have a nice sound to it.

Montcalm turned and looked to the rear of the frigate, towards the long line of other transports and warships that made up the convoy to see that they were faithfully following behind, their white canvas sails billowing in the strong breeze.

Two battalions of regular French soldiers and their supplies were with this convoy. Montcalm had brought with him from France a battalion from the Royal-Roussillon Regiment and a battalion from the La Sarre Regiment. He would combine these professionals with the Troupe de la Marine, who were already here, along with the Canadian Militia and the Indian allies.

After being brought to shore, Montcalm and his two senior officers made their way into Quebec City to report to the Governor General. Always the consummate politician, Montcalm presented a warm exterior as he greeted his assigned superior officer.

Maintaining a smile, Montcalm listened intently as Vaudreuil outlined his plan of action for the upcoming campaign, now that Montcalm and the reinforcements had arrived. Vaudreuil's concern was the increasing presence of English forces, their Provincials, and their Indian allies, who were growing stronger along the southern shore of Lac du Saint Sacrement at Fort William Henry. His main fear was that the English would soon attack the French position at Fort Carillon before it was completed. He ordered Montcalm and the two fresh battalions, along with additional Canadian Militia, to march to Fort Carillon and strengthen the defenses there. If the English attacked, the stronger forces would make them pay dearly. With a deep bow and flourish of his hat, Montcalm accepted his duty and departed to make ready for his march.

It was a different person who traveled to the encampment in the carriage than the man who had just met the Governor General. A deep scowl lined Montcalm's face.

"I am told to go on the defensive instead of striking against our hated foes," Montcalm thought, his brow knitting in concentration.

All the while, his senior officers silently stared or looked out at the passing scenery. Montcalm looked up from his thoughts.

"No, no, I will not just sit there and wait for the English to attack me. If he wants me to protect the fort, I'll do it by drawing the English away." With a smile returning to his face, Montcalm addressed his two officers. "Gentlemen, our first order of business is to march to Carillon, and there assess the situation to see if the great boogeyman of the English is a real threat or not. I believe they are not, and if so, then we'll take the fight to one of the other outposts to the west and draw the English Army away. We'll draw them out, destroy them, and then march on Albany and secure our victory!"

Both officers nodded in agreement while Montcalm clapped his hands together; he would have his victory and glory. Still, his plan was defensive, in a way. If there were no threat, then he wouldn't have to worry about drawing the enemy away.

Not waiting long, Montcalm began moving his men south towards Carillon in the cold wind that tussled the white uniformed men as they marched southward. The same wind turned and blew, its offspring blowing through the mountains and valleys to the south, where another wind was billowing the sails of a group of English ships arriving in New York harbor. Many of the residents of New York paused to look at the sight of the fleet disembarking the British soldiers and their baggage.

The English ships lowered their sails and longboats, beginning to transport the new arrivals to shore. One of these new arrivals was Lieutenant Colonel George Monroe, who after setting foot on dry land, assembled his 35th Regiment of Foot and waited until all of their equipment was unloaded. Once he accounted for all of his men and equipment, Monroe gave the orders to begin their march north towards Albany.

King George II was concerned about the stalemate and the French presence in the northern colonies. The king was unhappy about the previous year's failures, and he dispatched Monroe and the 35th from England to reinforce the Royal and Provincial forces and to take the fight to the French.

Monroe was uneasy though; his regiment was woefully under strength, having only 496 men instead of the normal 1,000. He was instructed to recruit from the locals in New York to fill his ranks, but he was concerned about what type of recruit would be available here in the colonies.

Even if he could recruit, he would not have the time to train the new men to the same proficiency as that of his regular soldiers in the line. This concern was still on his mind when he arrived at Albany and after seeing to his regiment, departed to report to General Webb to receive his orders.

The British grenadiers snapped to attention and presented their arms as Colonel Monroe and his second-in-command, Major Henry Fletcher, climbed the wooden stairs into the large home that Webb was using as a headquarters. Smartly saluting as they stopped before General Webb, they were asked to sit as Webb read their orders and dispatches from England.

"Gentlemen, I have an important task for you," Webb began as he placed the dispatches on top of an already growing pile of documents. "You are to march to Fort Edward with two companies of the 44th and one of these Provincial regiments. You will detach some of the companies' men to ensure there is an English presence there before marching yourself and the rest of your command to Fort William Henry. There you will assume command of the fort from Major Eyre and will be in charge of all forces present, English and Provincial alike. You will ensure that the fort is ready in case the French decide to make a push south."

Monroe nodded his head, understanding the instructions, and asked, "What is the condition of the fort and the men garrisoned there, if I may ask?"

General Webb turned and motioned to three men who had been standing in a corner on the other side of the room. Monroe noticed one was a short officer—a captain, he believed. There were also a lieutenant and a sergeant major.

"These men have been to Fort William Henry, and I am assigning them to your regiment to provide guidance and recommendations from what they have observed there. Captain Reynolds, you are to provide all the details that Colonel Monroe requires concerning the fort and the men garrisoned there."

Captain Reynolds snapped to a rigid attention and saluted, saying it was his honor to advise Colonel Monroe on the situation here in New York and at Fort William Henry. General Webb nodded as Captain Reynolds presented himself to Monroe; at least he had been able to finally get rid of that bothersome and boring Captain Reynolds and his insufferable sergeant major. This was turning out to be a good day after all.

While the French and the English were moving men and soldiers around on the great chessboard of the colonies, Jacob and his fellow Rangers continued to scout as the weather became more conducive for watching the French, though it was still a little muddy. The snow had melted, the spring rains had come and gone, and life had returned to the mountains and valleys.

Jacob and his men took their turns helping to create a second large garden on the island as well as to prep the regular garden near Fort Edward for the vegetables that would augment the supplies from Albany and the game the Rangers would get for the quartermaster.

As Jacob helped Charles with a plow, for he was the only one with experience using one, Samuel piped up from planting seeds.

"Do we get extra pay as day laborers," he griped, "or will they allow us first choice of the vegetables once they are ready?"

The group of Rangers, not really made out to be farmers, joined in voicing their opinions, though more playful in nature than serious. Most of them didn't expect to be tilling the soil at the fort, but it did help to break up some of the dull routine of garrison life. Spring was in the air, and they were enjoying the warmer temperatures much more than the frozen ones they had just endured.

In this time of renewal and growth, the relationship between Jacob and Maggie was also developing, and Konkapot and the other Rangers were trying to help out when they could. The Rangers took watching out and taking care of one another to a different level when it came to Jacob's relationship. Jacob was more confident and didn't blush as much or stammer around her, though his Ranger buddies did sometimes go out of their way to rib him about the relationship, for that's what Rangers did.

When time allowed, Jacob spent time with Maggie, sometimes sitting on Frederick's porch around his new two-story log house and store, or sometimes on walks along the fields or woods near the fort.

As the two walked, Rangers and some of the Provincials often waved and greeted them, Jacob normally waving back in response. It was on one of these walks that Maggie asked, "Jacob, what are your plans for the future?"

Jacob stumbled, both physically, as he tripped over a root, and mentally, not really expecting that question. Maggie laughed, but waited for his response.

"To be honest, I don't know," Jacob answered. "I have not really ever thought about the future because I am never sure I will be alive to see it." It was an honest answer, and Maggie accepted it. Most of the soldiers and Rangers serving out on the frontier were being lost or horribly mangled.

"I usually hope to see what happens in the next month, then so on and on," Jacob added.

"Where do you see me?" Maggie asked. "Where do you see us?"

Jacob stopped, and looking down into Maggie's eyes, spoke from his heart. "I hope to see you, if that's what you're asking. You give me reason to live, to stay alive; you give me a reason to come back."

Maggie smiled and simply replied, "Good."

The two continued their walk, until Jacob turned his head to look down at a still smiling Maggie.

"Why?"

Maggie stopped and looked up at Jacob again.

"As long as you see us together and you want to remain alive, that is good enough for me."

She raised up and kissed Jacob and turned, and after linking her arm in his, continued with their walk.

"We'll talk about us and the future later. For now let's just enjoy the moment and what time we do have," she said.

As they walked, Maggie thought about the tenderness that Jacob showed her, unexpected from this toughened fighter who had lost friends and family in these conflicts. She did think about their future and wondered if they would have one. The war continued, and either one of their lives could be quickly ended by shot or tomahawk.

For now, they would live for the present and worry about the future when it came.

Smoke, Raven, and Otto had grown into full-sized wolves. Smoke was a deep grey who was able to move as silently as his name, Raven was as black as night, and Otto was a mixed grey who was not as dark as Smoke. They went out on scouts with the Rangers, having proven their ability to spot a hidden enemy and having shown what the full fury of a wolf could do to that enemy.

As the Rangers worked in the garden and on their barracks on the island, the Provincials and militia were returning from their winter break. The Rangers noticed more families accompanying the columns of soldiers marching to both Forts Edward and William Henry.

Jacob, Konkapot, and Samuel were standing near the Albany road, with their wolves lying next to them, watching the arriving columns.

Samuel said, "Heard from some of the other Rangers serving up at William Henry that the fort is filling up with wives and children of the Provincials. Not much room in the fort there, and it's very noisy with screaming kids. The families are living with their husbands in the barracks."

Konkapot nodded. "They're scared. They want to stay with their men in the fort, and this is not a good sign."

Jacob nodded. "I've spoken with some of the Mohawks, and they said word has reached them from the north that the tomahawk has been struck into the war post; it's starting soon."

Konkapot and Samuel nodded as they watched the column snake past the fort, waving to some of the returning Provincials whom they recognized. The wives and the older children were scared because they, like the Rangers, expected the Indians allied to the French to strike soon at their homes and farms now that the weather was better.

"Glad to see you boys didn't all freeze up here!" one of the Provincials called out to the three.

"Well, it was close," Samuel yelled back, and pulled off his hat to show his bald head. "Froze my hair off though!"

The Provincials laughed, while some of the newcomers, who didn't know about Samuel's survival of a scalping, started quickly whispering to themselves. "Does it really get that cold up here, that you freeze your hair off?"

The three Rangers chuckled, overhearing the whispers. Then a sound of drums beating could be heard, and in the distance they saw snatches of crimson through the trees as another column made its way along the road.

Soon, they saw the unmistakable Union Jack and the regimental flag carried by soldiers in their red uniforms. Regular English soldiers, their muskets in perfect alignment, were marching towards the fort. "Well, I'll be. Regular English soldiers," commented Charles as he joined Jacob, Konkapot, and Samuel in watching the columns march by.

They were soon joined by Peter and James, who were returning from Frederick's shop, Peter with his ever-present pipe, puffing away.

"I vas wondering when dey vud show up," Peter said from around his pipe stem. "It vudn't be campaign season widout dem."

Jacob watched the English soldiers in the distance, thinking this could either be a good or a bad sign, depending on the point of view.

He had heard from other Rangers and from the Provincials that there was no love lost between the Provincials and Rangers on one side and the regular English soldiers on the other since General Abercrombie's dictate had arrived at the forts, giving the English officers seniority over all Provincial officers and decreeing that Provincials and Rangers alike were now subject to the same rules and discipline as the regular English Army.

To say there was some tension growing between the Provincials and the British would be an understatement. Jacob wondered which would be worse, living under an English tyrant or a French tyrant.

In any case, he was more concerned about keeping his men alive during the approaching fighting, which he felt would begin soon.

As they watched the column approach, Jacob led his Rangers back to the island. The stage was being set for the next game between France and England, who were placing their game pieces.

Just as the English were moving their pawns into place, so was Montcalm positioning his forces to begin the game anew.

Montcalm had ensured that his men were ready and their position at Fort Carillon strengthened. Construction on the fort was moving along splendidly now that the weather had warmed. The warmth also seemed to have drawn out those nasty little black flies, which he feared would eat them alive over time.

Their Indian and Canadian scouts had reported that the English were still at Forts Edward and William Henry and there was no sign of any preparation for an attack. They also reported on the removal of Governor Shirley and the growing discontent, reported by observers and some deserters, between the Provincials and the English.

Satisfied he had met the letter of Vaudreuil's instructions, Montcalm began planning for an offensive against the English to draw them out and away from Carillon.

Perhaps he could exploit the bad feelings between the Provincials and their English masters. He had also heard of the tension from supporters in the colonies; they told him there was a growing rift between the Provincial governments and the English crown.

After studying his maps and consulting with his officers, Montcalm decided that they would go after the English forts at Oswego.

As Montcalm began the game by heading towards Oswego in the western part of New York, in Albany, Colonel Monroe observed the rest of the 44th Regiment, some New York Provincials, and supplies depart for the three forts at Oswego: Ontario, Oswego, and George.

Instead of heading north to take command of Fort William Henry, Monroe was leading a detachment from his own 35th and from the 42nd Highlanders, escorting General Abercrombie, who had decided to visit Cohoes Falls.

Monroe later learned that the column from the 44th and the Provincials never made it to Oswego. They were stopped by men who brought the news from Oswego that the forts had fallen.

Villiers had arrived and had drawn the English away. Then a larger column of French had arrived and encircled the forts using large artillery pieces to batter down the walls. The British commander had ordered the men to abandon Fort Ontario and consolidate across the river at Fort Oswego.

The French promptly captured the heights and began raining shot and shell on top of both Forts Oswego and George, shattering their walls and the lives inside. The surviving British officers held a council of war and decided to surrender to the French.

All was going well until the Indians became enraged and attacked everyone who had surrendered—English, Provincials, and their families. These men who had brought the news had been able to escape while a French officer was trying to stop the Indians from killing and looting.

The news of the British defeat and massacre at the hands of the rampaging Indians made its way to Fort Edward and the Rangers. Jacob's life as a carpenter and gardener came to an end as he and his men were to be part of the next rotation of Rangers to Fort William Henry.

"You must have heard the stories already of what happened at Oswego," Rogers asked Jacob and some of the other sergeants being assembled to head up to Fort William Henry.

The Rangers nodded that they had heard.

"Then you know we must be extra vigilant. The French are going to be encouraged with their victory, and emboldened. That means their attention is going to turn and stare straight at us. We must be ready to meet this challenge and keep the commander up-to-date on the enemy as I have no doubt, they are preparing to come after us."

Jacob and the other sergeants returned to their men to make sure everything was ready to go. After packing their gear and preparing to march, the Rangers decided to throw a celebration before they left, just in case this would be their last time in Fort Edward.

As night fell, a large fire was built, and Frederick arrived with casks of rum and ale. Drums, pipes, and fiddles were brought out, and music began. Along with the Rangers were Provincials and Mohawks, drinking, singing, and celebrating life.

Maggie had come over with Frederick, and she sat next to Jacob, sharing in his mug of grog. She felt comfortable with these men, who made her feel like family. She bantered and joked with the Rangers, and they with her, accepting her as one of their own. Perhaps they accepted her because of her involvement with Jacob; in any case, it was good to feel so welcome.

Soon, the area was full of boisterous laughter and song, and some of the other ladies dragged their husbands out to dance around the fire, intermingled with Mohawks, Provincials, and Rangers alike.

Maggie grabbed Jacob by the arm, pulling him to his feet, which resulted in his spilling his mug of grog all over the front of his shirt. Maggie continued to pull, despite protests from Jacob about not knowing how to dance.

The other Rangers were hooting and yelling their encouragement for Jacob to dance. Konkapot grabbed Jacob's other arm as he himself was being pulled along by Ojistah, a Mohawk maiden.

Resigning himself to his fate, Jacob smiled and even began to laugh in spite of himself as he tried to follow the dance commands from the caller. Men and women linked arms and spun around one way, then another. Jacob stumbled, partially due to the rum and partially due to having two left feet when it came to dancing.

Charles, Samuel, and the other Rangers clapped their hands in time with the music, pipe stems clenched in their teeth as they cheered Jacob and Konkapot on and laughed whenever they stumbled or missed the step that had been called.

Peter and then James were pulled into the swirling mass of men and women. After stepping on Maggie's feet several times and crashing into James, Jacob decided he had had enough, and he dragged Maggie back to their places.

Collapsing onto the blanket that Jacob had laid out to sit on, they both were laughing and breathing hard.

"I am glad you're a better fighter than a dancer," panted Maggie, "or you would have lost your hair a long time ago!"

Jacob smiled and nodded his acceptance of the critique.

"Here, this will drown the pain of your poor feet," Konkapot said. With his arm around Ojistah, he brought Maggie a mug and then poured some grog into Jacob's empty cup.

Konkapot and Ojistah sat on the ground with Jacob and Maggie, and they all toasted to long life and sore feet. Peter had been dragged out into the maelstrom of the dance. He actually knew how to dance, but that didn't save him from the playful hoots and whistles of his comrades. Konkapot pointed to Samuel, who was sitting on a log with two Mohawk girls that were talking to him and touching his bare head where he had been scalped.

The dancing and songs continued, and their faces grew tired from laughing and singing. Eventually, it became quieter as the rum and ale had their effect.

Some of the Rangers and Provincials staggered back to the fort. The Mohawks and some other Rangers just fell over where they sat and commenced snoring. A few of the more diehard drinkers and revelers still played music and sang songs, just not as loudly as before and not necessarily in tune.

Jacob looked down at Maggie, who was leaning against his shoulder, her head resting gently. Konkapot was a mirror image, Ojistah leaning against him.

Peter was out trying to teach some dance called a waltz to a Mohawk maiden, mostly stumbling and laughing in the process. Samuel had disappeared with the girls, and James and Charles had fallen asleep leaning up against a log and competing to see who could snore the loudest. At the edge of the firelight, the golden eyes of the wolves were watching but not judging.

Jacob thought that even with all of the death and the tribulations they had endured, this was worth fighting for. His friends, comrades, fellow Rangers, and Maggie, snuggling close to him, her warmth reaching through his shirt, were all worth fighting for and worth trying to survive so he could have more time with them.

As Konkapot and Ojistah staggered off, Maggie once again pulled Jacob to his feet and dragged him off, but instead of going towards the music, she pulled him towards the new garden. With a giggle and a crash, they found themselves lying in the soft brush and the tall grass near the garden.

They embraced and kissed. Under the clear sky and stars, they loved with fire and passion. They fell asleep in each other's arms as the moon sank and the stars blazed above.

The following day, the Rangers assembled to begin their march to Fort William Henry. Much discussion occurred about the night before, with whistles and hoots, and sometimes applause, as Samuel and some other Rangers joined the assembled men with blurry eyes but large grins on their faces.

Lieutenant Waite would be leading the column. They were to meet near the lake with Captain Rogers, who had just returned from New Hampshire.

Some of the Rangers looked rough, with eyes bloodshot and a slight weave in their posture as they stood. Others, like Peter, Samuel, and Konkapot, had grins and were bubbly in their manner, which made the hung-over Rangers scowl even more.

Still though, the mood was joyful and the friendly conversations showed that morale was good and the men were ready for the march.

Maggie had accompanied Jacob to the formation; they stood a slight way off from the column, holding hands.

"Ah, go and kiss her already!" someone yelled from the column.

Jacob believed it was Samuel.

The comment caused the Rangers to turn, and they began to cheer and chant, "Kiss her, kiss her."

Without hesitating, Maggie reached up and pulled Jacob's head down and kissed him with passion to the merriment and cheers of the other Rangers. Blushing, Jacob turned and headed for the formation.

As Jacob walked towards his men, he heard from behind him Maggie yell, "Konkapot, Samuel, you men, you better take care of him, or I'll take care of you!"

This set off a whole new series of hoots and whistles from the ranks, which were soon followed up by assurances that they would all watch out for him. Even Rangers from other sections joined the chorus of "Yes, Ma'am!"

"You do that, and I'll make sure Mr. Best has a cask waiting for your return!" Maggie called.

The Rangers cheered and "huzzahed" and playfully formed a protective circle around Jacob until Lieutenant Waite ordered them to shoulder their rifles and begin the march.

She waved as they marched towards the forest, the wolves and other dogs marching along with the Rangers. It was all Maggie could do not to start weeping, concerned not just for Jacob, but also for the other Rangers, whom she considered almost like family.

The Rangers were in good spirits as they marched through the woods. They automatically took up their techniques of watching the woods, rifles and muskets at the ready. The dogs and wolves weaved back and forth, investigating scents and finding no enemies, though the wolves did chase down a few rabbits.

The Rangers passed through Halfway Brook and then through the ravine and past Bloody Pond. The ghosts of their dead no longer bothered them as much, many having accepted their loss and moved on.

When the Rangers arrived at the lake, Captain Rogers was at the shore with bateaux and whaleboats waiting.

"Guess we're heading back up north to see what the Frenchies are up to," said Peter as they halted. Spotting the boats, the Rangers nodded and some already instinctively began shrugging their shoulders to loosen them up, recalling how sore they had gotten from rowing.

"How were things in the valley, sir?" asked Jacob when Captain Rogers approached them.

Rogers shrugged. "Damn little doing, I'm afraid," he answered. "The expected Indian attack didn't happen so I was able to come back here where the fighting really is going to take place."

Rogers assembled the men, about fifty, and confirmed what Peter had suspected. They were heading up north to scout out the French at Carillon and Saint-Frederic.

"Well Rangers," began Rogers, looking at the assembled men. "Time to go see how our friends to the north weathered the winter and what they are up to."

With that, the Rangers moved to the shoreline.

They loaded five whaleboats armed with swivel guns, which Samuel gleefully spotted as he loaded his belongings into their boat, declaring that the gun was his. Jacob didn't argue with him, as Samuel had proven he was very efficient with a swivel gun.

After everything was loaded, they began their journey north. This trip was a refreshing change from their previous treks; the weather was decent, and it was not snowing or raining on them. The black flies had come out, but they stayed along the shore and were soon behind the boats, which skimmed along the lake.

After resting about halfway down the lake for a night on the shore, Rogers waited far into the day before starting out so they would pass Carillon in the dark. As they rowed and came close to the French position, Rogers had the men wrap the oars in cloth to silence them.

In the dark, the boats slowly and silently glided along the lake like giant water bugs, the Rangers crouching low. They could see the glow of fires from the French camp around Carillon. They could also hear conversations, music, and singing—typical camp life—from the French encampment as they floated past.

Once they were well away from the French, they began to row normally, and they landed about ten miles above Fort Saint-Frederic.

They pulled the boats close to shore and hid them under low-hanging tree branches.

Rogers took half of the men to observe a trail system close by, while the other half, including Jacob and his men, observed the lake from their concealed boats.

As the day wore on, they saw a lot of boat traffic on the lake, mostly heading north towards Canada from Fort Carillon. In all, they counted thirty boats of different makes that traveled past them.

At night, they took turns observing and resting in their boats. Samuel was watching the lake while patting the small swivel gun. Jacob just shook his head.

It was just before sunrise when Rogers and the rest of the men came back from watching the trail, and Lieutenant Waite reported what they had observed on the lake.

"Looks like we would have better luck on the lake than on the trails," said Rogers. "Man the boats, and get the swivel guns ready," he commanded. "Let's see what we can get today on the lake."

Samuel gleefully checked his swivel gun and prepared the slow match to be fired. They didn't have to wait long; a lookout passed word that there were two boats approaching from the north. The Rangers scrambled to their seats and ran out the oars; other men like Samuel were getting their slow matches lit and readying their swivel guns.

They had turned the boats so their bows were pointing out into the lake. The men were at their oars, and Rogers watched the lake with his hand raised. As soon as the boats were across from them, Rogers yelled "Now!" and dropped his hand in a chop.

The boats surged forward as the oars bit into the water, pulling them from under the trees and out onto the lake. The Canadians were caught by surprise, and they attempted to turn their heavily loaded boats away from the on-rushing Rangers.

A few of the Canadians began shooting at the Rangers, their balls splashing into the water or harmlessly whizzing by.

"Fire!" commanded Rogers, and all five swivel guns roared. They all had been loaded with grapeshot, which tore into exposed Canadian crewmen, shredding some of the sails and striking the sides of the boats in a shower of wooden splinters that caused injuries to the crews.

Some of the Rangers who were not rowing or helping to reload the swivel guns aimed and fired their rifles and muskets. Two Canadians fell into the lake from the accurate Ranger rifle fire. As the whaleboats closed to within twenty yards of the enemy, the swivel guns fired once more.

Most of the enemy crew fell like ten pins in a bowling lane, with two more men falling into the lake. One boat's sail crashed to the deck, the lines having been shredded by the grapeshot. It was enough to take the fight out of the Canadians; the few survivors quickly threw up their hands as the whaleboats pulled alongside. Rogers and some of the Rangers jumped on board the captured boats.

Between the two boats, only two men somehow were unscathed from the attack, and four Canadians were wounded.

Rogers ordered the Rangers to bind the wounds of the four injured Canadians and take them to shore, where, with luck, they might be picked up by French forces. The sound of their fighting more than likely had attracted the French, who would be sending forces to investigate, and soon. The two Canadians who were not injured would accompany Rogers as prisoners.

Jacob and a few of the Rangers searched both boats and found they were carrying wheat, flour, rice, wine, and brandy for the fort. Rogers decided to liberate as much of the supplies as they could fit on their boats, including the wine and brandy, and then sink the boats.

After the captured supplies had been moved to the whaleboats, the swivel guns were loaded with solid shot. Using brandy from the captured stores, they set some of the shredded sails and ropes on fire and then fired the swivel guns at close range into the hulls.

Soon the boats were blazing and sinking, and Rogers decided it was time to get moving before the French arrived.

The Rangers pulled with all their might on the oars, proceeding quickly to the other side of the lake and then traveling close to the shore and under the overhanging limbs. They spotted several canoes traveling towards the now sunken boats across from them, but they remained undetected.

Without incident, Rogers and his men arrived safely back at Fort William Henry with their prisoners and captured booty.

The prisoners and some of the casks were brought into the fort while the Rangers moved back into their old encampment, bringing some of the captured supplies for themselves.

After settling themselves into the same lean-tos they had used before, Jacob and his men started a fire, Konkapot using flint and steel to get the kindling burning. They warmed their rations and talked about their success on the lake. Samuel boasted he was one of the best gunners anywhere and speculated that perhaps he should join the artillery or even the navy.

"Don't the crews who capture enemy shipping get some of the prize money?" Samuel asked, wistfully thinking of a life on the high seas. "Some goes to the captain and the officers, most goes to the crown," explained James. "Now if you were a privateer, then you would get a share of the prize money.

Samuel nodded, whispering "privateer" as he thought about it.

Jacob just shook his head.

After a short while, Konkapot, Jacob, and Peter walked into the fort to see if it was really as bad as they had heard from the other Rangers. Before they had even entered the sally port into the fort, the smell hit them. A heavy odor came from so many people being crammed into what living space there was, mixed with the smells of waste, animals, and sickness.

Inside, the fort was a hive of activity, as men and women moved around. Provincials and their families were living in the barracks or in the bastions where they could find room. Animals squealed and bleated from many pens, and chickens ran all over the place, scratching at the dirt.

"This is insane," said Jacob, and the others agreed. "How can they live so close together like this?"

Peter replied simply, "Fear."

They observed some of the red-coated British regulars over at one of the barracks, separated from the Provincials. Jacob noticed there was an air of tension, with Provincials directing sidelong glances toward the British. You could almost feel the growing pressure in the air. They also saw some of the sick, men with smallpox who were being moved into a separate bastion that was being used as a hospital.

"Let's leave; it's not right in here," said Konkapot.

Jacob and Peter agreed, and they returned to their camp as evening fell and darkness covered the area.

CHAPTER 14

SARATOGA AND ALBANY: THE Ranger SCHOOL

A few days after the Rangers had returned from their successful raid, wagons from Albany arrived outside the fort with new clothes and equipment. Jacob, Konkapot, and the other Rangers who had been recruited originally were called to a meeting with Captain Rogers. Jacob noticed that there were still some familiar faces in the formation, but he also noticed there were a few missing.

"Men, we've come a long way," began Rogers. "A year has come and gone. When you signed with me, it was for a year, and that year is now over. You have done much and have brought fame and glory where others have failed."

Rogers nodded over towards the fort, and there was a light chuckle from the gathered Rangers.

"I see some hard years ahead of us, and I would like to ask you to reenlist and keep serving—serving the colonies, serving with me. I plan to stay here until the job is done. All I ask is for you to stay with me."

Rogers looked into the eyes of each of the assembled Rangers so they could see his determination. There was a murmur of discussion. Konkapot looked at Jacob and shrugged, and Jacob nodded yes.

"Guess I have a reason to stay and fight."

Konkapot raised an eyebrow. "Wouldn't have anything to do with Maggie, now would it?"

Jacob just winked and walked over to the orderly who had set up a small desk on some boxes.

Only a few men decided not to reenlist. Rogers shook their hands, thanked them for their service, and wished them well. He also shook the hand of every Ranger who had reenlisted to serve again.

After all had signed, Rogers informed them that they were now an independent company of Rangers, not belonging to one colony or another. Jacob and the Rangers moved over to a line of other desks, where they signed for their pay, which had been owed to them for some time. Each Ranger received a healthy sum of New York shillings and British coins in a leather bag.

After signing the receipt book, they moved over to the line of wagons where new clothes were waiting for them. Jacob looked down at his faded, threadbare hunting shirt and heavily patched breeches.

"Couldn't have come at a better moment," he said, and Konkapot nodded as he poked his finger through a hole in his shirt. All of their uniforms would have fallen off their bodies had it not been for the patching and thread barely holding them together.

Jacob selected a new coat made from green, a lighter, almost beige-colored hunting shirt, and breeches, which would breathe better in the hot weather to come. With his pay, Jacob went over to some of the sutlers that had been established near the fort to purchase lead ingots for bullet-making and other supplies he would need. Jacob had just finished paying for his supplies when a runner found him. "Captain Rogers wants to see you, Sergeant."

Jacob reported to Captain Rogers, who informed Jacob that he had a special task for him to perform. Jacob waited to see what this special task would be.

"Heading back up to Carillon, sir?" Jacob asked. Rogers looked up and gave him a slight smile. "That would be an easy task if it were the case." Jacob looked inquisitively at Captain Rogers.

"I want you to take your section and return to Fort Edward, where you will join with Lieutenant Spicer, and from there travel to Saratoga."

Rogers paused to see how Jacob would react, and smiled to himself at the confused look on Jacob's face.

"You are to assist Lieutenant Spicer in training British regulars on our tactics. General Abercrombie is concerned that their men are not fighting well enough, and he wants them to learn from us. You are to teach them how to build camps, how to scout, and in short teach them the New England way of fighting the Indians."

The instructions sank in, and Jacob nodded.

"Sir, you are aware there is some tension between us and these regulars?" he asked.

Rogers sighed and nodded.

"Aye, I know. Do the best that you can. I am not sure if they can learn what we have learned during our entire lives. Still, an order is an order. Good luck."

Rogers shook Jacob's hand and returned to planning his next raid against the French.

It was with mixed feelings that Jacob informed the men about their task of training the British regulars. While it would be a nice break from risking their lives against the French and their Indian allies, working with these British regulars could be almost as risky. They were all well aware of British discipline and their love of flogging for any infraction. At least with the French or the Indians, you could shoot them. It was a change of scenery though.

They assembled their packs and began their journey back to Fort Edward, the wolves trotting alongside. Everyone noticed there was a slight spring to Jacob's step as they began marching along the military road, and they snickered amongst themselves until Jacob told them, "All right, that's enough," which resulted in all of them breaking out into more laughter.

But when they arrived at Fort Edward, Jacob found that Maggie had gone with Frederick to Albany to get wares for his store. In any case, Jacob met with Lieutenant Spicer, and it was decided that they would depart in the morning for Saratoga. The English were sending men from different regiments to learn from them, and these men should be assembled at Saratoga when the Rangers arrived.

The Rangers departed as the sun rose on the following morning, the sky a crisp blue with no clouds. It had been some time since Jacob and his Rangers had marched in this direction; they had spent all of their time around Fort Edward or northward. Even the wolves enjoyed the different scenery and pranced around and played with one another as they kept up with the Rangers.

They relaxed slightly heading south. The chances of running into an Indian war party or Canadians this far south was slight. Even so, it could occur, so the Rangers didn't completely let down their guard.

The big difference they observed was that there were actual people living on the farms, and they passed farmers and their carts on the road. Most of the farms around Edward and William Henry had been abandoned, and the people had sought shelter either at the forts or down in Albany.

They passed small detachments of red-coated regulars marching north to join their comrades at one of the forts. While those men looked stoically ahead, it was easy to see the disdain of the officers as they looked down their noses at the Rangers they passed. It was going to be an interesting time at Saratoga.

The wolves watched them march by, getting some startled looks from the passing soldiers.

The difficulties became very evident when they arrived at Saratoga to find a mixed group of regular British officers waiting for them. Most of them had the detached or subdued look of having been told they had to do something that they really didn't want to do.

The Rangers met the officers, resplendent in their fine, tailor-made uniforms, on the commons in the center of town. There were officers from the 44th Regiment of Foot, the 42nd Highlanders in their military tartan kilts, the 60th Regiment of Foot, and the 35th Regiment of Foot. As Jacob walked past the officers, he spotted one he did recognize, Lieutenant Karl Manning.

Jacob walked up to Lieutenant Manning, shook his hand, and asked how he had ended up there. Manning looked Jacob straight in the eye and answered in a low whisper so only Jacob could hear.

"To be honest, if I had to spend any more time with Captain Reynolds, I would have killed him myself. Besides, it was you who said I should volunteer, and so here I am, volunteering."

Jacob welcomed him to the training.

Captain Rogers had been right. It would have been easier for Jacob to walk into Fort Carillon and count the number of French soldiers there than to try to train a group of the most stubborn and set-in-their-ways officers that he had ever encountered.

When the Rangers tried to explain to them that they needed to cut down their uniforms to make it easier to move through the thick vegetation, they adamantly refused, pointing out the cost to have these finely made uniforms tailored. The same complaint was made about removing all of the gold braid, buttons, and gorgets.

To prove their point, Lieutenant Spicer and Jacob led the group through the forests near Saratoga, stopping from time to time and having some of the officers move ahead of them to show how they shined with all of their gold braid and buttons.

The forest echoed with complaints about their precious uniforms becoming snagged and torn by the thorns and vines, and their hats were constantly being knocked off their heads by tree limbs. There were a few, Lieutenant Manning included, and who had followed the Rangers' instructions and had modified their uniforms and cut down their bicorn hats. These were junior officers, mostly lieutenants.

After a few days, more officers appeared with modified coats. They had been able to procure enlisted men's coats, which they had cut down and which had no shiny braid, buttons, or trim. At least their expensive, tailor-made uniforms would be safe.

The officers seemed to accept most of the discussions on tactics, on how to move, shoot, and communicate while in the woods. They were resistant, however, to some of the "Indian" tactics, having been thoroughly indoctrinated in European linear warfare. They also expressed their displeasure at the wolves, who watched with their golden eyes from a distance as the officers went through their drills.

When it came to marksmanship, they once again became stubborn and refused to learn, stating that officers and gentlemen had better things to do than to try to kill one another. The officers maintained that they had to lead the men, give orders, and maintain control. Without them, the battle would turn into a chaotic fight, no better than a tavern brawl amongst ruffians.

Lieutenant Spicer demonstrated his ability to shoot accurately, and he said that every rifle or musket was important in a fight up in the woods. The enemy would not refuse to shoot them because they were officers. Instead, they would go out of their way to find them and kill them, either with ball or with tomahawk.

"If you want to survive out there in the woods," Lieutenant Spicer said as he pointed to the north, "then you had better learn to shoot, and to shoot straight."

Lieutenant Spicer, Jacob, and his Rangers exercised as much of their patience as they could to help teach these officers how to shoot and load effectively. Just as the Rangers did, these men went through drills in which one would fire while the other covered him as they moved, taking turns shooting live balls at targets.

Most of the time, the senior officers complained that fighting was for the enlisted men and not for them, while Lieutenant Manning and the other junior officers proved they were quick learners. They quickly adapted and became proficient in their musketry, while it was a constant struggle with the senior officers.

The most frustrating part was the lack of respect some of these officers showed to Jacob and his men. They were trying to teach them skills that would save their lives and the lives of their men, but these officers wanted to constantly argue with them about what they knew about fighting.

In some cases, the officers became so frustrated that they lashed out at the Rangers and threatened to court martial them or flog them for disrespect. It was not a large group, only a small minority, but it did cause a rift to grow between the Rangers and these few British officers.

Peter asked, "When are we going to teach them about fighting with a knife or tomahawk?" but Lieutenant Spicer thought better of it. Jacob had to agree. It would be too tempting to have a slight accident with a tomahawk. These few officers were not worth it.

They decided to try something very unorthodox to finally drive home their point about surviving. Jacob and Lieutenant Spicer led the officers on a practice scouting mission in the woods surrounding Saratoga. Konkapot and the other Rangers, dressing and painting themselves up in Huron war paint, waited for them in the woods with the wolves.

As the officers entered the thick wooded area where Konkapot and the other Rangers were waiting, the "Hurons" rose up and gave blood-curdling war whoops and fired on the British officers.

While the balls went high, they did whistle and smack into the trees around the officers, showering them with leaves and bark. The Rangers were loading and rapidly firing, the whole time keeping the war whoops echoing from the trees. The wolves ran through the confused officers, growling and nipping at their legs, before running back into the woods, following the commands of the Rangers.

Some of the officers reacted, moving to cover; some ran away; and others just stood frozen. Konkapot, wearing only a loin cloth and leggings, his face and upper torso painted in black and red, jumped out of the woods with his tomahawk and knife.

The startled officers who still stood frozen were faced with this demon in their midst as Konkapot tapped them on their shoulders with his tomahawk. One of the officer's eyes rolled up, and he fainted on the spot.

Soon, the officers realized no one was hit, and no one was dead.

They had to revive the one who had fainted with water.

Konkapot and the other Rangers appeared out of the woods as Spicer and Jacob explained to the assembled officers that this was how it was done on the frontier; this was the kind of war they were going to face. While some of the officers seemed to understand, the looks others gave the Rangers could have killed.

Ignoring their scowls, Lieutenant Spicer paced in front of the British officers, pointing out what had happened, reinforcing their classes on scouting, on how to shoot, move, and communicate, and on how to work as teams, and they warned the men never to lose their heads in a fight.

"Now you see how it will be, and why you need to learn these tactics," Spicer instructed. "Now you see why you must never lose your head and use your old tactics. The linear tactics you know won't work in the woods!"

Most of the officers resigned themselves to the fact that what Spicer was saying was correct, and they accepted that the Rangers had been right the whole time. They would have to learn to adapt or die.

Still though, for some of the officers, the scowls remained. They would show these Rangers who their betters were. What the Rangers had done was beyond criminal in their eyes.

When the training was over and the Rangers had settled down for their evening meal, having a laugh at what had happened, a group of British soldiers marched into their camp. Lieutenant Spicer and Jacob looked up at the regulars, and the sergeant stepped forward.

"By order of Major Christianson, you are all considered under arrest and must remain in your huts here until a court martial can be convened."

The sergeant stepped back, having done his duty and posted some of his men as guards, watching the Rangers.

"That bloody tears it!" yelled Samuel. "Don't these fools know we're trying to save their miserable bloody lives?"

Lieutenant Spicer shook his head and said, "Rogers was right when he said this was going to be a challenge. Damn bloody fools!"

The Rangers began to talk over one another, airing their complaints.

Jacob raised his hand. "All right, that's enough!" he bellowed, and the Rangers quieted down. "Complaining about it won't change anything right now. We have to think straight and think smart if we're really going to have to face this damnable court martial."

Jacob looked at the Rangers who nodded.

"You have every right to be angry, but all that will do is give them," Jacob waved towards the houses where the British officers were living, "the ammunition to bury us. We'll get through this. We'll Ranger on!"

It took a day for the court martial to be convened. Until then, the British soldiers kept the Rangers penned in their camp, while Lieutenant Manning and some of the others stopped by to talk to the Rangers and show they supported them.

"This is all a sham," Manning said directly to Lieutenant Spicer. "These officers couldn't handle it, so they had to lash out at you and these good men."

When the time came for the trial, Spicer, Jacob, and the other Rangers were cleaned up and wearing their green uniforms. They marched together into the meeting hall where the trial would take place. Lieutenant Manning and a few of the other officers walked in to support the Rangers.

Sitting in judgment was Major Thomas Davies from General Webb's personal staff. He had ridden up to Saratoga from Albany, having heard the charge that the Provincials had tried to murder British officers. On one side of the room was the minority of the British officers, with smug looks on their faces and whispers behind their hands as the Rangers entered and took their places on the other side of the room.

Behind the Rangers stood Lieutenant Manning and some of the other officers who had learned and accepted the Rangers' tactics. The rest stood wherever they could behind the assembled officers, interested to see the outcome of the trial.

Major Davies looked up from the stack of papers in front of him. "Gentlemen, I have read your statements," he said as he looked at the British officers. Major Davies turned and addressed Lieutenant Spicer and Jacob.

"You men have been accused of taking unnecessary risks with the lives of these fine gentlemen and officers. You and your men constantly failed to properly show the respect warranted by these officers, you wantonly damaged their personal property, and you attempted to kill them. I believe you know the rest."

Lieutenant Spicer addressed Major Davies, "Sir, while we were aware that we were placed under arrest and confined to our camp, we were not informed of the charges."

"Do you deny any of these charges?" asked Major Davies as he laid his hand on the stack of documents.

They must have spent all night writing those statements, Jacob thought.

"Yes sir, we deny the charges. While we did run these officers through training, it was the same training we send our own Rangers through, no difference."

Then he turned and waved his hands at Lieutenant Manning and the other officers with him. "As evidence, I guess, here stand fine British officers who seem no worse for the wear from going through our training."

Then he turned to face the major. "Still, if I was in their position, I might believe these things happened," added Lieutenant Spicer.

The accusing officers were filled with a satisfied glee when Spicer confirmed their statements. Now, they would get to the part where they would flog the hides off these Provincial soldiers.

Major Davies turned and addressed the accusing group of officers, slowly shaking his head before he looked straight at their smug expressions. "What were your orders, gentlemen? Why were you sent here?"

The group of men seemed to have lost their smugness all of a sudden as they looked at one another before answering.

"We were ordered here to learn the ways of fighting like these New

England Provincials, sir," was their reply. "Who ordered you here?" asked Davies.

The group was now silent, and they looked unsure about what was occurring.

Major Davies boomed, "You were ordered here by General Abercrombie, and the order was confirmed by General Webb, to learn from these men who have been fighting here and winning for more than a year now! How many battles have you won? In fact, how many of you have won a fight against our enemies here on the frontier?"

Davies stared at the accusing officers, who were now looking at their shoes like school boys being scolded by the headmaster. The group looked sheepish as what Major Davies had said sank in.

"Did you men learn anything?"

Major Davies looked at all of the British officers in the room. Lieutenant Manning and some of the other officers raised their hands and said they had, and the now silent minority began to nod their heads in agreement.

"Then I don't see what the problem is."

Major Davies turned and addressed Lieutenant Spicer.

"I do not find any violation of law or discipline here. From what I can determine, you followed your orders to the letter, providing instruction to these men who seemed not to grasp what you were teaching. You men are found innocent and are ordered released to return to your command at Fort Edward.

"I would like to apologize for these fine gentlemen who have not yet learned that this country is not England and that we will not fight in the same style of warfare as we have seen at home. You may depart. The rest of what I have to say is for these officers only and does not concern you or your men."

Lieutenant Spicer saluted, and the Rangers followed him out the door, Jacob nodding and winking at Lieutenant Manning as they passed. As the drama of the Ranger School was playing out, additional training was being conducted to the south to prepare for the coming campaign. In Albany, Colonel Monroe was observing musketry drill and marksmanship training by his men of the 35th with Captain Reynolds at his side. During the musketry drill, one of the privates accidently fired his Brown Bess musket and shot two of his comrades through the legs. With accidents like this, Monroe wondered if he would have enough men to fight the French when he got to William Henry. Hopefully, the men he had sent up to learn from these Provincial Rangers at Saratoga would be valuable.

He had heard much from this Captain Reynolds about his experiences at both Fort Edward and William Henry. His major concern was the tales of the Provincial regiments who would be serving alongside his men. According to Captain Reynolds, these Provincials were an undisciplined lot, and they could not march or behave like regular British soldiers. They used mostly Indian tactics rather than the linear fighting tactics that real gentlemen employed. When in garrison, they were unkempt, dirty, drunken, and unruly.

As for these Provincial Rangers, Reynolds had possessed a grudging respect for them, but said they were the complete opposite of the Provincials. The Rangers were bloodthirsty and no better than the savages they were fighting. He told of his experiences watching them kill the enemy with their bare hands and take scalps.

They were also an undisciplined lot, allowing beasts like wolves and dogs to live with them in their camps. They associated freely with the Indians—the Mohawks and other tribes who were supporting the Crown. When Monroe asked if they could fight, Reynolds had to agree that these men could fight. They scared him, so they must scare the French and their Indian allies.

Monroe nodded. They better be able to fight, he thought, having recently learned of the loss of the three forts near Oswego. He felt the French would be coming soon, and they would need all the help they could get, even if it came from an unruly bunch.

Colonel Monroe attended a meeting with the British staff, with both Lord Loudoun and General Abercrombie present, along with the colonial officials. In addition to the various colonial government officials, there were Provincial officers including Major General John Winslow, commander of the Provincial army defending both Forts Edward and William Henry.

Most of the argument stemmed from the policy of British officers outranking any Provincial officers, including generals, and from the rule that all of the Provincial soldiers were subject to British discipline. Winslow argued that if these policies remained, the Provincial army would dissolve.

Abercrombie was in a tough situation. While an energetic and effective administrator, he still had a haughty and autocratic attitude towards these Provincials, who he deemed were British subjects and should not question British authority. But he knew he needed the Provincial army.

He did not have enough British regulars to take the fight to the French.

Abercrombie relented and stated that the Provincial officers were to be treated as senior captains, but the discipline was to remain. While

Abercrombie thought this was a most magnanimous concession, it did not sit well with Winslow and his fellow officers.

If the situation with the Provincial officers wasn't bad enough, General Abercrombie also had to deal with the colonial governments, who insisted on negotiating for all of his supply and manpower requests. Abercrombie thought he shouldn't have to request anything from these government officials; he should order them and, like good loyal subjects of the Crown, they should provide what he needed. It was becoming very tedious and time consuming to have to negotiate every time he needed supplies.

These problems had become even more critical with the news of the French victory at Oswego. Loudoun and Abercrombie were both worried that the French would follow up by attacking their positions at William Henry and Edward.

Colonel Monroe was not used to Provincial governments negotiating with the Crown. This was an entirely foreign tangle for him to understand here in the colonies, a tangle composed of the different Provincial governments, the militaries, and the climate in which they would fight the French.

CHAPTER 15

FORT WILLIAM HENRY: A GROWING CONCERN

Jacob and his Rangers were released from their duties and returned to Fort Edward, having completed their time as trainers and survived their court martial. Even the wolves seemed to be happier to be back at the fort than they had been at Saratoga. News of their court martial had preceded them. Now, Lieutenant Spicer continued on to report to Rogers and give him the details of the training and the trial.

As Jacob and the others crossed the bridge to their island, they could see that Captain Putnam had returned with an entire company of Stockbridge Indians, many of whom both Jacob and Konkapot recognized and waved to as they walked to their hut.

Rogers now had at his command two full companies of Rangers and scouts. A welcoming party was organized for that evening for the Stockbridge Indians and the Rangers, and it was also attended by some of the Provincials.

From the fort walls, the regular British officers scornfully observed the party out on the island.

As night fell and the bonfire grew, Rangers and Stockbridge Indians began to boastfully predict their upcoming victories over their enemies, the number of scalps that would be taken, and the total destruction of the French. The laughter grew, the music began, and the Rangers and Stockbridge Indians mingled, toasting and having a good time.

Jacob arrived with Maggie on his arm and joined in, but there were no couples dances this time. Instead, the Indians danced their war dances around the fire as they sang and chanted in their native language. Jacob and Maggie sat on a blanket, leaning against a log, and he translated the songs for Maggie. She listened intently, but mostly she just looked at Jacob and heard his voice.

"Well, at least you survived the assignment Captain Rogers sent you on," Maggie commented as she snuggled into Jacob's shoulder.

After taking a gulp of his rum, Jacob looked down into Maggie's smiling face.

"Barely," Jacob gasped. "We barely survived. Those bloody bastards wanted to peel our hides!"

Maggie leaned up and kissed Jacob on the cheek.

"But you did survive, and here you are," she said into his cheek. Jacob smiled back and sighed, "Aye lass, that I did."

As the night drew on, the party grew, songs were played, and mixed voices were raised in drunken choruses of tavern or traditional Stockbridge songs.

That night, Maggie led Jacob off by the hand, leaving the Rangers, Stockbridge, and Provincials, who sat shoulder-to-shoulder, swaying to the beat of the songs. She steered him inside one of the empty storage sheds, not wanting to be eaten alive by mosquitoes and black flies in the field, and they had their own personal reunion.

The following morning, Jacob, his men, and some of the newly arrived Stockbridge Indians traveled with Captain Putnam to Fort William Henry.

As they marched towards the lake, Jacob recounted their training experience with the British regulars, and Putnam scoffed, "The British will be no better than lost babes in the woods, if they can't learn to survive and fight in these lands."

The other Rangers chorused their agreement as they marched, alert and constantly scanning the woods as they had been taught.

When they arrived at Fort William Henry, they headed over to their encampment, the wolves going to their regular places as Jacob and the others greeted their fellow Rangers. He learned that Captain

Rogers was leading another group of fifty men on a scout of Carillon and Saint-Frederic and wouldn't be back for some time.

After getting settled back into their lean-tos, they got caught up on what had happened while they were away. The other Rangers told them that more and more regular British companies were arriving and that the tension between the Provincials and the regulars was growing steadily. Already a few Provincials had been publically flogged for disciplinary infractions.

"It's getting pretty rough around here," said Tom Parker, one of the Rangers who had been serving up at the lake while Jacob and the others were running the Ranger School.

"Now, it's not all of them, mind you," Tom continued. "Mostly, them there officers are causing trouble, and some of their sergeants as well. The private soldier seems to get along with us just fine. What was it like down your way at the Ranger School?"

Jacob and his men told them of their training adventure with the regular officers, and they all agreed that something bad was going to happen between the regulars and the Provincials, if the French or the Indians didn't kill them all first.

"Only time will tell," Jacob commented. "Until then, I guess we need to stay busy so we don't have an accident with our prickly comrades-in-arms."

The next day, the Rangers got down to business and began to conduct scouts around the area. Everyone was concerned that the French would be coming down the lake to attack them after being so successful at Oswego. The Rangers were tasked to continuously scout the surrounding area so as to be the early warning system in case the enemy arrived.

As Jacob and the other Rangers were getting ready for one of their daily scouts, they noticed two sections of British regulars heading out of the fort, marching past them and heading northward into the woods. Jacob and his men looked at one another curiously, and then over at some of the Rangers who had been at the fort for a while. They nodded their heads.

"Yeah, the 44th have been sending out their own patrols. They believe they can do a better job than us at scouting, seeing they're regulars and we're just Provincials," said one of the Rangers.

Jacob shook his head and led his men with some of the Stockbridge Indians, who were attached to get experience and knowledge of the area, out for a local scout to look for any sign that the French had been by.

They traveled east along the lake, skirting around South Bay, and then turned to head into the wooded hills to the north.

It did not take them long to notice signs that someone had been in the area. The Stockbridge Mohicans found moccasin tracks along game trails, which they followed to a cold campsite under a large rock overhang. Everyone became more alert, watching the trees around them. Jacob, Konkapot, and Wapekeniew, who was leading the Stockbridge Mohicans, knelt on the ground around the remnants of the fire, and the other Rangers and Mohicans knelt while watching the woods around them.

"What do you think?" Jacob asked, and both Konkapot and Wapekeniew looked around at what was the old campsite.

"It's a good-sized party," Wapekeniew said, Konkapot nodding. "Not sure if their intent was a scout or a war party."

Jacob pursed his lips as he thought. From the signs in the old camp, it was a large party, almost too large for a scout, but a good size to strike fast. "Let's keep our eyes and ears open and follow their tracks. The fact that they're not trying to conceal their tracks is troubling."

Jacob waved everyone up, and the Stockbridge Indians led the way, following the tracks away from the campsite. The tracks led to an overlook of the lake from which they could see Fort William Henry in the distance. Someone had definitely been at the overlook scouting. Again, the Rangers and Mohicans stopped, taking a knee and facing the woods around them, with Jacob, Konkapot, and Wapekeniew moving into the middle.

"How many?" whispered Jacob.

Wapekeniew replied in a low whisper, "Ten, maybe twelve. Not sure if this was all of them or some of them," and Konkapot agreed.

"That's a good-sized scouting party. We need to be careful," Jacob said.

He looked around the spot where the unknown men had made disturbances on the ground as they had looked at or towards Fort William Henry. His concern grew as he saw that once again the unknown men had not hidden their tracks or signs they had been there.

It was then that they heard the first crack of a musket in the distance, quickly followed by more. They all looked at each other and wondered the same thing. Had the scouting party found that patrol from the 44th?

As the sound of firing steadily increased, Jacob rose and waved them towards the sound of battle.

Jacob led his Rangers forward at a trot, the Stockbridge Indians keeping pace. Churning up the leaves as they trotted by, weaving their heads around and under branches, the Rangers and the Indians still stayed vigilant while moving quickly through the forest, hoping they would reach whoever was in trouble in time to help them.

The sound of the escalating fight got louder as they drew closer. While they may have been breathing hard, the adrenaline was pumping through their veins and the urge to fight was growing as the sound of battle came closer and closer. Someone was in deep trouble.

As they topped a ridge, they skidded to a halt to survey the fighting below them.

Easily spotted by their red coats, the patrol which they had seen leaving Fort William Henry in the morning had, in fact, gotten itself penned into a small ravine. On either side of the British were Canadians or Frenchmen in regular hunting clothes, with Huron and Abenaki Indians using the trees and rocks for cover, only rising to take shots at the British.

"Damn!" Jacob growled, then motioned for Wapekeniew to take his warriors to the right while Jacob took his Rangers to the left as they charged down the ridge towards their foes. He was hoping that the enemy was focused on killing the British and not suspecting an attack from their rear.

After informing the men of their plan of attack, Jacob raised his hand as they brought their rifles up and sighted on the unsuspecting enemy.

When Jacob dropped his hand, the Rangers and Stockbridge Indians all fired at once before charging down the hill while pulling their tomahawks from behind their backs.

All around them, the French, Canadians, and Indians froze as many of their comrades fell from accurate rifle fire from behind. As they turned, they were met with the horrifying specter of death as Rangers and Mohicans crashed into them with flashing tomahawks.

Moving fast down the ridge and jumping over the man he had just shot, Jacob focused on his next target, a Huron warrior painted in deep red, who was turning and trying to get his rifle up to fire. Jacob's tomahawk caught the Huron in the side of the head with a loud thwack, sounding like an unripe melon.

Continuing on, Jacob caught the next Huron's musket as it was coming around with his free hand and used the momentum to swing his tomahawk around to shatter the arm holding the musket. As the warrior bent in pain, Jacob followed through and struck the Huron in the back of his head with his tomahawk, finishing that fight.

With blood dripping from his tomahawk, Jacob stopped to take stock of the situation. The avalanche of his Rangers and the Stockbridge had broken the enemy's ambush. Most of the French and their allies were down. The few survivors were trying to run away, but they were being hotly pursued by the Stockbridge.

Seeing everything was under control, he motioned Peter and Samuel to come with him as he headed down to check on the British.

Lieutenant Kennedy of the 44th hadn't been sure what to do. They had been ambushed by demons, colorfully painted warriors who were screaming war whoops and killing his men. He had led his men into a ravine where he thought they would be sheltered from the enemy fire, but that had proven to be a false hope. His men were dropping all around him. Smoke was quickly filling the ravine as his men returned fire, no longer able to fire cohesive volleys, but rather firing independently.

Kennedy had taken shelter behind a moss-covered boulder in the ravine, with bullets ricocheting off the rock and sending rock splinters into his face and arms. Kennedy was cradling Cadet Henry Marr, who had taken a bullet in the shoulder, and he was trying to stuff his handkerchief into the hole to stop the bleeding.

The sound of the battle was deafening, and he could barely hear his men. There were shouts of anger and pain and men asking for orders.

Then the battle seemed to shift. There weren't as many bullets flying towards them, but it sounded like there were more muskets firing than before. Soon it became quiet, except for the ringing in his ears and his heavy breathing.

Kennedy looked up to see a tall figure step through the grey smoke, towering over him. A rifle barrel stuck up from behind his back, but a bloody tomahawk was in his hand. In the smoke, he couldn't see what color clothes the man was wearing, but he did see the blood splashed across his front and arms. Kennedy also noticed the bloody scalps hanging from his belt.

So, he thought, as he stared up into a dark face with a large scar running across it and piercing blue eyes that almost seemed to blaze, this must be what death looks like. Feebly, Kennedy began to raise his fusil, but it was taken out of his hand in a single motion by this nightmarish giant, and he thought he heard the apparition say, "Don't do that."

Kennedy could hear muffled noises, as if someone was speaking to him.

"Are you all right?" inquired the giant.

Kennedy's head and hearing finally cleared enough to realize this man was speaking to him in English. He then noticed the man was wearing dark green. He was one of those Rangers who were at the fort, and he was not death, but a savior.

Kennedy nodded his head that he was okay, and the large Ranger began giving orders for travois to be made for the wounded and dead.

It took all of the Rangers and Stockbridge Indians to assist the wounded and dead British soldiers from the 44th to return to Fort William Henry. Jacob took his turns pulling a travois with wounded or helping limping soldiers get into the fort. He had his Rangers and the Mohicans maintain a screen around them in case there were more enemy soldiers or scouts in the area.

The sentries on the wall spotted the column of injured coming out of the woods, and called down to the fort. Provincials and regulars alike poured out to help the wounded into the fort, while the travois with the dead were led over to the fort's growing cemetery.

Lieutenant Kennedy thanked Jacob for the rescue of his men, shook his hand, and went with his men into the fort.

Once the injured had been transferred, Jacob and Wapekeniew sought out Captain Putnam to report their discovery of the enemy scouting activity and their actions to rescue the patrol from the 44th.

Putnam and Jacob went into the fort to report to Major Eyre about the enemy activity. Jacob described the tracks, the observation position the enemy had used to watch the fort, and the activity around it. Major Eyre nodded, telling Captain Putnam they might have to rely more on the Rangers to watch these areas that the enemy scouts were using.

A few days later, Captain Rogers returned, his men pulling the boats onto the shore, and he held a meeting with Captain Putnam, Jacob, and the Rangers' other senior leaders.

Rogers recounted that they had been detected on the western shore of Lake Champlain when they had attempted to scout Fort Saint-Frederic. Jacob spoke of the enemy scouts they had detected and the rescue of the patrol from the 44th.

"Perhaps the French observed your departure with the whaleboats, and they were aware you were heading their way," he said.

Rogers thought about it and could see the correlation.

"The enemy is getting bolder, and that can't be good for us," he said. "We should expect more enemy scouts and attacks against us between here and their position at Carillon."

Jacob also reported about the training at Saratoga and the tension with the British regulars and officers. This was reinforced by the poor performance of Lieutenant Kennedy and his patrol with the 44th.

Luckily, Jacob and the Stockbridge Indians had been close enough to help them or, Jacob believed, there would have been no survivors.

Listening to the report, Rogers nodded.

"They refuse to listen to reason, even from those who have been living and fighting up here all of their lives," he said. "They think they have a good grasp on how to wage war here on the frontier. They're going to have a rude awakening real soon, I fear."

Captain Putnam reported about the addition of the Stockbridge Company, which now gave them four companies of Rangers.

"Thank you gentlemen, for your reports. With all of this activity, I will lead another platoon out to scout these French positions. Perhaps we can find a good ambush position so we can catch some French and ask them what's going on."

True to his word, Captain Rogers led a platoon on a patrol from the fort the very next day, and they headed east through the forest towards the site of the previous day's fighting.

After the morning roll call and orders for the day from Captain Putman, Jacob and his men returned to the encampment to fix their breakfast over the fire. Jacob watched Rogers and the platoon depart, silently wishing them luck and a safe return.

Summer was slipping away, and fall was starting to make its presence known with lower temperatures and changes in the color of the trees. Sitting on logs or on the ground, Jacob and the other Rangers were using tin cups and small pots they had procured from the sutlers to heat water and cook their rations.

Samuel and Konkapot were making fire cakes and biscuits while Peter and Charles sliced bacon and threw it into the pot. James used a long wooden spoon to begin stirring the snapping meat, filling the air with the sweet aroma of bacon and wood smoke.

Jacob leaned back with a steaming cup of tea that Konkapot had passed to him, savoring the smell and the warmth. All around, Rangers carried on conversations, talking of the attack and increased enemy activities.

"You think we're going to get attacked here, Jacob?" a Ranger from another section asked, and his comrades looked up to see how Jacob responded.

"Not sure, Patrick," Jacob answered. "But the signs are sure there. We're in the Frenchies' way, and for them to get south, they're going to have to get through us here at the lake."

The other Rangers nodded and returned to their meals and conversations.

What Rogers didn't know was that he was not alone in the forest this cool morning. A few miles away, Canadian officer Joseph Marin shivered as the cold morning dew that had soaked through his hunting shirt. He had returned from the victory over the British and their Provincial lackeys at Oswego.

When he had arrived back at Carillon, he had volunteered to lead another raid against the British on the southern shore of the lake. Perhaps he could get a crack at these legendary Rangers, who had made it difficult for the Canadians to achieve their victories here along the lakes. General Montcalm had agreed to the raid because of his desire to keep the English off-balance. Marin led a force of one hundred Canadian, Huron, and Abenaki warriors from Carillon to the southern part of Lake du Saint Sacrement, which he had learned, the English in their arrogance had renamed Lake George.

Marin watched his raiding force with satisfaction: first the tough and rugged Canadians, many of whom were trappers and hunters who were well attuned to fighting in the wilderness, and then the Indian warriors, their heads and necks painted in dark war paint, wearing hunting shirts, breechclouts, and leggings. They showed no sign that the morning cold was affecting them, their steely gazes searching for their prey and the chance to take scalps and earn honor.

It seemed the fickle god of war favored them that day, for in the distance, they could see their enemies heading towards them. Marin had selected the spot for its high vantage point, well concealed and along the route from the fight against an English scout the previous day. He had had a feeling the English would come out for a look.

Marin noted that they moved well and did not wear scarlet, but were dressed in dark colors. It was difficult to see the color of their clothes until they get closer, for they blended with the forest around them, observing silence.

Marin wondered if these were the phantom Rangers he had heard about as he slowly cocked the hammer back on his musket. Perhaps now he had his chance to hand these vaunted Rangers a sound defeat, to show them who had mastered the art of war.

Back outside Fort William Henry in their encampment, Jacob took the wooden bowl passed to him, filled with biscuits, bacon, and some gravy and was inhaling the smell, eyes closed, when he heard the roar of musketry in the distance. Everyone stopped and listened at the same time, looking in the direction the sound of battle was coming from.

"Damn, it's Rogers!" yelled Jacob as he dropped the bowl and headed over to where his rifle and shooting bag hung. He was quickly followed by the rest of the Rangers, believing their commander and fellow Rangers were in trouble. They grabbed their rifles and shooting bags, quickly falling in behind Jacob as he raced towards the lakeshore.

"Turn out, Rangers!" was being shouted throughout the encampment as the duty drummer in the fort began playing the long roll. Running, Jacob yelled for the men to head to the boats. It would be quicker going across in the boats than trying to get through the woods. A few other Ranger sections joined them as they threw their gear into the whaleboats and began pushing them out into the lake.

"Samuel, get on that gun of yours. We may need it!" commanded Jacob. Soon they were loaded and floating clear of the shore, and the Rangers took up the oars and began rowing as fast as they could. Like Samuel, other Rangers were loading the four swivel guns mounted on the other whaleboats as they cut through the water.

In the distance, the sound of the growing battle was easily heard. The prows of the boats cut like knives through the water, which curled around them in a white wake as the Rangers pulled with all their might to coax more speed from the whaleboats.

Back at the site of the growing battle, Captain Rogers had been shocked when the woods in front of him and to the sides roared with musket fire, and his men began to fall. Rogers dove to cover as balls whizzed and snapped past like angry bees, instinctively yelling out orders.

Damn, they got me good, he commented to himself, as he assessed his situation, which he had to admit looked bleak.

Rogers knew he was in trouble. The enemy had the high ground, and they were in a good position.

He yelled, "Fall back. Get away!"

From the sound of the muskets and the war whoops of the Indians, he knew that they probably had more men than he did.

"Fall back, fall back towards the fort!" Rogers yelled as he began leading his men in an angle away from the enemy ambush.

The Rangers began trying their leap frog bounds away from the enemy, one running while his file partner fired at the enemy. But the enemy was placing accurate shots, and many of Rogers' men were falling, so many that he could not drag them away. Rangers who stopped to help their wounded comrades were themselves hit.

Rogers shook his head in frustration and ordered, "Run for it.

Every man for himself!"

Rogers spat in frustration. He had never expected to give such a command. "Damn, they really got us!"

From their superior position, Marin directed the fire against the Rangers, who he had to admit were performing well and were trying to draw back in good order. His men's accurate fire was having obvious effects, as numerous Provincials were falling.

"You won't get away so easy my friends," he spoke out loud as he directed the attack to shift into a pursuit of the retreating Rangers.

Sensing the time was right, Marin gave a yell, and the Hurons and Abenakis were released to chase after their prey and satisfy their bloodlust. The Canadians and Indians rushed forward, screaming out their war cries and firing as they ran after the retreating Provincials. The Rangers were trying to carry their wounded away, but Marin's men were making them pay a heavy price.

Jacob knew it could not be a good sign when he heard the sound of battle slacking, and he pushed the Rangers on. Jacob was directing the whaleboats to follow the shore into a cove where they could see signs of the battle. Smoke was coming out of the trees on the ridge overlooking the lake, hanging like an ominous cloud.

"Head towards the shore!" ordered Jacob, and the five whaleboats turned and pointed their bows towards the rocky shore.

Rogers was running as hard as he could down the ridge, concerned that this could be the battle that ended his life. He could only see a few other Rangers running with him through the trees. As he broke out of the trees and onto a rocky shore, he could see their whaleboats a short distance to his left, and he turned towards them as balls still whizzed past his ears and around him.

Breathing heavily, Rogers mumbled "Thank God!" and began leading what few Rangers who were with him towards the approaching boats.

Konkapot spotted the first figure to break out of the woods. "There they are!" he yelled, pointing towards shore. Jacob nodded and turned the tiller so the boat headed towards the Rangers on the shore.

Konkapot yelled, waving his arms to get the other Rangers' attention. Rogers turned and scrambled over the rocks, jumping into the first boat that touched the shore.

"Watch for other Rangers," Jacob yelled. "Swivel guns watch the woods for pursuers, pick your targets!"

Jacob looked over at Rogers who was still breathing hard but had a disgusted look on his face.

"They were heading this way with me. Hopefully some more will make it," Rogers said, and Jacob nodded.

"Cover the woods. More should be coming!" ordered Jacob. Then in a low voice, he mumbled, "Hopefully."

Even Rogers, who had heard him, nodded his head in agreement as he watched for his Rangers to break from the woods and head for the boats.

Samuel watched the shoreline over the top of the barrel with his slow match glowing, scanning for targets. A few more Rangers ran out of the woods, splashed out into the lake, and pulled themselves into the boats after throwing their rifles inside. The Rangers in the boats spotted enemy Indians in the woods, and fired, keeping them back.

Fire from the enemy in the woods was starting to intensify. Balls were whistling and splashing into the water, and a few impacted into the boats with a thud.

Jacob, still watching the shore and giving directions, took a handkerchief out and pressed it to Rogers' head. Confused, Rogers reached up and took the handkerchief, which had blood on it. Reaching up and probing with his fingers, he realized his head had been grazed by a ball, and he was bleeding.

Rogers jumped as Samuel fired the bow swivel gun, followed by the roar of the other swivel guns and a few rifles. Only a few Rangers made it to the boats, and then nothing came out of the woods except the sound of enemy war whoops and cries.

Marin arrived at a spot overlooking the cove, where he could see five whaleboats with Rangers in them. He could see a few of the Rangers he had been chasing splash out into the lake and make their way into the boats. Then there was a series of booms.

The boats had swivel guns, and they were firing on his men. Raising his hands, Marin halted the pursuit. No need getting his men needlessly killed by those swivel guns. He had given these English a hard lesson in frontier warfare.

Marin saw a few overzealous Indian warriors dash out into the open, disobeying his orders, and they were shot down before they could fire their muskets. The swivel guns were playing havoc as well, solid and grapeshot crashing through the trees and brush. Not wanting to risk any more casualties, Marin ordered his men to seek cover but to continue to fire on the Rangers.

Soon the boats with the Rangers began to row away from the shore, their swivel guns still blasting into the tree line and along the shore.

Marin knew this was but a small number of the garrison at William Henry. They would be back with more.

Calling over the Indian captains, Marin instructed them to gather their scalps and trophies, to do what they wished with the enemy dead in order to let these Rangers know they were not safe, and to be ready to move quickly.

As the whaleboats pulled away from the shore and out into the safety of the lake, Rogers looked dejectedly at the far shore. He estimated that only he and maybe six others out of the original fifty had escaped that ambush.

Then he nodded his head towards the shore and mumbled, "You win this one, but I will get you next time. I won't make the same mistake twice!"

At least it was a welcome surprise when Rogers arrived at the shore and saw Major Eyre with his 44th and other regulars and Provincials waiting instead of blundering into the woods.

Along with the 44th, the entire force of Rangers was waiting, having gathered as many boats and canoes as they could. The regulars loaded onto bateaux while the Rangers filled all of the whaleboats and large canoes. Even the six survivors, after grabbing some extra powder, were going back to the battle site to help find any other survivors.

The entire flotilla moved out onto the lake. Jacob was still commanding his boat, and the other four that had started out with him were still right behind him, following his lead. The boats went ashore at a different cove from the one where they had picked up Rogers and the survivors, in case the French were waiting for them there.

Leaving a company of regulars to guard the boats, the rest of the British regulars and Provincials, with the Rangers leading the way, headed back towards the location of the ambush.

It didn't take long to find what was left of the dead Rangers. The Hurons and Abenakis had scalped them, mutilating the remains by cutting off heads, hands, and other body parts. Messages written in French and Huron warned the Rangers that their doom was at hand.

Even the toughened and hardened Rangers were affected by the wanton brutalization of their comrades, and the stoic and professional British regulars had a few men retching from the smell and sight of the killings.

The Rangers and the Provincials gathered what remains they could find and carried them to the boats to be returned to Fort William Henry. It was a somber flotilla that landed on the southern shore with all of the remains. The Rangers had continued with their practice of taking care of one another and had not left any fallen comrades behind.

Carts transported the remains to the cemetery as the Rangers and some of the Provincials with shovels went over to dig the graves.

It was a tough day for the Rangers. They had not truly been defeated before, but that had now changed, and it bothered Rogers. The French were getting bolder, and their victory out at Oswego and in these small battles was of great concern.

It was a somber day following the defeat of the Ranger patrol, and the mood was dark around the encampment and within the fort. Jacob was called over to Rogers's hut, where Captain Putnam was waiting along with Lieutenant Spicer.

"I need to salvage some good from this mess," began Rogers. "And from what I have been told and from what I have seen, you did a great job leading the men who rescued me. Sergeant Clarke, I want to promote you to Lieutenant. I need good leaders like you."

Rogers looked at Jacob to see his reaction.

"Sir, while I am honored," stammered Jacob from surprise, "I would much rather keep being a sergeant and leading my men. I'm not sure if I am ready to be an officer yet. Could I get back to you on being a lieutenant?"

Rogers understood and agreed.

"Think about it. Still, thank you for saving us—or rather me—out there. You're a good man, Jacob Clarke."

Rogers stood and shook his hand and returned to planning their next move. Jacob walked back to the encampment in a fog and told Konkapot and the others that Rogers had offered him the opportunity to become a lieutenant and that he had refused for now. There was a relieved look on his comrades' faces. They didn't want to lose their sergeant.

"Still though," commented Samuel, "you're a hell of a lot better than some of these lieutenants I have seen around here."

This was followed up by Peter who commented from around his pipe, "And heads above those there Provincial and British lieutenants over in da fort there, with the exception of maybe Lieutenant Manning." "I think I can say for everyone here," added Charles, "we'd much rather have you lead us one way or the other, either as sergeant or lieutenant. We'll follow you to the gates of hell if need be."

Jacob was humbled by the confidence shown by his men and nodded his head in appreciation "Let's hope it won't come to that," he replied. "But I have a feeling hell is coming our way, and soon."

CHAPTER 16

ISLE LA MOTTE: RAIDING THE NORTH

Seething from their losses, Rogers was determined to take the fight back to the French. They were getting the upper hand, and he was going to put a stop to it. He decided that he would lead another expedition north, scout around the French positions near Ticonderoga, and see what damage he could do.

He selected around thirty of his men, including Jacob and his section, to take part in the raid, and he left ten to watch the encampment.

Of growing concern was the fact that ten of his men had recently fallen sick to smallpox. As much as he had tried to keep his Rangers separated from the crowded and unhealthy conditions inside the fort, some of his men were still getting sick.

Rogers assembled the raid, and led the Rangers to the shore where they once again boarded their boats. The Rangers were now very proficient in small boat operations.

They departed just before sunrise on a smooth, grey, mirror-like lake. The boats eased from shore, their oars slipping quietly into the water, and the Rangers began traveling north. They had determined looks in their eyes, many wanting to get back at the enemy for the ambush and what had been done to their comrades.

It was a quiet, uneventful journey. This time, Rogers took a more deliberate and careful approach to the enemy's end of the lake. The raiding party stopped twice along the journey to encamp, arriving just before sundown and departing as the sun rose.

The Rangers were spared any late summer thunderstorms or rains. They faced only the hardship and dual curses of the New York woods, the vicious black flies and the tiny bugs most men called "no-see-ums," which flew around their faces and ears.

Rogers led the raid into a cove that they had never used before. The Rangers quietly landed, pulling the boats up and concealing them in the woods. Leaving some men to guard their boats, Rogers led the Rangers towards the French positions around Ticonderoga with Jacob and his section at the head of the column.

They came upon a well-used trail between one of the advanced French camps and the French position at Ticonderoga. Rogers set his men into an ambush, except this time he placed sections further down the trail on his left and on his right to serve as his early warning for the main ambush. Once they fired on the enemy, these sections would serve to protect their flanks from any counter-attacking French or Indians.

They hadn't waited long when their flank security, which was located towards Fort Carillon and Ticonderoga, warned of approaching enemies. Rogers crawled slightly forward and from under a thick tree, he was able to look down the trail and see the head of a column of white-uniformed French regulars.

Slowly moving back, he gave the signal to stay quiet. Rogers counted over a hundred French regulars, who marched by in columns of two. He noted that their uniforms, while slightly dirty, were in good shape. These must have been new arrivals who had not been on the frontier long. Soldiers who had been fighting there for a while were normally wearing threadbare and patched clothing.

The Rangers settled into the long wait of an ambush. The challenge was to maintain alertness while not moving and to avoid being lulled by the warm temperature, the gentle breeze, and the sounds of the forest around them. While they gritted their teeth and allowed the French to march past, they could see they were outnumbered and would have to wait for an easier target.

Jacob and his section were on one of the flank security positions, facing towards the enemy's advanced camp. When the column of French marched by, Jacob and his men sank as low as they could into the soft, mossy ground. They were well hidden under brush and pines, but with clear fields of fire and observation from their concealed spots.

Jacob let out a silent breath of relief that Rogers had not fired on this column, which greatly outnumbered the Rangers by three or four to one.

Jacob had learned through the harsh military school of experience that this ratio favored the enemy, not themselves. You wanted to outnumber your enemy in an ambush, even with the element of surprise on your side. Numerical superiority was important because it took a long time to reload the muskets and rifles.

Jacob settled into the routine of watching the trail and watching his men.

Konkapot was next to Jacob, with Charles and James on his right and Peter and Samuel on his left.

The comfortable conditions had gotten to Peter, whose head was slowly falling forward, his eyes closed. Without taking his eyes off the trail, Samuel reached over and placed his hand on Peter's head before he completely nodded off. Peter's eyes opened and his head snapped back up into position. Samuel patted his head and Peter winked back in a silent thanks. Jacob nodded to himself. With men like these, he felt that perhaps they could win this coming fight.

It had been a few hours since the French regulars had marched by, and the sun had passed its midday arc when Konkapot, quickly followed by Jacob, heard the faint sound of voices moving towards them from the direction of the enemy camp. A group of French regulars was walking casually down the trail, their muskets carried more for comfort than in readiness.

Jacob and his men slowly sank into the shadows as Charles slithered back to warn the main ambush line. These men were walking with ease, unaware their enemies were observing them from the cover of the woods.

Jacob assumed they must have been some of the French who had been relieved by the regulars who had marched by earlier. As these Frenchmen walked past their position, Jacob noticed that their uniforms were worn and patched. They had been there for a bit, and he was surprised by their lack of security or concern.

Jacob counted only twenty-two men march past them. In less than a minute, the woods behind them erupted in a roar as Rogers initiated the ambush. Jacob, Charles, and James ran across the trail and faced down the way the first group of French had come, while Konkapot, Peter and Samuel stayed on their side of the trail, facing towards the enemy camp.

Jacob looked down the trail at the carnage as Rogers led his men in an assault across the trail. The shock of the ambush had had a telling effect; Jacob could see several French soldiers sprawled out on the trail, while the rest seemed to have dropped their arms and were in the process of surrendering.

Rogers and the rest of the Rangers quickly disarmed the stunned Frenchmen and secured their prisoners. Rogers positioned himself to look down the trail at his flank security while sections of the Rangers began moving back into the woods pulling their prisoners with them.

Once all of the Rangers were clear of the ambush position, Rogers waved to Jacob who called out to his section, "Let's go," and led them back towards Rogers. As they ran past, Rogers counted each man to make sure no one was left behind.

After the other security party arrived, the entire force moved back to where the boats were hidden. Rogers decided that it was getting too close to sunset to start out, and he decided to spend the night there.

During the night, the prisoners were taken care of but warned that if they made a sound, they would be killed silently by knife. The night passed uneventfully. Each prisoner had a Ranger watching him closely. The Rangers were surprised that there had not been a determined pursuit by the French or the Indians after the ambush.

However, when the Rangers were getting ready to move out, one of the sections noticed that a Ranger was missing. Rogers didn't understand; he had personally counted every Ranger coming off the ambush. The missing Ranger, a private named Samuel Eastman, was not in the camp. Rogers called for Jacob and his section.

"I want you and your men to quickly head back towards the ambush line and see if you can find him. I counted everyone through, but I don't want to leave a man behind. Be quick though, and don't get caught!"

Jacob nodded and instructed his men to drop everything they didn't need so they could move fast. Rogers began organizing the departure, getting the boats back out onto the lake and the prisoners loaded.

Running quickly but silently, Jacob and Konkapot led the way through the forest, the tree boughs and limbs flashing by them as they made their way along the general direction they had taken from the ambush line to their camp. They stopped, each quickly taking a knee and facing out, trying to control their heavy breathing and listening for any sound of the enemy or the missing Ranger.

Not hearing anything except the forest, the Rangers ran on until they arrived at the ambush spot. With James and Charles watching out for any enemy patrols, Jacob and the others quickly went up and down the ambush line.

While they could see the blood spots and trails, there were no bodies; it seemed the French had arrived and taken their dead with them. There was no sign of the missing Ranger, and Jacob turned and led the section back to a waiting Rogers. The boats were on the lake, and all of the other Rangers were loaded.

Jacob led his section right to Rogers and reported that they had not seen anyone. Shaking his head, Rogers instructed that some provisions be left concealed in their old camp in case the missing Ranger found his way back.

Once the provisions were concealed, Rogers and the rest of the Rangers loaded the boats and began their journey back. Rogers had a look of doubt on his face, which concerned Jacob; Rogers was not having a good week.

It was a somber if uneventful trip back to the fort over the next two days. Rogers and the men had been almost euphoric with this victory over the enemy after suffering their heavy losses around Fort William Henry. Now, they were returning short a man, which did not sit well with either Rogers or his Rangers.

The raiding party arrived back at Fort William Henry, with Rogers and some of the Rangers leading their prisoners on to Fort Edward while Jacob and the rest secured the boats and moved back into the encampment to clean equipment and restock their supplies.

A few days later, a lone Ranger walked into the encampment and reported in, tired and slightly sheepish. Ranger Samuel Eastman, without informing anyone, had left the camp after the ambush to go back to find his haversack, which he had left behind. Fearing being chastised for leaving his gear behind, he wanted to find it and return, hopefully without anyone noticing he was missing.

He had become lost in the woods, and when he finally returned to camp, he found that Rogers and the Rangers had already left, but he found the provisions hidden for him. He had trekked back south over the last couple of days without incident, following the lake.

"Didn't see a soul, sir," he reported to Rogers, who still found the lack of enemy activity strange following their ambush so close to Fort William Henry.

Eastman's return pleased Rogers, confirming that he had counted correctly and removing the specter of self-doubt that had been haunting him.

Not resting for long, he decided to head back up north taking the same Rangers, except this time they took the new whaleboats that Rogers had personally designed based on their experiences on the lake.

The Rangers loaded their whaleboats and began their journey up the lake. Rogers decided to try a new tactic, and instead of continuing north, they crossed the lake and landed the boats about ten miles north on the east shore. He then had the Rangers carry the whaleboats overland for three-and-a-half days towards Lake Champlain.

While Rogers had considered this new design a "lighter" model, the boats didn't feel lighter to Jacob and his men, who were carrying them along with all of their other equipment. What impressed them was that Rogers took his turn at shouldering the boats over the rough terrain, which even included a deep gorge.

Simply, Rogers was cutting across the land between the two lakes in a spot where the enemy wouldn't be looking for them. The gorge was the most challenging, and when the men saw it, they groaned.

"We're going to feel this in the morning," remarked Samuel, and everyone nodded in agreement.

The Rangers had to use ropes to move the whaleboats over and along the gorge. Jacob and the others pulled, sweated, and worked in unity to move their boats six miles across the land, but they had achieved their goal and put into Lake Champlain.

"Where was this when they were recruiting us?" grunted Konkapot, and Jacob had to smile in spite of himself, sweat beading and dripping from his nose.

Rogers and the Rangers rested for a day before setting out on the next phase of their scout. There were numerous moans and groans from the Rangers, sore from the strenuous activity as they boarded their boats. With muffled oars, the Rangers moved quietly along Lake Champlain at night near a narrow point in an area known as South Bay. They were able to glide quietly by and get so close to the French positions near Ticonderoga that they could hear the French pass their watchwords at Fort Carillon.

By morning, they had silently passed by the French and taken up a position in the woods about halfway between Forts Carillon and Saint-Frederic at Crown Point. The Rangers had to remain concealed in the woods during both that day and the night, because a full moon made it extremely difficult to stay concealed while moving on the lake. The moonlight would have made it almost as clear as day.

The next morning, the Rangers were treated to a spectacular display as over one hundred boats of different sizes, all carrying French regulars, sailed past. They could see the white uniforms and stacks of supplies on the boats.

"That's a lot of men and supplies there," Samuel whispered and Jacob silently nodded. "Enough for perhaps a campaign?"

Jacob looked at Samuel and nodded, "Yes."

That evening, clouds moved in, masking the full moon, and Rogers led his Rangers back onto Lake Champlain, traveling up past Crown

Point for another ten miles before moving into another concealed position. The Rangers still used muffled oars and maintained men in the front on the lookout for any approaching enemy boats such as those they had seen the day before.

From their position, they observed another thirty boats and a schooner sail past heading north towards Canada. Keeping to moving at night, Rogers and the Rangers traveled another six miles north and landed at a place called Otter Creek. Rogers decided to send out patrols, leaving one group there to watch the lake and guard the boats.

"Let's see what they have been up to," said Rogers.

Jacob had been instructed by Rogers to follow the lake north and scout around the area known as Button Mold Bay. Rogers would lead a scout to the northwest, and a third patrol would head due west to observe any movement of French forces.

Jacob acknowledged his assignment and after briefing Konkapot and the others, he led them out on their scout. This was all new territory. Neither Jacob nor any of his men had been in this area before, or even on this side of the lake.

"Sure is a nice area," whispered Samuel, and Jacob had to agree.

They moved cautiously, knowing full well that they were very deep in enemy territory. It surprised them when they saw little activity as they made their way along the lake towards their assigned location.

The bay was large, offering good positions for observation along the shore. Jacob moved his men into a well-concealed position from which they could observe both the bay and the open lake. Again surprised by the lack of activity, Jacob took out his telescope and began observing the area through its lens.

Anchored in the bay was the schooner they had seen pass by the previous day, but there was no sign of any of the other boats they had observed. Jacob sat back and folded his telescope closed, almost disappointed by the lack of activity. Observing nothing else, he led his men back to their boats and reported to Rogers that all they had observed was the schooner anchored about a mile from shore.

Rogers quickly formulated a plan to attack and board the schooner, capturing it, its crew, and its cargo. As Rogers discussed his plan to board and seize the enemy schooner, Jacob found himself wondering when they had joined the navy. Or could this be considered piracy?

The following morning, the Rangers made ready for the raid on the schooner, loading their boats.

Just as they were about to push off, one of the sentries spotted two slow-moving bateaux that had just come around a bend in the lake and were heading straight for them. Rogers quickly decided to attack these smaller and slower boats first and then the larger schooner, and he ordered the men to make ready.

They could see that the bateaux were moving slowly because they were full of cargo and were each carrying six men. As the bateaux came even with the Rangers, Rogers ordered his men to fire, yelling to the Frenchmen to surrender. Even as the balls slammed into boats and men alike, the Frenchmen reacted by turning away and headed towards the western shore.

"After them!" ordered Rogers as they jumped into their whaleboats and took off in pursuit. The lighter whaleboats were able to catch up quickly, and they captured the bateaux without further trouble.

As the Rangers drew up, both crews quickly threw up their hands in surrender. The Rangers searched the boats and found wheat, wine, rice, brandy, and flour. They also found three men dead and two wounded, one of them mortally.

Samuel quickly interrogated the captured Frenchmen, who revealed they were from a force of close to five hundred French and Canadians, who were camped less than six miles from that very spot. They also learned from the prisoners that these five hundred were part of an even larger force of French, Canadians, and Indians who were all heading south under their new commander, a Marquis Montcalm.

Concerned about the size of the enemy camped nearby and this news about the large French force moving south, Rogers decided to secure the wine and brandy and sink the two bateaux. He rowed to shore and had to make an even harder decision. They had to move fast to get this information back to the fort, so he decided to move by foot and leave his new whaleboats hidden, hoping they could get back there to recover them.

He also made a difficult decision to kill the mortally wounded

Frenchman, who would only have slowed them down. Jacob volunteered. "I'll do it," he said, and Rogers nodded.

Jacob moved over to the prisoner and noticed that he had already died. Jacob closed his lifeless eyes and simply intoned, "Sorry. Fortunes of war, I guess."

Once Jacob returned, Rogers led the Rangers and their prisoners over land quickly and in a few days, they arrived back at Fort William Henry without any further contact with the enemy. Rogers quickly departed with the prisoners for Fort Edward, taking Jacob and his men along to take care of them.

Knowing the urgency of their information, Rogers stopped briefly at Fort Edward for provisions for the men and prisoners and then continued on to Albany. Jacob saw Maggie and waved as he moved quickly by on the road to Albany. Maggie gave a great sigh of relief. Jacob had survived another trip up north.

As the Rangers moved towards Albany, the French to the north were confused and concerned. How did the Rangers in whaleboats get around them to raid their positions? Was there a water route they were unaware of ?

Montcalm ordered his scouts out to try and find this secret water route the English were using and to stop them. He didn't need them reporting on his preparations for the coming campaign.

The French, who had been secure in their anticipation of beating the English, were now not so sure, and they began to look around them for these phantom Rangers who appeared from out of nowhere.

While at Albany, Jacob and his men took up a corner in a local tavern as Rogers reported to General Abercrombie on what they had found. The locals were of a different type than the men in the smaller village taverns they had visited in the past. These were "city people," who knew nothing of life on the frontier. They were well-to-do and sat with an upper-class air to them.

Jacob and his men didn't care; they sat in a corner away from everyone, smoked their pipes, and enjoyed their ale as they waited for Rogers.

Meanwhile, the meeting went extremely well for Rogers. He was now a newly promoted major, admittedly a brevet major, a courtesy title that did not carry higher rank or pay, but it was still a promotion. He was also told that two more Ranger companies had been formed under Captains Hobbs and Speakman. This now gave him four companies, almost a battalion.

General Abercrombie was concerned about the news that the French were massing. He thanked Rogers and dismissed him to return north to keep an eye on the French.

Rogers, with Jacob and his men, returned to Fort Edward. Jacob was able to spend time with Maggie while Rogers began planning his next raid.

Whenever Jacob had some free time, Frederick would let Maggie take a break, with a wink to Jacob. Even Maggie's sister nodded in approval of Jacob, as she helped Frederick around the shop. But it was only a short stay at Fort Edward before Jacob and the others made their way back to Fort William Henry.

Seeing the success he had had on Lake Champlain, Rogers wanted to take it to the next step and go after the French settlements along the Richelieu River, an outlet for Lake Champlain that connected to the main Saint Lawrence River, which in turn connected with Montreal and Quebec. He wanted to take the fight into the very heart of the French and the Canadian territory.

It took some time, but Rogers was able to secure permission for his daring raid from Lord Loudoun. After the messenger arrived from Albany with permission for the raid and before politics or other factors forced Loudoun to change his mind, Rogers ordered his men to move.

Departing from Fort William Henry, Rogers split his force into two columns for the march into enemy territory.

The first group under Lieutenant Stark would lead out with Jacob and his men included. Their mission was simple: move back to where they had concealed their whaleboats. Rogers would lead the second body, taking a different route. He would link up with Stark at the boats, and they would continue on to their raid in the French settlements.

With Jacob leading the way, Stark's expedition moved overland generally along the same route that the Rangers had returned on. Moving cautiously, Stark, with Jacob and his men leading, arrived at the concealed whaleboats, which appeared not to have been noticed by the enemy and were still intact. A day later, Rogers's column arrived at the boat site.

Rogers once again had his expedition carry their boats, much to the groans of Jacob and the others who had carried them before, but along a different route.

They entered the water on Lake Champlain at a different location. Jacob and the Rangers manned their boats, stowing their gear while watching the woods and the lake for any sign of the enemy.

Keeping to their earlier tactics, the entire force now traveled only at night, oars wrapped in cloth to silence them as the Rangers glided like wraiths up the lake.

They arrived off an island known as Isle la Motte, a small two-miles-wide by six-miles-long piece of land in the northern part of Lake Champlain on the eastern shore near the Hampshire grants. This was the farthest they had ventured, and the Rangers were being extra cautious, constantly scanning the woods and lake.

As they were approaching the island in the dark, a spotter on the lead boat observed a sailing vessel heading towards them. The Rangers huddled low into their boats as the schooner under full sail sped past, moving too quickly for them to board and seize it, and they hoped it was too dark for anyone on the schooner to have seen them.

Rogers was determined to board and capture one of these schooners; this was now the second time one had gotten away.

They continued northward in the dark for two more nights before stopping at a place known as Windmill Point on the Richelieu River. Rogers placed his Rangers into position for an ambush and waited for the enemy to arrive.

After some time waiting on alert, there was still no sign of the enemy. Rogers felt that since he had traveled this far, he did not want to go home empty-handed. However, they were quickly running out of food, even with rationing, and so Rogers reluctantly decided that they had no choice but to break their ambush and return home.

"Damn, one of these days my luck has to return, or at least some good luck," muttered Rogers. "Had enough of bad luck already."

Before he left though, he decided to leave a calling card. Rogers wrote a note and placed it on a post with one of their green bonnets on it, thanking the French for their hospitality and saying that they would be back soon.

While not capturing a schooner or a prisoner, Rogers's raid did have a major effect on the French. After they found this calling card, Montcalm was livid, demanding to know why his scouts, who boasted they knew every tree and flower in the region, could not find this secret waterway.

"How are these damnable Rangers getting up here?" Montcalm demanded from his officers.

His scouts insisted it did not exist, but Montcalm refused to believe them. He sent them out to find the waterway to protect his expedition. He didn't want the Rangers to discover his plans.

As a result, most of the scouts were out looking for this secret waterway and were not actively patrolling the English, which took the pressure off of the English. The French, civilians and military alike, were now very concerned that the Rangers were moving freely amongst and behind them, and that scared them. This fear was buying precious time for the English at William Henry.

CHAPTER 17

1757
FORT CARILLON: WINTER RAIDS

The year had not ended well for the British, who had not achieved much except for winning a few skirmishes. The French, on the other hand, had finished on top with the taking of Oswego and with handing Rogers and his Rangers their first major defeat and loss of life.

The dark, damp mood continued through the rest of the year as the Rangers and the garrison at Fort William Henry maintained only local scouting patrols while they tried to rebuild their numbers. While the Provincials and the British regulars would take anyone, Rogers continued to be very selective as to whom he would allow into the Rangers' ranks. Even the weather seemed to reflect the general mood as it moved from fall into a wet and dreary winter. Heavy snows and wind arrived early, and soon the lake froze over and ice covered the trees. The snow began to pile up against the walls of the fort as well as the encampment, which the Rangers had repaired after the previous winter.

The weather and low morale were having an effect on the men in and around Forts William Henry and Edward. Numerous fights broke out, mostly between Provincials and some of the British regulars, who were subjected to severe punishments.

Even the Rangers found themselves in some heated arguments and fights, but they were handled by Rogers and the other Ranger officers to avoid having the Rangers subjected to harsh British discipline.

Inactivity was one of the major culprits, along with the dull garrison routine the men were performing. Many of the Rangers decided it would be better to get into a fight with the French, even in the snow, than to remain cooped up in the garrison.

Major Eyre consulted with Major Rogers and the other Provincial officers on what they needed to do to keep the men from killing one another and to keep the French off-balance.

"I believe the French have moved into winter quarters, which would be a reasonable assumption after what happened towards the end of the year," said Major Eyre, turning to Major Rogers. "How realistic would it be for the French and their allies to raid during the winter?"

Major Rogers thought about it and replied, "We have had different winter raids here in New York over the years. While the regular French Army may have gone into winter quarters, the Canadians and the Indians have no problem with waging raids in the depth of winter. That is the threat we should be prepared for."

"It seems our commanding generals in Albany have also moved into winter quarters. We have not heard from them in a while," said Major Eyre.

Rogers looked at Eyre and replied, "Doesn't mean we have to go into winter quarters. We can keep pressure on the enemy using the frozen lake to move up and raid them while they're in camp."

Major Eyre nodded. "My concern is with most of the militia and Provincials gone home, we don't want to weaken our position at either Fort William Henry or Edward."

"We'll keep scouting around the southern shore, keeping to half a day's march out and then a half-day return until we can get our numbers stronger," Rogers suggested.

Major Eyre agreed. "We'll strengthen the walls and do what we can to keep the regulars and Provincials busy," he said. "You and your Rangers can keep up your localized scouts around the forts for now. Keep the French from observing our activities."

The following day, Captains Hobbs and Speakman and their Ranger companies arrived at Fort Edward. After Rogers learned of their arrival, he split the new companies between the two forts, reinforcing the Rangers in both. Rogers sent his brother out again to recruit more men to fill the depleted Rangers' ranks.

Jacob stayed busy. Early in the winter, he and his men headed to Fort Edward to gather their cold weather clothing, snowshoes, and ice skates. The snow was heavy enough that the Rangers were already using sleds instead of carts.

Supplies were going to be an issue again that year, both because of the weather and the bickering between the Provincial governments and the British military establishment.

When he was at Fort Edward, Jacob shared a few tender moments with Maggie whenever he could, whether it was sitting together on Frederick's porch or cuddling in front of his fire.

Frederick could see the developing relationship between the two. He treated Maggie and her sister like daughters instead of servants, and he liked this Ranger and approved of the relationship. He saw them together, smiled, and moved about his shop sharing knowing glances with his wife, who also smiled. As usual, their time together was short, so they maximized what time they had.

Back inside the fort, Major Eyre was still disturbed, not knowing if the French were going to descend on Fort William Henry or not. The not knowing bothered him the most. He called for Major Rogers and, contrary to what they had agreed earlier, asked him to lead another scouting patrol up to the French positions to determine whether they were in fact in winter quarters or were preparing for an attack.

Rogers understood, and the assignment was a great relief. He wanted to get back out there and take the fight to the enemy instead of waiting for them to attack. Rogers went back to his hut and began planning. He was going to hand pick his patrol in case his luck continued to run bad.

Jacob was called to a meeting, along with some of the other senior sergeants, and Rogers laid out his plan for the scout.

"Major Eyre wants information," Rogers began as he looked at his assembled Rangers. "We'll head north along the western shore on snowshoes and take a position where we can observe Carillon, the most likely place for an attack force to be quartered.

"I want you to pick your forty best, all experienced winter fighters. Captain Speakman, you will shadow me on this one so you can learn the ropes. Any questions?"

None of the Rangers had any, so Rogers dismissed them to go select their men and prepare for the scout.

When Jacob arrived back in his section's area, his men were already waiting with expectant looks on their faces.

"Are we finally getting to go do something and get away from this

God-awful place?" Samuel asked.

Jacob nodded, a small movement that received a resounding hoot of happiness from his Rangers. Jacob shook his head and muttered "savages" before getting down to business.

"Major Eyre wants information, so he tasked the major to go get it, and we've been selected to go along, seeing we all have experience in this fine weather."

Jacob looked at his men's faces, who were all smiling, their desire to get away from the fort bubbling out in their expressions.

"We're heading up on the lake, then crossing over on the western side to go look at the Frenchies in their camp, assess their numbers and, if possible, their intent."

Peter pulled his pipe from his mouth and asked, "Intent? In udder vords, the major will probably want a prisoner or two to ask, yes?"

Jacob nodded. "If we know our commander, yes. The French and Canadians might have won the last one, but now it's our turn. See to your gear and start cooking. Samuel and Peter, head over to the quarter master and draw about a week's worth of rations."

Konkapot and Charles got their fire going while Samuel and Peter went into the fort and returned with sacks of their issued rations. They began cooking their rations, packing extra shot and powder, and checking their cold weather clothing and snowshoes to make sure they were serviceable and would not fail. Jacob made sure his stitching was still good, the gear ready to face wet and cold.

They rested when they could, each man either brooding silently on his own thoughts or carrying on conversations with his neighbors about what they could expect on this scout. As they talked amongst themselves, Jacob thought about his responsibility to take care of his men and bring them all home, but he also thought about Maggie and his new reason for living. He needed to make sure he brought himself home, preferably in one piece.

As night descended, the Rangers curled up in their blankets and slept to be ready for the morning's adventure.

The Rangers assembled the next morning. After they were inspected by Major Rogers, they strapped on their snowshoes and began their journey northward. Jacob's section was selected to lead the way. As usual, Rogers was relying heavily on Jacob and his men to be prepared to "pull his bacon out of the fire," a phrase he frequently used when talking about Jacob since the scout at Saint-Frederic and the recent extraction on the lake.

Jacob and his men moved slowly and cautiously, ever scanning the woods around them, the Ranger column mirroring them, doing the same. The snow crunched under their snowshoes, and the wind caused the trees to creak as they swayed.

The Rangers tried to keep their rifles' and muskets' firing mechanisms dry and clear with leather coverings or with their gloved hands to protect them from the moist air, which could prevent them from firing.

It took several days to make the journey north, with security and vigilance the top priority. A specter of self-doubt still seemed to be sitting on Rogers' shoulder since his drubbing at the hands of the enemy, and he didn't want it to happen again. Jacob wondered if he was maybe a bit more cautious than before, and he asked himself if this was for good or for ill.

During the night, the Rangers maintained cold camps so that fires would not give away their position to the French.

Unfortunately for the Rangers' comfort, the weather remained rainy and misty, helping to mask their movements, but making the nights cold and miserable. Jacob walked up to a miserable looking Samuel, who was trying to stay dry, and whispered, "Still think this is better than garrison duty?"

Samuel adamantly nodded his head in the affirmative. "Bloody hell, yes! Out here you might die of cold, but back there the pox will get you, or worse."

They continued to move cautiously around Ticonderoga so they could get a good view of Fort Carillon and the area around it. Nothing seemed to be out of the ordinary. The fort appeared to be mostly complete, and there were numerous campfires within the fort and in the French encampment.

Using a telescope, Rogers surveyed the area. He noticed the defenses by the trace of the piled snow, and he counted the many cannons that had been mounted.

There were some small schooners and bateaux along the lakeshore, but the snow was piled up on them, indicating that they were not going to be used any time soon. There was no sign of any increased number of soldiers or of anything being prepared for an attack against Fort William Henry or any other place.

"If my guess is right," Rogers whispered, "there are fewer here than when we last visited. So I think Major Eyre can rest easy; doesn't look like any planned attack now in the winter."

It appeared that the French had in fact gone into winter quarters, but this impression still wasn't good enough. They needed to take a prisoner to find out what the French were up to.

"Still need to know for sure," Rogers continued. "We need to grab one or two if we can get them, so we can ask them directly about their intentions."

As Rogers and his Ranges endured the cold while watching the fort, a fire crackled in a large stone fireplace inside one of the large barracks in Fort Carillon. Newly promoted captain Joseph Marin paced in front of the room, deep in thought. He hated being cooped up in the fort; he needed to be out there fighting their enemies.

Having actually defeated the infamous Rangers in a battle, he was pleased by a rumor that the defeat had come with the Rangers' famous leader, Robert Rogers, in command.

The Marquis Montcalm was away at a meeting in Quebec, so Marin decided to act on his own. He was concerned that he had not heard of any activity out of Fort William Henry or received reports of any activity in their area for the last couple of months. Perhaps the English had gone into winter quarters, but these Rangers would not have done so. They had raided before in the winter.

"If I were in their shoes," thought Marin, "I would be out looking." Marin spun on his heels and headed to his room to gather his gear, yelling for his orderly to gather men for a scout around the area for security.

Back outside, overlooking the fort, Major Rogers had just lowered his telescope and was looking around the area when he spied a flash of light off to the north. Bringing the telescope back up, he looked in the direction of the flash and observed some sleds heading along the shore towards the fort. The flash had come from light reflected off metal objects in the sleds.

Sensing an opportunity to grab prisoners, Rogers began moving his Rangers towards an area where they could intercept and ambush the sleds. They were able to move quickly, and they took up a good position for an ambush. They had not been there very long before the sleds came into view.

"Get ready boys," whispered Rogers. "Wait until they get close enough to make it count."

Jacob looked along the sights of his rifle and began leading one of the soldiers in front of the sleds, who was wearing a white capote.

As the sleds drew closer, the sounds of the harnesses jingling and the horses' hoofs crunching through the snow were heard. The soft sound of voices as the men conversed between one another could also be heard as they came closer. Nothing indicated that they knew the Rangers were there.

As the sleds pulled up next to the hidden Rangers, Rogers gave the order to fire and the rifles thundered in response. Rogers was still concerned about possible roving patrols from the fort, so only half of the Rangers fired while the other half faced out and watched the countryside in case their ambush alerted any French or Canadians who might be close by.

Jacob pulled his trigger and was satisfied when his target dropped. He began to quickly load his rifle while Rogers and some of the Rangers ran out to take their prisoners. Rogers quickly went through the sleds and secured seven prisoners who were still stunned by the shock of the ambush. Some of the prisoners were soldiers, so they should be able to provide answers to questions, even if it required some extra persuasion to get them to talk.

The Rangers quickly searched the sleds for any documents or dispatches that could shed light on the French intentions. Not finding any, Rogers ordered a withdrawal, his men dragging their prisoners with them.

Jacob and his men covered the group led by Rogers as they ran by before taking up the rear of the column. Looking over, Jacob couldn't help but notice the big grin on Samuel's face.

"Damned better than garrison," he called as he jogged past. Jacob just shook his head and couldn't help but smile. Samuel was right. It was better than being cooped up in garrison.

As Rogers and his Rangers pulled their prisoners along or prodded them with blades to make them move faster, Joseph Marin had gathered a mix of Canadians, French regulars, and some Abenaki Indians. They were moving along their route when they heard the sound of musketry in the distance.

Marin felt a surge of excitement. He had been right to trust his instincts, which had warned him that the Rangers could not have stayed away for so long. The thrill of the hunt overtook him, and it spread to the rest of his men, who picked up their pace. The snow flew up in a powdery mist as they churned through it in their pursuit.

Marin led his men through the woods, and as they were cresting a slight rise, they saw their quarry heading towards them. It seemed that fate once more had brought victory to within his grasp. He quickly spread his men out into a large line facing the approaching Provincials. He could not see the color of their clothes, but he thought how fortunate it would be if he were facing the dreaded Rangers and their leader Robert Rogers again.

No matter, he thought. The result would still be the same.

The first indication that the Rangers were in trouble came when the woods to the front erupted into fire and a few of the leading Rangers fell. Two rose wounded, and two lay dead on the ground. The Ranger column turned away from the French, some of the Rangers aiming at the enemy while the others began to run away. In the center of the column were seven Rangers, each responsible for pulling a prisoner behind him.

The prisoners picked up their pace as French balls began whistling past them; perhaps they were concerned that they would be hit by their own comrades, who might not have realized that they were mixed in with the Rangers.

Rogers directed a section to fire and cover the column while the rest turned and began following the terrain down and away from the attacking French, who were pouring out of the woods and spreading out. As Jacob fired it occurred to him that there were a lot of men coming out of the woods.

"Bloody hell, once more into the fire dear friends!" Jacob growled as he took aim and fired at an approaching enemy soldier, who fell as Jacob's ball found its mark.

The French were pouring effective fire into the withdrawing Rangers, and a few more fell wounded. Some were able to get back up and continue running, but when another Ranger tried to help a comrade, he was often hit in turn, and he too fell. Jacob could see this fight was becoming desperate, and he hoped chance or fate would give them an opportunity to escape.

From the distance, the Rangers could hear war whoops from the Indians who were chasing after them. Jacob and his men were trading fire with the enemy while their file partners ran past and took up supporting positions before their next turn to run.

At least Samuel and the others were all business now, going through their well-practiced procedures for covering one another as they moved away from their pursuing enemy.

Jacob had just fired and turned, and he was in the process of loading when he heard Charles yell out and grab his shoulder. Jacob moved over to check on him. Charles was panting and holding his shoulder, and blood was beginning to seep into his coat. Jacob looked at his shoulder as Konkapot and Samuel came over and fired at the pursuing French and Indians.

"Keep going. Bunching up like this only gives them a bigger target!" commanded Jacob, who looked at Charles. "You're okay. It looks like it caught only the meat and didn't hit the bone."

Charles nodded, grunted, and began to trot off with Jacob following.

The ravine was beginning to narrow, and the Rangers were forced to bunch up. Rogers directed his Rangers to take cover and to return fire; they would make a stand and see if they could slow down the advancing French and Indians. He directed the seven Rangers with their prisoners to keep going.

"We could move faster without those damned prisoners," Jacob said under his breath as he took up a firing position behind a large tree.

His men also took up positions kneeling behind trees and boulders. The enemy bullets were smacking the trees and boulders, and rock chips and splinters were flying. Jacob felt a stinging pain in his left forearm; he had been leaning against a tree to steady his aim when an enemy's ball struck the tree. It threw his aim off, and when he looked down, he saw a large piece of wood sticking out of his arm. Bending down, he pulled it out with his teeth, spat it out and went back to loading.

Rogers was directing the defense when he was hit by a spent ball that struck him in the upper right arm but did not penetrate. His thick winter coat had helped cushion the blow from the spent round.

But Rogers' frustration level was building. He hated leaving men behind, knowing what the Indians would do to them, and he felt the same powerlessness he had felt after the fight near Lake George. Doubt was once more clouding his judgment.

The fight continued to be hot, both sides firing and loading, moving and trying to take advantage of the terrain. The Rangers held a slight advantage as they were in a defensive line, and the French were becoming channeled and easier for the Rangers to hit. Already there were many French and Indian bodies lying about, their blood pooling and being churned into the snow.

The Rangers were taking losses as well, and Rogers was concerned that the French advantage in numbers would soon prevail. Looking over his shoulder, he saw that the men with the prisoners were away, following the frozen stream through the ravine and out into the countryside.

They had held long enough, and Rogers yelled, "Break for it by sections, fall back and catch up with the prisoners!" Jacob and Konkapot worked as a team, with Peter and Samuel right near them, followed by James who was helping the injured Charles.

While Jacob kept on eye on his men, he also watched the French and Indians, who kept pouring out of the woods.

"Where in the hell are they coming from?" Jacob wondered. "It looked like no one was there."

Now it felt as if the entire garrison at Carillon had come out after them. The barrel of his rifle was so hot from continuous firing, it was becoming difficult to load. The air shimmered over the barrel from the rising heat, sometimes making it difficult to aim clearly. Hearing the command to fall back and seeing that the French and Indians were pressing their attack, Jacob ordered everyone to drop back.

"That's enough, bound back by teams!" Jacob ordered as he brought his rifle up to cover Konkapot, firing.

As Jacob rose up to run, he felt something slam into his midsection. It was like being hit by a club that spun him around and knocked him to the ground. The pain was sharp, and Jacob couldn't see, having fallen face first into the snow.

Pushing himself up, he began to shake his head, and the snow cleared from his face. He felt strong hands grabbing his back and helping him up. Konkapot had seen him fall and had run back to help. Jacob was having a hard time breathing, and his side hurt and burned.

"Are you all right?" Konkapot yelled.

Jacob nodded weakly and then started to trot in the direction everyone was going.

Peter ran up and grabbed Jacob's left side while Konkapot picked up Jacob's rifle, grabbed his right side, and began pulling him along.

Jacob's head cleared. It was still hard to breathe, but he was able to get his feet back under him and begin to run. He took back his rifle, and the Rangers continued to trot along the frozen stream, following the rest of the men.

As the Rangers withdrew, Captain Marin sensed the time was right. He looked around and saw that a good number of his men, French, Canadians, and Indians were sprawled out on the ground, a testament to the accuracy of the Rangers' marksmanship.

The Rangers were running now, and many of their men were either wounded, limping away, or laid out in the snow.

Marin gave the command to charge, and the line surged forward after the Rangers. Marin had brought his rifle up and was aiming at the head of a Ranger who stood up just as he pulled the trigger. The ball must have hit him, for he dropped to the ground. His comrades rushed up and grabbed him, and they continued to run away.

The Abenakis rushed ahead of the French and Canadians and soon caught up to some of the wounded, whom they struck with their tomahawks.

As Marin was loading his rifle, he yelled to take some prisoners. They didn't need to kill all of them; they needed to know what the English were up to. A group of French and Canadians were able to surround a Ranger who was helping to carry his wounded comrade and took them both prisoners.

The Indians, caught in the bloodlust, were still chasing after the other Rangers.

Rogers knew it was time to flee again, and it angered him. He hated tasting defeat again so soon after the first time. He was shaking his head in frustration, seeing some of the slower Rangers already being overtaken by the enemy and either being captured or killed.

Then he took another bullet in his upper chest near his collarbone that knocked him back into a boulder, which he bounced off of before hitting the ground. He was still dazed when a Stockbridge Indian and James helped him to his feet.

"Are you hit bad?" James asked. Rogers shook his head and wheezed he was alive and could run.

As Rogers began to run, he saw that Jacob was holding his right side but was running alongside him as he was helped back onto his feet. "You alive, Sergeant Clarke?" Rogers called out, and Jacob responded, "Barely, but I am still here."

They all ran for a bit, some in sections, others in two-and three-man teams away from the ravine. The sound of shooting diminished as they moved deeper into a thick section of the forest.

It appeared the French had stopped their pursuit. When they had caught up with the seven Rangers escorting the prisoners, Rogers felt they had run far enough to be safe, and he called a halt to get a count of his men.

As Jacob leaned against a tree to rest his painful sides, he looked over at Konkapot who simply winked as he breathed hard, and then Jacob looked at Samuel who gasped, "Think we won that foot race, thank God!"

Peter couldn't help himself. He started to wheeze and chuckle at the same time. It was contagious, and everyone began to chuckle around the perimeter.

The Rangers were pretty beat up, as they took cover breathing heavy, their breath clouds of vapor in front of them. Of the original forty who had departed for this scout, twenty were unaccounted for, including Captain Speakman. Six of the Rangers present were wounded, including Rogers and Jacob.

"Damned heavy butcher's bill to pay for seven prisoners," Rogers spat as he looked at his survivors, who were watching the woods for any pursuit by the enemy.

"I need to find that commander," Rogers said. "Shake his hand before I put a tomahawk in him!"

The prisoners were unscathed, as were the Rangers who had pulled them along through the snow, perhaps saving their lives. After resting for a short period, Rogers gave the order to move out and head for Fort William Henry. It seemed the enemy had returned to their warm barracks. "No doubt to celebrate their victory over me," griped Rogers.

"Again."

Jacob grunted when he got to his feet. He had been hit in the ribs. The ball had entered just to the side of his sternum and had followed the ribs around before exiting out his side. Samuel and Peter had wrapped the wound, Jacob shirtless in the cold air while it was being done.

He pulled his bloody clothes back on and worked his way into his coat. After slinging his gear onto his back, he took up his rifle and started the march. He gritted his teeth, because the wound still burned and it was hard to breathe. But he was alive and free, which was fine with him.

"If you feel pain," Jacob muttered, "you're still alive."

He would just need some time to heal once they got back to William Henry.

It took them a few days to get back, traveling carefully because they were concerned that the French would send out pursuers. As they made their way back, they saw a dark figure following behind them. Rogers sent out a party to see who was there. It turned out to be a wounded Ranger, who was brought into their night encampment.

Shivering from the cold, the man, who was one of the missing Ranger privates, explained what had happened on the field after Rogers had led them away. Having been hit in the hip, he had concealed himself in thick bushes as the French and their Indians stormed down into the ravine.

As he lay concealed, he explained, "Captain Speakman and two other men crawled down a gully, and I followed slowly behind them hampered by my wound here, so I didn't go too far, but stayed hidden in some bushes. I could see that the captain and the men with him were in a bad way, and I watched as they built a fire and the captain began calling for Rogers. The only reply came from a group of enemy Indians who surrounded them."

The Ranger continued with his tale. "The captain tried to surrender, but the Indians rushed him, stripped him entirely of his clothes, and as he knelt naked in the snow, scalped him while he was still alive. As the Indians danced around his bleeding shivering body, the captain asked for one of the men to give him a knife or axe so he could end his misery."

Pausing for a moment, the Ranger then continued on, "As one of the men tried to give him a knife, he was grabbed and carried off by the Indians. The last man, seemingly ignored and left behind, appeared to listen to the captain whisper something to him before he stopped shivering and appeared to die. I saw the third man depart, and didn't see him again."

Rogers took everything in, nodding, and he gave the Ranger a reassuring pat, saying, "You did good, lad, you did good!"

The Rangers continued their journey home and felt relieved when they saw the columns of smoke from Fort William Henry's chimneys, but they didn't totally relax until they had entered the encampment.

Jacob was wobbly on his feet; a fever had set in the day after the battle. After arriving in their camp, Konkapot and Samuel helped him to get his gear off and then helped him to the fort's hospital.

"No, not there," Jacob protested as he was being led into the fort, but they had no choice. They knew Jacob needed medical help. The hospital was located inside one of the fort's bastions, dimly lit by candles that flickered from posts and the walls.

The surgeon's mate directed Konkapot and Samuel to some boards laid across barrels inside of the surgery. As Jacob was helped up by Samuel, he noticed that the boards he was lying on were stained, probably from blood. Jacob moaned when he was laid upon the board, sweat pouring off him from the fever.

They removed Jacob's shirt to reveal the dirty bandages around his waist, and the wound in his left forearm, which had swollen and festered. Laying Jacob down, the surgeon's mate grabbed some medical tools in a bowl and brought them over. He told Samuel and Konkapot to hold Jacob with the command, "Steady him."

Using a small knife, he opened the wound in Jacob's forearm, causing Jacob to grimace and growl. Blood and puss flowed out of the opened wound, and the surgeon's mate tossed the knife back into the bowl and grabbed some forceps. Samuel turned a slight shade of green and grimaced at the site of the puss and blood.

Using his left hand, the surgeon's mate opened the wound farther, and with his right he pulled out a large wooden splinter that was black from blood.

Both Samuel and Konkapot, though veterans of many battles and fights, had never seen such medical procedures before, and they grimaced on behalf of Jacob, who was still caught up in his fever. For the surgeon's mate, it was a simple procedure that he had done a hundred times before, and he was unfazed by it.

"Miss Alice, could you wrap this for me as I work on the other wound?" asked the surgeon's mate in an almost bored tone.

A young girl came over with a basket of bandages and began wrapping Jacob's forearm as the surgeon's mate began looking at the black and blue wound along his right side.

"Now this looks a little tasty," remarked the surgeon's mate, which drew a concerned look from Samuel.

He probed with his fingers to see if the bullet had in fact passed through, which caused Jacob to sit up quickly with a groan, Samuel and Konkapot having stopped holding him down to watch the surgeon's mate. He knocked the poor girl who was wrapping his arm down, which didn't seem to faze her. She picked herself up and went back to finishing the bandaging of his arm.

"Hold him down," commanded the surgeon's mate once again, using the same bored tone.

"These bloody bastards are crazy," whispered Samuel as he held a thrashing Jacob down.

Konkapot and Samuel pushed Jacob back down and held him by his shoulders. Tracing the discolored rib bone with his forefinger and thumb, the surgeon's mate determined that the ball had indeed passed through. The rib had been cracked, but it was intact.

"Miss Alice, kindly bandage this as well," instructed the surgeon's mate, who went over to some bottles, poured medicine into a cup, and mixed some rum with it.

"Have him drink this," the surgeon's mate told Samuel. "What is it?" Samuel asked.

"It's laudanum, which should help with the pain," said the surgeon's mate. "Give this to him a couple of times a day with rum or wine until the pain subsides."

After he was bandaged and they were able to get him to drink the medicine, Jacob was brought into a large room where the other wounded were laid on a bed of planks and straw. His fever continued to burn, and Samuel, Konkapot, and Peter took turns watching over him and giving him the pain medicine when he needed it.

Jacob tossed and turned, sweating heavily from the fever. Miss Alice and a few of the other women, mostly wives and daughters of the Provincial soldiers garrisoned there, changed his bandages or helped wipe the sweat off of his brow as his concerned friends looked on.

The Rangers did not like being in the hospital. It was dark inside the bastion, it smelled of death and disease, and there was no fresh air. This was no place for Jacob.

Konkapot was worried that the hospital would kill Jacob, rather than the fever or wounds. He left and brought it up with Rogers, who agreed and instructed him to return to the hospital and bring Jacob back into their camp.

They moved Jacob back to the encampment after two days in the hospital. Konkapot, Samuel, and the others carried him into one of the few huts and placed him on fresh straw. They still took turns watching over him, changing his bandages, and keeping him covered whenever he thrashed around and knocked his blankets off.

Even Rogers checked in on him, himself healing up from his injuries from the fight. He frequently reminding Samuel and Konkapot, "Let me know if you need anything."

A few days after the fight, the newly promoted Captain Stark arrived with more men. His recruiting had been very successful. Along with the men and supplies that Stark had brought from Fort Edward, Maggie had come as well, having learned through the Ranger grapevine that Jacob was wounded.

She rushed into the encampment and to Jacob's side. Konkapot and Samuel both looked relieved.

"This should help bring him around," said Samuel as Maggie rushed past, followed by "Aye, that will surely do it," from Peter.

"You boys have done enough," said Maggie, "and I know you have better things to do than nurse Jacob."

Maggie looked up at both of them with an intent look on her face.

"Go back to being Rangers; go find who did this and make them pay!"

The intensity in her eyes made both Konkapot and Samuel quickly agree with a "Yes ma'am," leaving Jacob in her care.

Seeing Jacob laid out, sweating and mumbling, his eyes closed shut, both angered and scared her. She reminded herself that she had known this could happen, and she should be thankful that he was still alive, after what she had heard about how many Rangers had been killed in the last couple of months.

It had been Frederick who had actually learned that Jacob had been wounded, and he had told Maggie, "Go to him, girl. Go help him to get better. We can handle things here."

Audrey had squeezed her hand and given her a bundle with clean bandages, and Frederick's wife gave her a bag of healing herbs, which she said should help in the healing process.

Jacob was burning up, and his mind and body ached. He felt like he was in a dream from which he could not wake. All around him, he saw his friends and comrades falling, either hit by bullets or by tomahawks. A large Abenaki painted in red and black, the same one he had seen in his childhood kill his father and take his brother, kept chasing him with his blood-covered tomahawk.

"You can run, but you can't hide from me," the apparition yelled.

"I will get you in the end!"

Now and then, Patrick's ghostly visage would appear with a smile on his face, and a pipe in his hand. "You'll be fine laddie, you'll be fine. You'll tough this one out."

After a while, Patrick's comments were replaced by a soothing, almost recognizable voice, but Jacob could not wake up. However, that soothing voice soon became clearer. He was not as hot anymore, and as he finally opened his eyes, he realized he was looking into the face of Maggie, who yelled with joy, "He's awake! He's awake!"

Throwing her arms around his neck, she almost squeezed the life out of him, and Jacob finally realized where he was. Konkapot, Samuel, and the others rushed in upon hearing Maggie's cry.

"See," Peter said from around his pipe stem. "Told ya she would surely bring him around."

Once Maggie let him go, Jacob was able to learn about his injuries and treatment. He was told that he had been unconscious for several days.

Jacob felt something wet and rough on his left hand. Looking over, he saw Smoke showing how happy he was that Jacob was awake. Then he jumped up and pinned Jacob down as he licked his face.

Jacob spat and sputtered as the large wolf plopped down on top of his chest and stomach, continuing to lick his face. Jacob tried to fend off Smoke's efforts with a wheezing, "Get…off…me…you…ox," as his friends laughed, even Maggie.

Then they took pity on the recovering Jacob, and Maggie was able to get Smoke off of him, but they stayed close at hand, both Maggie and Smoke.

Jacob was forced to stay in the hut and in bed for a few more days, largely because Maggie threatened to do bodily harm to him if he got up too soon. A bandaged Major Rogers, along with Stark and Putnam, stopped by to check on him and wish him a speedy recovery. As they left, Jacob could here Rogers comment, "Wish I had a nurse like that," before he turned and winked at Jacob.

Perhaps it was the fresh air or the stew that Maggie spooned for him even though he could have fed himself, but he was getting better and his strength was returning. In time, Jacob was up and moving about. His put on his clothes, which had been repaired by Maggie. She made sure as he walked that she was by his side the entire time, though Jacob didn't know if she would be able to pick him up if he fell. But he wouldn't bet against that either.

Smoke was so happy that in his excitement and desire to play, he repeatedly knocked Jacob over and then ran around the camp. Jacob was better, but not strong enough yet to chase after Smoke.

Maggie had to keep shooing Smoke away, and began carrying a bag of jerky so she could throw him a piece to distract him. He would snatch it in midair, then go sit and chew on it for a little bit. Then he would come back, looking for more.

The winter had blanketed the area in a deep snow, with ice hanging from trees and buildings. After another week of constant care and supervision by Maggie, Jacob was almost up to full strength, and he would soon be ready to return to duty.

Samuel and the others checked in on Jacob regularly, telling him about their dull garrison routines of security for the work details or limited scouts around the area.

Maggie knew it was time for her to return to Fort Edward. If Jacob was healthy, he would go back to being a Ranger and would not need her nursing any longer. With night falling, Jacob had stoked up the fire in the small fireplace, bathing the hut with a golden hue. Jacob was sitting on the bed, and Maggie sat down next to him.

"So, you finally have your strength back?" asked Maggie.

Jacob nodded that he had. "Thanks to you."

"Good," was all she said before pushing him down and climbing on top of him. As they embraced, Smoke, who had been snoozing next to the fire, opened an eye, saw what they were doing, sighed, and went back to sleep.

Maggie returned to Fort Edward the next morning with some of the fort's sleds, Konkapot and the others hugging her and giving her kisses on her cheek to thank her for taking care of Jacob. She wished them all well before climbing on the sled and departing.

Jacob might have been better, but he was still restricted to stay around the encampment, since scouting might be too much for him. Jacob attended meetings with a healing Rogers, and Captains Putnam and Stark, along with a few of the other original sergeants, to determine how to prevent what had happened to them twice. The losses were too great. They had to learn from their mistakes.

They also had to plan what they were going to do next against the French, who had become very bold and had won too many victories. Rogers was concerned that these victories would embolden the French, who would turn their attention to either Fort William Henry or Fort Edward, or both. They had to come up with a way to keep the French off balance and to regain the initiative.

CHAPTER 18

THE SAINT PATRICK'S DAY ATTACK

As winter marched onward towards spring, Governor General Vaudreuil was angry. He was getting no recognition or credit for the French victories over the English. Rather, this upstart Marquis de Montcalm was getting all of the glory that should rightfully be his.

This was his land. He had been born and raised here. This Montcalm was from France, and he didn't understand the way of life here in the colonies. It had been the Canadians who had made the difference, not these regular French soldiers, who had no idea how to fight and survive here in the wilds of the new world.

However, Vaudreuil had to accept the fact that the goal was not personal glory, but the removal of the English. Chevalier de Levis continued to advise him on this matter, saying that it would take both the experience of the native-born Canadians and the might of the regular French forces to win the day.

De Levis had just brought a proposal for an operation against the English fort at the southern end of Lac du Saint Sacrement, Fort William Henry. Vaudreuil saw an opportunity here for bringing fame and glory to his family, defeating the English, and gaining recognition from the King. If fate was with him, this Montcalm would also get killed in the process. Vaudreuil had learned from his informants that two Irish regiments, the 44th and 48th Regiments of Foot, were garrisoned at Fort William Henry. His plan was simple: attack the fort on Saint Patrick's Day when the garrison would be either drunk or hung over.

They should be easy to take with his Canadian Militia assisted by the French regulars.

Along with this simple plan, Vaudreuil would also stack the attack in his favor by ordering Montcalm to have his own younger brother, Francois-Pierre de Rigaud de Vaudreuil, command the attack. If Montcalm didn't like it, he could take it up with the King, who had appointed him as commander-in-chief and Montcalm's superior.

Vaudreuil began drafting the orders, thinking that if he could take Fort William Henry, he would split the English colonies in half, making it easier for his forces to finally drive these English squatters from the French lands.

The orders, once affixed with his personal seal, were passed to de Levis who bowed deeply, turned on his heel, and departed. This would be his year of fame and glory, not Montcalm's, Vaudreuil thought.

When the documents arrived, the Marquis de Montcalm took the new orders surprisingly well, thought de Levis. At least he didn't break anything as he began to spit and sputter.

"Who does he think he is?" exclaimed Montcalm. "This Provincial-born peasant may outrank me, but he is not my superior. How many victories has he won? How many forts has he captured or destroyed? None!"

De Levis, the consummate diplomat, stood as Montcalm vented and, as he had done with Vaudreuil, he argued that the greater objective was to serve the King, to bring victory, and to drive the English out of the French lands.

Montcalm stopped pacing, gave de Levis a dirty look, and then nodded his head in resigned agreement. With a deep sigh, Montcalm called his senior officers together to begin planning the attack.

He had to admit that a St. Patrick's Day attack was a good idea, even if it had come from a peasant. With Irish regiments mostly garrisoning the fort, attacking on Saint Patrick's Day would make this assault easy. Perhaps Rigaud Vaudreuil could even pull it off.

After receiving the instructions from the Governor General, Rigaud Vaudreuil arrived at Fort Carillon to assume command of the attack force. Montcalm warmly greeted Rigaud and welcomed him with control and a fake smile perfected during years of courtly politics and intrigues back in France.

"If he wants to play at this game," thought Montcalm, "then let's play."

Rigaud and Montcalm inspected the gathered army, which was composed of 1,100 French regulars and Canadian Militia and around 400 Abenaki and Huron warriors. To support the attack, more than 300 scaling ladders had been built and would be transported on sleds down the lake.

The plan of attack would be simple: Use the lake to move the army to Fort William Henry as it was still frozen solid. While the garrison was drunk, asleep, or hung over, use the ladders to quickly scale the walls and take the fort.

They wouldn't even need to bring any artillery with them, which made logistics easier to plan. Once the fort was secured, it would serve as their base for an attack on Fort Edward and then a march down the valley to Albany.

The weather on the day of the army's departure was pleasant—a good omen, thought Rigaud. The army traveled along the frozen eastern shore of the lake, pulling their sleds with the ladders and their gear, each platoon responsible for a sled.

Rigaud sent scouts forward, mostly the Abenakis and Hurons, to make sure there were no Englishmen on their route to ruin their surprise attack. They moved cautiously, and the scouts continued to screen their movements until they arrived across from an island called Diamond Island. It was two days before Saint Patrick's Day.

Rigaud called his officers together to finalize their plan of attack.

The force would be divided into three columns, each carrying scaling ladders with them. In front of each column was a man with a lantern and a pick. His job was to chop holes in the ice to make sure it was thick enough to support the weight of the attack columns.

If everything went well and they were undetected, the columns would fan out, each column taking a wall. They would throw the ladders up and quickly get over the walls. Once inside, they would force the garrison to surrender.

When everything was in order, the army waited for the night of the 17th, with the attack planned for shortly after midnight on the 18th. As the French Army marched towards the south, at Fort William Henry, Major Eyre looked at the grey sky, and commented, "I so hate the winter." The season always made him feel isolated and alone. Supplies slowed down as the roads became impassable, and they had to rely on sleds to move goods between Albany, Fort Edward, and William Henry. The last message he had received from Albany was that a Lieutenant Colonel Monroe with his 35th Regiment of Foot would relieve him in the spring. To Major Eyre, that was still a long way off.

He was walking around the ramparts of the fort, looking to the north and trying to predict what the French were going to do next. "What is on your mind, my friends?" Eyre asked the cold air before him, as he faced towards the north. "What are you up to?"

Although the winter had put him in a bad mood, he was proud of his accomplishments, He had fought with General William Johnson on this very spot. They had then cleared the land and built this fort from the ground up.

"A lot has changed since then," Major Eyre commented to himself, and he saw the nearby sentry nod his head, having overheard him. "A lot has changed."

Looking over the fort, its walls and mounted guns, he felt the fort could resist a major attack. The only unknown was how the walls would fare against heavy artillery or siege mortars.

"It all depends on when, doesn't it?" Major Eyre thought, his gaze again returning to the north, as if trying to see up to the French at Carillon.

After completing a circuit around the ramparts and checking on the well-bundled guards, Major Eyre took one of the ramps down into the fort and went over to his office.

Waiting for him were the officers from the 44th and 48th Regiments and some of the few remaining Provincials as well. After Major Eyre sat behind his field desk, he asked what he could do for the fine gentlemen. "Sir, Saint Patrick's Day is only a day away, and we would like to request permission for a party, sir."

Knowing that most of the men in these regiments were Irish, Major Eyre understood the request. He called for the quartermaster, who promptly reported to his office.

"How are our stocks on ale and rum?" inquired Major Eyre.

The quartermaster paused in thought for a moment, then replied that they hadn't received any supplies of rum from Fort Edward or Albany.

"Mr. Best, who runs a sutlery there, confirms that the heavy snow has prevented any supplies from Albany, and even he has trouble getting to Albany and back."

Major Eyre nodded. "How much do we have on hand here at William Henry?"

With a sigh, the quartermaster replied, "Well sir, there are some small casks of rum and brandy being used in the hospital. The one large cask of rum that we have been using for the soldiers' rations is about empty."

Then the quartermaster looked up from his thoughts. "We do have some ale though, enough for the men to get a double ration."

Major Eyre looked to the officers who were smiling. "Will that do, gentlemen?"

They agreed it would do, since they really had no choice in the matter; they had to use what was in stock.

Saint Patrick's Day arrived, and the fort began with Church call, which the British regulars but only a few Rangers attended. The Rangers spent most of their time in their encampment. Jacob and his men had the detail to take a sled and go get firewood. Samuel and the others shouldered axes, and Konkapot and Charles brought their rifles along, just in case.

As they were chopping wood, the conversation turned to the day's festivities.

"Are we going to attend the Saint Patrick's Day festivities tonight, or not?" asked Samuel, supported by the others who said they thought it would be a good idea.

Since they probably needed to let off some steam, Jacob decided and with a resigned sigh, mumbled, "Why not."

"Once we're finished here and get this wood back," Jacob added, looking at an enthusiastic Samuel, "and if we have no other duties, then yes, we'll go to the celebration."

Samuel, James, and Charles all smiled at the prospect of going to the party, while Peter shrugged in indifference.

Samuel and the others smiled, nodded, and understood that they had a job to do first, before they could enjoy Saint Patrick's Day.

Jacob and his men brought the first load of wood to the encampment and went back out for the second load, which was quickly piled in the sled and brought into the fort. When they pulled the cart into the fort, they looked around at the celebration, which had already started even though the sun was still up.

They were surprised to see that there was some fiddle and pipe music already playing, and some of the men from the British regiments were sitting around drinking ale. After they dropped off the wood, the Quartermaster smiled and pointed over to the cask and told the Rangers to go ahead and get a ration of ale. They lined up with their cups and received their ration.

It seemed the tension that had been growing between the Provincials and the regulars was not being thought of that day, as both groups mingled and toasted one another with their mugs of ale.

"Perhaps we could settle this war," suggested Samuel as he took a long drink from his cup. "If we brought all the sides together and talked over a few casks, I bet we could find peace."

"Or pieces," remarked Peter. Both Charles and James nodded in agreement.

Jacob noticed that the officers, on the other hand, were absent, celebrating by themselves, segregated from both the enlisted men and the Provincials.

Well, that's how things are in the world, us and them, Jacob thought. He pushed it from his mind and decided not to dwell upon it. Instead, he hoisted his cup and toasted to good fortune with his comrades.

Then they took their second ration of ale, and returned to their encampment outside of the fort.

As the sun fell, the Rangers could still hear the faint sound of fiddles and pipes from the fort, but it was a relatively calm celebration compared to other Saint Patrick's Days they had experienced. In the Ranger encampment, voices and laughter mingled with the sounds coming from the fort as they celebrated a relatively subdued Saint Patrick's Day.

"Rather quiet celebrations this year," Samuel said, and James and Charles nodded. "Not as much excitement."

Jacob snorted as he sat on a log, sewing a tear in his capote by fire and candlelight. Looking up from his sewing, he asked, "How much more excitement do you want? Do you want to be out there on a scout or sitting here sipping ale?"

Samuel went through the motions to make it look like he was thinking, but then responded, "Well, if I have to choose…" He paused to take a drink from his cup. "I'll choose sitting here and drinking ale!"

"That's what I thought," said Jacob, and he went back to his sewing. There still was enough light at dusk that Peter and Samuel were engaged in a game of Farkle, a popular dice game, while James and

Charles watched, smoking their pipes.

Konkapot brought over some potatoes and beef in a small pot that had been cooked in the encampment for the party.

"Any cabbage?" Peter asked.

Konkapot looked in the pot and then back up at Peter, and shook his head no.

It was not as cold anymore at night, but it was still chilly. Spring was coming soon, which meant once more they would be heading out to take the fight to the French.

From time to time, Jacob's ribs twinged, reminding him that the time for payback would be coming soon.

"Maybe I need to take it easier on myself this spring," he groaned, knowing that would not happen.

When it became too dark to play Farkle, Peter and Samuel tried to outboast one another concerning women. Jacob and the others hooted and teased either Peter or Samuel, depending on whose story was the best. In time, they retired to their lean-tos, wrapped themselves in their blankets, and drifted off to sleep.

As the Saint Patrick's Day celebration waned, out on the frozen lake Rigaud waited until he felt it was dark enough, before giving the command to send out the scouts to probe ahead to check on the thickness of the ice, followed by the assault columns with their ladders. As they moved forward, they could hear the chopping of the ice, a pause, and then a signal from the lanterns that it was safe to proceed.

It was a good night. The moon was not up, and the weather was clear. They moved slowly, carefully picking their way across the snow and ice of the lake. A few more chops, then the signal from the lanterns. The columns slowly advanced forward across the lake, the scouts probing while the attack columns crouched, carrying their scaling ladders.

Soon, they could make out the southern shore and the faint outline of the fort with a light glow from the fires inside. As they paused for the ice probers to check the thickness, Rigaud could hear nothing from the fort. It was all quiet.

Their plan was succeeding. The garrison should all be snoring or in their cups, oblivious to the looming attack.

"All the better," he whispered to himself as a grin stretched across his face.

Whenever the signal was seen, the attack columns moved forward. They could see that they were only a few hundred yards away, and there had been no call from the sentries.

Soon, Rigaud thought, soon I will be bathed in glory as the conqueror of Fort William Henry.

As the French were creeping forward, within the fort, Private Henry McKenna kicked at a pile of snow on the cold rampart of the wall. He hated night duty, but at least it wasn't as cold as it had been. It was slowly warming up as spring came nearer. What little ale he had drunk during the party had had no effect on him, and it wasn't keeping the chill from his bones.

Ah, spring he thought. And we'll be relieved and return to Albany, away from this God-forsaken frontier. At least it won't be so cold anymore.

He paced slowly along the rampart on the northeastern side of the fort facing the lake. Down below, along the frozen shore, he could see the dark shapes of the whaleboats, bateaux, and schooners covered with snow. There was also a sound, a sound of ice being chopped, coming from the lake which caught his attention. Private McKenna paused and listened, and again he heard the sound of chopping ice.

That's odd, he thought, so he called for the sergeant of the guard. When the sergeant arrived, McKenna showed the sergeant the spot that the sound was coming from. First they both heard chopping, then it stopped, and then they heard it again. Next they witnessed a light out on the lake that came on briefly and then disappeared.

"Bloody hell!" exclaimed the sergeant, who turned and ran down the ramp into the fort's parade ground, yelling, "To Arms, To Arms!"

The duty drummer woke up, ran out into the middle of the parade ground, and began beating assembly, unsure what was going on other than the call to arms.

When the sound of the long roll began, Rigaud's vision of glory quickly evaporated. They were only a short distance from the fort and could see the dark shapes of boats on the shore, but they also heard the sound of men yelling and the call to arms coming from within the fort.

Any hope that they had not been spotted was quickly dispelled when one of the cannons roared from the fort and a ball flew over their heads. The element of surprise had been lost.

The gunners, having run to their guns, began firing their cannons at the surprised white-coated enemy on the lake, forcing the attack force to seek shelter on the ground. Rigaud had no choice but to order the attack, and he told his men to commence firing at the fort.

The three columns dropped their ladders, one column moving to the eastern side of the fort, one column to the west, and the third against the wall facing the lake. The French and Canadian column to the east moved forward, hiding behind the boats. The western column used the ten to fifteen-foot rise of the shore towards the fort to take cover, as did the middle column.

As soon as the first cannon roared, the Rangers rolled out of their beds, pulled their coats on, threw their bags over their shoulders, grabbed their rifles, and headed towards the sound of battle.

Rogers, Stark, and Putnam took charge of the Rangers and deployed them along the wall that stretched along the top of the high ground that their encampment was built on. Rogers was keeping the men within the encampment, concerned that in the dark, the cannon crews might mistake them for the enemy and shoot at them.

The Rangers spread out along the encampment's wall facing the lake, watching to see what was happening. The night was pierced by the flash of cannons firing from the fort. They stayed in their positions until the sun rose to reveal the mass of French and Canadians in three positions facing and firing on the fort.

"Well now," said Samuel. "Seems we caught some Frenchies in the open. How marvelous!"

Now that the gunners could see, they began firing solid shot and grapeshot at the enemy positions out on the open lake. The area between the fort and the lake began to fill with smoke, smoke from the cannons mixed with the smoke of several hundred muskets firing at the fort. The booms of the cannons echoed off the trees and even the mountains, as they began a sustained rate of fire at the stalled attackers on the lake.

From their position along the wall, Jacob, Samuel, and the others observed the flash and booms of the fort's cannons as the battle was being played out.

"You know," said Samuel. "It's nice for a change to be an observer and not fighting in these battles. From out here, they are rather spectacular, aren't they?"

Jacob had to agree, both because it was a sight to see and because it was nice being an observer not caught in the middle of the battle.

As the sun rose, the French were able to see the terrain they were fighting in. The rise from the shore to the northern wall was covered in snow, with stumps poking through. The shore ran for about twenty-five yards from the edge of the ice, and then rose slightly for another fifty yards before the rise to the fort.

Knowing he could not advance into the teeth of the guns, Rigaud had no choice but to order his attack columns to fall back. He would have to reassess the situation.

With the exception of the area along the shore where the boats were located, the ground was mostly open, broken with some snow drifts and stumps. The French moved back out onto the lake and took positions around Schooner Island, Rigaud using his telescope to observe the fort and reason out a new strategy. He still had numerical superiority; he just had to find where he could leverage it. A plan began to form in Rigaud's mind. Perhaps he could salvage the attack after all.

As the French withdrew, Major Eyre began moving additional infantry and extra artillery to reinforce the north and east walls, as well as the northwest and northeast bastions. He was sure the French would be back to try again, and he reasoned these would be the likely avenues of their new attack.

Believing the French and Canadians were positioned out on the lake, Major Eyre had some of the smaller mortars brought up to try and blast holes in the ice if they attacked.

That should slow them down, if the lake cracks open on them, he thought.

He also ordered hand grenades brought up and positioned around the walls. Hand grenades were hollow balls, each full of gunpowder, musket balls, and a fuse. Soldiers would light the fuses and then toss the grenades.

The gunners and infantry manned the walls, looking over the top of the ramparts, waiting for the next attack. Major Eyre knew that if the enemy were able to get up close to the walls, it would be difficult to fire upon them without exposing his garrison. So the grenades would have to be dropped on them from above.

The sun rose higher, and still there was no attack. Wanting more information, Eyre sent a patrol of British regulars to scout out the French and gather what information they could. Still, seeing so many

French, Canadians, and Indians in their thick white coats and winter furs was an impressive sight.

Major Eyre was wondering why they were not attacking yet. His concern was that the French might be moving artillery up, which would explain why the attack was delayed.

From their encampment on the high ground, Jacob and the other Rangers watched the red-coated regulars, their coats easily seen against the white of the snow, move away from the fort and out onto the ice.

"That's different," said Charles and they watched to see what happened next.

"Perhaps we're rubbing off on the garrison?" said James, an idea that was quickly scoffed down by the others as they continued to watch and wait to see what happened.

The patrol went out and in a short time returned, confirming the large number of enemy personnel arrayed against them, but reporting no sign of any French artillery, especially mortars.

Major Eyre nodded in satisfaction and continued to wait. The men manning the walls relaxed some, having conversations amongst themselves as they waited to see what the French would do next.

Over in the Ranger encampment, Rogers continued to keep the Rangers inside the wall in case the gunners couldn't distinguish the green of their coats from the enemy's white.

What's keeping the French? wondered Charles, as Jacob and the others leaned against the encampment wall, watching for the enemy.

They had seen the British patrol go out and return with no sound of firing, which the Rangers though was very odd. So they watched and waited.

"It's such a nice day for a battle," groaned Samuel, as he stretched before going back to leaning against the wall and watching for the enemy. "It would be a shame and a waste of a day if we didn't get back to trying to kill one another."

The Rangers chuckled up and down the wall, as they continued to watch and wait.

Around mid-morning, the French were on the move again as three large columns once again snaked away from Schooner Island and began moving towards the fort. When they could be seen from the fort's wall, the warning went out: "Here they come!"

The order went out to stand ready, men changed the flints in their muskets and rifles, extra powder and shot were distributed, and the cannons were manned and readied.

As the fort's garrison leaned forward in anticipation of the attack, the Rangers were also reacting to the news that the French were returning, and they prepared for the upcoming attack. One of the French columns had turned and was snaking towards the Ranger encampment. From their elevated position, the Rangers could see the approaching column before it was masked by the trees along the shore line. Then the cry of "Indians to the right!" was passed within the Ranger encampment, and all eyes and rifle barrels turned towards the right. Sure enough, Hurons and Abenakis as well as white-coated Canadians could be seen moving through the trees towards their wall.

Rogers ordered Stark to take half of the Rangers from the western side and reinforce the eastern side. Then he ordered Putnam to watch their rear in case the Indians got around them. Soon, bullets began to smack against their wooden walls, while war whoops echoed from the woods. There was no assault against them, just musket and rifle fire.

Staying low, the Rangers rotated from the wall, keeping up a sustained rate of fire from half of the men while the others loaded for them. Jacob and the others watched and waited, not wanting to waste their valuable powder and shot. They could see the movement but nothing directly near or opposite their position along the wall.

Jacob looked over the top of his rifle, seeking a target.

"Do you want to sit this one out as well Samuel?" Jacob asked, and then looked over at Samuel, who was also looking over his rifle barrel.

"No," he simply replied, but with a smirk on his face. "Was getting bored at just watching. Want to get into the fight now."

The Indians made no attempt to flank or go around the encampment, so the Rangers settled into a siege, just like the regulars in the fort.

Inside William Henry, Major Eyre moved around the fort to assess the situation, which was not good. They had only four hundred men at best, and from what it looked like, the French had maybe a thousand or more.

He could see the Ranger encampment firing on a group of French or Indians in the woods, and he could see two large groups facing the fort. Their advantage was that they had cannons and, luckily for them, the French did not.

This advantage became very apparent as the fort began firing its large 32-pound cannons at long range at the enemy columns, while their mortars began dropping shot and shell on top of the Indians and Canadians who were firing on the Ranger encampment.

The men of the 44th Regiment defended the walls of the fort, while the 48th Regiment remained as a reserve down in the parade ground. The Provincials helped by pulling carts loaded with powder and shot for the cannons up the ramps from the magazine to keep the cannons firing. During the day, there were several times when the French and the Canadians launched attacks carrying their ladders. The British waited until the attacking enemy got close enough for their combined artillery and musket volleys to cause maximum damage and then opened fire.

The combined weight of the grapeshot from the large cannons and the musketry was enough to push the enemy back, and the French and Canadians resumed firing against the fort's walls as they rallied for another attack.

Some of the attackers' bullets found their marks, either hitting the upper torso of a soldier as he fired over the ramparts or passing into the fort through the embrasures for the cannons.

The surgeons were busy working on the wounded, but so far only a few had been killed. The Provincials helped to carry the wounded down to the surgeon, their places filled by either the 44th Regiment, or by men from the reserves.

They still maintained a sustained rate of cannon fire at the enemy hiding behind the rise or other obstacles, and they continued firing the mortars with exploding shot. Major Eyre not only fired on the enemy, but he also fired cannons towards Fort Edward to alert them to the attack.

In the far distance, the sound of Fort Edward's answering guns could be heard. While they might not be able to reinforce them, at least Fort Edward knew they were engaged. Major Eyre smiled and returned to directing the defense.

The new attack had only achieved encircling the fort, and now the fight had settled into a stalemate and siege. French, Canadians, and Indians took cover behind stumps and logs and began firing on the fort's walls and defenders.

Rigaud knew he still had superior numbers, but the English had a walled fort with heavy artillery. He had suffered numerous casualties when his men had rushed at the fort and were cut down by the cannons and volleys from the walls.

He had also received reports that the Hurons and Abenakis, who were keeping the Rangers occupied in a walled encampment to the east of the fort, were having little to no effect, and the Rangers couldn't be lured outside of their encampment.

As it grew late in the afternoon, Rigaud called a council of war and directed that once the sun set, they would launch an all-out attack from all three sides. They would use their superior number of muskets to keep the English heads down as the ladders went up and they fought their way over with the darkness to mask them from the fort's artillery.

"We shall overpower them, and get under the guns so we can go over the walls, and the fort will be ours!"

After waiting long enough for the officers to disseminate his orders, Rigaud drew his sword and gave the command to charge.

As they surged forward, the dusk of the evening became very bright when all of the cannons facing the French opened fire and hundreds of small projectiles from grapeshot fell amongst the attacking French, hitting some of the soldiers or hitting the ground and throwing up snow. Somehow they had been spotted, and they were taking effective fire from the artillery, causing Rigaud's men to take cover or fall from wounds.

A roar rose from the French and Canadians as they charged up the slope and got underneath the cannons, so they could no longer be fired upon. As some of the attackers aimed up at the defenders on the walls, the other Frenchmen and Canadians began raising their scaling ladders. As was done in medieval sieges against castles, the French ladders thumped against the walls and the British simply pushed the ladders over using pikes.

With the French directly underneath the walls, the British soldiers rose up to aim down at the attackers, but that exposed them to the other French and Canadians who fired back at them, hitting a few of them, which forced them either to fall back into the fort or to fall forward and down to the ground where they were killed by tomahawks or bayonets.

Instead of tossing rocks down, as had been done in medieval sieges, the British used a new method; lobbing hand grenades over the walls without exposing themselves to the French. The grenades landed amongst the attackers, shattering bone and body alike when they detonated. With the exception of a few ladders bumping against the walls and even fewer French actually setting foot on top of the walls, the assault was stopped cold.

Both sides settled down into a second night under siege. The French built fires to warm themselves, which allowed the British defenders to watch what they were doing. There was still some musket and rifle fire keeping both sides on edge.

The Rangers also settled into a night of siege. The Indians kept moving around, which forced the Rangers to shift their positions to match where the Indians went.

Jacob and his fellow Rangers rather enjoyed being spectators and not being directly exposed to the enemy attacks, other than the Indians and Canadians firing on them from the woods, trying to draw them out into the open. Jacob and the other Rangers settled into the night, rotating between manning the wall and resting.

As Jacob leaned against the wall, watching for any movement against them, Peter came up with a steaming cup of tea.

"Helps to take the chill off," Peter remarked as he handed it to

Jacob, who thanked him and resumed watching the forest. "Do you think they'll attack again?" Peter asked.

Jacob shook his head. "They would have done it by now. I guess they figured they can't break the walls. I am surprised they didn't bring artillery with them to batter down the walls."

Jacob took another sip of the tea. "They're stuck out there on the ice, and they are running out of choices. That commander out there is going to have to make a decision soon."

There were no attacks during the night, and the French were still in their positions at daybreak. Rigaud decided to change tactics, thinking he could scare the English into surrendering.

"Offer terms of surrender to him," instructed Rigaud. "Make it sound as if we are only the advanced party, and the rest of the army will soon be here."

Then he thought, and added, "Tell them we won't be able to control the Indians. That should scare them!"

He dispatched Captain Le Mercier, who happened to be the chief of the Canadian Artillery, to deliver an ultimatum to the fort's commander, hoping his bluff would work. Rigaud had run out of options.

Rigaud watched as Mercier approached the fort under a flag of truce and was met at the sally port by a British delegation. He was blind folded and brought before Major Eyre. Rigaud's message was proposed to Major Eyre, including the warning that the French would release the Indians against them.

"The rest of the army will soon be here with artillery," Mercier lied. "We will not be able to stop our Indian Allies from seeking their rewards."

Major Eyre listened to the terms and politely refused.

"With respect, and as honor dictates, we will hold out at all costs. We have enough supplies and men to defend the fort. Besides, I have not received direct orders to surrender, so I must decline."

Mercier bowed to Major Eyre, was blindfolded, returned to the sally port, and released. While Major Eyre suspected Mercier had been bluffing, he did hope reinforcements were being sent from Fort Edward at that very moment.

"I hope he was bluffing," Major Eyre whispered to himself.

Mercier reported to Rigaud that the proposal had been refused. Rigaud asked Mercier, "From what you observed, could we take the fort without siege artillery?"

After looking back at the fort, then turning to Rigaud, Mercier shook his head no. Nodding, Rigaud called another council of war, and after a brief discussion with his commanders, decided that they were going to have to break the siege and return home.

This didn't sit well with the Indian chiefs who wanted their loot, but they followed the instructions to return north.

Rigaud decreed they would burn everything they could before heading north, at least causing some damage to the enemy.

The officers returned to their units, and while half of the force fired on the fort to keep the defenders' heads down, the others made torches and began burning all of the boats along the shore, along with a few huts and a sawmill.

At least a small victory, thought Rigaud. Their fleet of boats will be useless in the spring, and the destruction of the sawmill will prevent the British from building more anytime soon.

Major Eyre observed from the walls, helpless to do anything about the burning of the boats and buildings. He didn't have enough men to venture outside the walls. His first duty was the defense of the fort. He would just have to rebuild in the spring.

Better those boats, Major Eyre thought, than this fort. We can either get or make more boats.

Observing the blazing boats and buildings, Rigaud paused to look at the fort once more before leading his army home. Casualties were relatively light, and he had travois made to help transport the injured back to Carillon. To make the situation even more depressing, light snow had turned into a major snowstorm by nightfall when they departed.

Unfortunately, some of the Rangers who had been caught inside the fort because of the party and who had remained there during the attack had become infected with smallpox.

A newly arrived Ranger, Captain Hobbs, was one of those unfortunate enough to contract the disease, and he soon joined the company of the dead in the growing cemetery outside of the fort. The sick Rangers were segregated from the company until they either healed or died from the disease.

Major Rogers had to move some of his experienced men around to fill the vacancies due to the deaths of both Captain Hobbs and Captain Speakman. Another of Major Rogers's brothers arrived, Ensign James Rogers, who was promoted immediately to lieutenant and placed in Hobbs's old company. A Lieutenant Bulkeley was promoted to captain and took command of another company. The Ranger leadership was being decimated due to illness or combat losses.

The Rangers had to lick their wounds and get back into the fight. After the reorganization, the Rangers quickly got back down to the business of conducting scouts and patrols around the forts to see if the French or their Indians were close by.

Jacob, like the other Rangers, knew that even with the failed attack on Saint Patrick's Day, the French would be back. It had been a close one. Had the French brought artillery, the victory could very easily have gone the other way.

CHAPTER 19

FORT EDWARD: A GROWING TENSION

Following the French raid against Fort William Henry, Major Rogers sent patrols of Rangers out to scour the countryside to find any French or Canadian stragglers, and a few of the patrols brought prisoners back, surprisingly without a fight.

Rogers was glad that the French had not brought artillery with them. The raid had been large enough that the French could have taken the fort, but luckily for the British, they had thought surprise would give them an advantage and artillery wouldn't be needed.

Major Eyre was proud of himself; he had defended his position against an enemy with superior numbers. Although he had lost half of the boats and schooners, his causalities had been relatively light. The wounded included Captain Stark, who had been grazed by a musket ball. By the end of the month, five companies of the 35th Regiment, foot sore and muddy from a forced march from Albany, arrived at Fort William Henry. Leading the column was Lieutenant Colonel George Monroe, who had met a messenger on the road from Albany detailing the siege at Fort William Henry.

Monroe had ordered the five companies to leave their baggage with the rest of the regiment, and they had marched at the double to get to the fort quickly in case they were needed to stop the French attack.

The rest of the regiment was slowly making its way along the muddy road to Fort Edward. The 35th was welcomed with loud shouts of "Huzzah!" by the garrison, especially by the men of the 44th, who knew their relief had arrived and they could finally leave.

Unfortunately for Major Rogers, his tired body could no longer fight illness. He too was soon racked by fever as he fought smallpox. To ensure no one else would be infected, Rogers stayed in his hut and issued written orders that he passed through a slot in his door.

Jacob and his section returned to their island at Fort Edward, where he was reunited with Maggie. She ran out from the fort when she the saw the Rangers exit the woods and nearly knocked Jacob over as the rest of the Rangers marched past on their way to the footbridge to their island. She spun Jacob around and around, crooning, "You're alive! You're alive!" Konkapot and the other Rangers walked past with wide grins, and "Hello, Maggie" and "Nice to see you Maggie" was heard from the other Rangers as they passed. She ignored them, focusing solely on Jacob, finally finding relief from the fear that had plagued her since hearing of the fighting and siege around Fort William Henry.

Arm-in-arm, Maggie and Jacob walked across the bridge and into the encampment where a group of Rangers had gathered around Konkapot and the others in Jacob's unit to hear what had really happened at the lake.

Smoke and the other wolves who had returned with Maggie from the encampment, ran out to greet their Rangers as well, Smoke again nearly knocking Jacob over in his excitement.

That night, after cleaning their rifles and gear, the Rangers settled around a large fire to tell stories to other gathered Rangers who had been at the island and not in the fight. Maggie sat snuggled against Jacob, and Ojistah, Jacob noticed, was once again snuggled up with Konkapot, as each Ranger tried to outboast the others on their bravery or their marksmanship during the fight up at the lake.

"No kidding, there we were," Samuel started a version of the battle, "surrounded by hundreds—no thousands—of enemy soldiers, all trying to get at us and kill us!"

A Provincial who had joined the gathering asked, "Weren't you all scared?"

"Scared?" Samuel exclaimed. "Yes, we were scared, we were scared we would run out of balls before we killed them all and saved the day!" Both the Rangers and the Provincials laughed and threw scraps of items at Samuel, who ducked and swatted the attacks away, all with a smile on his face.

"Was it really that bad?" Maggie asked, and Jacob shook his head. "No," he answered in a low voice so as not to disturb the storytelling. "To be honest, compared to fights we have been in before, in this one, I have to admit, I felt the safest out of all of them. We had our walls, and the Frenchies and the Indians couldn't get at us. It was a rather nice, but boring, fight."

Maggie nodded, and replied, "Hope they all stay boring." Jacob had to agree.

The next day, Jacob, Konkapot, and the other Rangers were over at Frederick's shop, trading and replacing broken items, when they spotted the rest of the 35th marching out of the woods to the south, moving along the Albany Road towards Fort Edward.

Rangers and Provincials alike turned to watch the spectacle of the marching British regulars. With their regimental flag and King's colors snapping in the breeze and the drummers playing, the column closed on the fort. While their scarlet uniforms stood out in the spring sunshine, they looked weary from the hard march, evidenced by their leggings, which were mud-stained.

"Oh no! Look there," Samuel groaned, pointing to an officer riding a horse within the column. "Ah damn!"

The Rangers and Provincials alike looked to see where Samuel was pointing, and they all groaned.

Sure enough, Captain Reynolds, now of the 35th Regiment, had returned. As usual, his uniform was clean and well taken care of, and he had a haughty expression on his face. Jacob started to search faces, and towards the rear of the column he spotted Sergeant Major Lovewell.

"Knew he couldn't be too far behind," mumbled Jacob.

While the sergeant major faced straight ahead, Jacob could see his eyes were watching them as he passed, and a smirk played across his face. Things were about to become more interesting.

Spring was slowly arriving, thawing the ground. The snow was melting away, and the mud was drying into firm ground.

Considered one of the more seasoned Ranger officers, Captain Richard Rogers returned from detached duty recruiting to again take charge of his company and to run operations around Fort William Henry, serving as General Webb's eyes and ears.

Concerned about the boldness of the French, Captain Stark directed Jacob and his men to patrol along the Hudson River to see if there was any sign of French or Indian raiding parties in the area.

"They're bold enough," Stark said. "I wouldn't put it past them to get around us and start raiding and burning farms to draw our attention and men away from defending the forts."

Prior to departing for a scout, Jacob was saying goodbye to Maggie at the shop when he spotted Captain Reynolds and the sergeant major, with some of the regulars from the 35th, walking around the walls of the fort and yelling, mostly at the Provincial soldiers.

Konkapot and Samuel, who had also come over to shop, joined Jacob as they walked past the group. Captain Reynolds was in full form, dressing down a Provincial soldier whose uniform was in bad shape.

"Sergeant major, take this man to the stockade for failing to maintain a soldierly appearance!"

The sergeant major nodded his head, and one of the regulars marched the confused soldier into the fort, the prisoner stammering, "What did I do? What did I do?" Captain Reynolds had a satisfied smirk on his face when he turned and spotted the Rangers.

"You Provincials better take notice," instructed Reynolds with a satisfied expression. "Colonel Monroe has made me the provost here and charged me with cleaning up this rabble of an army!"

Jacob and the Rangers approached Reynolds and the sergeant major.

"What was he charged with?" Jacob asked the sergeant major. "For not maintaining the proper uniform of a soldier, of course," answered the sergeant major. "He'll get a couple of days in the stockade on bread and water, which will show him the error of his ways."

Reynolds gloated. "You Provincials are subject to British discipline now, so you better shape up! We'll whip you rabble into shape quickly enough!"

Reynolds turned and stalked off. Jacob noticed the sergeant major was staring at someone behind him. He turned and spotted Maggie on the porch of the shop and realized the sergeant major was watching her. The sergeant major saw that Jacob had noticed him staring at Maggie. He looked at him, licked his lips, and winked before hefting his spontoon and moving to catch up with Captain Reynolds. Jacob felt a cold hatred for the man, and he knew there would soon be trouble between himself and the sergeant major.

They still had a job to do, and Jacob led his Rangers on their scout and began to angle northwest towards the river. Smoke, Raven, and Otto accompanied the patrol, moving like shadows around them. The dogs' keen senses might prove effective in spotting any hidden enemy war parties.

Konkapot with Peter and Raven led the patrol, with Jacob, James, and Smoke in the middle, and Samuel, Charles, and Otto at the end of the column. As they strode through the tall grass bending to the wind, scores of grasshoppers flew before the Rangers as they made their way across the field to the woods.

The Rangers spread out. The trees were still mostly bare, so the men would have to move with care. It would be some time before the trees could conceal the Rangers from the eyes of their enemies. They followed the river as it turned northward and then westward.

By midday, the Rangers had concealed themselves in a thicket near a low waterfall to take a break and eat some food. There had been no sign of any enemy war parties or scouts so far, but that didn't mean they were not out there. After taking turns eating and watching the area around them, the Rangers continued their patrol.

By dusk, they came to a second waterfall, this one larger and wider. The water, cascading over grey granite rocks in a large horseshoe, filled the air with a loud roar and a cool mist. Konkapot and Jacob had heard of this area. The Mohawks called it Chepontuc, which meant "difficult place to get around." They could see what the Mohawks meant; it was an impressive sight.

Still, if it was known to the Mohawks, it might be known to the Abenakis or the Hurons, so the Rangers scouted around the shore of the river to see if there were any traces of activity. Other than animal tracks, there were no recent signs.

With the roar of the falls making it difficult to hear each other, Jacob pointed at Konkapot, signaling him to lead them out and away from the falls to find a place for the night. The wolves, after drinking from the river, took off running ahead of the Rangers.

Konkapot and Peter led the way with Raven running ahead, scouting until they found a suitable place to rest. It was far enough away from the falls that they could hear their surroundings instead of the falling water. They moved into a thicket and took turns pulling out their thick coats. The night was still cool, and there would be no fire to potentially give away their position.

Half of the Rangers took their turns eating their cold meals while the others watched the forest and the silent grey sentinels of the mountains in the distance. When the eaters had finished, they relieved the watchers. The sky turned black, the stars twinkled above, and the light of the moon shown down on them.

The evening sounds of birds and animals on the breeze were all that could be heard. The wolves stayed near their masters. Once in a while, one would raise its head, ears perked up, and then settle back down to snooze again once determining it was nothing, as only wolves could do.

The stars twinkling in the heavens could be seen through the tree boughs, which waved in the breeze. Jacob leaned against one of the trees, watching the woods around them, but his mind drifted to Maggie back at the fort and his growing concern about the sergeant major.

The roar of the falls was a faint sound in the distance, but it echoed what was in Jacob's soul, the turmoil he was feeling. He wasn't used to being in love, and his concern for Maggie's safety with the sergeant major around troubled him. He could rely on his fellow Rangers and the Provincials who knew him to watch out for her, but it was the British regulars he did not trust.

The night passed uneventfully, and the Rangers, after their traditional stand-to was completed, finished their cold breakfast and continued their patrol. The sound of the falls was well behind them now, and the normal sounds of the forest returned.

Jacob and the others constantly scanned the woods, listening for anything out of the ordinary, as the wolves darted about them, their noses busy.

The sun had just peeked over the mountains to the east when the wolves suddenly froze with their ears perked up. The Rangers froze too; it was not a good sign when all three wolves stopped at once.

The Rangers crouched and began looking around them when on the breeze, the smell of smoke reached them. It was not the smoke of a cooking fire, but a much larger fire.

Konkapot pointed in the direction the smell was coming from, and Jacob nodded for him to lead the way. As they moved through the woods, they trees became more open, and soon a column of smoke could be seen. The Rangers reached the tree line to see a farm in the distance. It appeared to be a newly constructed house, with smaller outer buildings. Around the house, brandishing torches and looting, was a war party of Hurons and Canadians. They were dumping out chests, hurling clothes into the air, and throwing items out of the house as the roof was beginning to catch on fire.

The outer buildings were fully burning, and the Rangers could see a man, a woman, and three children on their knees being bound by two Indians who were tying cords around their necks. The Rangers' anger rose. "Bloody hell!" said Samuel as they observed the raid.

Without hesitating, the Rangers quickly fanned out into teams of two while the wolves sprinted ahead of the charging Rangers. A Huron who was admiring a silver mirror saw a grey blur in the reflection, and as he turned, he was slammed down as Otto's teeth sank into his throat. Smoke and Raven had crashed into two other Hurons, which caused the others to stop to see what was going on.

Then, three more went down with the sound of rifle fire. The war party turned to see the Rangers charging them. Three were in the process of loading, and three more were rushing towards them. The Hurons were beginning to react when three more dropped as the second group of Rangers fired, and the wolves viciously tore into the arms of the three they had pulled down.

The shock of the assault had kept the Hurons in place as the Rangers struck, and Jacob reached one of the Hurons, who was binding the prisoners. As the Huron looked up, Jacob sank his tomahawk into his face and followed through into the back of his head.

Another Huron, who was also tying the prisoners, looked up just as Samuel crashed into him, stabbing with his fighting knife. As the Huron fell, Samuel left the knife in the body and knelt down to aim at a Canadian trying to run away. He didn't get very far because Samuel pulled the trigger and took him square in the back. The Canadian tumbled forward onto the ground. Then Samuel turned, quickly pulled his knife out, and began looking for another target.

Konkapot ran into a Huron who was raising his tomahawk to attack the male prisoner, knocking him to the ground. Konkapot rode him down, placing his knee in his chest and slashing his throat with his knife. Rolling off the dead body, Konkapot moved up into a kneeling position, aimed his rifle, and killed another Huron who was running away. Jacob rushed up and used his knife to cut the cords on the prisoners, and Peter moved up to cover him. James and Charles caught two more Hurons trying to run into the woods as the rest of the war party fled.

Jacob and Peter checked on the freed family while the other Rangers searched the rest of the farm to make sure there were no other raiders. The family clung to one another, still caught in the shock of both the raid and their rescue.

The farm was a complete loss. The house was now fully burning, the smoke mixing with that from the burning outer buildings. The wolves, their muzzles stained with blood, searched alongside the Rangers.

As Jacob and Peter took care of the family, Konkapot and the others went about the grisly task of scalping the enemy dead and collecting what they could from the bodies. Other than bruises, the family appeared to be in decent shape and could move without assistance.

"What happened?" asked Jacob.

The man explained that the war party had caught the farm at dawn.

"We were just finishing up breakfast when they just stormed through the door before we could do anything and grabbed us, dragging us outside and tying these ropes around us. I thought we were done for." No French regulars or officers were found among the dead. Jacob learned from the family that they were newly arrived Quakers from Albany, who had been told of this open meadow near the great falls, which had been described as a good place to settle.

"No one told us of these savages," the mother mumbled in shock, holding her children close to her and watching their life being destroyed around them by fire.

Jacob asked if they had not been told of the conflict here, and both the man and woman shook their heads.

"We have just arrived here in the colonies, and we were told the land up here was good land and free; the government needed settlers to farm it for the crown. So we took it. What choice did we have?"

Jacob could think of several other choices, but he understood how tempting it was to get free land and not be shackled to the rules of government up here.

They continued to explain that they were members of a pacifist sect of the Quakers and wanted religious freedom.

"We do not believe in violence, and we are not part of this conflict," said the man. "We thought we would be left alone. We came without violence and thought we could live without violence. How could we be so wrong?"

Jacob shook his head, and after securing what supplies they could, began to lead the family to the safety of Fort Edward. Jacob placed the family in the center, surrounded by the Rangers and their wolves, who were scouting ahead and around the patrol. The giant plume of smoke would draw unnecessary attention, and he knew they had to get away from there quickly before more war parties came to investigate.

Jacob could understand some of the beliefs of these Quakers, because he had heard about them from other hunters and trappers who had come across them. But to think that their beliefs would protect them out here in the wilderness was madness.

The Hurons and Abenakis didn't ask about beliefs before sinking their tomahawks into skulls and burning down farms. To them, anyone who was a settler was fair game, whether they were pacifists or not. It was a tough lesson these poor Quakers had to learn, but at least they still had their hair and their health.

As Jacob and his Rangers escorted the family to safety, Jacob thought back to the day the Indians had attacked their home, killed his father, and taken his brother. The sight of the Quakers being roped together made him wonder what had happened to his brother. Had he survived? Had he been adopted into the Indian tribe, a common practice at the time to replace fallen warriors? Had he been sold into slavery, another common practice?

Then Jacob thought that had his brother survived and been adopted into a tribe, or maybe worse, converted to being a Canadian, could he possibly be out here? That thought bothered Jacob. There was an odd chance that his brother was fighting for the enemy. If so, what would be the chance that Jacob would kill him, not knowing what he looked like now? Jacob shook his head and tried to chase the thought away, but it lingered at the back of his mind.

During one of the breaks to rest the family, Samuel came up to Jacob.

"What's on your mind, Jacob? You seem lost in thought."

Jacob looked at his friend, then nodded towards the huddled rescued family.

"Them."

Samuel looked puzzled at the response. "Not like you haven't seen this before?"

"No," Jacob explained. "I was thinking about the night my house was attacked, when they killed my father and took my brother. I understand how they feel."

Samuel nodded then looked back at Jacob. "So what else is it, Maggie?"

Jacob snorted. "No, not this time. I was wondering that if my brother survived, and either was adopted by a tribe or converted to become a Canadian, might I be fighting him out here, right now."

Samuel raised his eyebrows and softly whistled. "That is a tough one."

Jacob nodded.

"So what are you going to do about it?" Samuel asked.

Jacob replied, "Not dwell on it, stay alive, keep you alive, and see another day."

Samuel smiled and gave a reassuring squeeze to Jacob's shoulder. "Sounds like a reasonable plan."

Jacob escorted the rescued family to Fort Edward, not stopping in order to stay ahead of any other war parties in the area. It was dark when they arrived, and some of the family members of the fort's garrison came out to help the rescued family, after the sentries reported that the Rangers were bringing them in.

Once the family was taken care of, Jacob reported their action to Captain Stark.

"Like you said, sir, it wasn't past them. They are attacking and raiding along the river," Jacob said. "It's going to make it tougher on us here."

Stark nodded and agreed, thanked Jacob, and told him, "well done" for rescuing the family.

As word quickly spread of war parties possibly attacking up and down the river, decisions were being made in Albany and in London that would place the region in even worse danger.

Lord Loudoun had called a council of war with his leaders to discuss campaign plans for the spring. The British had to make up for their losses from the previous year, and they decided to take the fight to the enemy instead of waiting for the enemy to move.

With the new reinforcements of British regulars from England, Loudoun believed now was the time to strike at the very heart of the French and take Quebec. He would use his trusted and reliable regulars for this task, letting the remaining regulars and Provincials guard the northern frontier.

If this plan was successful, the war would be over in a single stroke, and the glory would be his to enjoy. Timing would be everything. He had to take Quebec before winter when the weather would place him at a great disadvantage.

However, the government in London did not support his planned campaign. They ordered Loudoun to follow a more timid two-year scheme in which the British regulars would first take Louisburg, the heavily fortified city that guarded the entrance to the Gulf of Saint Lawrence, and then attack Quebec a year later.

In any case, General Webb was still ordered to use the remaining regulars and the Provincial forces to secure the New York frontier from the French and their allies. To support this mission, new Provincial companies were gathered and trained.

In the meantime, the Rangers, Provincials, and British regulars at both Forts Edward and William Henry were busy. The Rangers were constantly scouting to find the frequent enemy raiding parties, whose numbers seemed to increase as the weather became warmer and spring began to shift towards summer.

Jacob and his fellow Rangers were out on constant patrols, many taking their dogs and pet wolves with them as Jacob had done, having learned that these animals could sometimes spot a hidden enemy in ambush before their human masters.

The Rangers were making frequent contact with the enemy; just about every other day, there was a report of a fight or skirmish between the Rangers and the Canadians or Indians.

Fort Edward was a hive of activity as spring bloomed around the valley. Major Henry Fletcher of the 35th Regiment had assumed command of the fort. Roughly three thousand soldiers now made Fort Edward their home, making it the fourth largest settlement in the colonies. There was constant motion as regulars and Provincials marched about or were kept busy in work details. A city of white tents was growing outside of the walls of the fort, which was no longer able to house all of the newly arrived soldiers.

Garrisoned at Fort Edward were five companies from the 35th Regiment and two hundred men from the newly formed 3rd Battalion of the 60th Regiment, known as the Royal Americans, as well as Provincial troops from New York, New Jersey, Connecticut, and Rhode Island. Jacob had not seen so many soldiers all in one place before, and it was a sight to behold.

Major Rogers was still weak, but he had won his fight with smallpox. Lord Loudoun sent word for him to come to Albany and get ready to lead the Rangers again. Captain Stark would accompany Rogers to Albany, which made Stark feel better, seeing the still-weakened condition of the major.

When Rogers and Stark arrived in Albany, they observed two newly raised companies of Rangers waiting, which were a welcome sight. However, Rogers learned these companies would not be joining him at Fort Edward. Lord Loudoun had stipulated that he could not conduct operations in Canada without the Rangers, and these companies had been assigned to support "foreign service" and would join the rest of the expedition that was being gathered for the attack on Louisburg.

Rogers also learned that a sixth company of New Hampshire Rangers had been formed under the command of Captain John Titcomb.

As Rogers reviewed the men in these two companies, he saw that while they were called Rangers, they had nowhere near the proficiency of his own Rangers. Lord Loudoun was taking his time, massing his fleet, troops, and resources at Albany. This allowed Rogers and Stark to try to give these new Ranger companies a quick "Ranger School" before they left for New York City.

While Major Rogers was away, tension was growing amongst the soldiers garrisoned at Fort Edward. Many of the British regular officers and some of their men looked down upon the Provincials as unprofessional rabble playing at being soldiers.

This situation was made worse by Captain Reynolds' position as the provost. He had never liked nor approved of the Provincials, and he took his dislike out on them daily. It seemed that he went out of his way to find several Provincials to throw into the stockade each day. There were also daily floggings or other punishments of both Provincials and regulars, but most of the punishments went to the Provincial soldiers. The stockade was always full of men who had been charged.

This tension was driving a large wedge between the Provincials and the regulars, and the desertion rate was rising. Even the men from the Royal Americans were not happy. They had been recruited under what they believed to be false pretenses. Most of the men were disillusioned and were beginning to vocalize their complaints.

Jacob and the other Ranger sergeants worked hard to keep their men away from the roving provost, not giving him the satisfaction of taking any of them to the stockade. The Rangers stayed busy. If they weren't out looking for enemies, many were hunting to restock the growing garrison's food supplies. Rangers even volunteered to escort supply wagons or sutler wagons, especially Frederick's, to stay safely away from Captain Reynolds and his trusty sergeant major.

The tension was even growing amongst the Provincials themselves like a disease worming its way through the whole body of the army. When a contingent of the New Jersey "Blues" marched by with martial music and flare, the column of wagons and carts also included their wives, mistresses, laundresses, and prostitutes.

This angered the more pious Massachusetts and Connecticut men. They had marched with no families and only their equipment, and seeing these women and prostitutes saunter past caused them to grumble.

Captain Reynolds and his trusted sidekick Sergeant Major Lovelace operated within this seething pot of tension. Along with punishing mostly Provincials, they tried to go after Rangers whenever possible. Jacob wondered if a good chunk of the tension felt throughout the fort could be attributed to these two, who seemed to go out of their way to make everything more difficult.

Prior to his departure, Rogers had known that Reynolds and the regulars were on the warpath against the Provincials, determined to bring them under regular British discipline. He instructed his officers and men to watch out for one another and to watch themselves. If there were to be any disciplinary actions, he—and not Reynold—would take care of it. But the timing was bad with Rogers and Stark away just as the tension had nearly reached a boiling point.

In addition, Jacob's fears about the sergeant major's obsession with Maggie were proving true. She frequently told him that Lovelace waited for Jacob to be out or away and then made his presence known to her. She found the man disgusting, and she made sure she was never alone when he was around.

"He strikes me as an awful, dreadful man," Maggie seethed. "There is something dark and sinister about him I don't like."

Jacob nodded, but knew he had to be careful with his growing hatred of that man, lest he fall victim to the waiting Captain Reynolds and his system of justice.

Frederick and his wife watched out for Maggie, as did some of the Rangers and even the Mohawks when Jacob was out on a scout or work detail. Whenever possible, someone was close by keeping an eye on Maggie and an eye out for the sergeant major.

However, with the French and Indians so active, many of the Rangers and Mohawks were out dealing with raiding parties. And even with all of these people looking out for her, the sergeant major was always around Maggie, stalking and watching.

One of the major problems with warming weather when so many people were living close to one another was disease. As had happened up at Fort William Henry, smallpox was breaking out throughout the garrison of Fort Edward, among regulars and Provincials alike. A long log building fifteen feet wide and eighty feet long was built to serve as a smallpox hospital out on the island away from the fort, but close to the Rangers.

Jacob and the others stood there and glumly watched the construction of the smallpox hospital near their camp.

"Do you think our beloved Captain Reynolds may be behind the location of the hospital so close to us?" asked Samuel, which got everyone thinking.

It would not be above Captain Reynolds to "advise" the fort commander about the location for the hospital, given his role as provost and his known dislike of the Rangers.

"It would be nice for the major to get back," commented James. "We need someone to stand up to these other officers and fight on our behalf." So many men and their families living in such close proximity helped the disease spread quickly, and the hospital was filling up. Additional smaller hospitals were built inside the walls of Fort Edward, run by the different regimental surgeons.

Along with smallpox, the men suffered from camp distemper, dysentery, diphtheria, typhus, and typhoid, all quickly spreading in the tightly packed living conditions of the fort and even out on the island.

Camp life in the garrison was not very pleasant with so many people now making Fort Edward their home. In addition to the different types of dwellings, ranging from log barracks and huts to lean-tos made from tree boughs, there were the soldiers' latrines or "necessities" dug around the perimeter and in between the huts.

There were no regulations on camp maintenance. Piles of garbage, rotting peapods, bones, and animal skins were scattered around the camps, and mixed with the necessities, they created a foul stench. That smell, together with unwashed bodies, dirt, and sweat, contributed to the unhealthy environment. With combat and the different diseases taking their toll on the men, numerous freshly dug graves appeared regularly in the fort cemetery.

Everyone was expecting an attack by the French, even as they were preparing for an offensive against them. Along with the Rangers, the 35th Regiment, the 60th Regiment, and the Provincials were sending out numerous patrols, mostly along the roads, and conducting sweeps near populated areas.

The Rangers and some of the 60th Regiment scouted the frontier and the deep forests on both sides of the lake. For a "regular" unit, the 60th seemed to work well with the Rangers, and they made numerous combined scouts of the area.

Still, enemy raiding and war parties were getting through. Rangers who were not out on patrols were normally assigned as security details for the work parties around the fort. British regulars on one of their patrols were attacked between Forts Edward and William Henry, and four regulars were killed, with another four captured. Even the Rangers were caught sometimes, having three men captured just thirty-five yards from the fort.

As spring turned to summer, the fighting began to heat up around the forts and the lake. There was also sporadic fighting between Provincials, Rangers, and even some of the regulars, though they feared punishment under the provost. The growing tension sometimes had to boil over.

Jacob could see the tension growing, even among his own men, and he had to separate Samuel and James after a prank went too far and they nearly came to blows.

"Remember the major's instructions!" Jacob growled as he pulled Samuel and James off of one another after their argument had grown into a tussling match.

"We take care of one another—we don't fight each other, we fight our enemies out there!" Jacob scolded the two, pointing to the north.

Then he looked at both James and Samuel. "Keep these shenanigans up and Reynolds and the sergeant major will be all over you, and I can't save you then. Do you want that to happen?"

Jacob looked at both of them, who seemed to look abashed, lowering their eyes and mumbling, "No."

Still looking at the two, Jacob warned, "Don't give that bastard the opportunity or he'll have the hide off of you, just because you're one of us."

Jacob also thought the sergeant major would love to get his sadistic hands on them because they were his friends and comrades. Jacob made the two shake hands and they returned to duty, and after a short time, it was as if nothing had happened. Jacob was still concerned though; this tension was only going to get worse unless they found a way to ease it.

Jacob and his Rangers were sent out to some of the villages to the south, partly for some recreation, but also to see if there were any signs that the French or their Indian allies were bypassing the forts and raiding the farming villages. It was also a safety measure to keep them separated from the regulars and Provincials to avoid any fighting.

While this route was normally less exciting than scouting northward along the lake, the Rangers took their responsibility seriously when checking the roads.

The taverns that they visited didn't mind the Rangers when they stopped by. They knew that when the Rangers were around, the enemy was not, and that the Rangers always seemed to have bags of coins on them from their back pay.

It felt good to let their hair down for a change, as Jacob and his Rangers drank and sang, sometimes including the local farmers, who were always looking for stories about the fighting. Jacob knew this helped to ease some of the tension for his men, and he joined them with the singing and drinking.

Peter, Samuel, and Charles tried to outdo one another with the storytelling, making the tales more and more grisly and epic. Konkapot and Jacob sat back, smiled, and watched from over their tall tankards, laughing at the locals' reactions to the stories.

Soon, they would have to return and the tall tales would turn into reality, so the Rangers enjoyed their time away, before they shouldered their rifles and returned to the frontier and Fort Edward.

CHAPTER 20

FORT EDWARD: THE MURDER

Jacob and his men returned to Fort Edward and went back to their routine of scouting or working around their island. Unbeknownst to them, the quiet would soon be shattered, as once more the enemy was bringing the fight to the English and the Provincials at Fort Edward.

A French and Indian raiding party was silently closing in on Fort Edward from the northeast. Moving slowly and silently, they crept forward towards their objective, getting close enough to attack one of the work details outside of the protection of the fort's walls.

Sergeant Michael De Lusignan slowly led his ra iding party forward. The party included seven French private soldiers and around ninety Huron and Abenaki warriors. They had spent most of the night crawling forward quietly, hiding from the numerous patrols of Rangers, Provincials, and regulars around Fort Edward. Their mission had two simple goals: spread terror and gather information.

Sergeant De Lusignan had moved his raiding party to a good position from which to watch over the valley and the fort. Most of the activity of the British and their troops was to the north and west of them. This sat well with Lusignan, who wanted to avoid a pitched battle with British regulars if possible.

Using a small telescope, Lusignan spotted his opportunity. A work party of men carrying axes and a small group of Provincial soldiers, perhaps totaling only thirty, departed from the fort and begin to walk their way. They were heading towards the woods close to Lusignan's position.

He silently signaled his men to get ready and to follow him.

While the unseen enemy was close at hand, Sergeant Major Lovelace was drunk, sitting in the shade amongst the empty wagons outside the fort with two empty rum bottles at his feet and his spontoon leaning up against one of the wagons.

"What a terrible place this is," he mumbled as he took a long pull from the third bottle of rum.

This was supposed to be easy duty, following that blowhard Captain Reynolds around, staying out of the fight. He had quickly learned that while Reynolds was a pompous ass, he avoided combat and knew how to stay alive. Reynolds also allowed him to belittle and abuse these pathetic, cheeky, slovenly soldiers. It was a win-win situation. Lovelace smiled. Oh how he relished the pain of others, especially those Provincial bastards he had flogged and punished out of spite.

But if he wasn't careful, he could be pulled into the fighting and get killed. Living out here among the savages and dirty Provincials was wearing on him. How he wanted to go home, or at least back to civilization! "This is no place for a professional like me," bemoaned Lovelace.

"It's starting to get dangerous out here."

He took a long pull and emptied the third bottle, which he tossed on the ground by his feet near the others. What he also wanted was a woman, and that little tart over at that sutler would do just fine. Staggering to his feet, he placed his hat on his head, grabbed his spontoon, and lurched over towards the sutler.

"Yes, she would do nicely," Lovelace whispered and licked his lips as he staggered towards the shop, thinking how it would also enrage that Ranger she seemed to be keeping company with.

"Yes, that would do nicely."

Maggie was working around the shop, stocking new items freshly arrived from Albany when Frederick came up and asked if she felt like getting some fresh air. He was sending one of his workers, Jabez Fitch, out to cut posts for the fence he was building around his now-popular shop. The day was pleasant and sunny, and he thought perhaps Maggie could use some time to get fresh air since Jacob was out on another patrol.

"It's a nice enough day lass," Frederick said as he looked outside. "Go get some fresh air and some time away from all this chaos."

Agreeing that it would be nice to have some fresh air and to hear the birds in the woods, Maggie went with Jabez. She pushed their small handcart as he shouldered an ax and a fascine knife.

As they headed out from the shop, they joined up with a work detail of axmen and Connecticut Provincials. They bantered back and forth, exchanging pleasantries.

"For some extra rum, we'll cut those posts for you miss," volunteered some of the Provincials, but Maggie shook her head and they headed off to where they would chop the firewood. She turned with Jabez to go to a less forested area where the trees were smaller and easier to make into fence posts.

Shadowing them was the sergeant major, who weaved as he followed but kept his distance, not drawing attention to himself. He licked his lips again, waiting for his opportunity.

"Yes," Lovelace said to himself as he lurched slowly behind, using his spontoon as a cane to keep him from stumbling. "The woods would be a nice place for a roll with this tart."

To the north of Fort Edward, Jacob and Konkapot were searching the ground for any signs of tracks. Their mission was to see if they could find those Rangers who were believed to have been captured after the recent ambush, but who might have escaped. Perhaps they were injured and could not make it back to the fort.

By accident, they found something more important: the trail of a large war party that was making every attempt to conceal its presence. They had just happened to come across a foot scrape, which led them to a campsite. Jacob had the Rangers spread out, and they found the war party's trail. They didn't like the general direction, which was towards the fort.

Jacob pulled the Rangers in, with Smoke, Raven, and Otto joining them. Kneeling with them in a small circle, Jacob whispered, "This is bad. We can't look for those Rangers anymore."

Everyone nodded. This trail of a possible enemy war party was more important.

"We'll track and follow the trail. If we can get to the fort ahead of them, the garrison needs to be warned."

The men agreed, knowing this was a risky opportunity, but they couldn't just let the enemy move around freely in their woods.

Jacob pointed to the direction to move in, and Konkapot, Charles, and Raven led the way, followed by the rest of the Rangers, moving carefully and on alert. While the enemy had tried to conceal their trail, there were still enough of them that it wasn't too difficult to find signs to follow, especially with the wolves tracking and leading the way.

As Jacob and the Rangers began following the enemy tracks, Sergeant Lusignan had already positioned his men well to ambush the approaching work detail. The hard part was keeping the Hurons and Abenakis quiet, because they thirsted for blood. It was a matter of patience and waiting like good hunters, which the Indians understood, so they settled into their hiding spots.

"Soon my friends, very soon" he whispered.

The woodworkers had arrived, and the axmen had begun chopping on trees. The sound of the axes mixed with the warm breeze and chirping of insects was lulling the Provincials and making them forget the possibility of nearby enemies. Lusignan still waited, wanting to watch and see if these Englishmen would let their guard down. That would be the time to strike.

Instead of actively watching the forest for danger, most of the Provincials were grouping together and standing around, resting on their muskets. A few appeared to be looking around, but their hearts weren't in it.

Lusignan watched the workers for a while, getting their patterns down. The axmen were collecting firewood, which they stacked in the middle of a clearing, possibly waiting for a wagon.

He could not believe his luck. They were actually working their way deeper into his trap. Using his hands to signal his men and the Indians, they slowly brought their weapons up and aimed at the unsuspecting enemy, fingers on the triggers, waiting for the command to be given.

"Just a few more seconds," whispered Lusignan.

As the French and Indians prepared to ambush the unsuspecting Provincials, Maggie was collecting the wood that Jabez had cut and shaped into fence posts with his fascine knife. Frederick had been right; it was nice to get away from the cramped camp and fort and to feel the breeze on her face, hearing the sounds of the forest mixed with the sounds of axes not far away.

As she placed the posts in the cart, she wondered where Jacob and his Rangers were and whether they were safe. She liked the men who were with Jacob. They were her friends as well as his, and they took care of each other. They were like a large family of big brothers.

Sighing and nodding to herself, Maggie chased those thoughts away and got back to work. From the shadow of a tree, the sergeant major watched with darkly intent eyes. With a grin, he thought that the boy wouldn't be a problem and then that young tart would know what it was to be with a real man, not that savage of a Ranger.

The sergeant major had quickly come up with a plan, even with his rum-muddled brain. He drew a tomahawk from his belt and slowly stalked forward towards Maggie. While unplanned, his timing couldn't have been more perfect.

The sound of wood axes quickly changed to the sound of muskets and war whoops as Lusignan commenced his attack on the woodworkers. The axmen were caught by surprise, and the bullets hit them and the trees around them, wood splinters flying through the air, which was filled with the sounds of firing, war cries, and the screams of the wounded.

A few of the axmen fell, spinning to the ground while the others dove amongst the trees and stumps to escape the fire. A few of the Provincials were able to get some shots off before they too were struck down in the hail of fire from the enemy.

The Indians charged forward with their tomahawks and knives raised, their blood-curdling war cries echoing from the trees, ready to take scalps. The sound reached the fort, and the officer of the day yelled to beat the long roll while the Rangers out on the island were shouting to turn out. Men grabbed their muskets and rifles and began to quickly form into their companies, while the Rangers began to move in their smaller sections.

Jacob and his men looked up as the sound of the firing reached them, and they all silently acknowledged that they had to pick up the pace. "Damn, we're too late," growled Jacob, and without his having to order it, the Rangers and wolves began to run, heading towards the sound of the fight.

When the sound of musketry and war whoops filled the air, Maggie and Jabez instinctively dropped their armloads of wood, first turned in the direction of the firing, and then turned towards the fort. That's when they spotted the sergeant major approaching them with the tomahawk and an evil glint in his eyes.

Both of them froze in place, and then Maggie yelled to Jabez to run. Instead of heading towards the fort, Jabez grabbed his fascine knife and charged the sergeant major. Oblivious to the sound of the nearby enemy raid, the sergeant major focused only on his prey. Maggie quickly looked for a weapon, picked up a freshly cut fence post, and held it like a club.

Jabez ran screaming at the sergeant major, swinging the knife. Even in his drunken state, the sergeant major deftly blocked the knife with his raised tomahawk, then pushed it past. When Jabez moved past him, the sergeant major turned and sank the tomahawk into the boy's head. The strike's angle was off, and the tomahawk stuck in his victim's skull.

No matter, thought the sergeant major.

He drew his knife and started towards Maggie, frozen from the horror of witnessing the senseless murder of Jabez. She quickly regained her senses, dropped the too-large club and took off in a dead sprint, hiking her skirt up and running through the woods towards the fort.

She ran as quickly as she could, branches slapping at her as she made her way through trees that were also being hit by multiple shots from the enemy attack on the wood cutters. She heard nothing of the ambush, caught up in her own need to run from the sergeant major and survive.

"Come here pretty. Don't play hard to get!" yelled the sergeant major, who was running in pursuit.

As Maggie turned to look over her shoulder to see how close he was, her skirt caught a branch and she fell. The sergeant major sensed his victory. Maggie was just getting to her feet again when he caught her. Maddened by his desire and oblivious to the enemy bullets whizzing around him, he grabbed Maggie and dragged her to her feet. As she struggled against his grip, she tore her chemise, but she clubbed him in the side of the head with her fist. Backing away, he growled as he shook his head to clear it from the strike.

"You'll pay for that, my little tart. I'll really make you pay for that." As he stalked closer, Maggie quickly grabbed a branch, pulled it back and let it fly into his face. The branch opened a cut and drew blood over his eye. His face was stinging, and with a predatory growl, he reached out and caught Maggie by the sleeve just as she turned, stopping her cold.

Jacob and the others were racing through the trees and bushes, the sounds of battle growing more intense as they got closer. Then the Rangers broke from the trees and entered the valley surrounding Fort Edward. They did not slow their pace; in fact, they sped up as they curved towards the growing battle.

The scene was utter chaos as Jacob and the Rangers arrived at the fight. Most of the woodcutters were down, along with some of the Provincials. The rest had found cover behind the trees and were returning fire to the French and Indians.

Jacob could also hear firing from the other side of the woodcutters. It sounded like the French were shooting at soldiers who were responding from the fort. The Rangers quickly paired up and began systematically taking turns firing and covering.

"Watch your targets!" Jacob yelled, "They are all mixed together!"

Jacob and his Rangers slowed, picking their targets before pulling the triggers on their rifles and then loading on the move.

The wolves were racing forward and snapping at the Indians, then fading back into the woods. When both Raven and Smoke suddenly froze, it drew Konkapot's attention. His eyes followed to where Smoke was looking, and he spotted the back of a red-coated soldier who had grabbed Maggie.

"What in the hell?" Konkapot growled. He believed he could identify the red-coated soldier.

Konkapot turned and yelled, "Jacob, Maggie is in trouble!"

This caused Jacob to turn, and both Raven and Smoke raced towards the sergeant major's back. Jacob couldn't believe what he was seeing in the middle of this fight, and his cold rage finally burst into a hot, molten desire to kill that man once and for all.

Jacob began to sprint towards Maggie, yelling, "Turn and face me, you bastard!"

The sergeant major, hearing, turned to face Jacob and Konkapot, pulling Maggie in front of him. Just as he turned to face the charging Rangers, three Indians ran out of the woods and into Konkapot, two of them knocking him down.

Konkapot quickly recovered, rolling to his feet in time for him to spin and catch one of the attacking Indians, throwing him over his shoulder. Seeing Konkapot in trouble, Jacob reacted quickly, throwing his tomahawk, which sank into the back of the Indian who was about to attack Konkapot from the rear.

Both Smoke and Raven hit the third Indian, their jaws locking on his arm, and the two wolves pulled him to the ground. Then Raven began to viciously tear the Indian's arm apart as Smoke let go and continued racing towards Maggie.

Raven, having finished with her first quarry, clamped her jaws around the throat of the Indian Konkapot had on the ground, killing him quickly. She then raced after Smoke, running towards the sergeant major. Jacob was closing the distance on the sergeant major, but he was afraid he wouldn't be fast enough so he brought his rifle up to his shoulder and took aim.

Sergeant Major Lovelace knew he would not survive and would not take Maggie as his prize. He saw the Ranger she cared for bringing his rifle up to his shoulder. He could also see the two wolves with bloody muzzles heading in his direction. In either case, he knew he was a dead man. With a grin, holding Maggie to his front and turning to face Jacob, he whispered, "Take your last look, bitch. If I can't have you…"

With a quick motion, the sergeant major drove his knife deep into Maggie's back as he looked over her shoulder and saw Jacob's rifle flash in front of him. It was the last thing he ever saw. Jacob's bullet struck him just above his nose and blew out the back of his head.

Maggie could see Jacob racing towards them, her heart beating for joy, when she felt the sharp, burning pain in her back. She didn't know what had happened. She had lost the ability to stand, and then there was an explosion and the sergeant major was dragging her down to the ground.

The ground rushed up, but she felt nothing. The sharp pain had gone away, but she couldn't move, and it was becoming harder to breathe. As he pulled the trigger, Jacob watched the sergeant major's head explode in a reddish mist, and then it looked like he had pulled Maggie down with him as he fell. Jacob ran over and dropped to his knees, sliding next to Maggie. She was lying on her side, facing him, but her breathing was raspy and she looked to be in distress.

Behind her was the body of the sergeant major, the bullet entrance wound just above his nose, his eyes looking up and crossed, and a stupid grin on his face.

Jacob lifted Maggie, and that's when he saw the knife in her back, buried to the hilt.

"No! No! No!" Jacob screamed and dragged Maggie towards him, pulling the knife out of her back. Raven and Smoke paced around Jacob, looking for anyone who might attack. They seemed to sense something was wrong and they had to protect both Jacob and Maggie.

Jacob could tell the damage that had been done. She hadn't much time to live. He cradled Maggie to him, tears falling, overwhelmed by a pain and sorrow he hadn't felt since his parents died.

"I don't feel so good … Jacob," Maggie gasped, and a small trickle of blood escaped from her mouth and down her cheek. Jacob reached up and gently wiped the blood away. He cradled her and rocked her back and forth, the tears flowing down his face and into Maggie's hair.

"I … love … you… " Maggie gasped one last time before her last breath wheezed out of her lungs, and she no longer felt anything but peace. It was as if Jacob's very heart and soul exploded into a bright white light, as all of the rage and pain he had been holding for years burst forth into a heart-wrenching scream. The battle, the sights and sounds of it, all disappeared as Jacob no longer focused on the event. He crashed into the depths of despair as his entire being separated itself from the reality of the fight and was consumed by the reality of Maggie's death.

The howl of anguish that came from Jacob, eyes closed and sending his cry towards the heavens, was so loud it actually caused a momentary pause in the fighting. Even Smoke and Raven jumped at the sound that came from Jacob's anguished throat. Three Hurons turned towards Jacob's kneeling form and ran towards him, their tomahawks raised to strike. Jacob, consumed, did not notice the approaching enemy, but his friends did.

"Jacob, watch out!" yelled Samuel, who had caught up with Konkapot, having heard his shout about Maggie being in trouble.

As one, Konkapot and Samuel fired at the same time as Smoke and Raven leaped. Two of the Hurons fell, and the two wolves in tandem took the third from the side, knocking him down with Smoke closing his jaws on the Huron's neck.

Jacob felt nothing, heard nothing. His world had stopped when Maggie died. Peter, Charles, and James joined Konkapot and Samuel, watching the woods as Konkapot and Samuel tried to get Jacob to stand.

Peter was shaking his head. "Jacob's out of it. We need to get him back to the island or the enemy will kill him," he said.

Samuel agreed and tried to help get Jacob to his feet while the others covered them. For the moment, the fighting seemed to have shifted away from them, and they had some space.

Jacob was still rocking back and forth, eyes closed and holding onto Maggie tightly.

Kneeling down and carefully placing his hand on Jacob's shoulder, Samuel said in a low voice, "It's all right. We have Maggie, so you can let go. We'll carry her to the island. We need to go now."

With a numb nod, Jacob slowly let her go, and then quickly rose. Before anyone could react, he yelled and headed towards the enemy. Peter and James quickly tackled him before he went too far, believing Jacob had lost his mind and was consumed by a death wish.

Jacob howled and thrashed, and Peter and James had to sit on him to control him. In a few minutes, the rage passed, and Jacob nodded that he was back to normal. Peter and James slowly let him up but stayed close to him as he returned to an almost catatonic state.

Gently cradling Maggie, Samuel turned to carry her towards the fort, escorted by James while Peter and Charles helped guide Jacob back towards the island, watching the woods around them. The three wolves circled the group, sensing that something was wrong and watching for the enemy as they moved.

Konkapot looked around. It seemed the French and the Indians had had enough and were fading back into the woods. The regulars and Provincials from the fort had not made it to their area of the fight yet, but they saw some Rangers close by, and Konkapot whistled. The Rangers turned and, seeing it was Konkapot waving at them, came running over.

When they saw Maggie's dead body being carried by Samuel, Jacob being escorted by Peter and Charles, and the dead body of the sergeant major, they understood what must have happened.

Konkapot whispered, "We need to keep this quiet, between us, and we need to get Jacob back to the island."

They nodded and began moving back with the other Rangers towards the fort.

As the group began their mournful journey towards the island, Konkapot turned, and drawing his knife, scalped the sergeant major of what little hair was left, so the British would think the Hurons or Abenakis had killed him. Konkapot then moved back towards the fort, tossing the bloody scalp into some dead trees.

"Not worth the shilling," he spat, not wanted anything to do with it.

While he was happy that the sergeant major was dead, he felt a brother's sorrow for Jacob, and he, too, mourned the loss of Maggie.

Using the wood cart, the other Rangers who had come over to help, loaded Jabez's body as Samuel gently laid Maggie's body next to him, and the group pushed the cart towards the fort. Jacob walked as if in a trance, his mind still lost in his despair.

Konkapot and Samuel stayed with him, while the other Rangers pulled the cart towards Frederick's shop. No one seemed to notice them as sections and platoons of Provincials and regulars passed by, heading out to where the fighting had occurred.

As the Rangers closed on the shop, Frederick's wife Martha, who had been watching the fight in case they would have to run into the fort, took notice of their cart being pushed towards them. She yelled for her husband and then ran out to the Rangers and the cart with a look of extreme fear on her face. Frederick had just reached the porch when Martha saw who was in the cart, and she let out a cry of loss.

Frederick took a deep breath and sighed. He called for some of the helpers to come out and give them a hand with Jabez and Maggie. Martha was weeping softly when Maggie's sister came around the corner and saw them lift her from the cart. She fell to her knees and let out an anguished wail. Martha ran over and wrapped her arms around the girl, and the two comforted each other.

Two of Frederick's helpers moved Jabez's body around behind the store and into one of the work sheds. The Rangers carried Maggie's body inside the shop and into one of the back rooms. Jacob just sat down on the porch and stared at the fort. Peter and James remained close to him, in case another suicidal thought entered his mind and they had to tackle him again.

Frederick asked Konkapot how it had happened. "Was it the French or the Indians?"

Konkapot shook his head slowly, and told him the sad story.

"During the fight we saw that a red-coated figure had grabbed Maggie, and then we realized it was the sergeant major. We were not fast enough to stop him from stabbing her in the back."

Frederick laid his hand on Konkapot's shoulder. "You did what you could lad, you did what you could." Then Frederick shook his head.

"So what happened to the bastard?" he asked.

Konkapot told him how Jacob's shot took him in the head and killed him straight out, but the damage had already been done to Maggie.

Frederick had known that the sergeant major was trouble, and he was glad that it had been Jacob who had finished him.

"Still too good for that sort of bastard. He needed to die a slow and painful death."

As Frederick was looking over at Jacob, he and Konkapot noticed Captain Reynolds riding by, asking if anyone had seen his sergeant major. Both Frederick and Konkapot placed a hand on each of Jacob's shoulders, keeping him sitting as he looked at Captain Reynolds with venom. His hatred was beginning to know no bounds. The captain was associated with the sergeant major, and at that moment, Jacob wanted him dead too.

"Not now, my friend. Now is not the time," Konkapot advised. Jacob's jaw was clenched in rage, but he stayed sitting as Captain

Reynolds continued on his search for his trusty sergeant major.

Frederick told Konkapot, "You should see to getting Jacob back out on the island. We'll take care of Maggie and Jabez."

Konkapot nodded and gestured for Peter and Samuel to lead Jacob out to the island. They helped Jacob to his feet and led him back to their hut.

Captain Putnam and Lieutenant Waite were discussing the morning's events when they saw Konkapot and the other Rangers lead Jacob across the footbridge and over to their hut. They could see by their expressions that something very bad had happened. They had received a quick word that some civilians had been caught in the fight and killed, but they hadn't yet associated the news with Jacob and his Rangers.

Konkapot and Samuel explained to Captain Putnam what had happened.

"It was Maggie and Jabez from the shop that were killed," said

Konkapot, which confirmed the report on the civilian casualties.

"It was that damned sergeant major," continued Konkapot. "He had attacked them during the fight, killed the boy, and stabbed Maggie in the back before we could stop him."

Putnam raised his eyebrows in astonishment. "That bloody bastard!

I knew he was no good."

Then he stepped closer to Konkapot and Samuel, asking, "Who killed him?"

Samuel nodded in Jacob's direction, saying, "Jacob did."

Putnam's face took on a look of concern. "Did anyone witness it?" he asked.

Konkapot shook his head no. "I made it look like the enemy did it; Jacob won't be associated with his untimely death."

Putnam nodded. "Good work. Look after him," he said, inclining his head towards Jacob.

Then, saddened at the senseless loss, he left to inform the rest of the company. He decided that Jacob would need to spend some time mourning before he went back into action. He made sure Jacob was under constant observation by his Rangers, and that he remained on the island until he could get through the period of mourning. Until then, he wouldn't be an effective Ranger, and he could possibly lose his life if he went out on a mission before his head was back to normal.

"If it can go back to normal," whispered Putnam to himself.

For a couple of days, Jacob stayed around the camp, with Konkapot, Samuel, or Peter staying close. Even Smoke stayed close, again sensing that something was wrong with Jacob. For Jacob, it was as if he were moving through a grey, misty world with sound muffled as his mind and soul dealt with his loss and his mourning for Maggie, a huge hole torn from his very being.

The other Rangers and Captain Putnam checked up regularly on how Jacob was doing, and Samuel reported he was dealing with it as best as he could.

It was a dark, grey morning when Maggie and Jabez were laid to rest alongside the fallen Rangers in the cemetery on the island. Most of the platoon, including Captain Putnam, attended the burial.

All who knew Maggie and Jacob were deeply moved by the senseless loss, even though most were hardened men who had survived years of fighting. They were angry that she had been killed in a cowardly act by the sergeant major, who for the most part had already been hated and despised by the Rangers.

To help with the mourning, Konkapot took Jacob across the river to the Mohawk camp. He knew he had to change the scenery, even if only to a different camp, to help Jacob's mind return to the present. Konkapot hoped that bringing Jacob back to the people he had, in a way, grown up with, might help his transition from mourning back to normal.

The word of Maggie's senseless death had already reached the Mohawks. When Konkapot explained that the sergeant major had died at the hands of Jacob, the Mohawks understood and nodded their approval.

The elders and medicine men worked with Jacob to help him complete his mourning, to accept her passing, and to rationalize what he was feeling. The timing was good, because Jacob avoided the military burial of the sergeant major.

While the fort garrison participated in the funeral, the Rangers were all absent, because "duties required them elsewhere." They knew it would be disgusting, with Captain Reynolds spewing about how Lovelace was such a great man, serving faithfully, while not knowing that he was actually a cowardly rapist—an animal.

The unfortunate side effect of the sergeant major's demise was the growing tension between the Provincials and the British regulars. The word had raced through the Ranger companies about what had happened to Maggie, and it did not sit right with any of them. They kept the tale to themselves, allowing the British and the other Provincials to believe the sergeant major had died at the hands of the enemy, an honorable death.

There were some heated exchanges between the Rangers and the Provincials who believed Captain Reynolds' story of the brave sergeant major, but then again, these were Provincial soldiers newly arrived, who were unaware of the sergeant major's general distaste for Provincial soldiers as a whole.

Captain Putnam and some of the lieutenants had to quell a few of these disputes and discipline the Rangers back out on the island, continuing with the policy of not letting the British get hold of them for disciplinary issues. Especially now when it seemed Captain Reynolds was even more extreme in searching out Provincials to punish, somehow blaming them for the loss of the sergeant major.

The grey mist of despair was beginning to dissipate from Jacob's mind. The sound of the Mohawks' drums and chanting reconnected him with his past and the Mohawks' mystical world.

He was beginning to accept the loss of Maggie, as he had long ago accepted the loss of his family. While the hole in his soul might be healing, it would take time for the hole in his heart to disappear. Jacob was conflicted on how to deal with his loss.

Part of him argued that it would not be wise to love anyone again, that he should harden his heart and soul and concentrate on killing his enemies. He thought he should just focus on revenge, revenge for his family and his new need for revenge for Maggie.

While the French and Indians weren't the direct cause of her death, he had to blame someone, and he couldn't kill all of these British bastards, who didn't respect the Rangers or support them.

However, his common sense side disagreed. It told him he would love again, just not now. Vengeance was still a double-edged sword; something he could focus on now but at what cost later in life?

Jacob knew that soon, the fighting would begin, and he would focus on his Rangers, keeping them alive as best as he could. He too must stay alive and not hurl himself into the face of the enemy, hoping for a warrior's death. Maggie wouldn't have approved of his throwing his life away without reason. His Rangers would be his reason now to fight and stay alive in order to fight again.

CHAPTER 21

QUEBEC: MASSING OF FORCES

Spring moved into summer, and the stage was being set for the next major confrontation between the French and the English in New York. As Jacob had predicted, it wasn't long before the two sides once again clashed in battle. The Rangers became very active, supporting the new British strategy of taking the fight directly to the French in Canada.

Captain Richard Rogers' new company of Rangers was not even close to being the same caliber of men that the Rangers normally took. He thanked them for their service and sent them to replace a New York Provincial Company under Captain Ogden, which was garrisoned at Fort Edward, taking Captain Ogden's company to augment his own Rangers. Richard led a combined raid with the New York Provincials under Ogden and his Rangers against a new French stockade position called Coutre Coeur at the northern end of Lake George. The raid achieved surprise, and they killed several of the enemy, but the French were able to rally quickly and prevent the raiders from entering the stockade.

Richard Rogers then contracted smallpox as soon as he arrived back at Fort William Henry. Unlike his brother, he did not survive, and he joined the growing ranks of the Ranger dead interred at William Henry. Lieutenant Noah Johnson assumed command of the company at the fort. Meanwhile in Montreal, Governor General Vaudreuil had a simple plan. He would send Montcalm, whom he had grudgingly come to accept as a gifted tactician, to take Forts William Henry and Edward.

Montcalm had been very successful against both of these forts.

When the forts were removed or controlled, Montcalm could release the Hurons, Abenakis, and other Indians into the south to burn and destroy, installing a sense of fear across the settlements. Then it would be simple to march south and take Albany. One of the strategic advantages of this plan was that it would force the English to drop any plans of taking Quebec.

Vaudreuil's plan was shaping up nicely. Thousands of Indian warriors arrived and massed around Quebec in preparation for the attack and the spoils of war they had been promised. While the English did not respect the fighting skills of their Indian allies, the French had learned that the Indians were efficient in waging war.

The warriors who had accompanied Montcalm to Oswego told tales of loot, scalps, and swimming in brandy upon their victory. These stories alone were enough to encourage warriors from across the north to move towards Fort Carillon during the winter in anticipation of the campaign to come.

Several hundred Ottawas, Ojibwas, and Potawatomis, enemies of the Iroquois who were known jointly as the "Three Fires," arrived to join the French for their campaign.

Vaudreuil had held a conference in Montreal during the winter, to which he had invited members of the Iroquois Confederation to show them the French might and to encourage them to abandon their English fathers.

"Why should you lose your young warriors to an English king who does not respect them as men?" he asked them.

Vaudreuil wanted them to warn their Mohawk brothers, who had refused to attend the conference, that if they did not abandon their support of the English, they would be shown no mercy when the fighting began.

This French buildup was placing the English in a precarious position. The Iroquois who had traveled north to Montreal and Quebec had brought back to the English news of the French military buildup.

The growing French strength was confirmed by the French prisoners who had been captured earlier, as well as by English and Provincial soldiers who had been captured and had escaped back to English lines.

With so many reports coming south, however, the British commanders in Albany thought the French were deliberately sending false information to draw English attention away from their real intended target.

Knowing that some of their English prisoners had escaped and were returning to the British forts with information about their plans, the French determined that they would no longer give rewards for captured personnel. If there were no prisoners, none could escape and report on their preparations.

Prisoners caused other problems for the French. They had to be housed and fed, which took supplies away from the stockpile needed for the coming offensive. Additionally, when an Indian captured a prisoner, he normally would not raid again. He would stay around the fort until he could take his valuable prisoner back home to be sold into slavery, eaten, or integrated into his tribe.

Montcalm shuttled between Quebec and Montreal, where he met with the governor general to check on the logistical support for the coming offensive, and Fort Carillon, where the force was being assembled.

His second-in-command, Louis-Antoine de Bougainville, had been busy organizing the French regulars, Canadian Militia, and Indian warriors. With such a large number of Indians becoming restless, Bougain-ville had released the Canadians and the Indians to raid around Forts William Henry and Edward, and if possible, to push south into the areas around Schenectady and Albany.

The success of the French raids into the area around Fort William Henry was turning the area along Lake George into a no man's land, with much of the area between Fort Carillon and Fort William Henry controlled by French-allied Indians.

These successful raids kept both the governor general and Montcalm informed of English activities around both Forts William Henry and Edward. Some of the prisoners told them that there was no indication of increased British activity in New York and that the buildings damaged or destroyed during the Saint Patrick's Day raid at Fort William Henry had still not been repaired.

In addition to the Canadians and Indians, even the French regulars began pushing out on raids. These raids were led by Joseph Marin, the regular officer who best understood la petite guerre or "Little War," as shown by his earlier victories, including twice defeating Robert Rogers.

Marin left Fort Carillon, leading an expedition of 380 men. This included 300 Ottawa warriors, some Chippewas, and some Iroquois guides. The other seventy or so were French regulars or Canadian Militia. He was leading them south towards the southern end of the lake to attack any British or Provincial patrols in the area.

The expedition moved along the lake and arrived near South Bay, an area which the Indian warriors were reluctant to enter due to the successful Ranger ambushes that had occurred there. The Indians spoke of bad dreams and bad spirits who occupied the trees, having lost their lives in ambushes by the Rangers.

To offset the reluctance of the Ottawas, the Chippewa medicine men performed a cleansing rite, made "magic," and hung a breechclout dedicated to one of their great spirits, Manitou. This was enough to satisfy the Ottawas, and the expedition carried on. They found no enemies so Marin led them around Fort William Henry and set up an ambush on the road between Forts William Henry and Edward.

Along their march, they stopped at the ruins of Fort Anne, which was still abandoned. This made no military sense to Marin. Both English raiders and French raiders used it as a landmark and rest area for their expeditions. Why hadn't the English built the post back up and garrisoned it to prevent enemy forces like him from using it? Marin just shook his head, and thanked the English for their lack of forethought.

While camped at old Fort Anne, Marin sent scouts to fan out, gather information, and report on any English activity. One of the scout groups of eight ran into a platoon of thirty Rangers led by Lieutenant Dormit of Massachusetts. The two groups met northeast of Fort Edward, and both froze in surprise at actually running into one another.

Dormit gave an order for the Rangers to spread out and attack, and then one of the Indians shot Dormit in the head and killed him instantly. These Rangers, freshly recruited and inexperienced, dropped their packs and ran back towards the fort instead of engaging the smaller Indian party.

Surprised by their good fortune, the eight warriors took Dormit's scalp, then chopped off his arms and mutilated his body. They went through the abandoned packs and took their spoils of war and then returned to the camp at Fort Anne.

Marin was amazed that the eight warriors had been able to escape with their lives. This was good information, showing that even the dreaded Rangers had been having trouble maintaining their ranks and now had more inexperienced soldiers than their well-seasoned fighters of the previous year.

Marin decided to send a hundred men back to Fort Carillon with the information they had gathered, which included papers from General Webb that had been found in one of the abandoned packs.

Three days after the chance contact with the Rangers, Marin made ready to push on towards Fort Edward. The Ottawa medicine men once again held rites and prayed for a successful raid from their great spirit Manitou, and then they moved on towards the fort. As he had done on the earlier raid, he planned to wait and ambush another woodcutting detail from the fort. One thing he had observed: the English didn't learn from their mistakes.

During the evening, Marin sent half of his men to a hilltop overlooking one of the areas that looked as if it were being heavily cut by the English. He placed the rest of his men in a wooded swamp nearby. This tactic had worked well for him in the past, so he employed this proven approach and waited for his game to arrive into the trap.

Marin didn't have long to wait. At around eight in the morning, the woodcutters came out of the fort, escorted by a covering party of around eighty Provincials. Marin watched them get organized.

As the woodcutters began their work, the Provincials were being broken into groups. Small groups of six to twelve were conducting roving patrols around the site while the others stayed near the workers.

"At least it seems they can learn a little after all," he whispered to himself, watching the Provincials.

The Ottawa warriors were knocking their arrows, and sliding forward on their bellies towards their prey. One of the guards near the swamp was killed silently with an arrow through his throat and five more in his chest. He died without uttering a sound as the Indians slid slowly forward to get closer to their intended targets.

Another guard, who had lowered his musket and was admiring the morning, was surprised to see brightly colored feathered objects fly by. Thinking they were a unique species of birds, he began looking for more when another flight of arrows flew by, just missing him. They were so fast though that all he saw was the bright colors of the fletching, and he continued thinking they were fast-flying, colorful birds. When one of the arrows thudded into a tree near him and vibrated before his astonished eyes, he finally realized what he was seeing and yelled, "Indians!"

The commander of the guard gave an order to "tree all," and the guards took cover behind trees and began to return fire. Marin, realizing the element of surprise had been lost, ordered muskets and rifles to return fire. While some of the Provincials were putting up a fight, others began to break and run for the fort along with the woodcutters.

The Indians charged out of the woods in pursuit, their war whoops echoing off the trees. As the Indians charged, many threw their tomahawks at the backs of their enemies, killing a few in the process. Within seconds, the covering party of Provincials was overrun by the Indians. Half a dozen had been killed and many others were wounded and could not escape. They were in the process of being taken prisoner or scalped. Marin could hear the sound of the long roll coming from the fort, which meant he would soon be facing many more British and Provincial soldiers. He gave the order to fall back before they themselves became outnumbered. He was satisfied that he again had met his objective of terrorizing his enemy, making them believe they were not safe even near their forts.

As the ambush was being initiated, out on the island, Jacob was getting back into the routine of being a Ranger. Major Rogers had recently returned from a failed expedition to try to take Fort

Ticonderoga and had learned of his brother's death from smallpox. He was himself wrestling with his grief and doing his duty with no real time to mourn.

Having heard of the vicious raid against Fort Edward and their losses in men and civilians, Rogers was briefed by Putnam and Jacob on what had occurred. Rogers nodded his head soberly, while giving his condolences to Jacob on the loss of Maggie, adding that the death of the sergeant major was a "good riddance."

As they settled down to the business of planning an expedition against the French at Carillon, they heard the sound of firing in the distance, quickly followed by the sound of the long roll from the fort.

All three looked up, and Jacob ran towards his hut to gather his men while Putnam began yelling, "Rangers turn out," and then ran towards the river. As Putnam neared the footbridge, Jacob, who was leading his section, came around the huts, followed by other sections that fell in beside Captain Putnam. Looking at Jacob's face, Putnam assessed that he seemed like his normal self, determined and focused on the moment. Waving his arm, Putnam led the Rangers towards the sound of the fighting.

Remembering the viciousness of the last raid, Jacob and the other Rangers did not want the French to get away a second time. They were moving so fast that instead of taking the bridge, Putnam led the Rangers into the river, which was low enough to walk across. The Rangers, holding their rifles, muskets, and shooting bags over their heads, splashed through the water right behind Putnam.

Inside Fort Edward, Colonel Lyman had mounted the walls after hearing the musket fire, and fearing that this was the expected all-out attack on the fort, began issuing orders to prepare to repel attackers and man the cannons.

Lyman spotted Putnam and his column of Rangers turning the corner of the wall heading towards the sound of battle. Yelling down towards Putnam, Lyman ordered the Rangers to halt and proceed no farther. Whether it was the tension between the Rangers and the British authorities or the fact their blood was up and the Rangers wanted to engage the enemy, Putnam quickly apologized and continued to lead his men forward, all of whom had intense looks on their faces as they ran by. Lyman decided that perhaps it would be better to let these Rangers go, and perhaps to feel pity for those who would run into them, because they all had murder in their eyes. It was about to get really bloody in the woods.

Putnam saw in the distance that one of the Provincial companies had formed and deployed in a line facing the woods. He angled his men towards the Provincials to provide support.

"Fall in to the left of the Provincials," ordered Putnam, and the Rangers angled towards the flank of the Provincial line.

The Provincials, Massachusetts men under the steady Captain Learned, were delivering well-spaced volleys into the woods, and the Indians and Canadians were firing back, using the trees for cover. Captain Learned was a seasoned fighter and veteran who understood his role well, inspiring his men by leading from the front. Putnam deployed alongside the Provincials and had the Rangers commence firing, though the Rangers were more openly spaced in pairs than in the shoulder-to-shoulder line of the Provincials.

Jacob brought his section into line with the Rangers and the Provincials and began picking targets, but they were not easy to hit. The enemy was using the terrain and the trees for cover to their advantage.

Putnam went over and conferred with Learned. He suggested that the Provincials keep up the fire while he led his Rangers around the end of the line to attack the enemy from the flank. Learned nodded his agreement and the Provincials kept up a withering rate of volleys as Putnam ran back to the Rangers.

Yelling, "Let's go get them boys!" and raising his tomahawk high, Putnam led the surge forward as the Rangers let out their own war whoops and charged into the woods.

Each Ranger became primal, his desire for revenge and his desire to kill his enemies taking over. They charged forward, weapons ready to deal out death and destruction. The fearsome sight and sound of the charging Rangers was enough to change the minds of the fighting Ottawas, who turned and began to fall back.

The crushing threat of the charging Rangers had a detrimental effect, however. Knowing that prisoners would only slow them down and that the Rangers were closing fast with bloodlust, Marin made the decision to kill all the prisoners except for one. He began to withdraw away from the ever-increasing number of enemy soldiers.

Jacob and his men pushed forward, their blood racing in anticipation of the kill. As they crossed the ground where the woodcutters had been attacked, they spotted an Ottawa race out. Having no time to scalp the fallen Provincial who had been overlooked, the Ottawa pulled out his tomahawk and chopped off the head of the fallen soldier.

Jacob and Konkapot raced off in pursuit and caught the Ottawa trying to scalp the head. He had the scalp halfway off when both Jacob's and Konkapot's rifles fired and ended the process.

As the Rangers were chasing the enemy in the woods, Colonel Lyman arrived at the fight, now realizing that it wasn't an all-out attack on the fort, but another raid. He ordered Captain Learned to take his company and pursue the enemy for ten miles.

Putnam had halted his Rangers to reorganize when they heard the line of Provincials advancing from their rear. The Rangers moved out of the way to let the line pass before following behind them.

They had not gone far when the company of Provincials was attacked by the Ottawa rear guard. To avoid giving away their position, the Ottawas again used only their bows and not their muskets. The Provincials reacted well; they halted and began once more to fire controlled volleys that drove off the Indians.

Putnam passed the Provincials as they were fighting the Indians and on a hunch, headed towards the ruins of Fort Anne. When they arrived, they saw that his hunch had been right. They could see there had been a large force camping there before the raid. There were some fresh blood trails, but they found only one dead body. His clothes and ruffled shirt told them the man was a regular French officer.

Putnam ordered the Rangers to fan out and search the area. Jacob, leading his section, moved into the woods and began looking for trails or any other signs of the enemy. Samuel and Peter looked at one another and winked. It seemed the Jacob they knew was back, and it appeared his mourning was not affecting his ability to lead them in the fight. He appeared focused and intent on doing the job right.

As the Rangers searched the area, Putnam searched the one dead Frenchman and could find neither wounds nor injuries on the man. He ordered that the body be loaded onto a travois and returned to the fort as the other Rangers continued to scour the area for any other pieces of information or equipment.

Jacob returned with his men, having not found anything other than tracks of their enemy going away from them and heading north. Putnam nodded and they returned to their island after dropping off the dead French officer at the fort. Out on the island, Putnam and Rogers went into conference, along with a few of the Mohawk chiefs who had come over from their camp.

The leaders decided that the French had been allowed too much freedom to move around and raid. In two days, the Rangers would depart for a raid against the French at Carillon. It was time to take the fight to the enemy.

"I am not sure why the command has not done anything but sit on their fat asses while our enemy has free rein to do as they please. We must put an end to this!" Rogers exclaimed, and they all agreed. Once the meeting was concluded, they departed to go pick their men.

There was some friction between Rogers and Putnam on how this mission should be handled. Rogers believed he had to keep most of the Rangers at Fort Edward, since half were inexperienced, while Putnam argued that this raid would give the new men experience. Rogers was also concerned about the growing strain between the Provincials and the regulars, who did not want any men traveling away from the fort because of the raids.

"One way or the other, there is trouble here, and we have to head it off before it explodes," said Rogers as he discussed it with Putnam.

"While I understand, sir," Putnam replied, "it would serve us better to go as the entire command, so the new recruits can be helped by the veterans. Everyone wants to take the fight to the French. Why not give them that chance?"

"We would be going against orders which would give the regulars the excuse they want to take us under their control and take away our ability to operate independently," Rogers replied.

Putnam nodded, realizing that Rogers was correct. It would violate the standing orders from the British commanders to remain around the forts. He relented, and it was decided he would hand pick about twenty men and join with the Mohawks. They would even wear Mohawk clothing to blend in so it wouldn't look like the Rangers were disobeying their orders.

Rogers would remain on the island and work on training the new recruits and keeping the British leadership engaged. This could become an issue, as General Webb himself was expected to arrive at Fort Edward. Rogers knew they didn't need to anger the commanding general by directly disobeying his standing orders.

Putnam selected Jacob and his Rangers to come on the raid and told them to wear Mohawk clothing.

"You need to keep this quiet. Make sure your men dress to appear as Mohawks in case the English officers see you. Even paint up to help with your ruse."

Jacob nodded and led his men across the river to the Mohawk camp. Jacob changed into deep blue leggings and a red breechclout, moccasins, and a plain shirt. He tied back his hair and then painted his face, neck, and upper chest in red and black war paint.

Konkapot painted up as well. Peter, a blond German, and Samuel, a trader not immersed in Indian culture, looked a little out of place, but they were all accepted by the Mohawks as they readied themselves for the raid, the Mohawks helping them with the paint so as to look like their own warriors.

Once they were all dressed and painted up, the Mohawks and Rangers departed from Fort Edward and headed towards Lake George. To help with their ruse, they left the wolves behind because the English knew the wolves traveled with the Rangers. There were about a hundred Mohawk warriors and Rangers altogether on the raid.

Once they arrived at the southern end of the lake, the raiding party stayed away from the fort and settled near the Ranger encampment, but in the woods where they could not be seen from the walls.

That night, they sang war songs, and the medicine men performed their spiritual rites to ask for victory. To the men at Fort William

Henry, it appeared to be another Mohawk war party, and there were no indications that the Rangers were mixed in with them. After the celebrations, the Rangers went to their blankets and checked their equipment, powder, and shot before they went to sleep.

As they relaxed, lying on their blankets or leaning on their elbows and talking, Samuel asked Jacob, "So, this was how you grew up, living with these people?"

Jacob nodded. "Well, I only lived with the Mohawks for a short time, but they are very much like the Stockbridge Mohicans that I did spend most of my time with."

Samuel nodded. "They are very unique and different, in a good way."

Jacob nodded, saying, "They are indeed."

In the morning, the Rangers woke, packed their gear, and had some breakfast before they journeyed northward. As they were eating biscuits and dried meats, they noticed a large party of Provincials march out from the fort and head towards the lake.

Colonel John Parker led five companies of the New Jersey Blues to the waiting whaleboats, and they began to load. They remembered watching that column march past Fort Edward, the accompanying women causing such a stir amongst some of the other Provincial units. The Rangers hadn't cared about the issue, one way or the other.

Jacob, Konkapot, and a few of the other Rangers, chewing on their biscuits and dried meat, watched the expedition depart and begin rowing northward. They looked at one another with raised eyebrows as the boats began to shrink in the distance.

"This could work in our favor," said Jacob to the others, who all nodded. "They will draw the French attention from us, and while the French concentrate on them, we'll get around them and bring the fight to their camps."

Samuel and the others smiled at the prospect. Jacob brought this to the attention of the Mohawk war chiefs leading the raid. He explained how this Provincial expedition could work in their favor, and the war chiefs looked at one another and agreed.

The war chiefs gathered their men and had Jacob explain in their language the potential advantage of having the Provincials on the lake. The warriors all whooped in agreement.

The raiding party departed the encampment and began their trek towards the enemy, traveling in the woods instead of on the lake. All of the warriors and Rangers were eager; everything was looking to be in their favor for a successful raid against their enemies.

CHAPTER 22

FIGHT AT SABBATH DAY POINT

The decision to send the Provincial expedition north had been reached in Colonel Monroe's office in Fort William Henry the previous night, just as the Mohawk raiding party was arriving.

Colonel Monroe needed information, and he was feeling frustrated about the order to remain close to the forts. All indications were pointing to a major French offensive, and it was more and more likely that Fort William Henry would be the object of that offensive. Monroe paced inside his office, a map laid out on the table and held in place by lead weights.

He paused and looked down at the map, scratching his chin with the stem of his pipe. What would Montcalm do? How would he approach the fort? His eyes traced the route from Carillon down the lake to where Fort William Henry was located. It was Monroe's responsibility to see to the defenses of the fort, which meant he needed to know what the bloody enemy was up to so he could plan accordingly.

Monroe shook his head, gave a heavy sigh, and asked himself if all this might be nothing more than a ruse to force them to stay here while the French attacked somewhere else. He had received numerous reports about the French buildup, both from escaped prisoners and friendly Cayugas, all of whom had said the French indeed planned to attack his fort during the summer. A French prisoner had also said that Montcalm planned to march soon.

Monroe sucked on his pipe, the smoke curling around his head.

Was this enough information to go on? Were these sources reliable? It was all pointing to what he feared, that he would be the target of a massive French attack, and he wasn't sure that his garrison could stop it. His garrison, thought Monroe, was on the verge of collapse, and he doubted the men's reliability.

The morale at Fort William Henry was low and getting worse, many of the men frightened by the successful French raids and by other horror stories coming from the locals. Several scouting parties had ventured out with only a few survivors returning to tell their tales.

If he could not rely on his own men from the regiment, whom could he place his trust upon to defend the fort? The Provincials?

While most of the Provincials relied on their Mohawk allies to scout, Monroe and the other regular British officers did not trust these "savages" or their fanciful reports that the number of the enemy "outnumbered the leaves on the trees."

To compound this increasingly desperate situation, Colonel Monroe had no confidence in his commanding general, General Webb. If Webb was too much of a coward to order a strike northward, then he would do it himself.

Monroe needed information so he could plan a defense if, in fact, the French were going to attack his fort. Monroe would order Colonel Parker, contrary to Webb's instructions, to take his force of New Jersey Blues along with some New York Militia.

He was to lead a sortie in strength, locate the enemy, and gather information on their strength and activities. Looking down at his map, it made logical sense to Monroe to send the Provincials while he kept his own regulars intact at the fort for later use, if needed.

Monroe had heard that Colonel Parker had some experience fighting the French and their Indian allies, having met them during the earlier King George's War. He knew he had to regain some of the initiative from the French; they had been running the fight long enough.

Monroe would have Parker lead his men forward and, if their luck held, take some prisoners from whom they could learn Montcalm's intentions. Monroe felt confident that with his combat experience, Parker would be successful.

After receiving his orders from Colonel Monroe, Colonel Parker began preparations in earnest and assembled his companies. On the morning of the expedition, Parker looked out over his massive assembled force as they loaded twenty-seven whaleboats.

It had been a great accomplishment of the quartermasters to replace the boats that had been burned during the St. Patrick's Day raid. Parker's expedition was composed mostly of his New Jersey Blues, some New York Provincials under Captains Ogden and McGinnis, and a single "gentleman" volunteer from the 35th Regiment of Foot.

Colonel Parker watched with pride as his Jersey men pushed their long whaleboats into the lake and lowered their oars to begin their journey north. He stepped into his own boat and proceeded confidently up the lake. While the expedition started out looking good, however, the boats soon began to spread out with many lagging different distances behind as some of the inexperienced boatmen tired from pulling on their oars sooner than others.

Around midday, Parker's expedition reached a section of the lake known as the Narrows, an area approximately a mile wide with numerous small, forested islands dotting the water. It was a nice area for an ambush, with many concealed coves from which to observe the lake.

It was from one of these hidden coves along the shore that Canadian Lieutenant Saint-Ours, who had been leading a reconnaissance of the lake, observed Parker's flotilla sail past. This was important news, and he dispatched runners to take the information to the garrison at Fort Carillon. They ran along the shore, concealed from sight, and made it to the garrison quickly, actually passing the boats, which were steadily decreasing in speed.

While catching their breath, they reported on the number of boats they had seen. The garrison was quickly called to arms, and the Indians, who were becoming bored from waiting around instead of attacking the English, responded quickly and en masse.

Within an hour, over four hundred Indian warriors, gathered from the Chippewa, Ottawa, Potawatomi, and Menominee tribes, had assembled with their war chiefs.

Leading the fifty French regulars and the Canadian Militia accompanying the Indians was Charles Langlade, who had been ambushed previously by the Rangers and was looking for some revenge, and Ensign Corbiere of the Troupe de la Marine. Once their force was assembled to meet this threat, Langlade ordered the Indians out to begin the intercept of the advancing Englishmen.

With their war whoops echoing from the encampment, the four hundred Indians and their allies departed at a trot. With the restrictions that had been placed on them by the Marquis to avoid engaging the enemy, they were all spoiling for a fight. They hurried down to the shore, loaded into their small fleet of birch bark canoes, and began to paddle down the lake towards the enemy.

The force broke up into smaller elements, normally along tribal lines, and they began to spread out in search of the English, like hounds chasing after game. The French and the majority of the Indians eventually landed at Sabbath Day Point, while the rest occupied some of the smaller islands leading to the point. There, they hunkered down to wait for the approaching Englishmen. Langlade liked the terrain; it was a good spot to ambush an enemy on the lake.

The Indians had pulled their canoes in off the lake and hidden them among the pines, and they observed the lake from concealed positions along the water that placed any passing boats in the firing ranges of their muskets and rifles.

However, the sun dropped, and there was still no sign of the English. The desire to attack their enemies had dwindled down to simple boredom as the Indians and French settled into the night. Still, they remained and waited. Perhaps in the morning, the English would arrive and they would have their chance.

As Langlade and his men waited, Parker's expedition, having been slowed by the waning strength of the men, had pulled into shore and camped before nightfall.

The Colonel felt frustrated as his plans for a glorious expedition against the enemy were dwindling as his men, not used to the rigors of rowing the large whaleboats, succumbed to exhaustion. He had no choice but to put in so they could rest. Had they met the enemy, he wasn't sure that in their tired state, they would have been successful in battle.

As the sun rose the following morning, Parker decided to send out a reconnaissance force to see if they had been detected or if there was any sign the enemy was close at hand. A group of three whaleboats was to travel towards the northern shore and the vicinity of the French positions at Ticonderoga and report what they had observed. While they scouted, Parker was getting his semi-rested men back into their boats to continue their expedition.

At about the same time, Langlade ordered two canoes to head south to see if they could find the English and report on their position. One Indian canoe returned with nothing to report.

Langlade knew he had to find the enemy. His Indian allies were becoming disheartened due to the lack of engagement. The challenge was that the morning was dawning with a thick fog covering the lake, making it hard to see an approaching enemy.

Unfortunately for the second canoe, as it came abreast of an island on which one of the Indian groups was waiting in ambush, the Indians mistakenly fired on the canoe in their excitement, having not seen anything through the fog. Two Ottawa chiefs were wounded, one of whom would die of his wounds. Thinking this was a bad omen, the Ottawas decided to pack their gear and leave the expedition.

Langlade, worried that he had just lost over half of his force, finally observed a group of whaleboats approaching the point as the fog partially cleared so they could be seen. As the boats pulled close, the Indians in their faster canoes broke from their concealment, charged out and surrounded them. All three boats surrendered and were brought into shore.

Fearful that they would be tortured, the captured Provincials quickly gave details about Parker's expedition and said that they were going to meet at Sabbath Bay.

Sensing an opportunity, Langlade pulled all of the Indians into the point, and had some of his men put on the blue coats of the Provincials to serve as bait. He would lure the expedition into the range of his muskets and rifles, finishing them off.

He allowed the Indians and their shaman to do their rituals to ensure victory before settling in their ambush. Once everyone was in position, Langlade waited patiently and hoped his Indian allies would be patient as well. The sun was starting to climb, but there was still a fine misty fog covering the water. Langlade hoped this would help in his deception and yet not cause problems as it had earlier.

His effort was soon rewarded as the sound of the approaching whaleboats could be heard over the lake, the slap of many oars in the water. The captured whaleboats with the men wearing the Provincial uniforms began to row out from one of the islands and head towards Sabbath Bay. Holding his breath, Langlade let it out slowly as the English began to follow the boats into the bay, the fog helping to mask his men. "They've taken the bait," he whispered excitedly, hoping his luck would last just a few moments longer.

He gave the whispered order to get ready, and over two hundred muskets began to follow the approaching whaleboats. The decoy boats quickly beached themselves and the men either jumped out of the boats and lay on the shore, or huddled deeply inside of the boats. The English continued to follow and were closing on the beach where the decoys had landed.

When Langlade believed the British boats to be close enough, he gave the order to fire. The woods along the shore erupted into a sheet of flame and smoke as hundreds of balls whistled towards the unsuspecting Englishmen.

From his boat, Parker was trying to figure out where his scouting boats had gone when the forest in front of him exploded. The balls whistled through the air, some striking and thudding into the wooden sides of the boats, some of his men falling over inside their boats or screaming, and some splashing into the lake as they were knocked over the sides by the musket balls.

Standing in spite of the balls flying around him, Parker ordered the boats to return fire. As they began to fire in sections at the shoreline, the forest echoed with the war whoops of hundreds of enemy Indians. They increased their rate of fire at the English, seeing many of their enemy falling from their effective shots.

Sensing movement, Parker turned to see fifty canoes with brightly painted warriors emerge from around the smaller islands, and they soon sealed the bay from the lake. Parker began shouting orders, but after the initial volley, all control appeared to have been lost. Some of the Provincials threw down their arms and raised their hands to surrender, while others dove into the water to try to swim to safety.

As Parker's expedition was lured into the trap and engaged, Jacob, his men, and the Mohawks were running along the lake. They heard the firing and turned towards the sound of the fighting.

They came to a small spit of land that poked out into the lake where they halted as the sound of the fighting continued. Jacob and the Mohawks crawled close to the shore where they could see what was happening.

Sure enough, it was the expedition that had departed from the fort.

However, instead of meeting the enemy, it was being overwhelmed and destroyed. They watched helplessly as numerous canoes boarded the whaleboats and began to tomahawk what appeared to be surrendering men. Some of the canoes were hunting down swimmers in the water. They were not leaving any survivors, at least from what they could see.

Some of the Indians dove into the water, swam under the whaleboats, came up on the other side, and pulled the boats over to capsize them. From what Jacob could observe, Indians rushing from the woods were attacking those who had swum to shore.

Only four of the whaleboats appeared to be making any effort to fight the attacking Indians, and they were actually pulling away and breaking through the canoes. The men in Colonel Parker's boat, in Captain Ogden's two boats of New Yorkers, and in one New Jersey boat were pulling for all their worth, and once they were able to break through, they quickly hid themselves in the fog, making good their escape.

Jacob and the Mohawks slowly crawled back into the woods, and decided that they should try to save some of these men, who if they weren't killed, would be taken prisoner and led to a camp somewhere. He quickly discussed this with his men and the Mohawks, and they all agreed.

Jacob led them out at a trot into the woods to see what they could do to save some lives and take some vengeance on the enemy. Jacob and the Mohawks followed the French and their Indians from the shore, keeping pace with the canoes loaded with prisoners and supplies captured from the whaleboats. Some of these supplies included casks of rum, and soon the shores echoed with the whoops and howls of drunken Indians, celebrating their victory.

Once the victorious French and their Indians arrived at Ticonderoga, they broke up and headed to their respective camps, dragging their prisoners and their booty of rum and spoils with them. From the dark of the woods, Jacob watched a group that was angling away from the main camps, and decided that their camp would be their target.

"We'll wait until it's darker, and then we'll hit them, rescue the prisoners, and be out of there before an alarm can be raised," said Jacob, and the Mohawk war chiefs nodded in agreement.

In preparation, they all took gunpowder mixed with water, which turned into a black paint, and began covering their faces, chests, and arms in a black shade that was then lined with deep crimson. They all did a last minute check on their weapons, from their rifles and muskets to their knives and tomahawks. Once everyone was ready, Jacob led the war party out and headed towards the enemy's camp.

As Jacob and the warriors were moving through the gloom of the dark, in their target camp was Father Pierre Roubaud, who had just arrived at the French encampment, having traveled with a group of Abenaki warriors.

He was visiting the Chippewa camp, which he observed was mostly empty because the warriors were out on a raid. He was speaking with one of the shamans, when he heard loud whooping and yelling as the victorious party led their captives into the camp. The shaman rose, smiled, and nodded at the successful return of the warriors.

The warriors who had stayed behind let out a war whoop of greeting to the returning victors and helped to secure their prisoners to wooden posts or trees. They pranced around and poked at the bound prisoners, welcoming the returning victorious warriors.

Father Roubaud was appalled by what he observed. The prisoners, whose faces were bruised and covered in grime and blood with streaks where tears had washed some of the grime away, stared in fear at their captors. The Indians began to build up a fire, and across it was suspended a great cooking pot.

The Indians continued to drink and pass the captured rum around, and they began to dance around the soon steaming pot. One of the prisoners was brought forward and stripped of his clothes, while ten others were staked close to the fire pit. The prisoner's hands, arms, and legs were quickly bound, and two warriors picked up the bound-but-struggling prisoner and tossed him into the great pot, from which a blood-curdling scream arose.

As he screamed, the other prisoners screamed in horror, and the Indians hollered their excitement. The cooking prisoner, his upper torso still exposed over the lip of the pot, continued to scream.

Father Roubaud grabbed a warrior who had just finished a long pull from his cup of rum and asked why they were treating the man this way. Wiping the rum from his mouth and trying to speak French, the warrior responded, "You French have your 'tastes.' Well, I am a savage, and this was what tastes good to me."

With that, he smiled at the priest and wandered off to find more rum. Father Roubaud had closed his eyes and said a silent prayer for the poor man when he heard a deafening explosion from the darkness.

Snapping his eyes open, Father Roubaud dove behind a tree in fear of the men covered in black and red paint who had fired from the woods and were now pouring into the drunken circle of dancing Chippewas. One of the first shots seemed to have hit the poor man in the pot, who had now mercifully stopped screaming.

The Chippewas were falling all around him as these black-painted demons, who had risen from the night, began to slaughter the dancing warriors. Father Roubaud observed one of these black demons, who with tomahawk in one hand and a knife in another, seemed to flow like water amongst the Chippewas.

His tomahawk flashed, striking one warrior in the head, and then he smoothly spun away and sliced the throat of another warrior with his knife. This whirling demon dealt death to the Chippewas; perhaps this was judgment for their cooking the young man alive.

Father Roubaud crossed himself and clasped his hands in prayer, praying for salvation from all these savages.

His eyes snapped open again as he felt a strong hand take him by his robes and pull him to his feet with a jerk. Inches from his face was a tomahawk, blood dripping from the edge and falling on his robes. He looked into the eyes of the black demon and met an icy blue stare. Breathing heavily, the demon slowly pulled the tomahawk away and, with a quick nod of his head, released the priest and pointed towards the woods. The priest nodded and ran from the carnage.

Jacob watched him run away as he caught his breath. They had made quick work of the warriors around the fire and were releasing the prisoners as the Mohawks continued to take the fight to the Chippewas. The prisoners cringed in fear of these black-and crimson-painted men, until Samuel and the other Rangers began to speak to them in English to let them know they were all right.

Soon, the Mohawks held the camp, and all of the warriors were either dead or had run off into the woods. As the Mohawks took scalps of the enemies, Samuel and the others began helping the prisoners escape while Jacob organized the withdrawal of the Mohawks. Satisfied with the carnage he had caused, Jacob followed with the rest of the Mohawks, and they formed a perimeter around the rescued prisoners.

They moved most of the night to get away from the enemy camp before they stopped to rest. As they washed their black and crimson war paint off, Jacob checked on the condition of their rescued prisoners, mostly New York men. Traveling with these wounded and traumatized men, the expedition took a few days of slow, careful movement to return to Fort William Henry, where the rescued men were turned over to their commands.

It had been a disastrous expedition that had started out looking so promising. Colonel Parker, and especially Captain Ogden, were thankful to Jacob for saving these men, but so few remained. From their accounting, Colonel Parker had lost over a hundred men killed or wounded, and one hundred and fifty men had been captured.

Along with the four boats, a few other survivors had been able to evade the enemy and make their way back to the fort.

The news of the disaster at Sabbath Bay reached General Webb, who finally decided that action was needed.

"Damn the orders," he remarked to an aide after reading the dispatch from Fort William Henry. "We need to stop these damnable French here and now!"

The day after receiving the news of the great loss of life, General Webb departed Albany for Fort Edward.

When General Webb arrived at Fort Edward, he was told of the enemy activity in the area and its steady increase between Fort Edward and Fort William Henry. Before moving on to Fort William Henry, Webb ordered two companies of British Grenadiers to escort him, along with a company of Rangers.

Lieutenant Putnam would lead the Rangers, which included Jacob and his men, who had only just returned to Fort Edward the night before. Very concerned that he might actually run into the enemy, Webb instructed the Rangers to lead the way and make sure there were no ambushes along the road.

"The general is concerned about enemy activity," Major Rogers explained to both Putnam and Jacob. "Actually, the general is more concerned that he will be attacked en route to the fort, so he wants our Rangers to screen his march to Fort William Henry."

Captain Putnam and Jacob looked at one another, shrugged, and nodded their understanding. They prepared for the march and were waiting for the general to give the command to move out.

As they waited, Samuel asked Jacob, "So, does the general want us to hold his hand through the woods?"

Peter added, "Perhaps he is afraid we find a bear or two in the woods?"

Jacob looked at his men and winked and continued to wait for the order to move. Once the column was ready, Putnam sent Jacob and his men forward as an advance guard, while the other Rangers flanked the column in the woods. At midday, they stopped at a place called "Halfway House" so General Webb could take a break.

The officers in the column relaxed as servants set up a folding table and chairs for their lunch. The grenadiers took up a perimeter around the resting officers, while the Rangers served as an outer watch and picket.

Samuel whispered, "Can you believe this? I wouldn't if it wasn't for the fact I am standing here and seeing it with my own eyes."

Jacob nodded as he observed the spectacle. "He wants us to screen him in case he is attacked, and yet here we are stopping for a picnic!" Jacob watched this incredible sight, as the gentlemen officers relaxed as if they were out for a Sunday stroll without a care in the world. In the back of Jacob's mind lingered the sounds of screaming men dying in battle and the recent poor soul who was being boiled alive by the Indians.

If this was how these English officers were going to fight this war, perhaps it would be safer to strike out on his own away from everything and everyone.

Jacob took a big sigh, and then turned to look at Samuel and the others who were watching the officers.

These are who I fight for, Jacob thought as he looked at his Rangers, and then turned to look back at General Webb and his staff lounging in the shade. Not these fancy pants officers.

Jacob continued to check on the Rangers to make sure they were watching the woods, in case they did in fact make contact with the enemy.

After two hours of relaxing, the column re-formed and continued its journey towards Fort William Henry. When the column approached and passed Bloody Pond, some of the British regulars began to whisper amongst themselves about this area being haunted by the slain whose bodies had been thrown into the water.

Jacob and the Rangers moved through the area, chuckling to themselves at the sight of the British regulars as they whispered and looked for the ghosts that were rumored to haunt the battle area. Jacob had already made his peace with the dead there, and none had ever bothered him.

Later that afternoon, the column finally arrived at Fort William Henry. Captain Putnam, Jacob, and the other Rangers were released. They headed over to the encampment and checked in with the Ranger Company currently stationed at the fort.

General Webb began an inspection of the fort with his advisors, so they knew they had some time to catch up on Ranger activities, though it had only been a few days since their return from the ill-fated expedition's destruction.

There had been no activity since, other than more rumors of a massive French force to the north, which were brought to the Rangers by Indian scouts and travelers.

After touring the fort and the grounds, General Webb held a council of war, which included Colonels Monroe and Young. Most of the discussion focused on what the French were going to do and what their plan would be.

General Webb believed that the French would do everything in their power to take Fort William Henry.

"If that is the case," asked Colonel Monroe, "wouldn't it be prudent to reinforce and man Fort William Henry with as many, if not more, soldiers than are at Fort Edward?"

General Webb had to agree with Colonel Monroe's assessment, and he replied, "I shall order an additional thousand men to reinforce the fort at the end of the month. Will that work?"

Thanking the General, Colonel Monroe nodded and asked, "If it would be possible, could four companies of the 35th be included with the reinforcements?"

Monroe wanted his whole regiment at Fort William Henry, but General Webb shook his head, saying, "While I understand your desire to have your entire regiment present, I need those regulars at Fort Edward and could not afford to spare any more regulars."

Colonel Monroe had to make do with what regulars were already at Fort William Henry.

Following the meeting with the general, Colonel Monroe then went to speak with Colonel Montresor about how long the fort could hold out, based on his expertise, with a French siege. Colonel Montresor turned to Monroe, and said that if the French arrived with siege artillery, "the fort would last twenty-four hours, maybe forty-eight at the best."

This confirmed Colonel Monroe's fears.

General Webb, having finished his inspection and confirming his promise of sending the reinforcements at the end of month, returned to Fort Edward. Colonel Monroe, who had seen the general off, had bowed and nodded his head, but he was already seething inside, concerned for his defenses if the French attacked.

Jacob and his Rangers accompanied the column back to Fort Edward, serving once more to protect the general's column. They stood off to the side until the general motioned for them to lead out.

Samuel leaned next to Jacob and whispered, "Think the general is going to stop for another picnic along the way?"

Jacob just shrugged his shoulders. Once the general was ready, the trip was uneventful and the general did not stop, but rather pushed on to Fort Edward.

When General Webb arrived at Fort Edward, instead of sending out messengers to instruct the movement of reinforcements, he sat and procrastinated. No one saw much of the general; he seemed to keep to his quarters in the fort.

The days continued to pass, and Colonel Monroe was kept waiting for his reinforcements as his men busily prepared the fort for a possible attack.

As for Jacob and the Rangers, they still struggled with the restriction on their operations, remaining localized for scouts or hunting expeditions. Major Rogers fought with the British command over allowing his Rangers to scout out and see what the French were up to, but they still refused.

"Don't you bloody well see that the French are getting ready to do something," demanded Rogers.

Major Fletcher simply shook his head. "The commanding general does not believe the sources of this information are reliable."

"Reliable?" Rogers exclaimed. "You better believe they are reliable."

Then Rogers paused for a moment and calmed himself before continuing on.

"Then at least allow my Rangers to go out and confirm how reliable the information is. We'll scout out the north end of the lake, and we'll tell you what we see, if the French are massing or not!"

While it made perfect sense to Rogers, Major Fletcher still shook his head no, saying, "Unless General Webb changes his mind, the orders stay in effect."

As Rogers tried to convince Major Fletcher to allow him to scout out the French, back at Fort William Henry, Colonel Monroe paced around the walls, watching the men clear the fields around the fort of any brush and limbs.

With the exception of the Ranger encampment on the hill to the east, all Provincial tents and lean-tos from the surrounding hills were moved into the ever-more-crowded fort. His concern was that the French and their Indians could surprise these camps and wipe out the men before the fort could respond. These included the remnants and survivors of Colonel Parker's New Jersey Blues and the New York Provincials. The promised day of Webb's reinforcements came and went, and Colonel Monroe began to question the reliability of General Webb.

"How does he bloody expect me to hold this position without the men that he promised?" growled Monroe to his aide, who simply nodded in agreement.

However, at dusk on August 2nd, the reinforcements finally arrived. Leading the column was Colonel Young, a wealthy American who led a hundred men of the Royal Americans. Following behind him was a column of over eight hundred Massachusetts Provincials under the command of Colonel Joseph Frye.

To support the guns of the fort, Webb had sent Captain William McCloud of the Royal Artillery with six cannons. However, there were no other British regulars in the column, and Monroe shook his head in dismay.

While appreciative of the extra men, Monroe felt they were not up to the proficiency of the regulars. Even these Royal Americans of the 60th Regiment were not truly English regulars, just Provincials placed in a British-numbered regiment.

Monroe slowly shook his head. How would he face this looming French threat? How would he defend his position with honor with this assortment of rabble the governors called troops?

Colonel Monroe looked out at the potential killing field around the fort. He faced northward up the lake, which he believed the French would surely use to move their army. Monroe looked at the mountains to the west and the rising ground from the lake towards those mountains.

With a deep sigh, he realized that the French could use either west or east approaches to their advantage. The more he looked, the more it appeared his position was even weaker than he had feared.

The now cleared area southwest of the fort, with the exception of the vegetable garden, wouldn't afford much cover for the attacking French. It would require extensive trench and modern siege craft for them to close in. This would be a slow process, and unless he was completely surrounded, he should be able to get a runner to Fort Edward to ask for help. Then he could squeeze them between the fort's walls and the force sent from Fort Edward.

Monroe turned and looked to the south, towards Fort Edward and General Webb. Unless he was completely surrounded, thought Monroe. He pursed his lips and recalled that the local natives had said, after their visit up north, that the French and their Indian allies numbered "as many as the leaves on the trees."

Monroe shook his head and scoffed. Still, if that were true, he thought as he turned and faced northward once again, he was in for a hell of a fight.

CHAPTER 23

PRELUDE TO THE SIEGE

At Fort Edward, General Webb paced around his room, worried about what he was supposed to do next. This was not working out as he had planned when he had agreed to accept this assignment. It wasn't supposed to be difficult to tame these savages and the French here in the colonies; it was supposed to have been so easy to gain glory.

As Webb moved about his room, the shadows cast by the flickering candles seemed to dance and mock him in his misery. His stomach ached. At least that was the story he used for the garrison commander and his staff so he wouldn't be disturbed or forced to make a decision.

Webb stopped to look down at the map showing the British forts and the French positions to the north.

"Why can't you just go away? Or attack somewhere other than here?" Webb asked Montcalm through the map.

Sighing heavily and rubbing his face with his hand, Webb continued to ponder how he could fix this situation without risking his career, or Lord forbid, getting injured or killed in battle.

The staff at Fort Edward left General Webb alone; he had ordered most of them away with the exception of the surgeon, who provided laudanum for the general's ailments.

Major Fletcher had assigned Captain Reynolds to see to the General's needs to simply get Reynolds out of his way. The man had never seemed to recover from the loss of his sergeant major, but it wasn't Major Fletcher's problem.

Captain Reynolds quickly got into his rhythm and was soon chasing or haranguing the staff to make sure the general was comfortable and well cared for. Most of the staff shrugged their shoulders or rolled their eyes when Captain Reynolds was not looking and ran off to do his bidding when he demanded it.

Like those at Fort William Henry, the garrison at Fort Edward knew something was afoot; it was impossible to ignore the tension in the air. From all of the rumors and indicators they had received, they felt the French were probably going to try something soon. It was the perfect weather for a military campaign. Seeing that General Webb was not launching one, it would more than likely be the French who would do so.

Rogers also believed that something was going to happen, and happen soon. He pulled all of the officers and sergeants together.

"I want every Ranger to be at the ready, their equipment in top shape. While these officers sit on their dead assess without moving, we need to be ready to respond, and respond quickly. You know as well as I do, the Frenchies are coming, and coming soon!"

Rogers personally inspected the arms and equipment of the Rangers, ensuring there was no rust on their muskets and the tomahawks and knives were well honed. Each man was required to maintain sixty rounds of shot and powder at all times in case they were called out. To keep his men occupied and ready, Rogers ran them through drills to maintain their proficiencies, veterans and new recruits alike.

Rogers, knowing the coming battle would be a big one, planned to use all of the Rangers fighting as a company instead of in separate sections. His Rangers were more flexible and could adapt to the changing battlefield, so he would use them to plug holes or gaps in the fight if needed. As Rogers walked through the camp and observed the men cleaning and repairing their gear, he commented to himself that this summer was going to be hot and bloody.

As he moved about the camp, he came across Jacob and his Rangers cleaning their muskets.

"You boys have everything back in order from your raid?" asked Rogers as he motioned for the men to sit back down and continue their work.

"Yes sir, everything's back in order," answered Jacob as he pulled a sharpening stone along the edge of his fighting knife.

Rogers sat on a log next to Jacob, who passed him a tobacco pouch. Rogers filled his pipe and accepted a burning stick from Samuel, and everyone reported that all was in order. They knew that it was always good to keep their muskets in top shape. Rogers nodded his head, pipe smoke curling around his green bonnet.

"What do you all think about the French and their friends? You think they are going to make a push?" asked Rogers.

He knew Jacob and his Rangers had seen a lot of action lately and that they were some of the few who would give honest opinions.

Jacob looked around at everyone and answered for the group. "Yes, sir. They're coming, and coming soon."

Then he placed his knife back in its sheath and looked directly at Rogers.

"From what we saw at Sabbath Bay, they are spoiling for a fight, and we don't think that was all of the Indians; we think there are more still up at Carillon."

Samuel and the others nodded in agreement.

Rogers listened as Jacob and his Rangers gave their account of what they had observed at the recent fight at Sabbath Day Point while he puffed away on his pipe. When everyone had finished, Rogers nodded and said that was what he thought too, but it was also good to hear it from other well-seasoned Rangers.

"I've tried to get these officers," Rogers said, pointing his thumb over his shoulder towards the fort, "to listen to reason. For some reason, this General Webb won't believe what the Mohawks are saying. He thinks they are unreliable."

Jacob snorted, as did the others who knew the Mohawks, and Rogers nodded.

"I even tried to get them to let us go north so we could confirm what the Mohawks have seen, but they refused."

Jacob and the others shook their heads as if in disbelief, yet they knew it was also very true.

"Dese officers don't know who to trust," said Peter. "They don't trust zee Mohawks, or us, so who do zey trust?"

Rogers nodded and grunted, "Yes, who do they trust?"

He stood, tapped out his pipe on the bottom of his shoe, and asked Jacob to walk with him. After a short distance, Rogers turned and spoke to Jacob when they were out of earshot from the others.

"If we're right, if we're all right, then the French are coming, and I don't know if we can stop them," Rogers said. "I have heard from the Iroquois and others who are adamant that there are thousands of French, Canadians, and Indians ready to pour down the lake and bury William Henry."

Rogers looked directly at Jacob.

"Webb doesn't look like he'll do anything, which means we're going to get caught in a massive fight. I want you and your Rangers to be ready, Sergeant Clarke. I may need to call on them to do what they do best."

Jacob nodded and asked, "Which is?"

Rogers smiled and said, "Why, killing Frenchmen of course."

Then Rogers looked seriously at Jacob. "It's also because I know you and your men can do just about anything, including saving my hide from time to time. I may have to rely on you to not only save my hide, but others as well. So be ready if I need you."

Jacob nodded and returned to his men while Rogers continued on to check on the rest of the Rangers and their preparations.

Had they been able to see very far to the north, they would have had proof that their fears were justified. Considering how close the French had come to almost taking William Henry during the Saint Patrick's Day raid, the governor general had agreed to Montcalm's plan to take a massive force south and finally finish off Fort William Henry.

The recent success at Sabbath Bay also reinforced their belief they could beat the English.

Montcalm's restrictions on raiding, scouting, and releasing prisoners were paying off, keeping information from British eyes and ears. Nearly twelve thousand men had secretly assembled around Carillon, with artillery and boats arriving daily. Two thousand Indians gathered from some thirty-three tribes were all coming to join and share in the glory of taking Fort William Henry. It was a mighty force that Montcalm had assembled, and strong enough to perhaps take him all the way to Albany.

Father Pierre Roubaud moved about the camp, observing the activity of the army preparing to march. He was still shaken by what had occurred in the Indian camp following the capture of the Englishmen at Sabbath Day Point. He had learned of forest spirits from the shamans, and he wondered if he had actually observed those forest spirits, if they were the black demons who had attacked because of the crimes the Chippewas were committing against the captured Englishmen.

These savages have brought the slaughter upon themselves, he thought. But as he walked around the camp, he sometimes could not distinguish French or Canadians from Indians, who had adopted their style of dress and mannerisms.

Montcalm called for a council of war, attended by all of the Indian chiefs and war leaders, as well as his French and Canadian officers. After all had assembled, the great chiefs arranged by their rank and seniority, Montcalm began by passing a wampum belt of 6,000 beads to the Indian chiefs as a symbol of the unity between the French and the thirty-three tribes. The belt was passed, and each of the chiefs from the thirty-three tribes spoke of the glory and the opportunity that had been laid before them by their French fathers, to turn the lake red with the blood of their English foes.

Once the orations were complete, Montcalm laid out his plan for the movement south. They did not have enough boats to transport the entire army, so he would split his force.

A lead element commanded by de Levis and composed of French regulars, Canadians, and about twenty-five-hundred Indians would move overland along the west shore of the lake. They were to screen the army, sweeping any enemy unit from the front and allowing the main force to move unmolested.

Montcalm would take another five thousand men in the boats and travel two days later to meet with de Levis. As a combined force, they would then march on Fort William Henry.

Nothing will bar our way to the fort, or southward to Albany. Victory will be mine, mused Montcalm, and he smiled at the prospect.

The following morning, de Levis assembled his force, and they began their movement towards their enemies. Helping de Levis was an Iroquois hunter named Kanaktagon, who knew the area extremely well and would lead them on the fastest paths to the rendezvous with Montcalm at Northwest Bay. They carried only what they needed. De Levis had decided to move lightly so they would be fast and quiet as they passed through the dense forest along the lake.

As Montcalm watched de Levis's column depart, he gave orders that no alcohol was to be given to any of the Indians from this point on. The campaign was on, and he did not want any alcohol-fueled situations that could warn the English and ruin the element of surprise.

The flotilla of two hundred and fifty boats was loaded with supplies and the implements of war, especially the artillery, which they would need to batter down the walls of the fort. The infantry checked their muskets, finished packing their packs and haversacks, and moved to their assembly areas. The Canadians melted lead and made shot, checked to see that all of their horns were filled with powder, and cooked their rations.

De Levis and his force traveled quickly and quietly, joining up with some smaller Indian bands along the way. They spotted no one who would give away that they were on the move, and they only rested briefly at night before continuing on to Northwest Bay.

Montcalm waited the two days agreed upon before issuing the command to launch the force. The army loaded its boats and began the journey down Lake George/St. Sacrement. De Levis had sent out scouts and, seeing no one, had lit three signal fires to inform Montcalm that all was clear.

The flotilla moved down the lake to Sabbath Day Point, where they were joined by one hundred and fifty canoes carrying more Indians, who led the expedition down the lake and into the gloom of the night. Montcalm was able to guide the flotilla by the signal fires provided by de Levis.

That night, the flotilla put to shore. The army rested until noon before sending de Levis ahead to continue screening their movements until they reached the fort, where they would begin to scout the enemy positions.

As the French Army made its way south on and along the lake, at Fort Edward and out on the island, Rogers was stalking around his cabin, deep in thought while smoking his pipe, the trail of smoke tracing his pacing back and forth. He wanted to know what was going on in the north near the lake; he wanted to know what those pesky French were up to.

Rogers stopped, took a pull from his pipe, and made a decision. "To hell with orders, and to hell with the general," he grumbled as he quickly moved over and looked at his map. Looking up from the map, Rogers yelled, "Get me Sergeant Clarke!" and one of his runners went to fetch Jacob.

Sprinting from the hut, the orderly ran up to Jacob, who was speaking with Konkapot and a few of the other Rangers from the company.

"The Major wants to see you, Sergeant," the orderly said. "Should we get ready to move?" asked Konkapot, and Jacob nodded as he followed the orderly back to Rogers' hut.

Konkapot raised his eyebrows and then headed over to let the rest of the section know that Jacob had been called by Major Rogers, which meant they probably had a mission coming up. Jacob arrived at the hut and went inside when Rogers, who was looking over the map of Lake George, waved him in.

"I am tired of waiting to see if General Webb will get off his damned indecisive ass and make a decision," said Rogers. "Everyone knows the French are up to something, and I intend to find out what."

Jacob nodded.

"You're going to have to take your section out of here in the dark. The fort commander and his generalship still don't seem to want anything but local scouts. Take your men, head towards and skirt around William Henry, and then push as far north as you can until you find the French. I want an accurate report of what's going on, and I want it done quietly."

Rogers looked Jacob directly in the eyes to emphasize his point. "That's why I want you to go. I know you have an uncanny way of getting in and out quietly. Avoid contact at all costs, if possible," instructed Rogers, "but if not, make sure no one survives to warn the French we have been there."

Jacob again nodded, and a grim look crossed his face. "That won't be a problem," he said.

Rogers nodded. "Get back here so we can provide reliable information that they will have no choice but to accept, unless they don't trust us."

Then Rogers thought about it for a moment. "If that happens, then to hell with all of them!"

He looked at Jacob.

"Any questions? It won't be difficult for you, will it?" Rogers asked, almost pitying any French or their allies who got in Jacob's way. "No sir," Jacob answered, his eyes intent. "No problem at all."

Rogers nodded and shook Jacob's hand, then handed him written orders to "scout the area between Fort Edward, Halfway Brook, and Fort Anne, then to return to Fort Edward," in case anyone asked about the Rangers' whereabouts.

"Good hunting," he said to Jacob. "I'll be getting the rest of the companies ready to respond. If we're right, they are going to need all of us ready to go at a moment's notice."

Jacob returned to his cabin to find the men were already assembled and waiting. Chuckling to himself, Jacob began laying out what Rogers wanted them to do.

"We're going on a local scout," Jacob began, and his men groaned. Holding his hand up, Jacob continued, "past Fort William Henry, and then we're to head north and find the French."

That seemed to draw his men's attention. They all looked at one another, then back at Jacob, smiles of anticipation replacing the previous groans of despair.

Jacob instructed them, "Make sure you have almost two weeks' worth of rations and that everyone has his sixty rounds of shot and powder."

Peter said, "We already have about a week's worth of cooked rations; we would only need another week's worth."

Jacob led the men over to the quartermaster, nodding to Frederick as they went by to draw the extra rations. Frederick remained leaning against a porch post, smoking his pipe, and he winked back.

The quartermaster looked dubiously at Jacob, who handed him the written instructions for a local scout from Major Rogers. The quartermaster then shrugged and started issuing out the salt pork, beef, hard biscuits, flour, and some vegetables from the garden.

They returned to the island, where they spent most of the afternoon cooking their rations and packing their equipment.

Once everything was ready, they sat around the field kitchen and waited for the sun to set. Even the wolves sat in readiness, sensing they were going out and getting away from the island. Rogers and some of the other Rangers came over to sit, smoke, and talk to pass time.

Rogers whispered to Jacob, "No one suspects?"

Jacob nodded. "Quartermaster thinks we're following your written orders. We only drew a week's worth of rations."

Jacob didn't mention Frederick. Rogers nodded. "Will it be enough?"

Jacob smiled and explained that they always maintained a week's worth of rations, so they had enough for two, and the quartermaster was none the wiser.

Rogers nodded and smiled. "Good thinking," he answered.

When the sun set and the day transitioned to night, Rogers nodded that it was time, and Jacob and his men shouldered their packs and rifles and headed towards the river where they loaded a large canoe. Even the wolves jumped in and took their places, sniffing the breeze on the water. Rogers shook the Rangers' hands and wished them luck as they climbed into the canoe.

Jacob nodded and pushed the large canoe off, and they began paddling up the river quietly. It was dark enough that it was hard to see the canoe on the river from the fort's wall. They only paddled a little way up river, enough to be away from the fort, before they landed. After unloading their gear, they pulled the canoe up and concealed it in thick brush. Jacob gathered everyone close and whispered, "We'll move up towards Halfway Brook and find a place to hide during the day near Bloody Pond. We'll avoid the fort and push past it and skirt the area to the west, then head north in the dark."

Everyone nodded. Moving at night in these dense woods could be difficult. They had done it several times, however, so they settled into the night scouting file, tighter than the way they moved during the day, but still following the same principles.

The wolves wagged their tails in anticipation. Jacob would rely on their keen senses that were better adapted to the dark than those of the men. With wolfish grins, they padded after the Rangers, noses and ears peaked, hunting.

They moved cautiously through the forest, constantly looking for one another as well as listening for any sound that might indicate enemies were nearby. The wolves moved silently, but with a keen alertness, ears up and noses sweeping the breeze as they stayed low to the ground. The Rangers could see each other's dark shapes in the night, and they kept close contact, whispering so no sound traveled away from them.

It wasn't all bad. There was almost a full moon peeking out from behind the clouds, making it easier to see, they were moving through an area in which the trees and brush were not as thick as in some other places, and they had traveled the area numerous times before and knew it well.

When they reached Halfway Brook, Jacob stopped the patrol, and they took cover behind the trees, watching and listening for anyone in the area. The wolves lay low but scanned the woods for any enemy that could be hidden there.

After a few minutes of careful listening, Jacob sent Konkapot, James, and Peter across while Jacob and the others covered them from the woods. The three men, along with Raven, moved cautiously across the open area, crossed over the brook, and entered the woods on the far side. After a few minutes, Konkapot made the call of a night bird, which indicated all was clear, and Jacob brought the others across.

The grey of predawn was beginning to spread over the mountains when they arrived near Bloody Pond. Using their well-practiced procedures, Jacob moved his men into a thicket where they would spend the day.

As Konkapot covered the tracks leading into their hide site, everyone listened to hear if anyone was close by. The wolves looked and sniffed, their golden eyes constantly watching the woods around them, but they made no indication that anything was near them.

Jacob nodded when he felt everything was in order, and they helped each other to quietly take off their gear and settle in for the day. Jacob took the first watch as everyone quietly wiggled a space in the thick brush and settled down to sleep. Konkapot curled up with Raven, and Otto lay between Samuel and Peter. Smoke stayed near Jacob, keeping the watch with him.

Jacob had an uneasy feeling about the days ahead. He was afraid they might get more than had they bargained for. As he watched the woods and thought, he scratched Smoke's ears, who sighed in satisfaction. He did not understand why these English officers had become so timid, compared to General Johnson, who was always spoiling for a fight.

Perhaps that's why we won more often back then, thought Jacob.

He sighed. Johnson had been one of them, a Provincial rather than some rich-born aristocrat from England. Well, Jacob thought, these fine English gentlemen better get their act together before the French teach them a hard lesson. The French seemed to be doing a better job of fighting this conflict than the English were.

Konkapot relieved Jacob, who nodded and patted his shoulder before squeezing into a soft section of ground under some bushes, Smoke joining him. The sun was coming up, so he used his bonnet to cover his eyes and after a couple of deep breaths, fell asleep. Smoke settled his head on his paws, and after one last look, closed his eyes and fell asleep as well.

During the day, they took turns watching, eating, and sleeping. As the sun sank behind the mountains and the inky blackness of night began to descend on the forest, Jacob had everyone up, packed, and listening, including the wolves.

Once they were sure no one was close by, Konkapot led them out, and Jacob steered them towards Fort William Henry. From Bloody Pond, it would be easier to head to the east of the fort to bypass it, and they could then continue their journey north.

A full moon was still out in a brilliant, star-speckled night with no clouds and a pleasant breeze. Jacob could not enjoy the scenery, however; his uneasiness was returning. There was tension in the air. It almost seemed like the mountains were holding their breath to see what was going to happen next on this giant stage.

As they closed in near the fort, Konkapot froze and held his arm up in a fist as Raven flattened on the ground, emitting a low growl. Everyone froze, and then slowly lowered themselves to the ground. The other two wolves did likewise, tuning in on some unseen object in the woods.

Jacob slowly and quietly made his way forward to Konkapot, who pointed off to their front. Sure enough, figures could be seen moving through the woods parallel to the Rangers. The Rangers quietly crawled into bushes and branches to conceal themselves. Jacob and Konkapot watched the group approach their position and then angle away heading east.

Jacob leaned over and whispered in Konkapot's ear, "Huron?" Konkapot slowly nodded yes. Their distinct silhouette meant

Rogers and most of the men were right; there were enemies close by. Jacob wondered if this was a scouting patrol, a small war party, or something else.

They waited until the Hurons were a good distance away before Jacob pulled everyone close. He once again poured some gunpowder into his hand, then some water from his canteen, and rubbed his hands together to mix the powder and water. Then he smeared the black mess on his face, neck, and hands to hide the whiteness of his skin.

Everyone followed suit, even Konkapot, darkening themselves so they could blend in with the night. The wolves stared in wonderment at this procedure, their tongues lolling out in a wolfish laugh.

Once everyone was ready, Jacob led the patrol forward, and they cautiously approached an elevated area to the west that overlooked the fort. The patrol stopped at the edge of the wood line and looked down at Fort William Henry in the distance.

From their observation point, they could see the light from the fort and smoke rising from the interior. They didn't see anything out of the ordinary, so Jacob motioned for them to head towards the western shore of the lake. Perhaps it was just a simple enemy scouting expedition they had passed, but that uneasiness still haunted Jacob.

It can't be that simple, he thought to himself.

They moved along a small ridge, staying on the reverse slope to hide their movement. The wolves moved ahead of them, searching for the enemy. As they traveled along the ridge, once again Konkapot motioned for them to freeze as another enemy patrol was observed. This time they could see what they assumed were Canadians, judging by as much of their clothing as could be seen in the dark, along with some French.

Jacob waited until the enemy was well out of sight before moving again. A third enemy patrol was observed as Jacob and his Rangers were near the southwestern corner of Lake George. Jacob knew this was not good: too many enemy patrols in one area.

"This place is crawling," whispered Konkapot to Jacob as they observed the enemy move past them.

They had to stop several more times to conceal themselves as more enemy patrols moved by, both men and wolves sinking into the underbrush. Jacob angled them away and moved to a higher vantage point to look down on the lake. They found a suitable spot, and Jacob and his men slowly crawled forward.

They were shocked by what they observed below them. Easily seen in the moonlight were thousands of the white uniforms of French regulars. Fires dotted the shoreline, where hundreds of boats were lined up, and a busy line of men were moving supplies from the boats to the growing camp.

"How is it Fort William Henry doesn't know about this?" whispered Samuel as they looked at the large army arrayed below them.

Peter crawled up next to Jacob and pointed out several large barges that had the shapes of large artillery pieces on them.

"Siege guns," whispered Peter, and Jacob nodded. Below them was the massive French Army of the Marquis de Montcalm.

"Our friends were right," whispered Jacob. "They do number like the leaves on the trees. I think the fort is in grave danger. We need to warn them."

Everyone nodded, and Jacob led them crawling backwards to the other side of the ridge. They had to warn the fort, but Jacob was concerned that with the large number of enemy patrols, it might be too hard to get through. They had to make an attempt. The fort needed to be warned.

But even moving quietly like shadows, they could see they weren't going to be able to get close to the fort. From their position behind the enemy patrols, they could now see that the French, the Canadians, and their Indian allies were sealing off the fort from the outside. They could see groups of the enemy taking positions to block anyone from leaving or entering the fort.

Jacob shook his head; the enemy was holding the line at the edge of the woods, unobserved from the fort's walls. Jacob looked at the enemy positions, then at the large open killing space from the woods to the fort. "That's why no one knows. No one is coming in or going out; the fort is blind," whispered Jacob, and Konkapot nodded. The fort was effectively sealed off from the world.

There would be no way they could pass through the enemy pickets without being detected, and most of them would not survive. Even if they were to try to send a message tied to one of the wolves, who in the fort would know these were Rangers' wolves and how would they get the wolves to run to the fort? They weren't carrier pigeons.

Jacob made a hard decision. There was nothing they could do for Fort William Henry, but maybe they could get help from Fort Edward.

Jacob motioned for them to head south away from Fort William Henry, silently wishing their fellow Rangers inside the fort and in the encampment the best of luck.

"Hang in there," Jacob whispered to the wind. "We're going to bring help."

They moved slowly, step by step, and stayed in the shadows of the trees. Jacob scanned the skies. It would be dawn soon, and they had to get away before it became too difficult to avoid detection.

As they moved, they came across one of the enemy pickets from behind. Jacob halted the patrol, and took stock of the situation. Behind them were more Canadians and Indians moving through the woods towards the fort. They had no choice. They had to go forward through the enemy picket.

Jacob slowly drew his knife, and they all understood what they had to do. Jacob pointed out one guard leaning against a tree to Konkapot and Peter; James and Charles were pointed at another to the left. Samuel would hold their gear so they could move silently. Jacob's target was what appeared to be a Canadian lying behind cover, but his head was down, probably asleep. Jacob motioned with his hand for the wolves to stay low.

Jacob nodded, and the three groups moved slowly forward, Jacob on the ground, slithering toward his target, followed quietly by Smoke. Konkapot and Peter stalked their target low to the ground, watched by the golden eyes of the wolves.

In a quick rush, Konkapot came up behind his target, placing his left hand over the man's mouth while sinking his knife into his kidney. Peter quickly grabbed his falling musket to stop it from clattering to the ground.

Jacob looked to his left to see James and Charles approaching their target when Charles stumbled over another Canadian lying prone whom they hadn't seen. Quickly, all three wolves sprang on the unseen enemy, jumping on the startled man and pinning him to the ground while sinking their teeth in his arms and his throat. He made no sound or movement.

Charles breathed a sigh of relief as James quickly moved up using his left arm to cover the mouth of his target, who had turned at the motion of the wolves. James kicked him behind the knees, and as the man bent back, James sank his knife into his chest while pinning his musket against his body so it wouldn't fall.

Jacob quickly leaped up and landed on top of his target, who seemed to be waking up. His head came up, but Jacob's weight crushed him down, pressing his face into the earth as Jacob stabbed deep into his kidneys.

Jacob looked around; all four had died quietly, and no alarm had been raised. He wiped his blade on his dead enemy's shirt as Samuel handed him his rifle and gear. The wolves padded quietly by with a satisfied look, blood smeared on their muzzles.

No sooner had they dispatched these enemies than another sound of approaching men was heard in the dark. Jacob, his men, and the wolves dropped to the ground and waited. As three shapes approached, their outlines were distinct, and they were not Indians. Jacob used a whippoorwill call, and the three shapes froze and replied with a different whippoorwill call.

Jacob slowly rose and approached the figures, who turned out to be three Rangers.

"Damn glad you didn't stick me with that," whispered one of the Rangers, pointing to Jacob's knife. "We have a dispatch for Fort Edward." Jacob nodded. "Luckily for you, we were here, or it would have been you on the ground," he whispered back, indicating the dead Canadians on the ground.

Jacob told the Rangers to fall in with his men , and they would help the Rangers get back to Fort Edward. Once everyone was reequipped and armed, they moved through the hole they had created and traveled quickly away from the area.

The Rangers continued silently through the early dawn, not seeing any more enemy patrols. Once they reached Bloody Pond, Jacob called a quick halt.

They discussed what they had seen, and decided they had to move even more quickly to warn Fort Edward. The three men, originally from Captain Putnam's company but detailed to Fort William Henry, confirmed that the French were having a go at them.

Jacob decided they would push through the day and reach Fort Edward as soon as they could. Speed would have to be their security as they pushed their pace up to a jog to get back and warn the fort. They settled into a distance-eating pace, still scanning the area around them as they moved.

After some time, they crossed over Halfway Brook and, feeling confident they were away from any enemy patrols, increased their pace even further. As they were moving towards Fort Edward, a single cannon shot could be heard from the vicinity of Fort William Henry, followed by the sounds of popping muskets.

Jacob paused and looked behind them, assuming the sound was the signal cannon warning Fort Edward that William Henry was under attack. "Well, that seals it. The French are attacking the fort. Let's get back quickly, and see if we can save the men at William Henry."

The Rangers began trotting to Fort Edward, hoping the soldiers in the fort were already in motion, reacting to the sound of the signal gun from Fort William Henry.

A lookout on the wall at Fort Edward spotted the Rangers and their wolves jogging out of the woods on the military road and alerted the fort that Rangers were coming in. When Jacob and the Rangers came up to the fort, they were met by Major Rogers. Catching his breath, Jacob quickly reported what they had observed.

Rogers motioned Jacob and the three Rangers from William Henry to follow him into the fort to the commander's office. The timing was perfect. Major Fletcher had assembled all of the Provincial officers and was in the process of a meeting when Rogers and Jacob entered.

The three Rangers reported their situation and passed the dispatch to Major Fletcher. Fletcher read the dispatch from Monroe.

"Sir, a large enemy force has landed with artillery and has begun taking William Henry under siege. We need reinforcements immediately before the enemy has time to invest in siege works and take this position under fire. Colonel Monroe."

"That explains the signal gun we heard. The French are investing William Henry," remarked Major Fletcher.

Major Rogers looked directly at Major Fletcher. "Now do you believe us? Is this information reliable enough for you?"

Jacob stood there in shock as the room exploded into shouts and excited voices. All of the Provincial officers like Rogers demanded to know when they would march out to save Fort William Henry. The British officers shouted back about following orders and stopping this continued lack of discipline and respect.

A sudden shout of "Enough!" stopped the heated argument, everyone shocked that the shout had come from Captain Reynolds. "You're disturbing the general with all of this shouting. He is ill and needs his rest!"

Jacob shut his eyes and shook his head, trying to figure what insanity this was. This cannot be really happening, he whispered. "Gentlemen, what is going on?" asked a new voice, and Jacob opened his eyes to see that General Webb had entered the room, accompanied by another gentleman, Colonel Montresor.

Colonel Montresor sat down and took charge, allowing all to report, while General Webb observed from the side. Rogers reported what Jacob had observed around Fort William Henry, supported by the three Rangers who had just arrived from the fort.

The British officers debated how reliable this Provincial Ranger's information was, which caused the room to explode once more as the Provincials yelled that the Rangers were more reliable than anything the British had provided.

Webb stood there and watched the argument between the British and Provincial officers go back and forth as he read the dispatch from Monroe. Their voices were raised, and their language was becoming more heated and foul.

"Thank you gentlemen!" yelled General Webb. "I will take this all under consideration and issue more orders when I determine the extent of this threat. That will be all. Dismissed!"

CHAPTER 24

THE SIEGE OF FORT WILLIAM HENRY

Rogers was livid, spitting and sputtering as they walked towards the island, even kicking a stone that got in his way.

"Why are they so blind?" growled Rogers. "Why won't they see the truth in it?"

Jacob walked alongside, nodding his agreement. Rogers noticed the front of Jacob's shirt was bloodstained. He stopped and pointed at the blood.

"Yours?" he asked.

Jacob shook his head. "Theirs."

Rogers nodded and continued walking across the bridge onto the island.

"See to your men, Jacob," Rogers directed and then turned to

Jacob. "You did a fine job once again."

After shaking Jacob's hand, Rogers continued on to his cabin.

"At least the major has it figured out," commented Konkapot as he joined Jacob.

Jacob nodded, and they continued on to their cabin to clean their gear and wait to see what would happen.

For the next couple of days, the Rangers and the garrison at Fort Edward waited for General Webb to make a decision. More scouts came in and reported that they had heard several artillery pieces and many muskets firing in the vicinity of Fort William Henry. Even with all of these reports, the old standing orders of only localized scouts were still being enforced, and no scouts were dispatched to the vicinity of the lake and the fort.

In the command office, the British officers and the Provincial officers debated on what their course of action should be. Many said they needed to march out and support Fort William Henry. Others cautioned that this could be nothing but a ruse or a small raid, not an actual attack. "You know how these Provincials have a tendency to over-exaggerate the enemy's strength," scoffed one of the staff officers.

The Provincials countered, "No different than the lack of aggressiveness of the Crown's forces."

The room echoed as both sides argued instead of finding a solution. The reliability of Provincial Rangers in providing accurate information was questioned again, mostly by the British officers. This started another series of angry debates with the Provincials, who shouted back that the Rangers' reports had been the most accurate reports provided by any of the forces here on the frontier. The debate moved back and forth, the voices rising and falling in anger and frustration.

Meanwhile in his room next to the office, General Webb sat on his bed, cradling his head in his hands. His headache was pounding. He wasn't sure if it was from the loud debate outside his door, the tough decision that he had to make, or maybe another one of these blasted frontier ailments.

He looked over on his table where several small bottles of laudanum were sitting, provided by the fort's surgeon. Webb rose from his bed and went over the table, poured a glass of wine, and then emptied one of the laudanum vials into the glass. He swirled it around and then drank it down.

Ah, that will make it feel better, thought Webb, but the loud debate from the other room again attracted his attention.

What am I supposed to do? he thought. I can march north and if this is nothing but a raid or a ruse, like my officers believe, then it's no trouble other than a march.

Webb continued to debate in his own mind. *If it is an attack, I could be heralded as the savior of the north if I march up there and catch the French between the fort and my forces.*

Webb's face brightened at that thought, then it fell once again as he continued to look at the problem from different angles.

If they are as many as these Rangers and Indians claim, then not only could we lose Fort William Henry, we could lose this force, which in turn would lose Fort Edward and open the way to Albany.

Webb shook his head; this would be the worst thing that could happen. *I would be the man who lost New York.*

Webb began to pace his room again. His headache was still there, but not as severe as before. *The medicine must be kicking in,* he thought. *They have heard the sound of cannon fire coming from Fort William Henry,* Webb thought.

He stopped pacing, and spoke out loud, "Instead of me going, why not send for the garrison from Albany?"

A satisfied look spread across General Webb's face. He knew he had no choice. All the other forces had been assembled for the expedition to Halifax under Lord Loudoun, and so he must rely on and call out all the Provincials and militia so as not to lose New York.

The door opened from Webb's room into the office, and the general walked into the now silent room.

"Gentlemen, I believe this is a major thrust, but we mustn't weaken our defenses here. We will wait here for further developments. Commanders, make sure your men are ready to march out if required, or if the enemy intends to raid towards us. I want localized scouts to provide early warning if an enemy raid is approaching."

Webb looked directly at Major Rogers.

"I want some of your Rangers to carry a dispatch to Albany. I will call upon the militia to turn out and march with all haste to Fort William Henry."

Then he turned to the rest of the officers. "I want a parade and inspection this afternoon. See to it, Captain Reynolds!"

Captain Reynolds snapped to attention with a loud "Sir!" and saluted the general.

Satisfied he had made a decision, Webb returned to his room. He was feeling much better, almost euphoric. Perhaps this was because the burden of making a decision was gone, or maybe he had mixed too much laudanum in his wine. In either case, he was feeling much better.

Rogers and his officers slipped out of the room, disgusted, and headed out to their island.

"They refuse to see, and they bury their heads in the dirt so they can't see!" growled Rogers. "And while they dither, Fort William Henry will be blasted into nothing."

Captain Putnam asked, "What do you want us to do?"

Rogers took only a few seconds to think about it. "Have everyone ready to go. Someone is going to have to save the day; it might as well be us!"

After the Provincial and regular officers dispersed to follow his instructions, Webb called for his aide de camp to pen a reply to Monroe's dispatch. His orderly arrived, and with his small writing desk set, with parchment and quill, waited on the general.

"To Colonel Monroe, from General Webb. Sir, we have fired our signal guns in reply to yours, so you know we have heard your signals. However, before I can determine a suitable course of action to support your situation, I require additional information concerning the strength and disposition of the enemy investing your position. Once we can determine the intelligence of your situation, we will respond with the full weight of the army if required and when it seems plausible. Until then, it is my sincere concern that you remain safe until we can render to you the appropriate assistance."

Webb looked down at his aide as he scribbled away on his tablet.

"Sign it and send a runner immediately to Fort William Henry," instructed Webb, who returned to his room and shut the door.

Back on the island, Major Rogers was discussing the situation with Captains Putnam and Stark, each with a disgusted look on his face. Major Rogers smoked his pipe while they looked at their options.

"I can almost understand why this Englishman refuses to support Provincial officers," commented Putman. "But to not support one of their own? This is insane!"

"What are we going to do, sir?" asked Stark. "We have our Rangers up there and Provincials as well."

Rogers stopped smoking and looked at Stark. To emphasize Stark's point, the low rumble of artillery could be heard in the distance.

"To hell with General Webb's inactivity," spat Rogers, who tapped out the bowl of his pipe on a stump. "We're going up there to see if we can at least save our own or some of the folks stuck at the fort. Stark, get your company ready; I will instruct you and your Rangers what I need done. I will also take care of any inquiries from the upper command."

Captain Stark nodded and rushed ahead, calling for his sergeants and lieutenants.

"Putnam, select two men and have them report to Major Fletcher so they can carry the dispatch to Albany."

As Stark and Putnam assembled their men, the situation to the north was becoming very dire. Montcalm's army was in full motion, establishing a field hospital and the initial buildup of siege artillery and lines and completing the encirclement of the fort.

Montcalm's siege engineers selected the firing line of the heavy guns to focus on the exposed angle of the fort's northwest corner. The engineers also looked at developing a second siege line where more guns could take the fort in a crossfire.

The French and Canadians began working in earnest, digging the siege lines and building the fascines and gabions in the style of true 18th century European siege craft. While the French and Canadians were digging, the thousands of Indians and the other Canadians encircled both the fort and the encampment and kept them under constant musket and rifle fire.

To interrupt this effort, Lieutenant Thomas Collins had Fort William Henry's twenty-four cannons at his disposal. The guns were crewed by experienced Royal Artillerymen as well as by gunners from the Royal Navy.

Collins positioned his largest guns, 32-pound pieces, in the northwest corner to fire directly on the French siege workers. Soon, the gunners took up a rhythmic cycle of sustained artillery fire, giving as good as they got from the French guns.

As Fort William Henry was fighting for its life, Stark had assembled the company on the island and instructed his Rangers to form a horseshoe. Major Rogers approached and pulled everyone in close.

"Rangers, we have a situation. The French have isolated Fort William Henry and are laying siege to it. You can hear the artillery in the distance. We have men there, and there are women and children there. General Webb will not march north to support Monroe, so I am sending you up there. I want you to gather as much information as you can, see if you can take a prisoner or two so we can figure out what the French will do next, and, if you can help anyone up there, then try."

Rogers looked at the assembled company of only sixty men, not much of a force to go up against thousands.

"Don't try to be heroes; dead heroes don't amount to much. I need live Rangers to carry on the fight, even if the British are too timid to do it themselves. Wait until dusk, and move under the cover of darkness. I'll cover you. If asked, I'll say that you're doing a march to Saratoga to escort supplies or lead the reinforcements from Albany to here."

Stark nodded. Rogers finished wishing them good luck and good hunting and returned to his cabin.

When the dusk had deepened enough to conceal their movements, Stark had the sections break off and leave separately, agreeing to rendezvous at Bloody Pond.

When it was time for Jacob to lead his men out, Stark wished them luck, and Rogers waved from his hut, the glow of his pipe illuminating his face. They moved to the end of the island where they could cross the river on foot, because the river was still low this early in August.

After wading across, Konkapot and Charles led their section into the forest with Raven once again ranging in front, followed by Jacob, James, and Smoke, and then Samuel, Peter, and Otto. They moved silently but steadily through the forest towards Halfway Brook.

As before, Jacob used half of the section to cover as the other half crossed the open field before catching up himself. It was past midnight when they arrived at Bloody Pond. A hooded candle was lit, allowing the light to be seen only from the south to guide the Rangers in. There, the different Ranger sections came together, while in the distance, the hollow booming of artillery could be plainly heard.

"Hang in there," Jacob whispered to the air. "We're coming."

Just before dawn, all of the company had arrived, and while the Rangers rested, Stark called in the sergeants and lieutenants to go over their plans. Jacob and his section would swing to the east, observe the military road to the fort, and see if the French had any positions on the eastern shore or on the high ground. If he felt safe, he was to try to make contact with their fellow Rangers in the encampment.

Stark with two sections would head to the west to see how strong the encirclement was, while one section would move up through the swampy area just south of the fort to see how close they could get. Stark stressed the need to be careful on this one. The hornet's nest was stirred up and broken, and thousands of angry French, Canadians, and Indians were out howling for their blood.

Once everyone understood their instructions, they returned to their sections and tried to get some rest. In the distance, the constant sound of a heavy artillery bombardment punctuated the desperate situation they were now facing.

As the Rangers rested and waited, up at Fort William Henry, Colonel Monroe looked out at the enemy positions as their heavy artillery boomed and heavy shot smashed into the walls of the fort. He had guessed right that the French would come from the northwest, since the east was covered by the large encampment and the swamp, which would have made it difficult to move heavy siege guns there.

Still, the encampment itself, protected only by a palisade, was surrounded and under constant musket fire. Most of Colonel Monroe's men were there. The inside of the fort could hold only 500, who were mostly the regulars of his 35th Regiment. Most of the Provincials were in the encampment.

For every one of his balls that flew, the French were sending back eight or ten more. He could see the French engineers digging their trenches and throwing up gabions and fascines to protect the diggers. All the while, the constant musket fire of the Canadians and Indians made it difficult for Monroe's men to return fire.

While most of his cannon shots were falling into the woods around the French position, some made impacts on the construction crews. The French simply removed the dead or injured and brought up replacements to continue the work.

The sun was beginning to climb into the sky, portent for another hot day. Where were his reinforcements? He had sent several runners to Fort Edward. It had been three days, enough time for a sizable force to make its way here and break the siege. Monroe turned and looked to the south, trying to see down to Fort Edward and glean what General Webb was up to.

There had been rumors that this Provincial General William Johnson, the same man who had stopped the French at this very spot once before, was marching with artillery and several thousand militia and Provincials to rescue them from this vise. However, he had not seen any hard proof that this was anything but idle rumors.

There was an ear-shattering explosion from behind Monroe, which pitched him forward into the wall, his head and ears ringing. Knocked to the ground, Monroe picked himself up. His head felt like it was full of cotton, and his ears were ringing, making it hard to hear. He felt something wet on his shoulder, and reaching up, he pulled off entrails that had landed on him.

One of the large 32-pound cannons had burst, sending large jagged chunks of metal everywhere and shredding the gun crew. In a haze, Monroe could see body parts and at least one man's upper torso scattered around the gun. A soldier came over and supported his injured shoulder and led him down off the wall.

"You must see the surgeon, sir!" he yelled over the din of the fighting.

To the south of the fighting around the fort, the Rangers were on the move, snaking silently through the woods, probing to find a way through the enemy encirclement.

While Jacob and his Rangers were moving towards Fort William Henry, another patrol from Stark's company had actually captured a Canadian prisoner, whom they quickly returned to Fort Edward. Once there, the Canadian was brought into one of the dark, damp bastions of the fort and was being interrogated in the dim light of a swinging lantern.

The Canadian, a Lieutenant Jacques Vaudry, had no problem spilling out the information the British officer and his imposing guards wanted. He slyly said that Montcalm had arrived with over 11,000 men and a large train of artillery, which included mortars.

This information was quickly sent to General Webb, who calculated that even if all of the Provincials and militia arrived, his force would still be outnumbered three to one. The staff could see the fire and energy leave General Webb; a look of desperation now lined his face. "Send a message to Colonel Monroe. Tell him that an attempt to move an army to his aide is no longer feasible based on new information just made available concerning enemy strength and disposition. We can do nothing until the entire army is formed with the reinforcements from the local militia and Provincials."

As the Rangers moved through the woods, the sun was coming up and it was becoming lighter as Jacob moved his section towards the military road that connected Fort William Henry with Fort Edward. They were close enough to hear the constant sound of artillery and musket fire, the wolves not liking the heavy thump and shock from the artillery, even in the distance.

As they were closing in on the road, Smoke growled and froze, which caused everyone to freeze. To their front near the road were several Indians and Canadians concealed in bushes or near trees.

That's why no dispatches are going out or coming in, thought Jacob.

"Damn!" hissed Peter who pointed down the road at an unsuspecting courier jogging towards the fort.

"Fire and close with them!" growled Jacob, and the Rangers and their wolves broke cover and rushed the enemy. An Abenaki was raising his musket to aim at the approaching courier when Smoke plowed into him, his jaws closing and crushing the Indian's throat and knocking him to the ground.

Jacob and his Rangers quickly picked their targets and fired their rifles, which were masked by the constant sound of the siege. Six Canadians and Indians fell, shocked that someone had hit them, and then Jacob and the Rangers fell on the other ambushers with tomahawks and knives. The courier, panting from the exertion of running to the fort, was surprised to see the flurry of activity and the close report of gunfire.

Then green shapes were wrestling with brown shapes in the trees.

"Get to the fort!" yelled Jacob, and the courier picked up his pace.

As he ran down the road, three more shapes detached from the trees, which he now recognized as Indians. They gave a war whoop, but all three were quickly knocked down as bullets whizzed past him to strike them. Jacob turned and slowed just enough to see the green uniformed men, Rangers he believed, load and then three more fired. The runner saw three more Indians fall.

His pace quickened. It seemed the courier had found a new burst of energy as he charged on towards the fort. He was almost to the bridge over the stream, when another group of Indians he hadn't seen rushed him and tackled him, their tomahawks doing bloody work on his head. With a triumphant war whoop, they took his scalp and the pouch and returned to the French lines.

Not knowing the courier had not made it, Jacob continued moving around to the east until they could see the old encampment on the high ground. Almost a brown wall of Indians and a white wall of Canadian hunting shirts encircled the high ground. They were keeping their distance, but also keeping up a sustained rate of musket fire.

There was a howling noise as heavy artillery balls flew overhead and landed in and around the barricades of the encampment. From what they could see, there was no way they could approach the encampment without being detected by the enemy.

Frustrated, Jacob growled, "Damn!" but accepted that there was little they could do. Then, he thought maybe they could help a little. They were in a good vantage point, elevated and concealed, with the enemy's back to them.

"We're going to try and take a little pressure off our comrades," whispered Jacob. "Engage the enemy, but time your shots so they are masked by the cannon fire."

Jacob directed that they pair up, Charles and James, Samuel and Peter, and Konkapot and himself, and, when an opportunity presented itself, kill the enemy.

They worked on their concealed position, and began to select their targets and pick off enemies slowly, one by one, in order not to give away their position. They waited until there were enough other noises to cover the sound of their rifles. The wolves lay low next to the Rangers, waiting patiently for any enemy to get close.

The Indians who had killed the dispatch runner ran into the camp and showed their prize. They also boasted how they had escaped from a large force to the south of the fort. A French officer and a Canadian officer approached and asked the Abenakis what had happened. They said there must be thousands of enemy soldiers coming from Fort Edward. They heard musket fire and saw comrades fall near the woods to the south.

The French officer took the dispatch and reported immediately to the Marquis de Montcalm.

"Enemy to the south?" asked Montcalm. "Thousands?"

The French officer repeated what the Indian had said. As an orderly read the dispatch, Montcalm ordered three companies of Grenadiers to march quickly to their southernmost position, and stop these reinforcements from arriving.

"Sir, this dispatch indicates that the enemy is aware of our strength and are not marching to their relief. They believe we are larger than we actually are!"

Montcalm accepted this news with a smile and clasped his hands together.

"How joyous! How simply joyous!" celebrated Montcalm, rubbing his hands together.

Then, Montcalm began to pace, concerned that the captured report said one thing and the report from the Indians another. Not wanting to wait, Montcalm grabbed his sword and hat and gathered another three companies of Grenadiers and Canadian Militia. They were preparing to march out when a runner arrived, saying it was all a false alarm. While they did find several Canadians and Indians dead near the road, there was no sign of any enemy force.

Relieved that it was a false alarm and buoyed by the report that Webb was not responding, Montcalm ordered an all-out effort on the construction of the siege lines. Four hundred axe men cut trees and dug trenches, expanding their first parallel.

More boats from the north arrived, and landed with supplies. They manhandled twelve heavy artillery pieces into position and some of the mortars were brought ashore. Concerned that the English might attempt an attack from the fort, three hundred French Regulars were assigned as a guard detail for the work parties.

As the French secured their stranglehold, Jacob and his Rangers spent the rest of the day and into the dusk in the woods sharpshooting, moving from one concealed position to another. Even the wolves got into the action, the three taking down two Indian scouts and a Canadian who had come too close.

They were slowly working their way around to the east to see how far the French lines and pickets stretched. There were no fixed positions as there were on the western side of the lake, but there were hundreds if not thousands of Indians and Canadians encircling the encampment.

Having spent time in the encampment, they knew the men would not be able to last much longer. The water source was outside of the camp, and the enemy controlled it. They observed a charge by a hundred or so Massachusetts Provincials, who poured out of the camp and engaged the Indians holding the water source.

From their vantage point, they could see that the fight was hot and heavy, but in the end, the Provincials were forced back into the camp. In fact, it almost looked like the Indians, caught up in the bloodlust, were going to try and carry the encampment, but artillery within the palisade sent them scurrying back down the hill.

Jacob, his Rangers, and the wolves spent the night in their concealed position. From their vantage point, they could see the far western shore aglow with fires and artillery. They rotated through guard shifts and a little sleep.

As Jacob watched, Konkapot sat next to him, and whispered, "They're doomed, aren't they?"

Jacob pursed his lips, thinking for a few moments, before slowly nodding his head.

"They have sacrificed everyone, all of their own regulars, the Provincials, the civilians; I don't think many of them will survive."

Konkapot nodded and watched the eerily fascinating light show of the cannons' bright flashes in the distance, followed by the echoing booms from the trees and mountains.

"Surely, the French will protect the woman and children, won't they?" asked Konkapot.

Jacob looked out at the siege and thought about it.

"I think the French will, but I can't say what their Indians will do. You know as well as I do, once their bloodlust is up, there is no stopping them," Jacob said, and Konkapot nodded.

This was no quiet night; the sound of the siege continued without letup. The crack and boom of the cannons, the sound of the exploding shells, the impact of the shots, and the constant popping of muskets and rifles echoed across the lake and off the mountains. The wolves still did not like the loud sounds of the siege, and they would sometimes growl softly as the heavy guns fired.

All of the activity appeared to stay on the western side of the lake and around the encampment. There were no signs of enemy patrols around their hide site. As the Rangers watched and listened from their vantage point, more Indians were arriving on the western side in the French camp. They wanted to see the "great muskets," which is what they called the mortars, fire on the British.

Through the night, the French engineers had completed their next firing position, closer to the walls of the fort. Then they manhandled the large siege guns into position, and the artillerists made sure the guns were leveled and readied for firing. Three of the guns were heavy eighteen-pounders, and one of the mortars was a large nine-inch mortar.

Montcalm, along with the gathered Indians, waited patiently as the gunners prepared to fire the mortar. One gunner using an angle measure calculated the angle required to lob a mortar shell so that it would fall into the fort's interior.

Once the gunner was satisfied, he nodded his head. Two men with tongs lifted one of the nine-inch shells and pushed it into the mortar after the powder had been poured and packed. Once the shell sat in the tube, the gunner gave the command to light the fuse. The other gunner lowered the linstock, the mortar roared, and the shot sailed in a hissing arch towards the fort.

From across the lake, as the sun rose just above the mountains to the east, the single boom of a heavy mortar could be heard. Jacob and the Rangers turned to watch what was occurring there. The shell fired from the mortar landed just outside of the northwest corner of the fort, where it detonated, throwing a large plume of smoke and dirt into the air.

After a few minutes, the mortar fired again. The Rangers observed the French continue to walk the shells closer and closer to the fort, until they finally started to fall on the wall and inside. Then the French line exploded as several large siege guns fired, and the northwest corner of the fort erupted in an explosion, with shattered sections of the log walls flying into the air.

Looking at the destruction, Jacob whispered, "They're done for.

The French have the range."

The other Rangers looked on and nodded, all understanding that the fort was doomed unless Webb and the reinforcements arrived immediately.

The French began a sustained firing rate of both heavy siege artillery and the large mortar. One of the French shots took away the pulley and line holding the British flag over the fort, the colors fluttering to the ground. In the distance, the Rangers could hear the French erupt in a great cheer.

Watching the drama around the flagpole through his scope, Jacob saw a soldier try to fix the pulley and raise the flag, only to be decapitated by another lucky French shot. Jacob lowered his telescope and shook his head.

"Any signs of the reinforcements from Fort Edward?" asked Samuel in a whisper.

Jacob brought his telescope back up, looked towards the military road to the south, and saw no sign of any troops, no red-coated British regulars, no blue-coated Provincials, and none of their own green-coated Rangers. Lowering his scope again, Jacob looked at Samuel and shook his head.

"Poor bastards," whispered Samuel.

As the situation worsened at Fort William Henry, to the south, the first group of militia requested by General Webb had arrived at Fort Edward. The hero of the Battle of Lake George himself, General Sir William Johnson, led fifteen hundred militiamen from New York and 180 Mohawk warriors.

Riding with General Johnson was a gentlemen officer, Colonel George Augustus, 3rd Viscount Howe, who was as travel-worn and uniform-stained as the militiamen who had marched up rapidly from around Albany.

General Webb, whose returning headaches and body aches had continued to confine him to his room, seemed to grow in spirit, and he was observed moving around the garrison at Fort Edward, trying to organize a relief column of supplies.

After Johnson and Howe reported to General Webb and inquired when they would march out, General Webb said he was not marching out until the rest of the reinforcements from the militia and Provincials arrived. Johnson insisted, "We must move now, before all is lost," but once again, General Webb stood firm and ordered Johnson not to move forward until the army was assembled.

Johnson, like Major Rogers, disregarded this order and marched his column towards Fort William Henry, but he made it only three miles before receiving a demand from General Webb to return. Exasperated, Johnson complied and returned to Fort Edward with an uneasy feeling of doom as he looked to the north.

As the potential reinforcements were turning around, to the north and inside Fort William Henry, Colonel Monroe steadied himself as the room shook from the constant shot and shells from the French. Monroe asked his chief of artillery the status of their guns.

"How many guns do we have left, and how much shot and powder?" "Sir, within the last day we have lost two ten-pounders, one twelve-pounder, and one of the large 32s as you are aware, and one of our mortars burst," replied Collins.

As Lieutenant Collins described the situation, a runner entered saying some Rangers had made it to the fort. Colonel Monroe instructed that they be brought in. The three Rangers, looking disheveled and bloody, reported they were nearly captured by Indians, forcing them to destroy the message by eating it.

"Damn it all to bloody hell!" exclaimed Monroe, but the Ranger held his hand up. "Sir, I memorized the letter before I ate it. It reported the immediate arrival of General Johnson and his reinforcements of militia and Mohawks."

A smile returned to Monroe's face. This was welcome news.

The Rangers explained that they had run ahead to alert the fort when they were ambushed by Abenakis and Canadians, who had forced them to fight through, losing several of their comrades.

"You're in a bad position. They have you completed surrounded and cut off until Generals Webb and Johnson can punch through to you."

"Yes, true, indeed you are," commented Monroe.

He then thanked them for their message and instructed his orderly to see to their needs. Monroe felt better. At last there was the good news that reinforcements were on the way. But as the walls shook from the bombardment, he asked the groaning timbers of the fort, "Will they make it in time?"

From their position to the east of the fort and the siege, Jacob and his Rangers continued to observe the siege, having moved to a new concealed position. Using his telescope, Jacob scanned the area between the encampment and the fort and noticed a bunch of Indians gathered in a group, concealed below the small ridge between the shore and the fort. They were moving slowly closer to the fort.

At the same time, a group of New Jersey blues had left the fort and were heading down towards the shore.

"What are those bloody fools doing now?" asked Jacob as he focused in with the telescope.

As the New Jersey men got close to the shore, the Indians rose up and overcame the Provincials. The fighting was brutal and close, with the Indians killing most of them and then leading two of the survivors off as prisoners.

Shaking his head, Jacob lowered his scope and slid it closed, placing it back in his haversack. He sat back and looked at the smoking walls of the fort. This was pure insanity, and it was catching.

During the night, Jacob, his Rangers, and the wolves continued to observe, perhaps to remember and report what they had seen. In the distance, the glow of the French camp showed more supply boats from the north, pulling up and discharging their cargo to the shore.

From their vantage point, they could observe that the second parallel and the second battery position were completed. Through the night, the engineers and the artillerists moved more heavy artillery and siege mortars into position.

As the Rangers observed French activities, Montcalm moved forward to the new line to monitor its progress. He was pleased with their success so far. His causalities had been relatively light, and the Indians were happy for the moment. But he was concerned that they were starting to get restless. They didn't approve of sieges and long waiting.

As the sun rose, Montcalm decided to welcome the morning by firing his guns from both positions at the crumbling northwest corner of the fort. After about an hour, the fort was nothing but columns of smoke, and the guns went silent. Montcalm smiled at the battered ruins of the fort as the smoke rose like the clawing fingers of a dying person into the morning sky.

The Rangers continued to observe, Jacob with his telescope. The firing had stopped, and all of the Rangers' attention was drawn to what was happening across from them. The silence was actually deafening, them having been so used to the constant booming of the artillery.

A half-hour later, the faint sound of a drum was heard, and a red flag was raised from the French lines. Jacob focused his telescope on the developing scene as the Rangers waited for him to explain what was going on.

"Looks like a parley," said Jacob.

He lowered his scope and drew a heavy sigh.

"The fort is finished."

Raising his telescope, Jacob continued to watch and tell the Rangers what he saw.

A small delegation from the French lines approached the fort and went inside. After a short while, the party left the fort, crossed the churned field, and entered their own lines. Seeing the way the delegation stomped across the lines, Jacob actually snorted and laughed. The cannonade resumed once again in a thunderous roar.

"Guess Colonel Monroe didn't like what the French had to offer, and he continues to fight," said Jacob.

"At least he has a spine compared to those other gallant officers back in Fort Edward," replied Samuel.

"Aye, that he does," Jacob said as he refocused his telescope on the French line, the spouts of the siege mortars bursting high into the sky from behind their protected works.

"How long it will save him remains to be seen," Jacob said as he lowered his telescope.

It now seemed that every two minutes, French shells were landing inside the fort, their gunners now having the correct angle and range calculated. The fort was erupting in explosions, with parts of buildings and log fragments flying in the air, and smoke obscuring everything.

The fort continued to reply in kind, but the strength of the fort's guns was diminishing, and they weren't firing as often.

Konkapot spotted a group of enemy Indians, a different tribe from the normal Abenakis or Hurons. He hissed a warning, "Indians coming from the left."

Jacob and the others sank to the ground and moved behind concealing bushes. The Indians were heading straight for their observation spot, and Jacob had no choice but to prepare an ambush.

"Get ready, pick your targets, make them count," whispered Jacob. They settled into shooting positions. The Rangers readied themselves, each aiming down his rifle and picking his target while the wolves coiled, ready to leap.

When the Indians were less than fifty yards away, the Rangers fired as one, then leaped out of their concealment, pulling their knives and tomahawks, the wolves rushing ahead with deadly growls. Six immediately fell. The others were momentarily stunned, which allowed the Rangers and wolves to crash into them, tomahawks, knives, and teeth slashing.

Blood flew in sprays as each Ranger moved from one enemy to another, knives and tomahawks doing their grisly work. The wolves leaped, knocking the enemies down before sinking their teeth into soft flesh. It was over in less than five minutes. Looking around to make sure there were no other approaching Indians, the Rangers took their scalps.

After securing their rifles and gear, they moved to a new location closer to the lake where they could still see the fort and the siege.

Being so close to the water, Jacob agreed to allow Samuel, Konkapot, and Peter to move down to the lakeshore to fish while the other three kept watch. The three fishermen crawled forward to an area where the bushes were thick, the wolves following quietly. They took their fishing lines from their haversacks and got down to business. While waiting for the fish to bite, they refilled everyone's canteens. Soon, they had eight decent-sized fish on the shore, even after the wolves had taken their ration.

They returned to the hide site with fresh fish to go with the hard, dried pork and biscuits they had in their haversacks. It was a welcome addition to the old stale rations they had been munching on.

Jacob doled out the rum to add to their canteens with the new water. He then pulled his telescope back out and looked over to the French lines across the lake from them.

Over in the siege lines, the French were busy putting the finishing touches on the third battery position and making repairs from the lucky British shots. While frustrated by the fort commander's stubborn refusal to surrender, Montcalm had to admire his determination to continue fighting, although he must have realized his position was lost.

During the night, two deserters from the 35th Regiment were brought before Montcalm, who confirmed his suspicions about the conditions in the fort. They also told him of the message received that General Johnson had arrived with reinforcements from Albany and was at Fort Edward.

This news about the reinforcements concerned Montcalm, and he wasn't sure if it was true or a lie. In either case, he might have to push his timetable up to take the fort before these reinforcements caught his men between them and the fort.

"Send scouts out to watch the road and notify me immediately if they detect any English heading this way," Montcalm ordered.

The news that two men had deserted and were presumed captured also reached Colonel Monroe, who could not believe his own men would desert. He had always believed that it would be the Provincials who would desert. This didn't help his gloomy mood, as reinforcements still had not arrived.

"Where in the bloody hell is Webb and the reinforcements?" Monroe growled as he looked at the map. "Why have I not heard any other news than what these Rangers brought me?"

The only response was the groaning of the walls from the impact of the enemy artillery.

The sun rose pale, trying to burn through the thick black smoke pouring from the fort. Now that the artillery was closer in the second battery, the French split their guns to focus on both the fort and the encampment, which was taking heavy fire. The small palisade around the encampment was not designed to stop artillery fire, just musket fire. The cannon shots were crashing through the barricade as if it weren't there.

The mood inside the encampment was tense. Many had not slept in a couple of days, and though there had been rumors of reinforcements on the way, they had never materialized. It wouldn't be long before the willpower of the men defending the barricade was sapped or destroyed entirely.

Tension was also spreading inside the fort. While the British soldiers were performing their duties, many of the Provincials were showing early signs of a potential mutiny. The Massachusetts Provincials resisted manning the walls. When they did man a wall, or what was left of it, they lay as flat as they could, firing their muskets into the air instead of riskily exposing themselves to the Indian sharpshooters, who were even closer than the day before.

Colonel Monroe, a heavy look of exhaustion on his face, paced in front of his tent, his office having been destroyed by a French shell and turned into a smoldering ruin. Lieutenant Collins reported to the colonel, having taken a survey of the fort.

"Sir, the walls on the north, northwest, and west have all been severely damaged. Some of the timbers have been destroyed for a depth of three to four feet."

Monroe acknowledged the assessment and asked about the status of the fort's guns.

With a heavy sigh, Collins reported, "Sir, the passageway to the magazine has collapsed from the fire, and the magazine in the other bastion's roof has been destroyed. In my honest opinion sir, we do not have enough guns or ammunition to make a defense tenable."

With his own heavy sigh, Monroe accepted the report. He had already lost ninety-seven dead and another two hundred wounded. Monroe had to accept that he no longer had a choice but to surrender.

"Gather the officers for a council of war in the morning. We'll decide our fate then," ordered Monroe. Unless Webb arrived with his promised reinforcements in the next few hours, he thought, all was lost.

As the sun rose, Lieutenant Collins and his remaining guns continued to fire on the French lines, which were now even closer, and at a third battery, which was almost complete.

Monroe's council highlighted the desperation. Most, if not all, of the Provincials, with the exception of the Rangers, had given up the fight. Either in the fort or in the encampment, they lay as low to the ground as possible, shooting into the air to avoid exposing themselves, accepting that all was lost. Their willpower was slipping steadily away, and they were grumbling that they were sacrificial lambs being sent to the slaughter.

The officers in the council included the Royal Americans, the Massachusetts Provincials, the New Hampshire Regiment, the New York Provincials, the New Jersey Blues, and the 35th Regiment of Foot.

The atmosphere was subdued. They all knew they had done as well as they could, but they also realized they were in a bad position. If the third French battery went into action, then they would just be throwing their lives away uselessly if they held out any longer.

While surrender was a bitter pill for Colonel Monroe to swallow, the officers, after a brief debate, agreed that it was their only choice. Concerned that he would be court martialed for losing Fort William Henry, Colonel Monroe had them sign an affidavit confirming the unanimous decision. Once the council was over, a white flag was draped over the wall, since the flagpole had been blown into splinters.

Jacob and his Rangers continued to observe the situation at the fort from their position. The firing again seemed to have stopped, which drew their attention. Jacob and the others watched and waited to see what would happen, Jacob scanning the lines with his telescope.

"Do you think it's over?" asked Charles, and Jacob shook his head. "I don't know," he replied, "but it doesn't look good. In fact it looks a lot worse than the last time the guns stopped firing."

The fort was hardly recognizable. It was mostly a smoldering heap of timbers with some, but very few, portions of the walls intact.

By midday, there was a commotion as the French regulars in their white uniforms, their flags snapping in the breeze, marched out to the open field between their lines and the fort and formed a long line.

"Here we go," commented Jacob as he focused his telescope on the action. "Looks like a more formal parlay this time, and with more people in attendance."

The other Rangers shuffled closer so they could listen to Jacob describe what he was seeing through the telescope.

After a few minutes, the doors opened on one of the walls, and a crimson line of British regulars marched out, their flags also snapping in the breeze. Jacob followed them with his telescope and began telling his men what he was seeing. The British formed a line parallel to the French line. Jacob wondered if they were going to fight it out on the field in some odd duel. Instead of firing, the lines presented arms to one another.

Looking through his scope, Jacob saw a finely dressed French officer with two staff members approach the British line. Jacob assumed this must be the dreaded Marquis de Montcalm.

He observed a British officer, whom he assumed to be Colonel Monroe, and his staff approach from the British line. The two men rendered salutes and appeared to have a discussion. After a bit, a French aide read a document that seemed to irritate Colonel Monroe.

Jacob focused as best as he could with his scope. It seemed Montcalm was having an intense discussion with Colonel Monroe, having closed to within an arm's reach, and he actually appeared to touch Monroe's arm. The discussion went on for a few minutes, and then both men faced each other, bowed, and then saluted before returning to their own lines.

Both lines presented arms one more time and then turned and marched into their respective areas. Jacob looked at the expressions of his Rangers.

"What do you think?"

Opinions varied on what Monroe should have done, ranging from a continuation of the fighting to the surrender of the fort. Jacob heard their opinions and then decided.

"We had better move to a better position to support the men in the encampment, just in case."

They spent the rest of the day observing, noticing no bombardment or fighting, which led Jacob to believe the fort had actually surrendered. Once the sun set, he led his Rangers back around the encampment, moving deep into the woods to avoid contact with the numerous Canadians and Indians out there. They found a good position overlooking the encampment, the road, and the fort from a distance and settled in for the night.

CHAPTER 25

THE MASSACRE AND RESCUE

It was a quiet and uneventful night, the Rangers eating their cold rations while taking their turns at watching the woods, their wolves watching intently alongside them. They were getting low on food. They were going to have to leave soon and return to Fort Edward or find some game to eat.

The night passed into the glow of morning, the Rangers not used to a quiet evening with no artillery. The sun rose as it normally did over the mountains in the east, except this time, the morning was still quiet. The only sounds came from the songbirds in the trees. The guns had remained silent throughout the entire night, which reinforced the Ranger's assumption that the fort had capitulated.

The Rangers followed their morning ritual of standing to and observed no enemy activity.

"Let's move closer to get a better look at what's going on," Jacob whispered to his men. "We'll find a spot where we can provide support if need be."

The Rangers nodded, and Konkapot led them out of their hide site to an elevated position closer to the road. From there, they could see the fort and the encampment better.

Once they found and occupied the new observation position, they heard a faint sound of drums from the vicinity of the smoldering fort. The drums became louder as a column of British soldiers marched around the northeast corner of the fort and began moving down the road. A column, four men abreast, was marching down the dirt road, muskets shouldered and royal flags unfurled and flapping in the breeze.

Jacob looked over to Peter and whispered, "Maybe I am wrong, but when armies surrender, don't they lay down their arms or flags?"

Peter nodded his head. "Normally, unless perhaps Monroe had been offered the honors of war." They both thought this was very strange.

The column continued, followed by any injured and wounded who could march, limp, or lean on one another. Behind them came the Provincials and their families. Hundreds of painted Abenakis and Hurons, along with other tribesmen, lined the road or were watching from the field in groups. Jacob spotted a couple of green-uniformed fellow Rangers in the column.

"That's it," said Jacob as he lowered his telescope. "It's all over here."

Konkapot tugged Jacob's sleeve and pointed towards the groups of Indians. Jacob trained his scope and focused in on the Indians, who appeared to be gathering into larger masses.

"This doesn't look good," said Jacob. "The Indians seem angry about something."

Jacob described how the Indians were grouping. The leaders appeared to be having a heated discussion as their arms waved about, pointing at the fort, the encampment, and the column. Jacob closed his scope and put it back in his haversack.

"I don't have a good feeling about this," he said, and the others agreed.

The Indians were joining into larger groups, mostly away from the white-uniformed French regulars, who had formed up into lines on either side of the road to render the honors of war. Jacob was concerned that there were more Indians than French regulars—a lot more.

By agreement, Monroe had indeed surrendered the fort to the French, so the British and Provincials marched into the encampment.

Jacob's concern about the Indians was confirmed as he spotted a few of them harassing the wounded, taking their packs and haversacks, grabbing items from their pockets. Emboldened groups of Indians even followed the soldiers into the encampment and continued to grab items from the defeated men.

Jacob was surprised to see a company of French Grenadiers fix bayonets and drive the Indians from the encampment as the British and Provincials continued to march in. From his scope, Jacob could see the expressions on the faces of the Indians, denied their plunder, begin to turn ugly. The Indians skulked off while the Grenadiers remained as guards.

Soon, it appeared that French officers were visiting the encampment and going inside. Jacob could not see what was going on.

Peter explained, "Sometimes these gentlemen officers will call upon one another at the conclusion of the fight."

Jacob snorted and shook his head. That was a strange way to fight a war: one day trying to kill one another, and then having a social gathering once it was over.

Jacob couldn't see what was happening up at the fort. The Indians, driven away from what they thought were their spoils of war at the encampment, had entered the fort. They started looking for other plunder to take, searching the damaged buildings and passageways, even as the end of the column was still marching out.

Those at the end of the column were mostly the severely injured who needed assistance to walk, Provincials, and militiamen with their families. They looked on in horror as the Indians went about their search for plunder. The Indians found some rum and began to drink heavily.

Then they found the wounded who could not be moved inside one of the bastions that had not been destroyed. The Indians fell upon them, killing the wounded and taking their scalps. The screams from the wounded of "Murder!" and "Help!" could be heard coming from the fort's hospital.

The end of the British column, out of fear or shock, ignored the pleas for help from the wounded and quickened their pace out of the fort. Some word must have gotten out. As Jacob continued to observe, a French grenadier company left its post at the encampment and began to jog back to the fort. Jacob could also see the end of the column, which was moving more quickly, with soldiers or their families looking over their shoulders towards the fort.

"The Indians are up to no good," remarked Jacob as he watched through his telescope. "There is fear on the faces of the people leaving the fort, looking over their shoulders. Those Frenchies are running into the fort, so something must be going on."

This did not feel right, Jacob thought, as he continued to observe through his scope. Even Smoke seemed agitated, growling low and fidgeting next to Jacob. Jacob spotted the Indians, who had returned once again and had entered into the encampment looking for plunder.

After a while, the French officer whom Jacob had assumed to be the Marquis de Montcalm arrived on the scene, and peace seemed finally to settle over the encampment. The Indians departed to go to their own camps near the road to Fort Edward, which worried Jacob as he tried to determine how many of these Indian camps were between him and his Rangers and Fort Edward.

The Rangers continued to observe the events playing out before them at the encampment, remaining in their hide site. There seemed to be a constant movement of the French officers coming to the encampment, apparently meeting with their British and Provincial counterparts.

During the night, Jacob was awakened when there was a single shot from a musket near the encampment, followed by a huge volume of musket fire. All of the Rangers were alert, having quickly awakened, rolled over, and placed their rifles at their shoulders, watching the woods.

"Is there a change of heart?" whispered Samuel.

"Don't know," whispered Jacob back. "Could be some nervous militiamen shooting at shadows. There is no other shooting, nothing from the French."

The wolves sat with their ears peaked, listening and watching for any movement. When it became quiet, the Rangers returned to their rest site for only a short while before Konkapot woke everyone.

"The British are forming outside the encampment," Konkapot whispered to Jacob.

It didn't look like they were forming for battle, but instead for a march. They appeared to be waiting for something. After a while, a French officer came out to speak to the soldiers, who then returned to the encampment.

In the woods, Paugus, an Abenaki war chief, was not happy. His small band of thirty warriors felt they had been denied what they had been promised by the "Great Ontario," their name for Montcalm. They had done their part, fighting the English while dodging their large guns. His warriors were angry, feeding off of each other's rage, which continued to grow into a bloodlust.

Paugus decided that he would not fail his warriors; he would keep his promise of plunder and spoils. They worked themselves into a frenzy, passing around the few bottles of rum they had plundered and dancing around a fire in praise of their gods of war. They applied black and red war paint, grabbed their tomahawks with promises to color them red with the blood of their enemies, and asked their great spirit to give them strength to carry off the entire promised plunder.

Paugus and his group of warriors moved through the woods towards the encampment, and they were not alone. Other groups of Indians were moving and massing around the road between Fort Edward and the encampment. Some of the groups were even standing just outside of the encampment. They all seemed to be of the same mind.

Jacob and his men had performed their stand-to and were again observing what was occurring around the encampment. Jacob did not like what he saw through his scope. Many of the groups of Indians that he could see were heavily armed with knives and tomahawks. Some were even openly priming their muskets.

Through the gaps in the palisade surrounding the encampment, Jacob could see that the British and the Provincials had their muskets clubbed, that is, barrels pointing down or slung with their barrels down. This probably meant they were unloaded, a deduction that was reinforced when some of the groups of Indians became impatient, climbed over the barricades, and began to once again loot the camp. Jacob could see the Indians pulling packs off soldiers and leading horses out of the encampment.

Some of the men tried to resist, but they were overwhelmed by the Indians. The Indians became even bolder when they realized that the French were not stopping them. Most of the soldiers just stood there, as if in shock, and allowed the Indians to take everything, from their muskets, to their gear, and even their clothes until they stood naked in the line.

Jacob continued to observe and pass on to the others what he saw through the scope. The British column began to move quickly out of the encampment and onto the road, shuffling towards Fort Edward.

"If there is mercy in the world," Jacob whispered, "let these poor souls return safely to Fort Edward."

Most of the British seemed to have had their packs taken, and there were Indians who were running up with war whoops and taking hats, pistols, swords, and even the officers' hats. Some of the officers and even some of the enlisted had their coats and shirts torn from them by the Indians, who ran off waving their prizes.

Then Jacob noticed what he feared, men being led away from the column, hands bound and ropes tied around their necks, and no one was putting a stop to it. The Indians were taking prisoners, mostly other Indians or Negro servants.

The Indians seemed to explode onto the scene as they all became caught up in the feeding frenzy, taking everything they could from the soldiers. They grabbed muskets, personal items, halberds and spontoons from officers, even drums from the musicians.

Jacob watched to see what the French would do, and it appeared they were doing nothing to stop the wanton looting of the defeated British and Provincials. Some even just stood there and watched, leaning on their muskets.

"Get ready to move," said Jacob. "It's about to get real ugly down there. Grab your kit. We're moving, so be prepared to go in heavy if someone needs help. No one has been killed yet, but those warriors are working themselves into a lather down there."

The Rangers checked their rifles and tomahawks while they shouldered their bags. All three wolves sat with anxious faces, wanting to get into the action. Once everyone was ready, Jacob nodded and

Konkapot led them out towards the road. A bad feeling kept nagging Jacob, which made his senses even sharper. They moved at a quick pace, constantly looking about them as they closed on the road.

As Jacob and his Rangers moved through the woods, some distance away Paugus was watching the road, and he smiled as the British column began to move down it. He waited until the soldiers were past and the Provincials and their families had come onto the road. Now was his time to fulfill his promise to his warriors.

He gave a war whoop and thrust his tomahawk into the air, and his warriors took up the war cry, following Paugus towards the road. They burst into a group of startled Provincials and their families.

The Indians quickly moved in amongst the Provincials, who were mostly unarmed. If they had muskets, they were unloaded. The Indians' tomahawks made bloody work of the men. Then the warriors went after the women, grabbing them and dragging them into the woods. The warriors were using their knives and stabbing the women in their stomachs, pulling their entrails out.

The Indians also went after the crying and screaming children, grabbing them by the ankles and smashing their heads against trees. Soon other groups of Indians, caught up in the frenzy, joined the wonton massacre of the helpless soldiers and families.

The shock and horror of the attack caused some of the soldiers and civilians to just freeze in place, not moving until they too were grabbed by the attacking Indians.

The Indians poured out of the woods and grabbed everything they could that hadn't already been taken by other Indians. Men were being stripped down to their stockings and shirts, having everything they owned torn off them. Some of the English soldiers ran to the French guards, who sneered, "English dogs," and pushed them back towards the Indians, laughing at their troubles.

The front of the column, now realizing that something terrible was happening towards the rear, turned to try to provide assistance. However, as part of the surrender agreement, their guns were unloaded and they had no ammunition. All they had were their bayonets, so they fixed them and charged towards the rampaging Indians.

The column was breaking up, however, and units were losing cohesiveness. Some groups tried to fight, while others fled in every direction away from the marauding Indians.

Jacob and his Rangers jogged through the woods and into this chaos as men and women, some carrying children, were running past them, almost blinded by pure terror. The Indians were enjoying plundering without any consequences. No one was fighting back effectively, making it almost too easy.

The scene that came before the Rangers' eyes was something out of hell itself. The road was covered in bodies, blood, and discarded weapons and gear. Some of the Indians were in hand-to-hand combat with a few of the Provincials who were trying to make a stand. Some of the Indians had beheaded victims and were carrying their bloody, dripping trophies. Konkapot yelled "No!" when he saw the dead women and children, their entrails covering the ground, their crumpled bodies lying around the trees with the smeared grey matter of their brains oozing down the tree trunks. Maddened by the sight, Konkapot raised his rifle and shot a warrior who was about to stab another female victim.

As Konkapot rushed into the carnage after firing his rifle, Jacob yelled to wait but knew he couldn't stop him.

"Pick your targets, cover one another!" yelled Jacob, who quickly took out a warrior who was about to tomahawk a fallen Provincial soldier.

The sound of rifle fire drew the attention of all the warriors, who had felt invincible up to then because their enemies were unarmed. This quickly changed as three large wolves in full fury charged into them, teeth tearing at their legs and, if possible, their throats when they were pulled down.

Groups of Indians were dragging shocked prisoners, men and women, off into the woods towards their camps. Paugus and his warriors had secured a few men, women, and some children, whom they would take to the slave markets in Montreal.

Now Paugus heard real fighting. Perhaps he could gain more honor and prestige by taking prisoners while really fighting. Giving a command and letting out a war whoop, Paugus led some of his warriors, not burdened by plunder and prisoners, to meet this new challenge.

Jacob and his Rangers were loading as fast as they could, but they were being quickly overwhelmed. They had to begin using their tomahawks and knives, and the wolves closed in next to them, growling and snapping at anyone who was attacking one of the Rangers or seemed about to do so.

Jacob could see that Konkapot was in trouble, and Raven was too busy wrestling with an Indian to help. Using his knife and tomahawk together, Jacob flowed from one attacker to another toward Konkapot, making quick work of the enemy and moving on.

Samuel and Peter were fighting back-to-back, tomahawks flashing and trailing bloody arcs, with Otto striking from behind. Charles and James were also fighting as a pair, while Jacob tried to get closer to help Konkapot. Many black and red painted warriors burst from the woods, and six of them tackled Konkapot.

"No!" yelled Jacob, who became more enraged and went almost berserk, cleaving an arm from one attacking Indian while his knife slashed across the throat of a second, whose blood splashed out in a warm fan.

Quickly spinning around, using the momentum of the attack to carry him around the Indian who had lost his arm, he struck a third Indian in the head who had been raising his axe to attack Charles.

The fighting was close and brutal. Jacob looked around, and it seemed as if time had slowed to a crawl. He could see Peter and Samuel holding their own. Samuel had his hands wrapped around an Indian's throat as they were falling to the ground, while Peter's tomahawk was being buried into the back of an attacker.

All three wolves were wrapped up fighting Indians, caught up in the massive free-for-all. Konkapot was struggling under the weight of six warriors pounding on him and trying to take his weapons from him. They were trying to take him prisoner, which drove Jacob to press harder to get close enough to render help. A blood-curdling yell burst from Jacob's lips as he charged to help Konkapot.

As Jacob turned, he could see that Charles was down, using both of his hands on his tomahawk to block and keep an enemy's axe from hitting him in the head, and James was jumping on Charles's attacker. As Jacob was moving to get closer to help Konkapot, a Provincial soldier, maddened by the carnage, swung his musket like a club and struck Jacob in the head.

It was a staggering blow. Jacob saw stars appearing before his eyes as he fell to the ground, his head ringing. He fell, lying on his side as the world began to dim. He could see Konkapot struggling, but losing, and being dragged off. Jacob could hear the sound of screaming, yelling, and fighting all around him. The ground smelled of earth mixed with blood. The sound of battle became more muffled as Jacob's view of the world became grey. Into this grey scene, he saw Montcalm enter the field, yelling at the Indians and tearing open his blouse, exposing his chest.

French soldiers were pouring around Montcalm, physically dragging Indians off soldiers and pushing them away. In Jacob's foggy mind it seemed odd that the French were now trying to stop the carnage, though it was well past late.

Jacob was trying to rise up, shaking his head to clear it, when he felt Smoke's wet tongue clean the blood from his head. "Thanks lad," Jacob groaned as he got to his feet, his head clearer.

Peter and Samuel ran over, each taking hold of one of Jacob's shoulders and helping him to his feet. Jacob's sight and hearing, and the sights and sounds of the fight, were returning. Except that now, the Indians were leaving the survivors alone, at least the ones near Montcalm and his soldiers.

"A little bloody late!" yelled Jacob at some French soldiers running by, who simply ignored him.

Jacob looked around, and Konkapot could not be found. "Where's Konkapot?" he asked, and then he realized that James was standing there, but not Charles. "Where is Charles?"

Samuel pointed towards the woods.

"The Indians took both Konkapot and Charles and dragged them in that direction."

Jacob's head cleared, and he looked at his men.

"We're going after them," he said. "We're not leaving any Ranger behind. Find extra weapons. This is going to be a tough fight to get them out of a camp, if they are in one."

The Rangers spread out and grabbed what weapons they could. It seemed the fighting had moved away from them. They were almost alone; even the French had returned to their lines. The wolves were pacing, apparently anxious to go after Konkapot and Charles, especially Raven.

Samuel found a pair of silver pistols that he loaded with some rifle shot that fit and stuffed them into his belt. Jacob found a blunderbuss that he loaded with powder, then buck and ball, making it into a large shot gun. He loaded his rifle and made sure it was primed.

Peter found a small jaeger sword that an officer had carried, and he slung it over his shoulder. He picked up one of the dropped muskets and loaded buck and ball into it as well.

James found a few more pistols, which they loaded and distributed to everyone except Samuel, who already had two. James also grabbed two more muskets that he loaded with buck and ball, and then he slung them over his back.

Once everyone was armed and ready, Jacob looked his men in the eyes.

"We have to strike hard, and strike fast, and they are going to outnumber us. We hit them, and we get our people back, and, if possible, any other people they took prisoner. Everyone ready?"

All of the Rangers nodded that they were, with determined looks in their eyes.

"All right, let's go."

The Rangers had to move carefully, to avoid making contact with the numerous roving bands of Indians or their camps. Jacob froze the section as a group of Indians approached, the Rangers seeking concealment in the bushes. They had to physically hold the wolves, who wanted to tear into the Indians, who were shouldering their plunder, swilling bottles of rum, and leading a string of six prisoners as they moved past the concealed Rangers.

It was a hard pill to swallow for Jacob, but they were searching for their men, and there was nothing they could do for these detainees. Perhaps the French would influence the Indians to return them, since this bloodbath had hopefully not been sanctioned by the French.

Once they felt the group was far enough away, Jacob led them out, and they continued to search for their friends.

As the sun began to sink, the clouds thickened, and the wind picked up. Jacob scanned the clouds. It looked like one of those fearsome summer storms was brewing. The low light made it easier for the Rangers to blend into the shadows, as well as to spot the different Indian camps by their fires.

Some of the camps were huge. The Rangers moved close enough to look, but not close enough to give themselves away. The Indians had built large bonfires and were celebrating their victory and sharing in the spoils of war. Casks of rum and bottles of liquor taken from the fort or from the encampment were being passed around, and the Indians were becoming roaring drunk. This large group did not appear to have any prisoners, so Jacob led the Rangers on into the growing darkness.

They searched a few more camps, until they spotted a smaller one away from the main camps. Jacob vectored his Rangers towards it. As it grew darker, the Rangers paused momentarily to mix powder with water and blacken their faces.

This camp was in a small clearing, a fire burning brightly with sparks dancing above the flames and catching in the increasing breeze of the night. Paugus watched his warriors dance about the fire, their well-bloodied tomahawks waving in the firelight.

He had kept his promise; he had led his warriors into battle against the hated English dogs, beat them, and taken their plunder as promised by the "Great Ontario." He could lead his warriors back to their home village of Panaouske with glory and honor, securing his place as a great war captain.

He had come a long way from his youthful days, raiding the English settlements and taking plunder and prisoners. He didn't care what these French or English were fighting about. It was war, and he reveled in it. He took pleasure in the suffering of the white devils who were spreading through their lands like a plague.

Paugus snorted a short laugh as he took a long pull from a bottle of captured brandy, the burning liquid further heating his burning blood.

He remembered an incident, a raid near a town the English called York, where he had begun to prove himself a capable warrior. It had been so easy. He had walked up to the door and knocked. The Englishman simply opened the door for him, and he had shot him, grabbing the youth who stood near him and seeing the look of fear in the eyes of the other boy standing there.

Ah, that feeling of ultimate power, thought Paugus, as he looked over at their prisoners.

The Mohican, who wore the green uniform of these Rangers, and his comrade he would save to be presented to the village, so they could partake of their flesh. Konkapot and Charles were bound, their faces heavily bruised and cut from the beating they had taken from Paugus' warriors.

Then there were the three other men they had taken, the six women, and the three children. They should fetch a good price in trade from the slave markets. Paugus watched as three of his warriors grabbed one of the young women from the prisoners, and dragged her screaming into the woods. There was a sound of tearing clothes, and then his warriors were yelling in enjoyment.

Perhaps some celebrating tonight is worth it, thought Paugus, who ordered two of his warriors to place the pot on the fire and get the water boiling.

Motioning to two of his warriors, Paugus walked over to the frightened, huddled group of bound prisoners and pointed at one of the men. Two warriors grabbed him, cut his bonds away, and led him over near a tree.

A third warrior approached with a tomahawk and a large nail, which drew Paugus' attention, and he smiled and nodded his head. Paugus went up to the prisoner, his arms held by a warrior on each side, and as he drew his knife, the prisoner stared at him, horrified.

Paugus faced the prisoner, and stared into his frightened eyes. With a quick motion, he sliced the man's shirt away, exposing his chest and abdomen. Then with another quick motion, he sliced open the man's abdomen and reached in with his hand as the warriors held the prisoner in place, and pulled out a section of intestine. The third warrior ran up and with the tomahawk, nailed the intestine to the tree.

Paugus looked at the man, shaking in fear and pain, and said,

"Run!"

The two warriors who had been holding the man's arms let go, drew their knives, and began to poke the prisoner in the back. Out of fear, the man took off running, being chased by the whooping, knife-poking warriors.

As he ran, the intestines came out in a long, stretchy, reddish/purple line that eventually ran their entire length, before tearing the rest of the digestive track out of the lower body in an explosion of blood and flesh. The other warriors who witnessed it took up the whoops as they continued to drink their rum. Paugus went up to the twitching, dying man, grabbed his head and with a quick motion of his knife, scalped him and joined the celebration by waving his bloody trophy.

The third warrior walked up, used his tomahawk to sever the man's head from his body, and began to butcher the corpse and toss the flesh into the pot. The prisoners screamed in terror and huddled together for the little protection they could give each other from these black and red demons.

Unknown to Paugus and his warriors, in the darkness there were other eyes, some golden, watching for their chance. After seeing this brutal execution, Jacob and his Rangers became hardened in their resolve not only to rescue their friends, but also to kill as many of these Indians as they could.

"Samuel and Peter, swing right and attack from that direction; James, you're with me, we're swinging left," Jacob instructed in a low whisper.

Everyone nodded, cocking their muskets and pistols as quietly as they could.

"No prisoners, hit them hard, and hit them fast!"

Jacob's eyes were burning with an icy blue determination, and everyone nodded back, their own eyes steely. The eyes of the wolves mirrored Jacob's, also hard and determined.

"Good luck!" whispered Jacob and motioned for them to go.

Samuel and Peter began moving to the right, generally towards where the prisoners were huddled together. Jacob, with James following and all three wolves after him, began moving toward the left where Konkapot and Charles were.

The wind was starting to pick up, the trees swaying and creaking, and there was a crack of thunder. Paugus, in his alcohol-sodden mind, thought the Great Spirit was speaking to him and congratulating him on his victory.

As Paugus swayed with his eyes closed and smiled at that thought, he was shocked to hear a new sound, a crack of musketry instead of thunder. Paugus's eyes snapped open to see several of his warriors fall as green-clothed, black-faced men charged into his camp, tossing smoking muskets down and pulling pistols from their belts. Three large wolves also tore into his men.

What is this? thought Paugus as another crack of musketry came from behind him.

He turned to see two more green-clad, black-faced men enter his camp. One had dropped a musket and was unslinging a second, while another appeared to have a large, stubby musket pointing at his warriors, who were standing in shock.

The green-clad, black-faced demon pulled the trigger and the gun exploded, almost sounding like a small cannon. Several of his warriors fell, as many balls smashed into them, one even losing his head in a pink mist. At the same time, the wolves were pulling his men down and tearing their throats open in sprays of blood.

Jacob dropped the blunderbuss and turned to see the war chief standing and staring at him. Something deep from his past recognized the pattern of the black and red paint on this warrior. An image he thought he had buried deep in his consciousness exploded into his mind. Then it all came back, that night in his home when his father was killed and his brother taken. With a bestial scream, Jacob charged and tackled the chief, striking him hard in the face with his fists. His time had finally arrived.

Paugus fought back, trying to throw Jacob off and get to his knife. In the struggle, Paugus got loose, and both men rolled to their feet. Paugus pulled out his knife, but before he could use it, Jacob had closed and caught his wrist in a grip like an iron vice.

Spinning to the side of Paugus, while holding the knife hand with his left, Jacob struck Paugus's arm with his right hand where it joined with the shoulder. The force was so hard, it dislocated Paugus's shoulder, who screamed out as the burning pain quickly sobered him.

Striking a second time, Jacob hit Paugus's elbow, shattering the arm and forcing him to drop the knife. Paugus swung at Jacob with his left arm, but Jacob ducked, and catching the arm against his chest, drove his right fist into Paugus's chest while kicking his legs out from under him.

Paugus hit the ground hard, and the air was knocked out of him. The pain was excruciating. He was having difficulty breathing, and a red haze covered his sight.

Jacob took Paugus's throat in his steely grip and began to squeeze the life out of him. Paugus, using his left hand, tried to tear Jacob's fingers from around his throat, but they would not budge; they only became tighter. Jacob sat on top of the squirming Paugus, watching his eyes twitch and begin to roll back into his head.

Releasing some pressure, Jacob moved so he was nose-to-nose with Paugus, and while looking in his eyes, whispered, "This is for my family, and all the families you destroyed."

The last sound Paugus heard was the snapping of his throat as Jacob choked the life out of him.

It was as if a heavy weight was lifted from his soul, and Jacob sighed with relief. However, this was short-lived, as something hard struck him in the left shoulder area and spun him off the dead body of Paugus. As he rolled to his feet, he faced a warrior who had gotten close enough to stab at him with a knife.

Jacob moved his body out of the way as the knife just missed his center, but caught him in the side, leaving a searing pain. The blade luckily hit a bone, and slid along it, cutting Jacob's side deep. The warrior quickly withdrew his blade and slashed again at Jacob, this time towards his face. Jacob moved his head back, but the blade caught him along his nose and down the right side of his face at an angle.

With his right hand, Jacob caught the warrior around his throat, and lifted him off the ground and threw him to the ground. Quickly pulling his pistol, Jacob shot the Indian at close range, then quickly flipped it over and grabbing the barrel, used the grip as a club to smash another attacking Indian.

While Jacob was fighting Paugus and the warriors, James had moved around and was approaching Konkapot and Charles when he came across the three warriors who were raping the young girl. They had stretched her over a log, two of the warriors holding her arms while the third took his turn with her.

James brought the musket up, took aim at the startled Indian, and fired, blowing his head clean off. The two others who had been holding the young girl let go in shock. James dropped the musket, grabbed his tomahawk, and in one swift motion, threw it and caught one of the Indians in the forehead. The third one turned to run, but from the darkness, the wolves leaped and brought him to the ground screaming.

James went over to the traumatized girl to render assistance. She was shaking and crying, hugging herself with her arms.

"It's over. They won't hurt you anymore," James said softly as he approached.

She looked up through tear-streaked eyes, gave a sniffle, and then before James could do anything, she grabbed a pistol from his belt and shot herself in the head as James yelled, "No!"

There was nothing for him to do for her, so James went over to help Jacob, who he now realized was hurt.

Peter and Samuel were moving quickly, working as a pair. Peter was using the jaeger sword effectively, stabbing and slashing the Indians, while Samuel, with pistols in both hands, fired one and then the other, killing two warriors quickly. Then he tossed the pistols to the ground and pulled out his knife and tomahawk to join Peter in dealing death and destruction to these who had a butcher's bill to pay.

The two worked in harmony, moving and swaying as Indians charged them. Peter blocked a tomahawk with his sword while Samuel sliced the throat of the attacker. Soon, the Rangers were left alone, the Indians either dead or running away from these mad men, especially since their war chief lay dead.

Samuel and Peter moved over and began to untie the shocked prisoners. As they were freed, families hugged one another. Samuel and Peter returned for their pistols and reloaded them. Placing them back in their belts, they held their rifles at the ready.

"Can you move?" asked Samuel, and the released prisoners nodded that they could.

Jacob's arm hurt like hell, more than either the cut in his side, which was bleeding through his shirt, or his face. James asked if he was all right, and Jacob nodded that he was.

"See to Konkapot and Charles," ordered Jacob as he stuffed in some linen to stop the blood from the knife wound, tightening his belt to hold it in place.

Jacob went over to check on Konkapot and Charles, who had been released by James. They were in bad shape. Their faces were bloody and bruised from the pounding they had taken from the Indians, and they had multiple knife wounds—not deep, but painful. The Indians had tortured them a little; Konkapot seemed to have lost a finger from his left hand that James was helping to bind up.

Though his face was swollen, Konkapot looked up at Jacob and said, "You look bad."

Jacob snorted and said, "And you look worse. Can you move?"

Charles stood up and said, "I'll bloody well walk out of this damned place!"

As Raven licked the blood from Konkapot's face, overjoyed he had been found, they located Konkapot's and Charles's rifles and gear. Once they were reequipped, Jacob formed them up. Jacob's left arm was in a sling, but he carried his rifle in his right.

"Let's move before they bring back any friends," he said, and the Rangers, with the liberated prisoners, moved out of the camp and into the woods, escorted by their wolves. They faded into the blackness of the night, and moved towards the safety of Fort Edward and their island.

CHAPTER 26

FORT EDWARD: SURVIVORS

The rescued men, women, and children were surrounded by the battered Rangers, Peter and James in the front, Konkapot and Jacob in the center, and Charles and Samuel covering the rear with the wolves ahead of them all. They moved through the woods away from the scene of the bloody massacre.

Several times they had to stop. There were still roving bands of Indians out hunting English soldiers and Provincials so they too could gain some slave money or trade items.

The weather was getting worse; the wind was picking up, and there was more thunder and lightning, making it easier for the Rangers and their wards to escape the notice of the Indian bands.

"We have to move further west to avoid any band that is, more than likely, between us and Fort Edward," said Jacob, which his men agreed to.

The recovered prisoners stayed huddled together in the center of the Rangers.

"Head towards Bloody Pond, then keep heading southwest from there until we reach the river. That should take us well away from the roving bands," Jacob told Peter and Samuel, who nodded and led them in the prescribed direction.

As Jacob and the Rangers with the rescued civilians moved away towards the fort, Colonel Monroe and some of his officers had found sanctuary in Montcalm's French camp. Meanwhile, some of the survivors were able to evade the rampaging Indians and make their way back to Fort Edward. Beginning as a trickle, some individually, some in small groups, British regulars and Provincials were straggling into the fort.

After some time, a group of thirty men from the 35th, carrying their regimental flag, burst out into the open field around Fort Edward and entered the fort, reporting what had happened to them to Generals Webb, Johnson, and Lyman. These men were in bad shape, desperate, out-of-breath, some with clothing torn off them.

The news of the massacre spread like wildfire through the fort and out on the island to a troubled Major Rogers. The tale of horror grew with each telling as new groups arrived at the fort. A second large group, with Lieutenant Collins of the Royal Artillery and Captain Cunningham of the 35th, arrived. These survivors were quickly battered with questions about friends or comrades at Fort William Henry.

General Webb sent out a guard force of three hundred men under the command of Major Augustine of the Royal Americans to serve as an early warning in case Montcalm decided to follow up his victory and come after Fort Edward.

General Johnson looked at Webb.

"This could have been prevented if you had let me continue on to the fort," he argued, but Webb simply ignored him and returned to his office, closing his door in General Johnson's face. Johnson looked at the closed door, whispered "bastard" under his breath, and went outside to see if he could gather any more news from the lake.

Rogers called out all of the remaining Rangers and sent them out to look for and help any other survivors coming back to Fort Edward and also to serve as an early warning in case the French decided to attack.

"To hell with the standing orders!" he yelled to his Rangers. "Go find and help any survivors you can, especially any Rangers in need!"

Most of the survivors were being brought out to the hospital on the island, and the Rangers helped where they could. They brought food and water, helped tend to the injured, or simply listened to the tales of horror of the siege and massacre. It was a dark and bloody picture the survivors painted for the Rangers, and this greatly concerned Major Rogers and Captains Stark and Putnam, who had returned and had reported on what they had observed at William Henry.

As the survivors made their way to Fort Edward, Jacob gritted his teeth. Everything hurt, especially his arm and shoulder. He must have been hit by a spent ball, but it had been close enough to have possibly broken the bone. Then he looked at the survivors. Charles and Konkapot were also in bad shape, but they kept Rangering on.

The rain and thunder were growing in intensity, trees bending under the power of the rain. They were all being drenched, and it was difficult to see where they were going. While this helped to conceal them from any Indians still bold enough to be out in the storm looking for prisoners, or for them specifically, it was making it difficult to travel.

During one of the rest stops, Jacob gathered the Rangers together.

They were dripping and soaked through.

"We're going to have to stop somewhere soon before we drown," said Samuel, and Jacob agreed.

The storm did not look like it was lightening up at all. After their break, they kept moving until there was a low, steady rumble to their front, not just thunder.

"Do you think it's *Chepontuc?*" asked Jacob, and Samuel shrugged. "Seems about the right spot for it."

After moving a little way, they came out on a ridge, and less than a mile away was the waterfall they knew as *Chepontuc.* Samuel and Peterled the Rangers and the survivors down a trail that cut through the high ground and brought them out next to the river with the falls roaring in the distance. The sides of the ridge were like small cliffs made from grey stone and shale.

After moving a short distance, they found a large cave in the shale, which had been carved out by the river ages ago. Samuel and Peter went inside, and using a candle and their flint and steel, made a light and quickly explored the cave to make sure it was clear. They came out and signaled it was all right to enter.

The Rangers went inside and found there was enough room for themselves and the survivors. The Rangers pulled out a couple more candles and lit them from the first one, shining some light inside the cave. While damp, it was a lot drier than being out in that raging tempest of a storm.

Jacob sat heavily down on the rock floor and leaned against the wall of the cave. Smoke sat next to him. He sent Peter, Samuel, and James out to try to find some dry wood or branches for a fire. In a short while, they had a fire crackling in the center of the cave, smoke rising to the ceiling and traveling out the cave entrance. Otto and Raven stood watch at the entrance, sitting on their haunches.

We should be safe, he thought. An enemy would have to be right in front of the cave to see the light, and the smoke was blending in with the mist of the rain.

Peter and Samuel were shaving tree limbs with their knives and tomahawks to get to the dry center to help feed the fire. Around the fire, they stacked thicker pieces of wood they found in order for them to dry. When one smoldered, it was dry, and they threw it onto the fire and set a new piece next to the fire to begin drying. Between Samuel, Peter, and James, they had found enough wood to last them for a while.

Jacob looked down at his side. The blood that had seeped through his shirt had dried. Samuel came over to look at the wounds in his side and on his face. As soon as they moved the linen from the knife wound, it began to bleed again.

Seeing his wound, one of the women came over and pulled a small sewing kit from her skirt pocket.

"Maybe this could help?" she asked, and Jacob nodded.

"It may hurt," she warned, but Jacob said, "I'm already hurt, so it shouldn't be a problem."

Samuel helped Jacob out of his gear and removed his shirt to expose the wound. The knife had sliced deep and the cut was a good four inches long, the blade having followed the line of his rib. Taking a deep breath, Jacob once more gritted his teeth as the woman sewed the wound closed, which helped control the bleeding.

Samuel washed the blood away with a damp cloth. Then he cleaned the wound on Jacob's face and saw that it would not require stitching.

When the woman finished tying off the last knot, she thanked Jacob and Samuel for what they had done for the prisoners, and then hugged them both, hurting Jacob's shoulder, before returning to the other survivors huddled around the fire for warmth.

Jacob looked over to one of the small children, whose eyes were vacant and staring off to nothing, haunted by the horror he had witnessed. Jacob wondered if the children would ever be the same.

Samuel went over and helped clean the wounds of Konkapot and Charles, who looked much better than when they had first seen them. The Rangers shared what little food they had left with the survivors, and then Peter and Samuel grabbed their fishing lines and went out into the storm to fish for fresh food, the wolves following.

James went around and made sure the survivors were helped out, cleaning any injuries. Most were suffering from the shock of what they had gone through.

After a bit, Peter and Samuel returned with some large trout, which went onto ramrods and were cooked over the fire.

Jacob looked outside at the rain, which seemed to be coming down horizontally. He wondered if this was God's, or the Great Spirit's, way of washing the blood of the massacre away. Soon, the cave filled with the smell of cooked fish, and the Rangers made sure the first fish went to the survivors, who gratefully accepted.

They spent the night in the cave, trying to rest as well as they could.

The Rangers dried their rifles and their newly procured pistols and loaded them with new powder and balls. They took turns standing watch at the cave entrance and kept the fire going, which now had warmed the cave to a comfortable temperature.

Jacob even took his turn on watch, sitting near the entrance with a pistol cocked and ready, his left arm in a sling, and Smoke by his side. The rain had stopped, the wind had quieted down, and the storm had moved on.

As Jacob sat, the images of what he had observed over the last couple of days played out in his mind. One of these was the black-and red-painted warrior, both from his past and from his present merging together in his mind. He had kept his promise to his dead family to avenge them by killing the Indian who had killed his father, taken his brother, and ultimately killed his mother.

After some time, Peter came to take Jacob's place on watch. Jacob noticed that Peter had kept the jaeger sword. Peter squeezed Jacob's good shoulder and nodded; Jacob returned the nod and moved into the cave, Smoke plodding silently next to him.

Jacob went over to check on Konkapot, who was leaning against the wall, going over his rifle. Jacob sat next to him with a groan and asked how he was doing.

"Much better now, thanks to you."

Jacob just shrugged and looked at his damaged left hand.

"Could have been a lot worse. At least they didn't go after my shooting hand," Konkapot said.

Then he looked at Jacob.

"You need to learn to duck better," he said, pointing at the new slash on Jacob's face and the wound in his side.

Jacob snorted and nodded his head yes, and then sighed heavily. "Are we getting too old for this?"

Konkapot shook his head. "We're not that old yet."

Then Konkapot reached over and squeezed Jacob's uninjured shoulder.

"Really my friend, thanks for coming for me. I don't know how to repay you. I owe you my life."

Jacob grunted and stood up.

"Ah, buy me a drink sometime, and we'll call it even."

Jacob continued around the cave and checked on Charles, who was being looked after by the woman who had helped stitch him up.

"You seem to be very good at this, miss," said Jacob.

She and Charles looked up. She wiped her forehead and pushed back some of her hair, which had fallen into her face.

"I used to work in the fort's hospital, helping the surgeon treat the injured from the fight."

Jacob nodded and looked at Charles.

"You seem to be doing better. How are you feeling?"

Charles nodded his head, his face bruised and battered, but his smile shining through.

"Much, much better. Thanks for coming for us." The woman also nodded her appreciation.

"Yes, thank you. We all thought we were done for, never to see our homes again."

Jacob squeezed Charles's shoulder and nodded his head to the woman.

"Try to get some rest. We're heading out in the morning. Hopefully, the rain will be over by then."

Jacob continued around and checked on the rest of the survivors. While most of them seemed to be recovering from the shock, the children still had a traumatized look in their eyes. The survivors all nodded to Jacob and voiced their thanks for the rescue and for the food. Jacob nodded his acceptance of their thanks and went over to his spot.

He settled into a comfortable place with a grunt, and then the exhaustion of the day took him, and he quickly fell asleep. His Rangers let him sleep through the night, and Jacob didn't seem to mind. Through the cave entrance, they could see that the sun was coming up and the rain had stopped. The food and rest seemed to have rejuvenated everyone.

The Rangers took care of clearing the cave and removing any signs that they had been there. Once everyone was ready, Peter and Samuel led them out along the river, followed by the survivors, Konkapot and Jacob, and then James and Charles bringing up the rear.

Back up the lake, the Marquis de Montcalm was beside himself in frustration. How could he extricate himself from this and still bathe in the glory that was rightfully his?

His engineers went through the ruins of the fort and documented all of the captured equipment, which Montcalm was loading onto barges to be brought north to Carillon. At least these captured guns and supplies could be used by the fortification there.

Most of the Indians had departed, many with the prisoners and plunder that he had not been able to prevent them from taking. He was able to liberate some of the captives, but many of the Indians quickly took to the woods and headed back to their home villages.

The Canadians were saying that they must return north soon. It was almost harvest time.

The French and Canadians went through the fort, the passageways and casements filled with the dead, scalped, and brutalized. Montcalm ordered the fort burned and the encampment destroyed.

With the loss of the Indians and with the Canadians having to leave soon, Montcalm had no choice but to return to Carillon and try Fort Edward at a later time.

"So close…so very close," Montcalm whispered. "The game is still afoot and must be played out."

To the south, General Webb felt relieved when some of the Ranger scouts who had been observing the French reported the fort on fire, the encampment destroyed, and the French Army withdrawing, heading north. Some other Ranger scouts brought in several French deserters, who confirmed what had happened with the Indians, the destruction of the fort, and the plan for the army to return to Carillon.

General Webb quickly penned a note to Lord Loudoun, reporting on the situation at Fort Edward. Mostly, it was a letter justifying his lack of action, reporting that the enemy forces of over 11,000 greatly outnumbered his 4,500 men fit for duty. In the letter, Webb praised the activity of the British regulars, but vilified the Provincials, who failed in his mind to do their duty for King and Country.

With survivors steadily coming in, Webb instructed that a signal gun be fired every couple of hours to help guide stragglers to the fort.

A few more officers arrived, who had followed the signal gun to safety after living off wild berries in the woods.

It was around midday when Peter and Samuel led the Rangers and the survivors up over the riverbank and into the valley, Fort Edward and their island visible in the distance. They too had heard the signal guns, but they knew the area well enough to find their own way.

They had picked up four more stragglers near the river, including Major John Gilman from the New Hampshire Provincials, who had been forced to swim across the Hudson River three times to evade capture until he ran into Jacob and his Rangers.

A heavy weight seemed to fall from everyone's shoulders when they sighted the fort, the Union Jack still flapping in the breeze. The survivors began to talk excitedly with one another. Even the children appeared to be returning to a sense of normalcy. Jacob felt more at home when he saw their island sitting out in the sparkling river, the silhouettes of their huts in the distance.

"French on the left!" yelled Peter, and everyone's feeling of ease quickly changed to alertness. The survivors cringed and some screamed as a group of thirty French regulars in their white uniforms came into view, but they were carrying a white flag. The Rangers had their rifles at the ready, both groups vectoring towards the fort.

Lieutenant Savournin of the La Sarre Regiment and Joseph Marin, of all people, had been tasked by Montcalm to go to Fort Edward to negotiate the transfer of the British prisoners they had recovered from the Indians or who had sought shelter within the French camp from the rampaging Indians. They were marching, their muskets slung barrel down, and the white flag in the front.

As they came out of the woods, they could see the fort in the distance, as well as a group of people moving parallel with them near the river. Marin saw they were clothed in green uniforms and had their weapons at the ready as they escorted a group of civilians.

Marin also noticed the angry, almost animalistic looks these men, Rangers he believed, were sending their way. The civilians' faces showed fright. Marin could understand that, but these were the fortunes of war.

Still, they were instructed not to appear aggressive, and he told his men not to make any sudden movements as he pointed to the group, then towards the fort, hoping they got his meaning.

Jacob and his men warily watched the French, who seemed to be halting just outside the fort. The recovered survivors had mixed emotions on their faces; the children cringed slightly in fear, and the adults' looks threw daggers at the hated French. While it may have been the Indians who had done the damage, they had been serving the French.

They arrived at the fort, and the survivors entered, once again thanking the Rangers and shaking their hands. Then Jacob turned and led his section across the bridge and over to their island.

Other Rangers announced that they were coming in and yelled that someone should fetch the surgeons. Jacob and his men stopped at their cabin to drop off their equipment. The wolves curled up and lay down outside the cabin, and the Rangers proceeded over to the hospital.

Along the way, fellow Rangers arrived to slap their backs and welcome them home, asking what had happened and what they had seen. They arrived at the hospital, and the surgeon and the surgeon's mates began to fuss over them, working on their injuries.

Jacob was sitting on a bench, leaning up against the hospital wall, a surgeon looking at the stab wound in his side, when Major Rogers and Captains Stark and Putnam arrived. While the surgeon worked on his injury, Jacob described what they had seen, both the siege and the massacre.

Rogers had an orderly there taking notes. After Jacob was done describing what he had observed, Rogers sent the orderly with the notes to the fort to keep Generals Johnson, Lyman, and Webb informed.

Rogers looked at the orderly. "Make sure General Johnson gets the report first, then Lyman, and if time permits," Rogers paused, "then Webb."

Rogers, Stark, and Putnam spoke with Jacob, Konkapot, and Charles, asking about their injuries.

"Surgeon said my arm's broken, but not too bad. The other wounds will heal," said Jacob.

"When will they be fit for duty?" asked Stark, and the surgeons said not for a while. They asked if Stark wanted the men to die from infections.

Rogers nodded. "Well, get some rest and heal up," he said. "We're not done yet."

As Jacob and his Rangers were being worked on and were reporting what had really happened at the fort, General Webb sent a delegation out to speak with the French and to work through the negotiations to have the prisoners, including Colonel Monroe, returned. The British sent a detachment of regulars to Half-way Brook where the exchanged prisoners were received and returned to the fort.

Jacob, Samuel, and some of the Rangers watched the column enter the fort. "They don't seem so proud and invincible as they did before," commented Samuel, observing the body language of the returning soldiers and survivors. It seemed fitting that the day seemed to weep as the dejected survivors made their way into the fort, looking for friends or loved-ones who may have survived as well.

At the lake, in the same pouring rain, Montcalm's soldiers began loading the boats to return north. Montcalm had no choice; he needed to leave. What few soldiers remained with him at the ruins of Fort William Henry were growing unruly, and discipline was becoming an issue. The Canadians were loading their boats, without Montcalm's permission, to get back to their homes for the harvest.

The men were also jumpy from the extreme smell of the decay of corpses in and around the forests. While the flames that had consumed the fort had cremated many of the dead, there were even more bodies scattered through the woods.

Montcalm looked at the smoldering ruins of Fort William Henry, the smoke mixing with the grey of the rain. Under the grey veil that covered the area, the cold was piercing everyone on the boats and on the shore. Montcalm wondered if this was God's way of punishing him. Could he have done more to prevent the massacre? Still though, he had done exactly what he had intended to do. He had destroyed the English fort, and he had driven them from the southern shore of the lake.

As he looked at the ruins, a smile played across Montcalm's face. Yes, now that he thought about it, this had worked out to his advantage. He nodded, and the oars lowered and began to pull the boat north.

"I'll be back soon. Don't worry my friends."

CHAPTER 27

FORT EDWARD: THE AFTERMATH

Montcalm returned to Carillon, and General Webb began to dismantle the army he had gathered at Fort Edward. Webb released the militia so they could return home. The survivors of the Massachusetts Regiment marched south to Albany, along with Colonel Monroe and the remnants of the 35th Regiment.

However, the rift that had been growing between the British and the Provincials continued to worsen and solidify. This came to a head when the Provincials who had garrisoned Fort Edward were not allowed to go home. They felt that since the French had returned north, they should be released as well.

The growing discontent reached such a level that the New York Provincials attempted to desert, and they warned that if any of their officers tried to stop them, they would kill the officers. This mutiny was quickly quelled, and the ringleaders were court martialed, some jailed and others hung.

A month after the massacre, the first of the ransomed British and Provincial prisoners were released from Montreal and returned to their homes. Their journey home was almost as bad as their capture. A number of the prisoners were held in temporary prisons as they were being moved south, and the prisons were rife with smallpox.

In a twist of irony, the Indians who had massacred those in the hospitals at Fort William Henry had attacked the smallpox hospital and, unknowingly, contracted the disease and brought it back to their villages.

It soon began to spread and decimate the Indian villages. In a way, the massacred dead were able to reach from their graves and get vengeance. The Indians had never before been exposed to this European disease, which quickly raced through the Indian Nations. Unknowingly, the returning victors were carrying smallpox on the scalps they had taken, the clothes they had plundered, and the prisoners they had brought back with them. The epidemic would reach as far west as Indian villages along the Mississippi.

Jacob's wounds and injuries took time to heal, as did those of Konkapot and Charles. Jacob was concerned about the dissention growing between the British and the Provincials.

"You said this was going to happen," remarked Konkapot, and Jacob nodded his head. "The one time I didn't want to be right."

Colonel William Haviland assumed command of Fort Edward. Replacing Lord Loudoun, General Jeffery Amherst was appointed Commander in Chief, North America.

Jacob and the other Rangers remained at Fort Edward as the strategists in England, severely stung by their loss of Fort William Henry, were trying to determine what they should do next about the French.

The seasons continued to march onward, the mountains observing patiently from their lofty positions. Summer ended, fall arrived, and winter followed, closing out the year 1757.

Major Rogers once again asked the veterans of the heavy fighting around Lake George to reenlist and continue fighting the good fight. After a quick discussion, Jacob and the others all agreed to stay on and help Rogers.

Rogers approached Jacob once again about becoming an officer. Rogers said he could really use a man like Jacob to lead and teach the Rangers. Jacob declined, saying he could lead and teach with the best of them, but it didn't feel right for him to become an officer.

Rogers understood that Jacob's ambition was not like his own. At least he still had the trusted sergeant he could rely on to bail him out if he got into trouble.

Rogers nodded his head. Trouble was coming and everyone was going to get a heavy dose. As long as the French, the Canadians, and their Indian allies had access to New York and held Carillon, the fighting was not over.

Major Rogers walked away as flakes of snow began to fall. He was going over some ideas in his mind on how they could not only take the fight to the French and Canadians, but maybe also do enough damage to change the tide in their favor, or at least to keep the French from attacking south towards Albany.

Jacob, whose arm had healed and was mostly back to normal, worked with Konkapot and Samuel to chink their cabin with mud and straw as snowflakes danced lazily around their heads.

"Snow is starting a bit early this year," said Konkapot as he brought another bucket of mud and straw to close all the gaps in the cabin. "It's going to be a cold one, I think."

Jacob nodded and took a handful of mud, which he squished into the space between the logs and patted into shape. The wolves, who were watching the activity, raised their muzzles to the sky and sniffed the air, snowflakes landing on their fur.

"You think the French will come back?" asked Samuel. Jacob shook his head no.

"Not this year, but who knows what the spring will bring? We have a new English commander, and they all get fascinated with Carillon, or Crown Point, or even Quebec. If I was a gambling man, I would bet we will be heading north this spring. Which means …"

Jacob paused for a second to pat another handful of mud into a crevice between logs.

"We'll be going back out soon, scouting and gathering information for the next push."

They nodded their heads and finished chinking their cabin and then went inside to warm up next to their fire. The spring would tell what would happen next.

As fall shifted to winter, the situation between the Provincials and the British continued to simmer. The situation exploded when two Rangers were accused of stealing rum and were imprisoned. Their comrades, angry over the incident, chopped down the whipping post on the island and attempted to break their comrades out of the guardhouse.

They were yelling, "If they are flogged, then there will be no more Rangers!"

This led to six more Rangers being arrested. The new commander, Colonel Haviland, threw these Rangers into the jail inside Fort Edward. Major Rogers tried to intervene on behalf of his men, but Colonel Haviland refused to listen.

Haviland held an inquiry, but the Rangers remained silent, and he could not determine guilt or innocence. Rogers warned Colonel Haviland that unless he put this situation to rest, he could not guarantee that his Rangers would not desert en masse.

Colonel Haviland did not make the situation any better by saying that if Rogers could catch one of these deserters, he would hang him. Rogers promised that if that happened, then he would resign. As the situation grew tenser, General Abercrombie intervened and defused the situation, arguing that without Rogers, the four companies would be useless anyway.

Rogers was instructed to raise five more companies to support the upcoming spring campaign. He also ran another Ranger School, though this time, the school would be held on the island, and a group of fifty volunteers would receive special certificates issued by General Abercrombie to the fifty British Cadet Volunteers, who were formed into a cadet company.

While the instructions were being presented, Rogers began penning his rules of ranging, which the cadets could take with them back to their units. During the fall and going into the winter, work was conducted around Fort Edward to improve the fort's defenses. In early winter, one of the barracks in the fort caught fire, and it was a quick response by Captain Putnam and some Rangers that prevented the fire from spreading to other buildings and possibly destroying the fort.

Frederick Best was placing the finishing touches on his two-story house/sutler shop. Business had been going very well for Frederick, enough so and because of a fondness for the Rangers, that Frederick had opened a smaller sutler shop out on the island.

From time to time, when Jacob and the others visited the shop, Maggie's sister Audrey checked on Jacob, like he was a brother to her. He thanked her for her concern, and said he was dealing with it day by day, but was doing fine.

As for Audrey, she seemed to have found comfort with one of the other men working for Frederick, and like Jacob, was coping with the loss of her sister day by day.

Frederick was also seeing the tension growing between the British and the Rangers. Not surprisingly, Captain Reynolds could still be found somewhere in the middle of all this tension.

This was one reason Frederick had created the small, separate shop on the Rangers' island. He believed it would be prudent to keep the Rangers and the regulars apart, especially if he sold alcohol. Maybe the new location could lower some of the tension, he thought.

Jacob and his Rangers conducted localized patrols and hunting expeditions. One of their patrols took them back up to the ruins of Fort William Henry. When they arrived, they found nothing but piles of burnt timbers. The barracks, the outer buildings—all were in ruins. Jacob and his men observed that the French and Canadians had already taken anything of value. What was very abundant were the bones of the dead scatted about the entire area, the bodies having been picked apart by wolves and other scavengers.

Colonel Lord Howe went out on a few scouting patrols with Rogers to observe Ranger tactics firsthand. Howe was impressed with what he saw, and he learned from these scouting patrols. He began to understand the importance of these specialized Ranger companies.

In November, Captain James Abercrombie, nephew to General Abercrombie, arrived at Fort Edward to organize what he called a "grand scouting party." The strain of all the activity had been hard on Rogers, and he was sick once again, this time with scurvy. Captain Stark was to lead the grand expedition with three hundred Rangers, including Jacob and his men.

Stark had been looking forward to getting back into action, having just recovered from smallpox, but Captain Abercrombie insisted he would lead this expedition since it was his idea. When Jacob told the other Rangers that Stark had been superseded, they all rolled their eyes and prepared for the worst.

Captain Abercrombie was leading their grand scouting expedition towards Fort Carillon to "see what trouble they could stir up." When Jacob heard this, he mumbled, "Abercrombie should be careful what he wishes for."

The scouting party departed Fort Edward and moved northward in a long column of twos, staggered and separated. The word that Abercrombie was in charge had a strange effect on the Rangers, who decided to violate every principal that Rogers had instilled in them. The men hunted game along the way, even though Abercrombie ordered them to stop.

Jacob and some of his men thought that this rebellious spirit might be due to the constant tension between the British regulars and the Provincials.

The wolves had accompanied them, much to the displeasure of Abercrombie, but his dislike didn't seem to bother the wolves. Captain Stark refused to intervene, saying that this was Captain Abercrombie's expedition and his leadership challenge.

After moving northward for six days, Jacob was surprised that they had not run into any enemy activity, even with the Rangers shooting at game. Captain Abercrombie halted the expedition and selected Jacob and his men to accompany him and two other British regular "gentlemen" officer volunteers to scout closer to the French position.

Konkapot and Samuel led their section forward. Jacob watched Abercrombie and the two British officers in the middle, and then James, Charles, and Peter covered their rear with the wolves. It was a blustery day, grey and overcast, with light snow blowing, which assisted the small scouting force to come within nine hundred yards of Fort Carillon.

They could see some activity from the fort, but what drew Abercrombie's attention were the twenty to thirty boats pulled up on to the shore.

"There is our target of opportunity," said Abercrombie. "We'll move down there and burn the boats!"

Abercrombie was excited and inexperienced.

"Sir," began Jacob, "we're only nine men, and it would take time to burn all of those boats."

Then to emphasize his point, Jacob pointed to the fort and argued, "Those guns up there would tear us to pieces, and for what? Burning boats?"

Abercrombie and Jacob debated back and forth, experience finally winning over the "buck fever" excitement of youthful inexperience. Jacob suggested that they set an ambush and take prisoners to gather information. Abercrombie relented, and they returned to the main camp of the Rangers.

Abercrombie directed that the Rangers split the watch, one man sleeping while the other kept watch. During the night, Abercrombie woke to check on the camp and found, to his horror, that all of the Rangers and their officers were fast asleep, wrapped snuggly in their wool blankets. Only the golden eyes of the wolves showed any interest in him. Abercrombie's frustration level with these Rangers was growing. They were supposed to be the best, but they were nothing but ill-disciplined Provincials.

Before the sun rose, the Rangers moved down to the vicinity of the road where they were going to set up the ambush and settled into their positions. They did not have to wait long. Soon a group of six armed men approached the area near the ambush, possibly out hunting.

The Rangers waited to see if they would come closer to the ambush position. The men appeared to be staying out in a field and then moving towards them. After thirty minutes, Abercrombie instructed one of the Ranger officers, Lieutenant Robert Rose, and ten Rangers to sneak up and take the men prisoners.

However, as the Rangers were closing in on the men, they were spotted, and the six men took off running. Abercrombie hesitated, unsure of what to do. Stark jumped up, let out a war whoop, and sped off in pursuit with the Rangers and wolves joining in the chase.

The six men were heading for the fort, and the Rangers were running hard to catch them before they reached the safety of the French position. Some of the Rangers took shots at the fleeing men, which drew the attention of the fort.

As they closed the distance, there was a loud boom as the fort fired one of its big guns, followed by a second one. Both balls skipped into the earth, throwing up snow, dirt, and debris, but no Ranger was hit.

The Rangers halted, and began chanting, "God save King George," as well as hurling insults at the French for refusing to come out. The French responded by firing eleven cannons in rapid fashion, forcing the Rangers to seek cover and quickly withdraw into the forest.

After returning to Fort Edward, Captain Abercrombie wrote dispatches to his uncle and other senior leaders in the British Army, detailing the lack of discipline he had encountered on this "misbehavior scout."

Captain Abercrombie sent a dispatch to Lord Loudoun, recommending that regular British officers assume command of the Rangers all the way down to the Ranger companies.

Jacob and his men sat around a fire, cleaning their gear, and he commented that it had been one of their more unique, almost fun, scouts. But as he thought about it, Jacob realized that things might have gone too far. In fact, he realized that it may have increased the friction growing between the Provincials and the regulars. While the scout had broken most of Major Rogers' Rules of Ranging, it had been a good time and a great stress reliever. However, it might have damaged their well-earned reputation.

Major Rogers recovered from his bout of scurvy, and organized a scout in mid-December. Leading an expedition of 150 men, Rogers placed Jacob's section in the front, heading towards the southern shore of Lake George. The wolves were ranging to their front and their sides, looking for the enemy.

The Rangers were bundled up in their blanket coats and fur-lined wool caps. When they arrived at the charred ruins of Fort William Henry, the broken logs jutting like white-covered bones from the ground, the Rangers conducted a sweep of the area. During this sweep, they discovered a cache of cannon balls and shells the French must have forgotten and left behind.

Leaving the ruins of Fort William Henry behind, Rogers lead the Rangers northward around the eastern side of the lake, but the sky turned dark, the wind grew cold and fierce, and soon thick flakes of snow filled the air. Soon, it was difficult to see one another as the blizzard crashed upon the Rangers, the canopies of the trees not protecting them from the onslaught.

Rogers halted the men, who took up what shelter against or under the trees from the relenting storm, trying their best to watch the forest around them. Looking at the shivering men, men who were already tempered and hardened to the northern conditions, Rogers grudgingly decided that mother nature won this one, so Rogers decided it was better to return before more men suffered cold weather injuries. He knew he had to maintain his fighting strength, and the enemy wasn't going anywhere soon in this same weather.

After a week, the weather turned better, and Major Rogers decided to try another expedition north. Gathering as many of the available Rangers as he could, which only numbered about one hundred due to illness running through the ranks, Rogers once again began traveling north towards Fort Carillon.

They were again surprised to see no activity along the shore of the lake, and they were able to once again move close to Fort Carillon. Jacob had decided to leave the wolves behind, and it almost seemed that they hadn't minded not having to travel through the deep snow.

Rogers had decided to set up a series of smaller ambush positions around the area in an attempt to capture a prisoner to gather information. Jacob and his men moved close to the fort, pretty much in the same area they had visited during the Abercrombie expedition.

As they lay concealed in thick firs and bushes, Peter tapped Jacob on his shoulder and whispered, "Frohe Weihnachten, my friend. It's nearly Christmas."

Jacob realized that in fact it was December 24th, and he shook Peter's hand, before he slowly moved back to his concealed position. Fate smiled on them when a lone French soldier appeared, walking down the road from the fort. Quickly jumping out, Konkapot and Peter tackled and overpowered the man, found out he was unarmed, and took the prisoner to Major Rogers.

The prisoner, a sergeant from the Troupe de la Marine, was interrogated and gave up that there were only 350 men garrisoning the fort due to the winter. Quickly, Rogers formed a council of war and decided to try and give them all a big Christmas present and capture the fort.

Jacob was selected to serve as the bait, to lure the garrison out from the fort. As they pursued Jacob and his men, the rest of the Rangers with Rogers would enter and take the fort.

Jacob looked at Rogers and asked, "Why me?"

Rogers grasped his shoulder and said, "I know you can pull it off." "I appreciate your confidence; I hope I am around to enjoy it," replied Jacob as he moved off to inform his men about their mission.

Jacob and his men moved along the tree line until they came within six hundred yards of the fort. Fate once again smiled on the Rangers as another man left the fort and was walking down the trail just like the first. Except this time, when Charles jumped out to capture him, he slipped and missed the grab.

Skidding to a quick halt, the Frenchmen turned around and began sprinting towards the fort. Jacob drew a bead on the running man, and he heard the click of his men's rifles not firing. Their powder was wet from the snow. Grimacing, Jacob increased his lead and fired, hitting the running man in the back and knocking him forward into a spray of snow. The rest of the Rangers began to hoot war cries and fire at the sentries on the wall, with James repriming his rifle and getting it to fire. While they could see the French looking at them from the walls, none of them would venture out. Instead, just as they had on Abercrombie's expedition, they fired cannons at them.

The Rangers made loud noises and fired at the walls, but the French would not take the bait. Jacob returned to Rogers, who moved them away.

Rogers still wanted to harass the enemy, even if they would not venture out. He spotted a herd of seventeen oxen.

"Anyone want some fresh meat today?" asked Rogers, who led the Rangers over to the animals.

The French remained safely behind their walls as the Rangers shot and butchered the seventeen oxen. They also found a nice stockpile of cut firewood that had been stacked, waiting for sleds or carts to haul it to the fort. Using the firewood to cook the oxen, the Rangers waited to see what the French would do. They still refused to come out to confront them.

Jacob and his men sat, enjoying freshly cooked oxen meat as some of the Rangers took shots at the French on the walls. It became a contest to see who could hit the farthest moving target. This eventually drove the Frenchmen from the walls, but they still would not come out.

As the sun dropped behind the mountains and night set in, Rogers decided to return home. They burned all of the firewood in a great bonfire, which provided enough light for Rogers to pen a receipt for the oxen and firewood.

"I am obliged to you sir, for the rest of you have allowed me to take the fresh meat and firewood you sent me and my men on Christmas. My compliments to the Marquis de Montcalm for the fine oxen."

Rogers stuck the receipt on a horn of a dead ox, and turned his Rangers around to head south.

As the winter began to thickly blanket the north, covering the scars from the year's battles, the leaders in Albany began planning their next moves for the spring of 1758. The militia and Provincials were released to return home while the regulars moved into their winter quarters. Major Rogers released the cadet company, and the members returned to their normal units.

Jacob and his men finished winterizing their hut and inspecting and repairing their snowshoes, ice skates, and other winter gear. They visited Frederick's sutlery and traded items they had taken in battle for items they needed for the winter.

There were some social functions held in the new shop. Though Jacob and his men attended, Jacob remained more aloof than ever, observing from the side. As he watched at one of these parties, fire crackling and a multitude of candles shining brightly, fiddle and flutes being played, Jacob thought back to all of the trials and tribulations that had befallen them.

This had been a tough year, and Jacob thought the next year would be just as bad. He missed Maggie and his comrades who had fallen during this bloody, ugly conflict. He resolved to harden himself, harden his heart and soul, and focus on bringing defeat to these hated men who had killed all he had loved.

EPILOGUE

As Jacob and the other Rangers continued with their duties, in England, Prime Minister William Pitt was taking more control of the war against France. Pitt realized that France was strong in Europe but weak in the colonies, so that's where he would focus England's military might against French interests.

General Abercrombie was directed to develop a plan of action for removing French influence and power from the colonies, which meant Abercrombie had to take Carillon. To support these efforts, Pitt promised Abercrombie that he would send additional regular British forces to reinforce his command.

Orders were written, regiments were assigned to be sent to the colonies, and the logistics of gathering supplies and filling the ranks began. The regiments moved to the coast to await the arrival of transport ships to be escorted by the Royal Navy. Commanders looked forward to the coming campaign, to the chance to bathe themselves in glory, which would lead to promotions and status.

The King, the government, and even the people of England wanted the war to be over; it was beginning to wear on the finances of the country. The King was also receiving reports of the friction growing between the Royal forces and the Provincials, but he was convinced the reports were nothing to be concerned about because he believed all loyal subjects would rally to their cause and, as a nation, work together to force their enemy into submission.

North at Ticonderoga, Colonel François-Charles de Bourlamaque had assumed command of Fort Carillon. The construction was nearly completed, and the extra supplies and artillery that had been captured at Fort William Henry had been dropped off by the Marquis de Montcalm before he traveled north to Montreal.

Joseph Marin remained at the fort to lead the scouting expeditions, hoping to tangle once more with the Rangers and beat them at their own game. The French position at Carillon was strong, well positioned, and well stocked with supplies.

In Albany and other colonial capitals, the Provincial Royal Governors and their ministers were gladdened by the promise that England would pay most of the cost of keeping the English soldiers fed and housed and that the English would do most of the fighting instead of requiring the Provincials' men and money.

As the leaders moved their pieces on the great chessboard, back in the colonies the mountains, the great grey sentinels with shoulders covered thickly in snow and ice, settled in for another cold winter. They continued to look passively down into the valleys as men and animals went about their business.

In quiet testimony, the great peaks judged neither side in the conflict, only observing the carnage that was wrought in the valley. The two combatants, like the great bears that lived in their peaks, had settled into their hibernation to wait for spring. The wind howled, the rivers froze, and the trees waved to and fro as the storms passed through the mountains and into the valley. The silent mountains watched and waited to see who would be victorious in the end.

About the Author

Erick Nason was born and grew up in Glens Falls, New York, spending much of his childhood in the Lake George region and the Adirondack Mountains. He served in the United States Army, serving with the 2nd Ranger Battalion and the 10th Special Forces Group for twenty years. While in the service, he received a Bachelor's of Arts Degree in World Military History and a Master's of Art Degree in Military Studies: The American Revolution, both from the American Military University. He retired from the Army in 2005, went to work for TATE Incorporated as an instructor, specializing in personnel recovery, and earned a Doctorate in Education, specializing in military history from Walden University. He previously published his autobiography *From Desert Storm to Iraqi Freedom: One Soldier's Story*. For a hobby, he has been a living historian and reenactor since 1987. Nason lives with his wife Karin and daughter Samantha in Virginia.